ORACLE

Ian Stewart and Jack Cohen

Joat Enterprises

CONTENTS

ORACLE

Ian Stewart
and Jack Cohen

1

Dune Encounter

A small patch of brown and black moved against a backdrop of swirling sand. A jackal was slinking across the desert floor in the lee of a barchan dune, deep within the flat, open region cradled in the twin cusps of its crescent arms, dwarfed by the towering slope of the dune's main mass. Circling vultures and the smell of a freshly dead hare, the abandoned prey of a snake, had alerted the jackal to the presence of food. It crouched low to the ground, haunches angling above its compact body, more machine than animal in appearance.

It looked up the dune's steep slope, which terminated in a sharp crest. Windblown sand, trickling up the far side, was blowing off the crest in a spray of fine powder and settling back on to the desert floor in the calmer conditions downwind. More powder trailed from the tips of the crescent. As the windward slopes eroded, layer by layer, the lee side gained what was lost at the crest. The entire dune rolled imperceptibly forward, a million tons of desert marching inexorably towards an unknown future as the crescent shape reformed itself instant by instant.

The jackal's sensitive nose led it into the central void between the advancing arms, where a vast counter-rotating bubble of air had scoured away the finer particles to leave a basin of coarse grit. The circulation scattered the hare's scent-trail, but a cluster of vultures made it obvious where the remains must be. Spotting its prize, the jackal chased the ugly birds off, and they settled resentfully a few wingspans away as it made short work of what little flesh remained.

Suddenly, the jackal pricked up its ears. Disturbed by something it did not recognise, it raised its blood-streaked head from the carcass.

The hairs on its body stood on end, and the air seemed to *crackle*.

A shadow swept across the ground, as if a passing cloud had blotted out the sun. The jackal glanced nervously skyward, and froze. Then it began to back away, out of the shadow towards the bright, familiar sunlight of the desert.

Above, a shape unlike anything the jackal had clapped eyes on was hovering, unsupported. It was reddish orange in colour, a massive, unearthly mix of hard angles and soft flowing ruffles like a baroque palace engulfed by a frozen waterfall. The air beneath the floating giant seethed with static electricity, and sand writhed in strange, slow patterns, rising in puffy clouds and falling like drizzle.

The jackal howled, turned tail, and ran for its life. The vultures scattered, screeching.

If man or woman had been around to observe the ponderous form, they might have recognised it as the sky-boat of an all-powerful solar deity. Or a giant beetle, flying on invisible wings. Or a temple that floated on thin air. Or a cloud—itself a rare sight in the desert—turned to stone by a vengeful god. Or —

Whatever they might have thought the shape to be, they would have *known* it was nothing natural.

They would have been right.

But no human was there to wonder at the awesome sight. That was why this particular dune, one indistinguishable crescent amid an entire field of desolate barchans, had been chosen. And not by any human agency.

The ochre giant advanced into the scoured-out depression, the only sound that of a trillion grains of sand being rearranged. It lowered itself between the slopes of the arms, where the dune rose to greater heights. Its strange, irregular bulk reshaped, becoming rounder and more compact. Even so, it was half as high as the dune's central ridge, and similarly wide.

Its colour changed, chameleon-like, to match the desert sands.

Metamorphosis complete, the object sank into the ground without apparent resistance, stirring up huge clouds of dust that inexplicably failed to rise above the crescent walls, as if surrounded by a vast transparent bag. The descent stopped only when the giant was almost buried. Then the entire dune began to vibrate, a subsonic hum. A wind, rising from nowhere, howled over and around the dune. The sand began to accelerate. It flowed like thick honey, like water; then, gathering momentum, it surged like the Great Wet Way in flood. In a few heartbeats, the dune advanced a distance that would normally have taken decades. A barchan can overrun a village, given time. Generations later, the ruins emerge again in its wake. This one lapped like liquid mud against, around, and over the strange, huge object, engulfing it in less than a minute. Sand rushed onward, surging like winter storms across a lake; the next instant, all was still. Unnaturally still. Not a breath of wind.

There was an almost tangible hesitation, as if the laws of nature had temporarily been interrupted. Then the world returned to normal as the barchan resumed its ponderous, imperceptible march. Once more sand trickled over the crest, to settle on the steep slopes that now concealed the Sun-god's sky-boat. Or whatever it had been. Not a trace of the enigmatic structure remained. The hare had vanished, buried beneath the gigantic wave of sand. The vultures had fled to the four pillars of the world.

The jackal came to a decision. It would seek dinner elsewhere.

Preferably as far away as possible.

2

Speaking-Stone

A few hours after setting out on his initiate's pilgrimage, with the great capital city of Ul-q'mur now just a blurred haze of urban sprawl on the horizon, Hatsutmer had left the river basin and was approaching the edge of the cultivated land. There he came across a poor family scratching a precarious living from straggling crops and skinny goats. The man was nowhere to be seen. His woman was as skinny as their goats, outlines of her bones clearly visible, her eyes desperate. A good-natured mob of naked children scrambled around her feet, covered in dirt, yelling and arguing. One had a pronounced limp, another had lost a finger. But she had cut their hair in roughly the recommended fashion, to keep down lice, and she held herself upright with a brave show of pride.

He uttered the customary greeting: *"Ym hut'p, syn't!"* Peace be with you, sister.

The woman grunted something vaguely similar to the time-honoured reply "And with you, brother." She gestured towards a stack of bricks and dried vegetation that Hatsutmer belatedly recognised as a badly built hut. "You want stay night?" Her accent was so heavy that most of Hatsutmer's colleagues would not have understood a word. But he had spoken like that himself, not so long ago. "Is straw, corner under roof," she added, to show that he wasn't expected to sleep on the dirt outside the tiny hovel that she would call a house. "My man come back soon," to make it clear that only shelter was on offer.

The roof was interlaced palm fronds, the straw most probably infested with biting insects and lice, and the corner was faced with poorly made mudbrick. Hatsutmer was used to those, but he understood that the woman was making her offer only out of reflex politeness and respect for a priest. If he accepted, she would also feel obliged to insist on feeding him, which her family could ill afford.

The small pack with a few belongings lay uncomfortable against his spine, and he flexed his back to adjust it. Then he changed his mind and slid it from his shoulders.

"You're generous, sister," he said, rummaging through the pack's meagre contents. "But the *rau*-priests have commanded that tonight I must sleep on bare ground beneath the wheeling stars."

With visions of his own childhood flooding back, he took pity on the woman and her family. "Ah, here it is!" He took a twist of papyrus from the pack. "Sister: I have salt. I will trade it for food, if you can spare any. Just a little." Her eyes lit up. Even such a small quantity of salt was valuable. He knew she would sell the salt, and the proceeds would feed her family for many days. He had anticipated such an encounter, and he had brought salt because it had high value and was easy to carry. He gave her more than was necessary, out of a mixture of compassion and painful memories of what her life was like.

It had been his life, once.

The woman recognised a bargain, and had the sense to accept it. Hatsutmer blessed her, and they exchanged goods and conventional farewells.

He continued on his path until sunset, thinking about his former life in the village, wondering how his childhood friends had fared since he lost touch with them, remembering now-dead relatives. As dusk drew a veil across the far horizon, he found a dead tree and sat, leaning his back against it. As the last light faded, he prostrated himself and chanted prayers for the Sun-god's safe rebirth as He sank into the underworld, and for the continued protection of Tuwrat, goddess of the Hippopotamus Cult.

Soon starlight lit the land. The initiate cleared stones and dry vegetation from a patch of ground, extracted a thin sleeping pad from his pack, unrolled it, and lay on his back, watching Heaven wheel slowly overhead. The stars were bright and crystal clear. He picked out familiar groupings: the spear-bearer, the lion, the cobra twins, the Heavenly Goose soaring along the glittering dust of Heaven's Wet Way. The Moon-goddess Ythriz had a propitious aspect.

Hatsutmer inhaled the desert air, and its familiar many-layered smells quickly lulled him into a deep sleep, untroubled by dreams.

Next day, the trainee priest moved on without a backward glance, heading in the general direction of the Great Dune Sea. Trees, bushes, and undergrowth gave way to sparse, wiry scrub. The further he ventured from the swampy river, the drier and more barren the land became. The path was marked by occasional stone cairns, but it had clearly borne few travellers. Thorny shoots obscured the track, sometimes requiring a detour between snake-infested clumps of spiky yellow grass.

As the journey continued, he soon became accustomed to this nomadic existence. He had not seen another human being for days. He found that he did not mind being alone. His spirits rose as his isolation increased, and he became one with the deserted land.

Hatsutmer adjusted the coarsely woven *nammu* that covered his head and shoulders to protect him from the worst of the sun. His face already bore a few lines, even though he had outgrown his youth less than a year before. He was striking rather than good-looking, clean-shaven as were all who served in the Temple, and several fingers taller than the norm. A dozen days ago his dark hair had been shaved to the skin, but now stubble covered his head. He carried a razor of black volcanic glass, but only enough oil to shave twice: the morning of the Ceremony he had been sent into the desert to perform, and the day of his return to the Temple.

Born river-dwellers would have found this harsh terrain intimidating, but Hatsutmer loved the dry lands, the slightly oily scent of the *shiba* bushes, the thorned cacti, the small scuttling lizards and beetles, the sandy crust breaking noisily into fragments under his feet. His village had been close to this barren world, and as a boy he had spent many an hour exploring it.

Grandfather Ka'a had once told him that somewhere beyond the far horizon there stretched W'alq Hamda, the Great Dune Sea, an endless waste of drifting sand and exposed bedrock scoured by fierce winds, where none save the *bidd'hu* dared venture. Hatsutmer had loved his grandfather and the old man's tall tales, which had kept him entertained for many evenings, sitting beside the communal fire at the centre of the village. In the Great Dune Sea, Ka'a had said, there were mountains of sand so high that it took a man half a day to clamber up their loosely packed slopes, only to find—yet more mountains of sand, stretching away to the horizon of the Sun-god's nightly battle for survival. The child's eyes widened, as he attempted to grasp such immensity, while Ka'a embarked on long, convoluted stories of gods and demons and less credible creatures such as winged snakes and three-headed cats.

But Ka'a was long dead of the wasting sickness, his brief childhood had passed, and Hatsutmer's goal was not the Great Dune Sea. That way lay only a slow death. Even the *bidd'hu* would hesitate to venture into such a wilderness. They preferred to stick to the many desert trails, most of which only they could recognise. For Hatsutmer, the desert's edge was a more reasonable option. Here, life still clung with a rugged tenacity. A few scrubby bushes struggled through the surface scattering of shattered rock; a few hardy weeds, tough and spiny, braved the arid conditions and the oppressive heat of the sun. Insects scuttled into hiding at his approach. Small reptiles fled to the shade of the rocks, their beadlike eyes watching him as he passed.

Their hold on life might seem fragile, but Hatsutmer had come to realise that the spiked plants, scrawny lizards, and reclusive scorpions were at home in this desolate wilderness.

He was not, even though he felt a deep affinity, even affection, for this place. He was an intruder, and knew it. But he was a man, not an insect or an animal, and he did not need to be at home to survive. There were ways, and from early childhood Hatsutmer had known enough of them to remain relatively comfortable and relatively safe.

He had food and water and tools to make fire; he had clothing to shield his body from the sun and a *nammu* to wrap his head. He had his obsidian razor, his chert-bladed knife, and a fire-hardened wooden spear. He had his courage.

And he had his goddess.

Tuwrat's principal avatars preferred the cool waters of the Trackless Swamp, but even a novice such as he knew that Tuwrat could make herself manifest in aspects more appropriate to this wasteland. So, when he saw vultures circling high overhead, he took it as a sign of Tuwrat's protection, not an omen of foreboding.

At least, not for him. But circling vultures boded ill for something.

Or someone.

Three *khar* ahead, a little to his left, a dramatic outcrop of sun-blackened rocks stood out against the cloudless sky. He nodded in satisfaction and turned his steps towards it. This was why he had ventured into the wastelands, this was where he would pray to his goddess and perform the Ceremony of Five Stones. This was the Mound of the Lifegiver, and it was here that he would advance beyond the novitiate, goddess willing—for Hatsutmer had grown in ambition since the *rau*-priest had taken him from his home village to train him in the rites and beliefs of the Hippopotamus Cult.

He saw the smoke before he smelt it. Thin white tendrils were rising from the far side of the outcrop, and he berated himself for not noticing them sooner. His heartbeat quickened: smoke meant fire, and fire meant travellers, and travellers might mean danger. To calm himself, he recited a prayer under his breath. There was, he told himself, no need for alarm. It was probably no more than another initiate, walking the holy trackways of the wilderness in reverence for his chosen deity, stopping to build a fire. But as Hatsutmer neared the outcrop, this pretence began to falter. No initiate, he realised, would dare to defile this sacred place with fire. And no Temple novice was due to make the pilgrimage, save him.

Perhaps it was a band of desert *bidd'hu*, in which case he had already approached too closely. Most *bidd'hu* were peaceful, most of the time. If these were the other kind, he was already a dead man, though final death would not be quick. But the protective vulture-aspects of Tuwrat reassured him, and he marched briskly towards the cluster of rocks, picking his way across the stony ground with a fresh urgency.

Whoever had made the smoke, he would soon find out.

Even as a child, Hatsutmer had always possessed a quick mind, with a degree of curiosity that his village teacher found unhealthy. It often got him into trouble when he asked questions that the teacher could not answer. But it also got him into the lowest levels of the priesthood when a passing *rau*-priest, more perceptive than the pedestrian and hidebound teacher, took notice of the slim boy who kept asking penetrating questions. Now, Hatsutmer's curiosity was once more in charge, and the purpose of his pilgrimage was cast aside until he discovered who was making fire in this sacred place, and why.

As Hatsutmer neared the Mound of the Lifegiver, he slowed his pace, seeking a gap between the rocks that would lead him to the source of the smoke. There should be one... Yes, a boulder-strewn slope, half-hidden by *shiba* bushes, formed a natural footpath that led up a narrow crack between huge granite boulders, their weathered surfaces flaking off in thin slabs like petals from the dried bud of a sacred lily.

Grit crunched beneath the soles of his feet. There was no way he could conceal his approach from whoever had lit the fire. He clasped the amulet hung round his neck on a string, took a deep breath to calm himself, and began a dogged climb towards the summit.

No club smashed his brains, no knife slit his throat. No hands seized him to peg him atop a nest of devil-ants with his eyelids cut away to let the sun fry his eyes. The flat top of the outcrop was deserted. The smoke, he now saw, was ascending from a steep-sided depression in the rock, to whose flanks vegetation clung. There must be water nearby, beneath the sand. Not enough to dig down to and drink, but enough to create a miniature oasis.

A high-pitched, erratic babble came from the pit, seemingly located immediately below him, its source hidden by the pit's rim. He recognised it as the noises made by feeding vultures. As he watched, two more fell from the sky to join their fellows.

With his blood pounding in his ears, Hatsutmer crept carefully to the edge of the depression, trying to make as little noise as possible. Despite the vultures, there might still be people down there. If so, perhaps they had *not* yet noticed him approaching, for the racket that the vultures were kicking up might have concealed the sounds of his footsteps.

Seeing a few weedy clumps of thorn growing at the very edge, he moved silently towards them. Parting the dry stalks with care, he peered down into the depression.

The first thing he saw was a grey ring of ash, with charred sticks. At its centre, the remains of a *shiba* bush were smouldering. This was the source of the smoke, but it did not resemble any fire made by man. It looked, for all the world, as if the bush had caught fire of its own accord, and was now burning out.

Hatsutmer knew that fire sometimes came from the sky when the gods were angry, accompanied by terrible noises and torrential rain. There were tales of trees and bushes being set aflame—though how they could burn in such a downpour, the stories never explained. But he had seen no stormclouds, heard no thunder. No mud from flash floods defiled the sacred grove.

Another vulture descended, only a stone's throw from where he crouched, and disappeared behind the lip of the rocky plateau. Hatsutmer edged forward again... and saw the corpse. A dozen vultures were picking it over, and even allowing for their attentions, it did not look much like a man. A shiver ran along Hatsutmer's spine. It looked like—what *did* it look like? A jumble of shredded clothing, flesh, *fur*?

It was too far away, and the feeding birds obstructed his view as they tore off strips of carrion.

With another silent prayer to Tuwrat, Hatsutmer took his courage in both hands, and slipped down into the depression, landing lightly on the balls of his feet, ready to respond to the first sign of any threat.

There was none. Aside from the noisy birds, he sensed only stillness and an overpowering stench of death.

Propelled now by pure curiosity, wanting to flee for his life but wanting even more to know what this strange thing was, he edged closer to the corpse. A wisp of smoke wafted his way, bringing the sharp oily taint of smouldering *shiba*. The vultures cackled at him, their beadlike eyes—featureless black discs ringed with yellow—watched his every move. They were adults, their once-white feathers begrimed with the dirty pink of desert ironstone. He shooed them away, and knelt to take a closer look at their meal.

It had... the head of a jackal. And some of the body. But there were other parts that looked like hyena, oryx, and wild sheep. There was a *second* head—that of a baboon. And was... that... the tail of a *crocodile*?

Could it be the body of a *dead god*?

He had been taught that despite their wondrous powers, gods could be killed—though only by other gods, as Wozer had been slaughtered by his step-brother Zhef at the Dawn of the World. But Hatsutmer had also been taught that while gods were often depicted on Temple walls as people with animal heads, or fusions of different animals, this was a human attempt to represent their divine attributes, not a true likeness. Of course, a god could manifest himself as a crocodile's body with the face of a baboon if he so wished, but on the whole gods didn't do that sort of thing. Only the ignorant and the superstitious imagined that they might, thereby confusing holy iconography with reality, and symbols with facts.

So Hatsutmer thought it unlikely that this decaying mess was truly the corpse of a god. A closer examination confirmed him in this belief. He found it hard to imagine a god incorporating assorted pieces of desert hedgehog into its earthly manifestation. Certainly there was no such god depicted on any temple wall he knew of.

Was it just a pile of dead meat, the remains of some bizarre hunt or gruesome feast? It would have been easy for Hatsutmer to convince himself of that, and so explain away the puzzle. But the youthful initiate was a careful observer, and by poking at the remains he soon found that the animal parts were not separate. They were knitted—or had grown— together, merging seamlessly into each other. And there was a curious kind of logic to their arrangement, as if this had once been a creature that walked on its legs and held its head— heads—high, with eyes that gazed on the world from the now-empty sockets. So what—

There was a harsh *scratching* noise, and Hatsutmer whirled round, spear raised to defend himself. But he saw no one.

Just as he was deciding that the noise had been an illusion, a creation of his own fear, he heard it again. Not so much scratching, he thought, as *crackling*, like dry wood thrown on to a fire.

The noise was coming from the smouldering bush.

No: from the ashes of the bush. Were they, perhaps, settling as the fire died down?

He had never heard of ashes crackling. Burning branches and twigs, yes. But not ash.

He poked at the ash with his spear, until it lodged against something solid. There was something buried in the ash. A rock? He dug with the tip of the spear to uncover it.

No rock. This was something that a man had shaped, not a natural form. A flat, square slab, half a cubit across and the thickness of his hand. He pulled it out, brushed away the grey powder that clung to it.

The slab bore curious markings, but nothing resembling writing. He could neither recognise what it was, nor of what material it had been made. Not wood, not clay, not metal, not any stone that he could put a name to...

Any simpleton could see what it was *not*.

What it was... even the wisest of men could not say. This, he knew instinctively, just as he knew that each night the Undead would battle to hold back the Sun, striving to engulf the World of Man in eternal darkness.

But he knew what the strange slab exuded. He could feel it, quickening his blood, tugging at his lifesoul.

Power.

His whole body was shaking. Thoughts flashed across his mind so quickly that he could not identify them. He had never felt like this before, a strange mix of fear and exhilaration, terror and awe.

Hatsutmer knew that his life was changed, forever.

After a suspension of time that for all he knew could have lasted a heartbeat or a year, a semblance of rationality returned. Hatsutmer thought to hide the strange artefact among the rocks, so that he could return another day when the omens were more favourable; which was to say, when the *rau*-priest did not have any idea where his subordinate might be. His excitement was tempered by hard-learned caution: for all he knew, the object might be some cunning piece of underworld trickery, a trap to steal his souls.

He needed to *think*. For that, he needed time. And to buy time, he needed to make sure that the strange artefact was safely hidden from prying eyes and thieving hands.

Most likely, the slab truly was a gift from the goddess, as he hoped and feared—but if so, was the gift intended for *him*? He rather thought it was, for why else would Tuwrat have led him to stumble upon it? But such self-centred thinking, he knew, could be a snare.

He decided to conceal the object, and depart, and to pray as fervently as he had ever prayed in his whole life. He would ask for enlightenment, not answers... for had the *rau*-priest not told him that when enlightenment came, answers would not be far behind? But all such thoughts fled from his mind in an instant when, unwittingly, he spoke them aloud—

—and the object spoke back.

Hatsutmer dropped it.

Angry with himself for showing fear, he picked it up again, and this time, when once more it spoke to him, he asked it what it was.

There was a silence that stretched interminably, and then a rush of strange words. Then more silence. When he questioned the slab again, it seemed to him that it heard his words, considered them for a moment, and then answered.

He did not recognise its tongue. It was not the tongue of Qus, so much was evident. Neither was it that of Nabish or Bat-alamalaba, of which he had learned a smattering in his youth: when his mother was dying from the blind fever, he had been sent to live with an uncle who did menial work for a merchant who traded in scents and spices, and this had brought Hatsutmer into contact with wayfarers from distant lands.

No, the language was another mystery, but language it

most surely was. It had the cadence of speech.

Long into the night Hatsutmer spoke to the object, using the tongue of the highborn: the priests had taught him that this was mandatory when addressing miraculous beings and their magical talismans. And it spoke back to him in a tongue all its own, though for all he could tell, neither understood a single word uttered by the other. The slab baffled him, and frightened him, but he would risk eternal torment to keep it— for one thing he did understand: this was an object of immense significance and power.

As the Sun-god ascended triumphant into the light of a new dawn, Hatsutmer held what he had come to think of as the speaking-stone in his hands, and stared at it, wild-eyed. This was strong magic. In the hands of an ambitious young man such as he, magic represented a future of position and power, and strong magic represented great power indeed. By now Hatsutmer *knew* that the goddess Tuwrat must have sent him this magical stone that spoke, for who else could have done such a thing? And since she had sent it for him, and him alone—which must be so, because *he had found it*, and there were no witnesses save for a dozen irritated vultures—then she must want him to make use of it.

In that timeless moment, Hatsutmer's destiny was forged.

He knew exactly what was required of him; there was no shadow of doubt in his mind. He would stay to perform the Ceremony of Five Stones, as was only proper; that was why the priests had sent him here. He would return to Ul-q'mur and the Temple, to its ministrations and teachings, for that was expected of him, and to do otherwise would draw unwanted attention. But on the way back he would search the wadis, and hide the speaking-stone where he alone could find it. Then he would wait for the goddess to inspire him as to its proper use.

Already he knew its power would propel him rapidly up the ranks of the priesthood. The goal of becoming High Priest, the cult's leader, seemed eminently attainable now. And that could be a springboard to wealth, and land, the political power of the nobility... perhaps a high-level appointment among the King's closest associates.

His eyes returned to the enigmatic, impossible corpse. Should he hide that, too? But within a day the vultures would have consumed most of it. It would be hard, messy work to drag the remains out of the pit, and then there was nowhere sensible to bury them, and he had no tools for digging. He could improvise with bones, if suitable ones could be found...

No. Hatsutmer looked again at the vultures. Two dozen on the ground, many more overhead. No novice was due to make this pilgrimage until the next frowning Moon, when it would be Patuki's turn. By the time that fat fool arrived, all that would be left would be a pile of assorted animal bones, whitening in the sun. The novice would put it down to hyenas, if he noticed it at all—

It was another sign from the goddess! She was protecting his discovery for him.

Hatsutmer would aid her by dispersing the ash—if only to make sure there were no other magical treasures buried beneath it. But he did not expect to find anything else.

One miracle is all it takes to change a life.

Much later, with the speaking-stone safely hidden, when he was back in the Temple and the Moon's frown had changed to a smile and back again a handsworth of times, he finally worked it out.

What manner of inanimate object spoke—albeit incomprehensibly—when addressed in the tongue of the highborn?

There could be only one answer.

3
Swamp-Pig

Chill morning draped swirling mist over the reed beds of the Trackless Swamp, like goat's milk left too long in the dish. Cenby copperbeater watched the reddening sky, and knew that the most dangerous phase of his vigil could not be put off any longer. He slapped at a biting insect and rolled his sleeping-mat into a neat bundle, securing it with thick string. He had twisted the string himself from the fibrous pith of the *y'my* plant, as his grandmother had taught him. Normally woman's work, on occasions such as this it was traditional for a man to make his own string. It propitiated the gods and brought good fortune.

Cenby, nervous as a cat and trembling with fear, was desperate for all the good fortune he could get. He took a deep breath to calm himself. As the ripe stench of rotting vegetation hit his throat, it felt as though he had inhaled the entire swamp. His head swam.

With a conscious effort, he pulled his thoughts together. *Time to move*. He always felt better when he was *doing* something, not just sitting and waiting. Perhaps that was why he always looked thin and wiry, except for his muscular arms. Or maybe it was the physical labour involved in beating copper, which had given his arms their strength. At any rate, action seemed to dispel the demons.

Speaking of which... As he slung the bundle over his back, his gaze was drawn to the horizon, where the blood-red disc of the Sun-god was dragging Himself out of the clutches of the demons of the underworld, back to the freedom of a clear blue sky. Cenby's heart soared at this inspirational sight. Once more the Sun had struggled against the infinite Legions of the Undead; once more He had emerged victorious, thanks to the rites of the priests and the offerings of the people.

The Sun-god had won his nightly battle with real demons. Surely Cenby could win a few skirmishes with imaginary ones?

Cenby's people saw the world in many different ways, and had no difficulty entertaining several of them at the same time. There could be no logical contradictions while the magical powers of the gods ensured that the world was as it should be, for magic trumped logic. So to Cenby, the smoky tendrils that bedecked the swamp were, in their most mundane aspect, ordinary mist—but in another aspect they were simultaneously the ghostly remnants of the snake-goddess Mahumat, striving even now that the battle's outcome was beyond dispute to wrest victory from defeat and drag the fiery disc of Akhnef back down into everlasting darkness. Her success would condemn Cenby and his people to unspeakable horrors for all eternity. But once more the offering-rituals had triumphed, Akhnef's fire burned hot, and the snake-spirits were visibly withering in the fierceness of His glare.

The further Akhnef climbed to safety, the hotter his fire would become, and the quicker the snake-spirits would fade, sucked back into the solid roof of the underworld.

The Land of the Water People was safe for another day—

With a start, Cenby realised he had been daydreaming. In sudden panic, he tore his gaze from the sunrise, and cast a fearful eye over his immediate surroundings. His breath, quickened by fear, slowly became more regular. Nearby, all was still. The swamp continued to smell like swamp. Not far away, he heard the shrill calls of ibis and the raucous squawks of ducks, which always made him want to laugh; but today's task was no laughing matter and their rasping quacks sounded oddly menacing, reminding him how quickly the innocent pursuit of life might be brought to an abrupt end by predators lurking unseen in the muddy waters.

Even while daydreaming, he probably would have sensed danger approaching—but *probably* had put too many good men beneath the sand before their time and turned their skin to leather. Among them his erstwhile Master Hopthor, who had ventured too close to a crocodile's nest without observing that it contained young.

There were no crocodile's nests here: Cenby had made certain of that before laying out his sleeping-mat, and checked twice more after doing so. But still fear dragged at his bones, and his strength turned to vapour as he contemplated the dangers in store.

Between Cenby and the rising sun, matted vegetation spread as far as the eye could see. It seemed as if it could never end, but this he knew to be an illusion. While haggling over a sack of copper ore, he had heard from a Nabish trader that the swamp's erratic boundaries, which stretched either side of the meandering braided tracks of the Great Wet Way, extended more than ten hundred *khar* to the south—a distance beyond any man's comprehension, in Cenby's opinion. His father Ukash had once ventured an even greater distance northwards and returned safely; from him Cenby had learned that a few hundred *khar* saw the swamp merge with Qus-ni-Tuwrit, the Inundation: a vast, noisome, fly-ridden delta perpetually discharging its cargo of silt into the Saltwater Sea. And the wise men of the city affirmed that on the far side of that vast sea, ten hundred or more *khar* beyond the Inundation's northern shore, there was a region of misty marshes and strange blue-grey rivers. Beyond loomed the vast wall of Maab-ul-Qusqus—endless towering cliffs of solid water that signalled the borders of Habd-ul-Zamet, Wolfland.

Solid water! It was said to be pale blue, where it was not encrusted with dirt, if it caught the sun just so—

The marshes adjacent to the ice wall were fertile and

packed with deer and antelope, but these attracted the attentions of wolves and sabretooths, which roamed the region in vast numbers. Few ventured into those lands, save for fur hunters with more courage than sense, and occasional highly organised and well-armed hunting parties aiming to capture live animals, such as baby mammoths and sabretooth lion cubs, to be raised to adulthood for the delectation of the King and his people in the royal zoo and the Arena. Cenby gave thanks that he was not so desperate as to hunt white bear or shaggy mammoth in a land of lion prides and wolf packs. There would always be safe work for a copperbeater in the Land of the Water People. Cities meant customers, and the cities of Habd ul-Qusnemnet—Qus for short—stretched westward from the Trackless Swamp's edge, scything across the grasslands of the cool savannahs, until the encroaching sand sea made it too precarious for even a poor man to scratch a living from the infertile soil. The broad river of the Great Wet Way threaded a twisting path through the marshes and linked the cities together, an easy route for transportation and trade.

He had heard tales—traveller's tales, wild boasts made over a pot of thick beer, not to be taken literally, but possibly wrapped round a kernel of truth—of entire towns being submerged by the relentless march of sickle-shaped dunes, creeping across the desert like a slow but invincible army.

While farmers reaped grain, the remorseless desert reaped cities—

His mind was wandering *again!* Was he falling under some enchantment?

Here on the margins of the swamp it was wise to be alert for crocodiles, and unlike his former Master, Cenby was careful to check the soggy ground for signs of their passage, and especially for egg-laden nests. An enraged mother crocodile was a sight he preferred to witness from a safe distance; better, not at all. The ubiquitous snakes, he fervently hoped, would stay away from him. They would not attack unless they felt threatened—or he accidentally trod on one. He placed his feet carefully, all senses alert for any sign of danger, and mumbled a childhood prayer to Uadj't the viper-headed god for protection.

Cenby was not looking for snakes or crocodiles. What he sought was far more dangerous, something that he hoped would secure him a goddess's blessing for a forthcoming commission. More precisely, he was looking for a hippopotamus, which he and the other locals inaccurately named the giant swamp-pig, a beast both sacred and deadly. Out of respect for the former he was obliged to accept the risk of the latter.

Paradoxically, in the sunlit fields of the afterlife, the swamp-pig goddess Tuwrat was the bringer of children and the protector of pregnant women. In the worldly reality of the swamp, however, the goddess's mortal aspect was more likely to bring sudden, gory death. He knew that he would not become a swamp-pig's meal—the creatures subsisted only on vegetation. But being killed by mistake, out of misdirected anger, was no improvement.

To the unwary, a dozing swamp-pig, nine tenths submerged, appeared harmless. Cenby was extremely wary, but he carried no weapons. Against a swamp-pig, a wooden spear, however fire-hardened its point, would offer no advantage to a solitary wayfarer. Wielded by a hunting-party of hundreds, such weapons might offer some assurance of safety, but even then their protection often proved a delusion. In any case, weapons were strictly forbidden when carrying out the ritual preparation for capturing the swamp-pig's image. Weapons would offend the goddess.

His foot slipped through the bed of reeds into a shallow pool, sinking into thick mud. He wiped the mud away with a handful of leaves, and resolved to take even more care.

In a basket slung from his shoulder, Cenby carried what he needed to complete the ceremony—a few sherds of pale limestone, a reed stylus, and a small pot of black ink, all of which he had made himself; save for the pot, which had come from a market vendor. He had decorated the pot with an image of Tuwrat for good fortune. He hoped to improve upon that image, if the fortune he sought smiled and he encountered one of the goddess's mortal avatars—and survived the experience.

As an undersmith, subservient to the dictates of his Master, Cenby had been taught the proper way to fashion the stocky form of a swamp-pig by beating sheet copper with a hammer of hard rock, bound firmly to a hardwood handle by twisted goat sinews. He was a sufficiently careful observer to recognise that the traditional outlines were not a faithful representation of the animal, but Hopthor had explained many times that what mattered were the souls of the goddess's earthly aspect, not its mere physical shape. Now, with Hopthor dead and buried a thirteenmoon, Cenby was his own Master, but Hopthor had trained him well, and he was determined to follow the traditions of his trade. Part of him yearned for the freedom to create a new image that would dazzle all who beheld it, making them think for an instant that the metal had come to life—but he accepted that this could never be. To break with tradition was unthinkable, for his people's lives depended on respect for the ancient ways, which were to be followed without question, lest the gods should become angry. Those ways had served his people well, for countless generations, which proved their correctness. So new ways could not even begin to compete.

Furthermore, he would not wish to anger a powerful deity by confusing either of her souls with a mundane avatar.

At the back of his mind there lingered a stubborn feeling that despite these time-worn excuses, the old traditions did not adequately portray the swamp-pig's ferocity, its overwhelming *presence*, which surely should be apparent in at least *one* of Tuwrat's souls—perhaps the lifesoul, but more likely the selfsoul. However, such a thought was surely heresy, and Cenby shied away from it. Certainly he would never give voice to it.

In any case, he had received a commission that absolutely demanded the traditional portrayal—more than a dozen copper panels, carefully cut and shaped, glued firmly to a core of dried mud reinforced with straw—much as mud-bricks were made, but shaped like a swamp-pig's souls. It would be the largest artefact he had ever made, a trophy worthy of the skill and courage of the victorious combatant in the most significant of all contests—*i'khsid-chyh*, the Festival of the Frowning Moon. And to prepare for its creation, to be pure in souls and body, he must undergo the traditional vigil and creative transfiguration in the Trackless Swamp, risking injury or death for the sake of his craft.

He was vaguely aware that many inundations past, the trophy had been cast in solid copper, a fortune of rich red metal and an act of sculpture beyond the abilities of a mere copper*beater*. But time had eroded the value of the object, while preserving its symbolic form and external appearance.

It was still a lot of copper, enough for a man to live on for many years. Better still, it was within his powers to make, and unlike many Qusites he had no interest in wealth for its own sake. Cenby had no family: his parents were long dead, he had been their only child, and he had never been able to attract a wife. He was accustomed to his lonely lifestyle, and it had some advantages: this commission would feed him for a sixmoon. To be honest, he would not have wanted the responsibility of handling the quantity of copper required to cast a solid trophy. Such wealth would attract the attention of professional thieves. The regular patrols made by the city police deterred amateurs, but they would offer him scant protection against truly determined criminals.

No, it was better by far to be a copperbeater. Even if it occasionally made your life distinctly dangerous. *Trust in the gods,* he told himself. *They will protect you.* He swallowed, mouth suddenly dry. *If they so will it.*

With his heart beating so strongly that he feared the noise would attract crocodiles, Cenby began to wade through the shallows of the swamp, intent on getting dangerously close to a swamp-pig so that he could scribe the enormous animal's bulbous outlines on his fragments of limestone. He ignored the certainty of leeches; he would take them off later with a firestick. Leeches were the least of his worries.

His heart was thumping fit to burst. The opaque waters were becoming deeper at every nerve-racking stride, and he could not see what else he shared them with. Now his life truly lay in the hands of the gods—and their assorted paws, hooves, and talons—however carefully he trod.

The swamp noises *changed*, and the hairs of his neck stood on end.

Ahead, past a thick stand of reeds, he could hear much splashing, accompanied by flatulent grunts and snorts. He was too short to see over the reeds, but he knew it was a swamp-pig, and his heart sank even as he crept towards his goal. Torn between prudence and precaution, he stopped voicing his prayers, repeating them soundlessly within his own head. Then he stopped even that, because he needed to remain fully alert.

Strange...

As well as the splashes, there was a distinct humming sound. A swarm of bees? No, more like a Temple chantress warming up.

While his mind gibbered at the prospect ahead, his body moved forward of its own volition. Cenby parted the reeds, and came face to face with a gigantic swamp-pig. Its huge mouth gaped, showing the daggers of its teeth. He caught a foul waft of partially digested vegetation, and nearly choked.

Then he realised what was causing the splashes, and he did choke.

It was just too much.

Was Tuwrat toying with him?

The splashes were not being made by the swamp-pig. Instead, they came from a torrent of muddy water cascading off the terrible beast's flank. The water flowed from a bunch of reeds tied firmly to a long stick. At the other end of the stick was—a man.

No, a boy.

A *young* boy.

His age, Cenby guessed, was about ten years.

The child was scrubbing the hippopotamus.

Standing up to his chest in crocodile-infested water, surrounded by ideal snake habitat, yet showing no sign of fear, this defenceless child... was... *scrubbing the hippopotamus!*

With a crude but effective mop.

And he was singing. That was the humming sound. It carried a simple, repetitive tune, which Cenby found vaguely familiar.

The boy waded round to the swamp-pig's head, apparently unaware that his arm was less than a cubit from its teeth. He stopped, peered into the animal's cavernous mouth— and *reached in,* to pluck out something dark and glutinous. His tawny hair, tied in thick braids, brushed the animal's teeth. For a moment his head was *inside* the mouth.

Cenby shook with fear. Surely the swamp-pig would kill this presumptuous, foolish, suicidally ignorant child!

It did not.

It showed every appearance of enjoyment.

The boy turned to dip his mop in the water, saw Cenby, and registered his horrified expression. He dropped the leech he had extracted from the hippo's mouth, letting it fall back into the swamp, and a broad grin split his mud-spattered face.

How did he do that? Cenby wondered—for pulling leeches free without a firestick was, if anything, a task even more daunting than scrubbing swamp-pigs.

Then the child's coarse features, his straight ginger hair, and his unusual combination of abilities, struck home. Most Qusite children had black, curly hair, and their faces were fine-boned. Cursing himself for the slowness of his wits, Cenby began to relax.

The boy is no true human, but a lionface.

Lionfaces did that kind of thing.
Lionfaces were beastmasters.

The boy's elders called him Bentankle, in reference to a slight deformity of his right leg. It didn't even slow him down: he was quick and agile on his feet. Cenby, who had been told that lionface names were more like life histories, was puzzled by the brevity of this one, until the boy started to recite his name in full. After a minute or so, Cenby stopped him.

Bentankle would do nicely.

"My mother Stormcaster-Lightfoot sent me here to help her father," Bentankle explained, making the instruction seem very serious. "My mother's father serves the King! He is called 'When but a mere child this one sucked snakebite from the hindfoot of a—'"

"*Haiyah!* I've heard of him!" Cenby said in surprise. "He's Jackalfoot-Snakebite, and he's the King's Beastmaster. He—"

"*Everyone* has heard of him," said Bentankle. "My grand-father is famous!" He gave a nervous grin. "When he graces our home, mother calls him Jackalfoot."

A strange supposition was forming in Cenby's mind. He was beginning to think that he knew why the boy was here, deep among the reeds, and why he was scrubbing a hippopotamus. "We have something in common, you and I," he said.

The boy started to shake his head in incredulity, for he knew that lionfaces and Water People were separated by a gulf far greater than the Trackless Swamp, but Cenby pressed his claim. "You disbelieve me? Then let me tell you why your mother sent you here. Your task is to prepare a swamp-pig for the coming festival, to cleanse it thrice daily, so that it may be a worthy opponent for the gladiators who will do battle for the honour of becoming Grand Champion."

Bentankle's mouth opened in surprise, confirming Cenby's supposition. Cenby went on: "In my own way, I'm also preparing a swamp-pig for the Championship. But while yours is made of blood, flesh, and bones, mine will be made of copper. While yours is life-sized, mine will be the length of a man's arm. While yo—"

The boy emitted a lionface laugh, a throaty rumbling sound. "I have never seen a metal swamp-pig! Nor one so small! How will you accomplish these miracles, Cenby beater-of-copper? Will you chant prayers in the Temple like the priests, to bring your dead metal to life?"

Cenby smiled, and gave a shake of the head. "My swamp-pig will remain lifeless," he said. "It will be merely the image of a swamp-pig, moulded from burnished sheets of copper by the strength of my arm and the heft of my hammer. The King himself commanded me to make it!"

"The King spoke to you?"

Cenby looked slightly abashed. "Well, not in person. The commission was delivered to my workshop by a servitor of the Third Assistant Overseer of What Is and What Is Not. But it's an official commission, well paid, and it bears the King's signature!" Cenby paused for breath, and then he was off again. "My swamp-pig will be sacred to Tuwrat! It will grace the house of whichever gladiator survives holy combat with the goddess's avatar and defeats all other contenders, to become Grand Champion! His family will treasure it for generations to come!"

Bentankle's grin faded. "I have never understood why a swamp-pig must be killed," he said. "My grandfather tried to explain it, and my mother told me to stop asking foolish questions. But... I still cannot stop wondering... swamp-pigs are sacred to the goddess Tuwrat, they are her holy avatars, and yet... one at least must be killed?"

"The symbolic role of swamp-pigs must not be confused with their daily existence," Cenby explained, sounding pompous even to himself. "For do not the King and his Regent hunt swamp-pigs, crocodiles, and jackals, even though all are *sometimes* divine avatars? The priests will ensure that the divine presence has withdrawn from the beast before combat begins—that it has reverted to being no more than a mundane swamp-pig. At the Festival of the Frowning Moon, its ritual death will then become a form of sacrifice, its life dedicated to the goddess herself."

Bentankle's puzzled look did not fade.

"It's a complex matter," Cenby admitted. "I don't fully understand it myself. Like you, I do as I'm bid. I leave fine points of theology to the priests. You cleanse the swamp-pig to ready it for combat. I capture its essence in metal, to commemorate the battle. And a gladiator—"

"Slaughters it," said Bentankle sourly.

"Performs a sacred rite as ancient as the Moon herself, and sacrifices the earthly semblance of the goddess to honour her immaterial heavenly form," Cenby contradicted, repeating stock phrases from his own initiation, many years before. Wondering how much of it he truly believed.

The boy reverted to scrubbing, and Cenby took out his stylus, ink, and a sherd of limestone. He stroked his hand across the smooth face of the rock. "Uh—Bentankle?"

"Yes?" came the muffled reply.

"Can you persuade the animal to turn a little more sideways, to give me better light?"

4
Magnetotori

The Herd was a stream of violet pinpricks against velvet dark.

In most Galactic cultures, direct contact with magnetotorus Herders was forbidden. Looking too long at a Herder could cause severe mental problems. Indirect contact, mediated by technology, was fine. *Knowing* that Herders existed, and what they were, was fine. Minds could accept mere knowledge. But the stark reality of physical contact was so dramatic that it often destroyed them.

The senses of normal-matter beings could not form an accurate representation of a Herder, because Herders were not made of normal matter. They were partly quantum-mechanical and partly not. Unlike most entities in the Living Galaxy, a Herder's wavefunction did not decohere into a unique classical state when it was observed. Neither, however, did it exist as a superposition of classical states, as would be the case for a fully quantum entity. A Herder's quantum state did not respond to an observation, except in the negative sense of rejecting it. What collapsed was not the Herder's wavefunction, but the attempt to observe it, along with the mental state of the would-be observer.

No classical being ever truly 'saw' a Herder. Instead, their senses received a sequence of random samples of the Herder's wavefunction, each sample a classical projection of its state from an infinite number of possibilities. So a Herder was perceived as an ever-changing series of forms, each presenting itself for a fraction of a second. The usual result was nausea: the sight of a Herder literally made the observer sick. The fleeting shapes made no physical sense, but the observer's brain tried to pigeonhole the incoming visual signals into a recognised category anyway, because that's what brains *do*. The attempt usually failed, and the perceptual dissonance did serious damage. A few species could handle the dissonance, and even fewer could extract a shape that resembled something to which a name could be put. These species universally described the result, using their own similes, as a gangly spider about ten metres across with too many legs.

Herders had no difficulty perceiving other Herders, because their senses responded to the entire wavefunction as a single *gestalt*. They also had no difficulty perceiving classical entities, although the flimsiness of such creatures' wavefunctions did give them a ghostly appearance, as if made from mist.

The same went for ordinary matter, but a vacuum is an absence of matter, and here Herder perception differed considerably from the classical. In cultures whose creatures are made from ordinary class-one matter, which includes all planet-based civilisations, the default perception is that the space between the stars is a vacuum, so total that even the most sophisticated technologies fail to match it. Of course, the planetbound must first be aware that there *is* space between the stars, but having finally decided that the sky is not an upturned bowl, no matter how much it seems to resemble one, they quickly conclude that interstellar space is *empty*. Empty, and vast. Too vast to imagine, too vast to comprehend.

Cultures advanced enough to contemplate spaceflight, or sufficiently intelligent ones that happen to be obsessed with natural philosophy, usually come to a grudging awareness that this image is flawed. They don't *believe* it, for old habits die hard, but they find themselves forced to come to terms with it. Their theorists model a vacuum in many ways—as a crystalline solid so rigid that vibrations travel through it at the speed of light, through which matter can move because it, too, is made from vibrations; as a vast store of potential, waiting to be made real; as a seething foam of creation and annihilation, where quantum particles flicker in and out of existence like moths in a street light. Some consider space to be the mind of a god, and its inhabitants to be the god's thoughts. Polytheists may see it as some sort of divine group mind—the mind of the gods. Some believe it's all a mistake, or a cosmic joke. Some insist they can prove it.

Whatever the theories, the engineers and the political classes soon begin to dream of extracting boundless energy from 'the vacuum'—as if there were only one of it, as if empty space were full of... *something*.

Herders do not theorise about vacuums. They live in them. And they know exactly what they are full of, and how to exploit it. Except that 'full' is the wrong concept.

To a Herder, the space between the stars is like a grassy meadow, dappled in sunlight, with butterflies that skip from blossom to blossom, and grazing animals that eat the grass and are nourished by it.

The grazers are magnetotori, the creatures that the Herders herd. The fields that the tori graze are magnetic. Their grass is ionised hydrogen—naked protons. Between the stars, the grazing is sparse, but the creatures' mouths are huge. They are made of self-organised plasma, coiled into thick rings, spiralling perpetually through the central hole. Magnetotori are quasi-living Bussard ramjets, and they power their magnetohydrodynamic metabolisms with the protons they scoop up as they traverse the void.

Magnetotori are the baleen whales of the interstellar ocean, feeding on particle plankton.

It takes a lot to bore a Herder, who will happily contemplate an abstract problem in gravitoceramics or a photonic mould-sculpture for the best part of a sunspot cycle without breaking concentration. But, even to Herders, magnetotorus migrations did become tedious after a few centuries.

Migrant Herders passed the time in different ways, depending on personality. Some vacuolated, some read the great epic wavepoems, some thought about philosophy, some built ceramics, and some merely slept. Their analogue of sleep is a low-energy torpid state in which high frequencies are filtered out; their version of reading is too complex to describe, except to say that they store information as standing waves confined within a small ellipsoidal force field. Their philosophy would make no sense to any classical entity, and usually makes very little sense to the Herders themselves.

Their ceramics, however, are another matter entirely. Ordinary, solid class-one matter, to be precise. The raw materials for Herder ceramics are a waste product of magnetotorus metabolism. Along with the required intake of protons, tori occasionally ingest entire atoms, even molecules. When these build up in sufficient quantity, the tori excrete them. Somewhere in their distant, forgotten past, Herders acquired the ability to mould the resulting substance and rigidify it with radiant heat. They sculpted ceramic artwork, and they manufactured useful tools. Paramount among them were the Herder's shuttlecraft, which looked at least as puzzling as a Herder, despite having a single fixed shape. The logic of Herder shuttle design was apparent only to a Herder. To everyone else, they were a mess.

Implement-of-Consensus was one of those who passed voyage-time by moulding ceramics. It had been working on a sculpture for nearly three decades, a conceptualisation of Nay-yum-within-Qqan's celebrated Third Fundamental Eigenform. But some subtle aspect of the great liar-philosopher's abstraction kept eluding it. The Herder emitted a cloud of neutrinos, the quantum equivalent of a sigh, and set the unfinished sculpture aside, replacing its tools in their storage loops.

Admit it, {self-identity}: you're bored.

When even an activity as exciting as moulding ceramics loses its interest, it's time to become dormant. This didn't imply loss of consciousness; just a reduced level. Some components of the Herder's quasi-quantum mind would remain active.

Implement-of-Consensus cancelled its future commitments and went to sleep.

After a time—how long had not registered—the conscious part of its mostly-dormant mind sensed dimly that something was *different*.

A Herder's long life was mostly uneventful, and the few events unusual enough to be considered as happening followed a regular rhythm, the cyclic pulsation of a migrating Herd. Now, even while most of it slept, Implement-of-Consensus was becoming disturbingly aware that the Herd's pulse was slowing down. Each successive phase of the cycle was taking longer to complete.

Implement-of-Consensus sensed change. And that implied a corresponding change in space-between-stars. The change, it suspected, lay in the status of *between*. Space and stars were relatively permanent. Between was not.

The Herder had good reasons for this suspicion. It knew from long experience that the apparent slowing of time was an illusion. It was experiencing the changes subjectively, so its senses, paradoxically, must be quickening. If everything around it appeared to be slowing down, that meant that subjective time was *speeding up*. Along with the Herder analogue of metabolism.

Arrival. The Herder's carrier waveform was emerging from the semidormant mode appropriate to space-between-stars, where an alert mind would go mad from tedium. Soon Implement-of-Consensus would become sufficiently awake for its conscious mind to register the reason for this awakening. Its fuzzy thought-patterns would sharpen.

Soon it would be conscious that the migration was nearing its end.

And *that* would mean—

—Some aspect of its infinite-dimensional mind overran a tipping-point. The Herder awoke, and so did the thought. However, Implement-of-Consensus was not yet ready to accept it. The quasi-quantum entity was still too sluggish for such unpleasant observations to register.

That did not prevent its awakening proceeding ever more rapidly.

It had been a quick journey by Herder standards: little more than twenty thousand years. But even with such unseemly haste, there had been no clear demarcation between approach and Arrival, and that had confused Implement-of-Consensus's torpid mind. Yes, the potential target star was now a visible disc—but it had been like that for several decades. And the size of the disc depended on the size of the star as well as the distance yet to be covered. The question was, did any of this herald *Arrival*?

That was a complex issue.

Implement-of-Consensus did not doubt that the Herd's arrival at its intended destination was *impending*... but in a sense it always had been, for impending arrival was implicit in departure. But had it ceased to impend, and become actual? Was the actual Arrival process genuinely about to occur?

Following timeless precedents, Implement-of-Consensus waited until it was properly awake, and as soon as it was, it sought advice from Those Who Decide.

The advice was inconsistent.

The Herd was indeed approaching a plausible target system, but it was unclear whether it had yet arrived. In a sense, the Herd never had a destination until some collective quasi-quantum process decided that the system they had reached had always been the intended target. There were subtle clues, perceptible only to a Herder collective, that might indicate that such a decision had been reached, or was soon to be reached. Unfortunately, the clues were irreducibly ambiguous, because the Herd itself was not aware that it was deciding on its destination until it had done so. Only when the magnetotori plunged into a star's photosphere would the probabilities solidify, causing a superposition of hypotheticals to crystallise into a definite fact.

But—there were clues, and the job of Those Who Decide was to integrate the probabilities and locate the amplitude peaks.

So Implement-of-Consensus superposed its mentality with those of its colleagues, among them Instrumentality-of-Corroboration, Expediter-of-Mutuality, Ratifier-of-Assent, and Concurrence-of-Opinion. Hoping that they would manage to get on the same wavelength, basically. But on this occasion, there was disharmony. The Herd was still well outside the orbit of the largest planet, often a sign that the journey would be continuing. However, there were other, contradictory, signs. When the Herd was passing through the innermost portions of the new system's cometary halo, the Herders had taken the opportunity to use nets woven from monofilament fibres to snare a few of the icy bodies for later use as reaction-mass for their shuttles. Later, they would pick up a few asteroids in the same way. Historically, these activities correlated closely with Arrival. Moreover, once the last few stragglers had passed through the halo, the Herd had begun to decelerate, and deceleration almost always heralded Arrival.

The Herders' sensoria desperately desired the ongoing comfort of informed, balanced procrastination, but their sensorial clocks told a different story. They were fooling themselves. Given the choice, torus-herders preferred everything to stay exactly the same. Boredom was infinitely preferable to change. And most of the time it was so, for there were few choices in the space-between-stars, so everything stayed the same by default. Even on those occasions when there was a choice, prudence dictated that hasty action—and as far as a torpid Herder was concerned, *any* action was hasty—should be avoided at almost any cost. Unless there really was *no* choice, of course, and the time had come to carry out some specific task, such as disentangling over-twisted field lines, discharging burnt-out plasma to keep the Herd healthy, or collecting excreta for the ceramicists. But those were not actions, merely routine activities.

However, there was an exception. When—as now—the level of urgency passed the rather arbitrary tipping-point that had evolved over the course of countless similar voyages, Consensus veered away from comfortable maintenance of the status quo, and settled on the necessity of short-term discomfort, change, and—perish the thought—*doing things.* Just in case the Herd was deciding that it had arrived at what it now believed had always been its destination.

And... it rather looked like it was. In fact—

For the past two hundred centuries, the Herd had been rambling across space in an irregular spherical clump, several light hours in diameter. But now the migration from Umbbseg to—it definitely appeared to be Shool, the current location—was coming to an all too abrupt end. And when Herders finally managed to arouse themselves from their habitual inertia, they went to the other extreme.

Yes, it was Shool. Always had been, of course. And everything went wild.

In a *mêlée* of creative chaos, hundreds of ramshackle ceramic shuttles began buzzing about on trajectories that made sense only to the Herders, as they obeyed the iron whim of Consensus by prodding recalcitrant magnetotori with sudden pulses of magnetic force, driving their herding mode away from the Cometary Halo towards the Inner System. The Herders could not change their beasts' migratory routes, which had evolved and stabilised a hundred million years before the creatures had been domesticated. They could not change when the Herd chose to migrate—a mysterious event triggered by some poorly understood complicity among the toroids' magnetohydrodynamic mentalities. They could not change where the Herd decided it had been heading all along, once it finally did so. Most assuredly they could not prevent Arrival once the Herd decided it had arrived. But the Herders could make fine adjustments to location and timing, better to suit their own purposes; even adjustments that to the uninitiated might appear to be actively influencing the magnetotori's free choice. And that was what they were now doing.

From long practice, they had become very good at it. This Herd had followed the same circular tour from star to star, repeating the same itinerary every two hundred thousand years or thereabouts. It had completed the same cycle of seven stars at least sixty times, though not with the same individual tori, long-lived though the creatures were. But the precise timings were erratic, and even the Herders had never computed a pattern.

The Shool system had eight planets in roughly circular orbits, in almost the same plane. The ninth was an oddball, eccentric and inclined. Although it seemed perfect for coldlife, it was uninhabited, perhaps because it was geologically active despite its near-zero absolute temperature. But even colder bodies further from the star were also devoid of life, be it silicoid or metalloid. Presumably, life had never evolved there. The third world, much closer to the star, was very different. It hosted diverse species of warmlife, some in huge numbers, but showed no signs even of level-one technology, ranking it as 'primitive'. The only advanced creatures in the system were hotlife, living in Shool itself: plasmoids. These impressive entities occupied about one sixth of the stars in the Living Galaxy, a proportion that was slowly increasing as they broadcast themselves to new systems. The Herd's traditional migration route included two such stars: Shool and Xeraxol.

After a period of apparent confusion, the Herders began to achieve a semblance of order. Slowly the glowing lavender toroids started to align their axes towards the bright disc of Shool, drifting together to form a single glowing shaft, aimed directly at the heart of the star. Inevitably, that could spell danger; it was one of the risks every migrating Herd had to accept. Such a formation might easily be misinterpreted as hostile, so once it had secured permission from Those Who Decide, Implement-of-Consensus would have no choice but to open negotiations with the local plasmoids. And so the bargaining time began, as the Herder had known it must from the moment it first began to wake, but had desperately tried to ignore.

Such negotiations were always delicate, prone to misunderstandings and crossed purposes, and emotionally stressful. But they could no longer be avoided. They would be complex, tiresome, and annoying. And horribly quick. Implement-of-Consensus had no fear of complexity, but undue haste was another matter altogether, and it shrank from the prospect.

As the swarming ceramic junkpiles that the Herders called spacecraft continued to chivvy stubborn magnetotori into something resembling an arrival-stream, Implement-of-Consensus took time out from the fray to sharpen its wits for the coming discussions.

The Consensus had already selected those parts of the photosphere that its tori wished to graze. As the Herd drove towards Shool, and the magnetotori's living ramscoops sucked in ever-more-abundant hydrogen ions, the beasts became proportionately more excited. Arrival meant endless supplies of raw plasma, giving the Herd a rare opportunity to breed. Implement-of-Consensus knew that it must conclude negotiations quickly, before the Herd became uncontrollable.

On Shool's third planet, the only one bearing lifeforms (other than assorted jellies and algal wisps in the subsurface oceans of a few satellites of the gas giants in orbital positions five and six), the approaching Herd went almost unnoticed. The most advanced local technology was barely post-mesolithic, and as yet the Herd was no more than a faint violet smudge, almost invisible to the unaided eye.

On that planet's lone satellite, a few sentients equipped with considerably more advanced technology (level-five symmetrogravitic, for the record) did detect the Herd's approach, but those entities were much more concerned that the magnetotorus Herders might notice *them* than they were about what the Herd might be doing, or why. So they stealthed their equipment with wrappings of negafrax and waited for the magnetotori to make their inevitable rendezvous with the system's star. Provided the Herders did not take umbrage, all would be well. In the unlikely event that they did, Shool-3's satellite was made of rock so dense that nothing short of a direct hit on their moonbase would cause significant damage. In the event of any less destructive attack, their bodies—which were locally sourced, making them susceptible to excessive radiation but expendable—might need to be swapped for new ones, but that was routine anyway.

Provided the exchange was made quickly enough, the entities' brains—the physical sites of their individuality—would not be adversely affected.

Implement-of-Consensus took great care to follow the protocols. Plasmoids could easily become violent, their most favoured weapon being a coronal mass ejection or hyperflare. They would stretch their star's magnetic field lines to breaking-point, then let them go with a snap, an MHD catapult propelling a trillion tons of flaming gas into space like a life-seeking missile.

According to persistent rumours, plasmoids possessed weapons more deadly even than hyperflares. There were tales as ancient as the magnetotori themselves, tales of entire stars being transformed into beams of unimaginable energy and destruction. But no living entity had ever witnessed such a transformation, and Implement-of-Consensus had always disbelieved this particular myth, considering it to be mere exaggeration. It was, however, wise to be prudent.

A torus-herder's identifier was not a name in any conventional sense, but a wavefunction that described a characteristic quantum state, which the Herder could assume when required. Implement-of-Consensus fashioned a disposable component of its wavefunction into a sharp pulse of electromagnetic radiation and squirted a message in quantum pidgin at the looming star:

{{Approach | Herder$^{\text{seven-squared}}$} | <creation-operator> | request | permission(immigrate) + temporary} | {respect | plasmoid + local?}}

The delay of several days between sending a message and receiving a reply was so small, compared to the normal delays experienced when herding, that the negotiating process would be worryingly rapid. When negotiations were carried out with such unseemly speed, mistakes could be made. *Would* be made. Herder lore included innumerable instructive examplars in the form of collective wavechants. *The Inglorious Fate of the Unconsensual Herd*, for instance, clarified the dangers of provoking misdirected coronal mass ejections, while *The Unseemly Archive of the Noncompliant Implement* made it clear that promises to star-owners, even if unintended and ruinous, must be kept.

It knew that Shool's plasmoid inhabitants would already have sensed the Herd's approach, but as yet it was too far from the star for a mass ejection to be an effective deterrent, so in principle the Herd and its Herders would be safe from the stardwellers' defensive reflexes for a few more cycles. It was obviously important to get an opening message on its way before transgressing acceptable bounds. Protocol demanded as much.

Implement-of-Consensus followed up its initial contactploy with a longer, more detailed message, identifying each Herder and each magnetotorus by its wave-id, stating the purpose of the visit, and humbly requesting grazing-rights for potential sites. The message consisted almost entirely of sequences of base-7 digits, converted into conventional opticode for easy reception and packaged according to their importance. Then it readied itself for the reply, hoping that the delay of a few light-hours would be enough for it to redirect the negotiations along favourable lines. Plasmoids were notorious for obscuring their true intentions; a common trick was to include ruinous terms and conditions in low-frequency components in the hope that the recipient would overlook them. Implement-of-Consensus would need time to apply appropriate signal filters.

It wanted very little: mainly to convince the plasmoids to allow the Herd to occupy regions of their star's photosphere that would normally have been uninhabited, wastelands where MHD turbulence exceeded the plasmoids' ability to adjust to the variability of ambient fields. Magnetotori were adapted to such unproductive regions, and could find rich grazing in the stream of energised particles that the turbulent flows emitted. By consuming the particles, they would calm the turbulence. So ultimately the plasmoids would benefit from the exchange, once the tori departed for their next migration.

It followed—and this was standard negotiating procedure—that Implement-of-Consensus's best tactic was to ask permission to enter only turbulent zones. but it had to list specific locations, not a generic descriptor. This task resembled nothing so much as weather forecasting, but with magnetic storms and surging sunspots in place of rain and wind, so it was a black art, impossible for any classical mind. Quasi-quantum organisms, however, lived parallel lives, so *thinking* in parallel was easy. Implement-of-Consensus could simultaneously contemplate an infinite ensemble of predictions, integrate the results, and assess which was the most probable.

The trouble was, the most probable option might not be the one that was ultimately realised. Plasmoids were far less predictable than turbulence.

5

Sacred Duty

Thirteen years after he had discovered the speaking-stone, Hatsutmer—now High Priest Shephatsut-Mer (Give Thanks to His Divine Majesty)—was searching.

The desert floor was strewn with stones of every size. Here it was scoured to bedrock where the wind blew unimpeded, there it was heaped with sand where the wind's hot breath was stilled. Over centuries, abrasive sand carried by the swirling winds had carved outcrops of rock into fantastic, surreal, top-heavy forms, the sculptures of an insane genius. They created fierce eddies and patches of calm air, mingled seemingly at random.

A plateau, riddled with currently dry wadis, formed a backdrop to the field of wind-shaped rocks. There was no easy way to distinguish one wadi from another, as they branched and twisted and carved their way through the crumbling red sandstone—here blocked by boulders tumbled by a flash flood, there ending in a wall of intrusive basalt. The heat of the sun had burnt a dark patina on to the surface of the rock, and generations of would-be artists had scribbled graffiti—giraffes, boats, naked dancing-girls, always popular—by scratching away the dark surface to reveal the paler tones beneath.

Shephatsut-Mer had realised many of his ambitions, but was not yet satisfied. He was unsure what *would* satisfy him, but whatever it was, he was careful to conceal any wish to rise beyond the priesthood. By ruthless exploitation of the power of the speaking-stone, he had become High Priest of the Hippopotamus Cult, with a high-born wife, three concubines, and two young sons: one in rude health, one sickly. He had been married to Nemnestris for six tempestuous years.

He wore the holy garments of his station—a linen kilt and a cloak sewn from the skin of a juvenile sabretooth lion, its eyes replaced by gemstones, its scimitar teeth still the originals. The cat's head, flattened by the removal of its skull, hung over his right shoulder; the boneless tail hung down his left thigh. His sandals had ox-hide soles and uppers made from braided thongs of goatskin. Three thick bunches of hair were coiled against his head: one on top, one over each ear. The skull between was shaved, every morning and again every evening. He had anointed his body with *syssa*-seed oil, and his every move was accompanied by its heavy scent, reminiscent of dried almonds.

Today he was looking for a very specific rock-inscription, a sacred symbol known only to the upper echelons of the priesthood. He was sure that he knew where to find it, having followed the same path many times before, but the maze of wadis could deceive even the most knowledgeable visitor, and every rainstorm could change familiar landmarks into enigmas.

He tapped his foot against a rock to dislodge an annoying stone, and tried to concentrate on the shapes of the rock formations, searching for one shape in particular... *Haiyah!* Just where he had expected. For a moment, the harsh shadows had fooled his eyes. Confident, now that his memories were confirmed, he stopped and turned.

Not far behind him there followed a troop of the Royal Guard in combat uniform: brown leather kilts and jackets, armed to the teeth. They were there to protect His Divine Majesty Son-of-Akhnef Chosen-by-the-Sunsouls Insh'erthret (May He Shine Forever), who was nearly thirteen years old, almost adult height, but already plump from overindulgence. He slumped in his carrying-chair, fractious and uncomfortable.

Beside him in an identical chair was his uncle Sitaperkaw, who reigned on his behalf as Regent, and would continue to hold that office until Insh'erthret's seventeenth birthday.

His Divine Majesty sat up, looked out at the dry, dusty desert, and made a royal pronouncement.

"I'm *bored.*"

Sitaperkaw glared at him. "A King is never bored, Insh'erthret. There are always vital affairs of state to occupy His mind."

His Divine Majesty pouted. "You never let me decide any affairs of state, uncle."

Sitaperkaw grunted irritably. "You're too immature to *decide* things, boy."

"So *why*—"

"I've told you before, you should still *think* about them. In preparation for when you *are* old enough to decide." *Assuming you're still around by then.*

The Regent was tall, and his bearing exuded nobility. His facial bones were finely chiselled, with a hooked nose above a thin, cruel mouth that seldom smiled. His dark features and greying hair gave him the predatory air of a fish eagle, and in this they did not mislead. With four more years of power guaranteed, Sitaperkaw had not yet decided whether the child-king would be allowed to live that long. The gods might well intervene before the difficult decision needed to be taken—especially if men helped the gods do their work.

The previous King, Insh'erthret's mundane father Sh'erthret-Amt, had been killed six moons earlier when he flushed a pregnant swamp-pig from its daytime hideaway in a papyrus marsh, and his spear-cast missed. The child-king's skyfather was of course Akhnef, traditional god of the Sun and its souls.

"Why are we hanging around in this horrible place, uncle? I'm hot! I want my servants!"

"You've got a fan-bearer. That's all you need. Learn to be patient, Inshy. Learn not to show your true feelings."

Trying to ignore Insh'erthret's whines, Sitaperkaw leaned back nonchalantly in his gilded carrying-chair, held aloft by a dozen muscular Nabish bearers. Their bodies, black as the silt of the Great Wet Way, glistened with sweat. Shephat-sut-Mer gestured to the Commander of the Royal Guard, and the company came to a halt. The bearers thankfully lowered the carrying-chair to the ground, taking care to ensure that it came softly to rest in an upright, stable position.

"I want to go back to the Palace," Insh'erthret complained.

"The bearers will carry you back to the Palace when we've finished our business here," the Regent told him. "But not right now."

"Why not?"

Sitaperkaw was starting to show signs of exasperation. "I explained why before we set out, Inshy. The King must pay respect to the gods. Tradition demands that twice every year you must venture into the desert, in person, to obtain answers to vital questions. The rest of the time you can stay in the Palace if you want."

"What questions are those?"

"No business of yours. I've already given the list to Shephatsut-Mer. To obtain the gods' answers, the High Priest must continue alone."

"Why?"

Gods, this child is persistent. "Because only the High Priest may know the location of the holy artefact. Only the High Priest may witness its glory."

"Why? I'm the King! I'm a god! The priests must do *my* bidding!"

Sitaperkaw glared at him. "You're not King yet! Even when you *are* King, you may not be elevated to godhood. It's not automatic, you have to *earn* it. And if you want to be elevated to godhood, you don't give orders to the High Priest. Ever. Your tutors have explained this many times, Inshy. Royal power depends on maintaining a delicate balance between the

Palace and the Temple."

Isnh'erthret waved his hand dismissively. "Tutors? What do *they* know? I want to see the oracle!"

"No. That would be sacrilege."

Sitaperkaw knew full well that the main reason was the absolute certainty that someone would steal the item under discussion if its whereabouts became known, but the official Temple position was that the gods and goddesses, in their infinite wisdom, had commanded that neither Regent nor King should know where the sacred object was hidden. This precaution was necessary for His Majesty's own safety. Such arcane knowledge was inherently souls-threatening, and Shephatsut-Mer had often declared his pride in facing that danger on His Majesty's behalf.

So Insh'erthret and his retinue waited, under Sitaperkaw's command, as the High Priest made his way into the further reaches of the wadi, disappearing from their view.

The child-King started to fidget. "I want to go too!"

"Shut up, Inshy."

His Divine Majesty Son-of-Akhnef Chosen-by-the-Sun-souls Insh'erthret (May He Shine Forever) saw the look on his uncle's face, and shut up.

The dog had once been energetic and sturdy. Now his fur was thin and mangy, his ribs stood out beneath stretched skin, and he trailed one hind leg as he walked.

He pined for his master, a middle-aged widower who subsisted on whatever he could grow on the small plot he had inherited from his father. Originally the field had been large enough to feed a family, with some surplus left to sell in the street markets, but it had been shared among six brothers. Being the youngest, his master had received a plot that could barely feed him, so it was fortunate that his wife had already died and they had no living children. Moreover, the widower was an accomplished craftsman, and the wooden amulets and votive statues that he carved kept him and his dog in meat. Until the heart attack.

The dog had dimly realised something was wrong. His master wasn't moving; the expected bone failed to materialise. Whines and howls had no effect. Eventually he abandoned his dead owner to scavenge whatever food he could find.

That morning, he had taken a drink from a muddy puddle in the marshy ground beside the river. He had tried to catch a duck, but the bird was too quick for him, rising skywards with fluttering wings, quacking a warning to all the other ducks.

The dog was starving.

That was when it chanced on the carcass, lying at the edge of the marsh beside a rock. Once a young oryx, it was now a mass of disarticulated white bone held together by a tattered bag of skin and hair, drying in the sun. The dog smelt it from a hundred paces, as even a man or woman would have done. But the dog also smelt something that a human would have missed: a strange, pungent scent, wafted into its nostrils by the morning breeze. In the dog's crazed mind, the scent was received as a message, loud and strong.

Food.

Investigating, the dog discovered that the enticing smell came from one part of the noisome carcass—a bunch of purple spheres, each the size of an onion. A human might have realised that such organs were not normal in an oryx, but the dog sensed nothing amiss. The spheres had thick, leathery skins, too tough to bite through, but the combination of hunger and the chemical temptation of the scent was irresistible. One by one the dog swallowed the spheres, whole. Its belly now replete, it trotted off.

Within a day, the dog looked healthier, its fur thick and sleek. A new intelligence glowed behind its eyes, and it prowled the rural area just outside the city with a new sense of purpose. It seemed to be seeking something more specific than mere food. Late one evening, in a remote corner of an over-grazed pasture, the dog came across a sick sheep, lying on its side under a stand of date palms, its belly distended by the toxic leaves it had foolishly eaten.

What happened next would have baffled any human observer, and in this superstitious culture, created feelings of awe and dread.

First, the dog clamped its jaws round the sheep's throat until it suffocated—a typical tactic for a lioness, but not for a dog, which normally would have tried to rip the throat out if it was going for a kill. It gnawed at the animal's neck until the head fell off, and dragged it aside. Then it settled down on the ground with its own neck pressed against the bloody stump of the sheep's. After a time, the dog's skin began to crawl. Waves of movement rippled through its body, and its neck began to merge with the sheep's. Cells of muscle, nerve, and skin flowed into new configurations as the dog's head disconnected from its body and re-connected to the sheep. Now the waves had transferred from the dog to the dead sheep.

As dawn broke, a sheep bearing the head of a dog staggered to its feet, emitted noises somewhere between a baa! and a bark, and loped off across the field. The purple spheres knew that the composite creature's body parts would slowly decay, but new bodies could be reassembled using whichever creatures were most convenient.

You can't trust people to heed warnings, Shephatsut-Mer thought. *However dire. Especially a child-king.* So he kept making nervous backward glances to check that no one was following. From time to time he stopped, and listened for the crunch of sandals on gravel.

Nothing.

Now he could concentrate on the search. He was looking for a cunningly concealed niche at the base of the high rocky wall, the entrance to a contorted tunnel that opened out into a small, low cavern. The cave had been hollowed out by the swirl of flash floods, dark water laden with sharp stones that had ground away at the sides of the wadi for millennia, whenever a god became angry and unleashed one of the infrequent but ferocious rainstorms. Rocks, which he had artfully arranged, protected both the cavern and its contents.

He slipped inside the cave. When his eyes adjusted, there was just enough light to see the expected heap of boulders. It seemed untouched since his last visit, and he began to breathe more evenly.

Carefully, he dismantled the heap. Scorpions often lurked beneath desert rocks, and even though their stings were seldom fatal to a healthy adult, they were excruciating. Horned vipers and other snakes were an ever-present danger, too. So he removed the sacred stones one by one, making the appropriate ritual gestures, taking care to keep his fingers clear of any crevices. As he slid the stones aside and inspected the ground beneath for poisonous reptiles and arthropods, he chanted a prayer to Tuwrat. As the Hippopotamus Cult's High Priest, this was his right, his duty, and his pride.

Five hundred paces away, the King, his Regent, and his soldiers waited impatiently, but even royalty must defer to divinities. The Oracle would deliver its verdict in its own time, and not at all if the proper forms were not followed. The ceremony could not be rushed. Insh'erthret had no real idea what was happening, and tried to stave off boredom by playing idly with a wheeled goat carved from ebony.

The Regent was nervous, so his High Priest was nervous too. Shephatsut-Mer had seldom seen Sitaperkaw in such an indecisive mood. When the Regent was indecisive, his decision was awaited with bated breath. When the Regent frowned, mortals trembled. When the Regent was worried, they feared for their lives. It was thus all the more imperative that his questions be answered wisely. Which was to say, answered according to the demands of Tuwrat, as interpreted by the *shep-*

priest of the Hippopotamus Cult. This was Shephatsut-Mer's sacred duty. The goddess would inspire his lifesoul with her answers. He would recognise their truth, and convey them to the Regent, and through him to the King.

None but Shephatsut-Mer knew where the Oracle was hidden, for he was the one who had first found the strange stone in the ashes of the *shiba* bush. He was the chosen one to whom the stone had first spoken. At first, not understanding what it was, he had thought of it as his speaking-stone. He had been young, then; torn between greed and fear, and greed had won. He had hidden the speaking-stone and returned to the Temple.

Moons later, he had finally understood the obvious: what the speaking-stone was, and why it spoke. It was an oracle.

The Oracle. The holy Oracle of the goddess Tuwrat.

It still spoke to him. Sometimes the words were in his own tongue. Such direct advice from the goddess thrilled him to the core, and he always made certain that his actions conformed to the Oracle's pronouncements. But the words were often incomprehensible. He had deduced that what mattered, then, was the interpretation he placed on them. For only this could turn unintelligible sounds into clear advice from the goddess. The words were magical, the stone was a thing of power—and it was power that he, Shephatsut-Mer, could channel towards his own purposes, by turning magic into sense.

Thus it ever was with oracles and priests.

He quickly understood that the Oracle would greatly augment the power of the Cult of the Hippopotamus, so its possession would greatly augment his own power within the Cult. He exploited the Oracle so effectively, and with such speed, that his competitors withdrew in stunned disbelief. He rose to the level of High Priest, changing his name to Shephatsut-Mer. And he kept the Oracle's whereabouts, and its physical form, secret—especially from his principal wife.

Nemnestris was High Acolyte of Nefteremit the Lilypad

Prophetess, earthly intermediary of Ythriz the Moon-goddess. Who in turn was the Sun-god Akhnef's Divine Great Wife. They both knew that the prophecies were a fraud, as Nemnestris had long suspected before she became High Acolyte and was made privy to the cult's secrets, confirming her suspicions.

Shephatsut-Mer had known all along that you can't get public credit for oracular revelations without telling everyone you have an oracle. The superstitious and credulous populace would believe this without further evidence. There was an inner circle of nobles who would be more sceptical, but to some extent they could be fobbed off with the usual excuses —the god had forbidden anyone but the priest to see it, approaching it too closely was dangerous... that sort of thing. Nemnestris was a prominent member of this inner circle, but initially, as a matter of course, she had made the natural assumption that his oracle, like hers, was fraudulent. He dropped hints to encourage her in this belief, while trying to do the opposite to everyone else; it had been a tricky juggling act, and he must have dropped the ball at some point. Never one to keep her nose out of other people's business, Nemnestris had convinced herself that the Oracle, and its magical powers, were genuine. Shephatsut-Mer had never worked out how he had slipped up. He had been grudgingly impressed by his wife's cunning, and even more so, annoyed by it.

His mind returned to the issue at hand. Sitaperkaw was no doubt becoming more impatient by the minute, and more nervous. This was dangerous, but also an opportunity. It made him more receptive to oracular persuasion. The High Priest rolled away the last boulder, checked once again for deadly vermin, and dragged the Oracle into the open. He set it upright on a flat slab of basalt, which he had long ago placed at that spot, for that purpose.

He rubbed his hands on his sabretooth-skin cloak to purify them, knelt before the Oracle, poured water from a goatskin pouch on to the sand as a libation, and chanted the holiest prayer he knew. Then he put the questions to which the King desired answers. The Oracle responded, its words no more comprehensible than they had been the first time it had spoken to him. But no matter: Shephatsut-Mer would *interpret* its words and convey them to Sitaperkaw on behalf of the child-king. That was his function and his holy duty. And he would tell the Regent...

What would he tell the Regent?

He would tell the Regent whichever words the goddess chose to place in his mind. Which, on past experience, would be whatever was most beneficial to the Hippopotamus Cult and its High Priest. Which was only fitting, for the High Priest was the Water People's sole channel to the divine wisdom of Tuwrat.

With the High Priest away on royal duty, and not back until late evening, the High Acolyte could safely play. Nemnestris ran her fingers through Khuf's long hair, planting a kiss on his thick, sensuous lips. Satiated by the fulfilment of mutual lust, they lay side by side on a soft, broad couch in a secret chamber to the rear of the Temple of Nefteremit. The door was barred and their clothing was scattered on the carpeted floor.

The gladiator was sleeping, his muscular chest rising and falling in a slow rhythm. His bronzed skin bore many scars, honorable signs of his profession, and evidence of his skill, since he had lived long enough to acquire them. He was of powerful build, with a broad chest and slim waist. If there was any spare fat on his body, Nemnestris had never found it, and she'd checked him over thoroughly and repeatedly. She rolled away from him, wishing that they could have dared to make use of a fan-bearer. She could have done with a cooling breeze wafted by an ostrich-feather fan, but not with the attentions of the servant who would wield it. Perhaps the Vizier could persuade one of his craftsmen to make a fan that didn't need a servant to operate it? Perhaps powered by a heavy stone on a rope, wound round several wooden cylinders, like the clever toy that one of them had made for the boy-King, a bull that moved across the floor of its own volition.

But what excuse could she offer for wanting such a device?

No, it was folly.

So is this, she thought. *But only if my husband finds out. And he's far too obsessed with his cult and that confounded Oracle he's so proud of.*

The problem was that when not on cult business, Shephatsut-Mer spent too much time with his concubines, especially the shapely one who claimed to be from the island of Keff'tu across the sea to the north of the Inundation, and not enough time with her. He could hardly complain if she lavished her frustrated affections on a substitute. Especially one so virile and handsome.

The people called him Khuf the Shrewd, but his key characteristic was more an instinctive animal cunning. If he'd been less powerfully built, he would probably have been known as Khuf the Crafty or Khuf the Devious. But few would have risked insulting this muscular man, unusually skilled in swordplay and ever ready to sneak in a disembowelling knife or toss a handful of sand in the eyes. He was unusually tall for a Qusite, and there were rumours of Nabish ancestry; but the Nabish were slim, with skin such a dark brown that it seemed blacker than the night sky. Khuf's build would have been stocky, were it not for his height, and his skin colour was the pale bronze of most other Qusites.

Khuf had first come to Nemnestris's attention when he won a famous battle against a water buffalo in the Arena, using only a knife. He had distracted the animal by unwinding his loincloth—the only garment he wore—and throwing it over its head, where it became entangled in the horns. Then he vaulted on to its back, and thrust the knife into its brain. As well as revealing astonishing bravery, the attack also revealed his manly physique, and several of the ladies of the royal court swooned, though Nemnestris noticed that they all kept their eyes open. Nakedness was common in the Arena, indeed in most parts of the land, if there was reason for it. The Qusites had few body-taboos, and both sexes often bathed together in public pools.

Instantly smitten, Nemnestris had enough sense of self-preservation to use extreme caution. Under the pretext of wishing to place a bet for her husband on Khuf's next bout, she employed the Temple's extensive network of informers to investigate his background. He had, in fact, been born in a small farming village some sixty *khar* south of Ul-q'mur, to the village potter Nyjl and his fat frumpish wife Kyran; their ninth child and the second to survive to puberty. The potter was so short as almost to be a dwarf, but the mother was taller than most women of the villages. She had been a beauty when young, but ran to fat because the potter was good at his trade and much of his income came in the form of food. They ate well, and both showed it.

Rumours abounded. Had some tall stranger fathered the child on Kyran without Nyjl's knowledge? Or with it, for that matter, since the potter was inordinately proud of the strapping son that towered to nearly twice his height. But Kyran was already a fat frump when the child must have been conceived, and there were plenty of available young women in the village that would surely have been more likely prospects.

It must have been the will of the gods, an explanation that satisfied most of the inquisitive neighbours, even though *anything* could be explained as the will of the gods. There was some speculation regarding which god, but as the boy grew into manhood, he acquired a fiendish reputation as a street fighter, so it had obviously been Zek-Mek, the goddess of war whose commonest aspect was a near-naked human female with the head of a lioness. Zek-Mek played many roles in Qusite religion, and in particular she was the guild-goddess of gladiators. So there was little surprise when Khuf entered the annual series of amateur bouts in the Arena, whose winners would receive automatic acceptance for gladiatorial training.

Khuf snorted, and instantly became fully awake, as he always did. Nemnestris, a little cooler now and less sweaty than before, snuggled close again.

Khuf reached for her, hands already roving. "My love, you are insitiable," she murmured. "But remember, you have an appointment in the Arena at noon. With Bil."

Khuf laughed. She loved it when he laughed, it was deep, rich, and resonant, a real man's laugh. It was one of his many manly attributes, and one in particular was coming to her attention. Well, coming to attention. "The promoter can wait a little longer, you minx!"

Nemnestris pursed her lips as if in thought. "If you say so, my love." As he kissed her, she squealed with pleasure.

"Perhaps he can wait *much* longer," Khuf amended.

"Bil might," said Nemnestris. "But I'm... not sure... I can."

6
Thanatography

The encrypted signal had been travelling at six hundred times the speed of light for just over a year, compressed into a narrow tightbeam. The Ship allowed the pandemons to use ansibles, which are instantaneous, but long-range ansible signals are omnidirectional and would inevitably be intercepted by Effectuators. It would take even the best-equipped fex a considerable time to break the encryption, but they could cause a lot of trouble without doing that. They would undoubtedly be intrigued to find a level-five technology signal emanating from a region of the Galaxy that seldom stretched to level-two, even if they couldn't read it. They would investigate.

The pandemons were confident they would spot the fex coming and evacuate in time, but they would find traces of unauthorised installations, collect evidence of who had put them there, and discover they had been pandemons. If the signals could be decyrypted, which was probable given enough effort, the fex would also find out what class of crimes the pandemons had been committing. Then they would do everything in their considerable power to track the criminals down and punish them. The penalties for these particular crimes were severe. The rewards were correspondingly great, and pandemon greed was unbounded. It outweighed their fear, provided the chances of being apprehended were sufficiently remote. They were keen to keep them that way.

This particular signal, retransmitted from a relay station in the cometary halo for extra security, originated deep in a crater on the solitary grey moon of an obscure mottled planet known as Shool-3, well away from the civilised regions of the living Galaxy. Several pandemons had gathered in their moonbase, while the rest carried out their usual duties on the planet itself. KrajMajJazj was testing the tightbeam alignment, using an optical telescope to check the configuration of nearby stars around the target direction.

"That's funny."

"Something wrong?" BuzgRuzgMofz asked.

"Not sure. There's something out there that's not in the datalogue. Some sort of fuzzy purple nebula thing."

BuzgRuzgMofz shook his horned head in irritation. KrajMajJazj was imaginative, prone to bursts of genuine creativity, but no technician.

"Offal. No such thing. Let me take a look."

He wandered over, and put an eye—which until a few days ago had belonged to a baboon—to the scope's viewfinder. "You need to sharpen the focus, can't you see the stars are blurred?" He extruded a blue tentacle and tapped at a command pad. "That's more like it. *Yuz!*"

"Yuz what?"

"What you're seeing, KrajMajJazj, is a rare event. Migrating magnetotori."

The other pandemon took a quick look. From Shool-3 the approaching magnetotorus Herd would be barely visible to the naked eye, and then only as a lavender smudge in the night sky. But from the pandemon base on the back of the Moon, the now-focused scope showed KrajMajJazj parallel lines of purple rings, glowing beads threaded on an invisible string, all pointing towards Shool.

"Pretty. What's a magnetotori?"

"A magneto*torus* is a magnetic plasma ramjet that feeds on electrons. This is a whole herd. They migrate from star to star. Very slowly. First time I've ever seen them in the wild."

"Never heard of them."

"No reason you should. I only know about them from a hydet I experienced, years ago."

"Intelligent?"

"Not enough to be sentient. They're not exactly alive, but not exactly dead either, if you get my meaning."

"No. Does it matter?"

"Might." BuzgRuzgMofz fiddled with the command pad, took some measurements. "They're definitely coming this way. Heading for Shool, it looks like."

"Close?"

"Not yet. Still outside the orbit of Shool-6."

"Which planet's that?" KrajMajJazj asked. He was always weak on detail.

"The one with the big ring system."

"Oh, yuz, that one. Trouble?"

BuzgRuzgMofz thought about that. "The Herd's harmless enough, but we need to keep an eye on the Herders. They're seriously weird. Hyperintelligent and as technologically advanced as you can get, but you can never tell what they're going to do next. Mostly nothing, but then they surprise you."

"What sort of surprise?"

"You never know. That's why it's a surprise, right? Thing is, if they discover we're in this system, they might ignore us completely, scream for the fex, or cause trouble in their own inimitable ways."

KrajMajJazj scratched an ear with his own tentacle. "So what do we do?"

"*You* go and tell the boss. Then he'll decide what we do."

KrajMajJazj relayed the discovery to MasgNasgOsg, who didn't seem terribly interested. "No reason those wierdos would call the fex," he said. But just to be sure, he ordered his gang to install another layer of negafrax and tighten security procedures.

You could never be too stringent about security. That was why MasgNasgOsg had decided on the tightbeam. The transmitter, despite being level-five, was obsolete, but it happened to be ideal for this particular application: sending large quantities of ultra-high-quality immersive hydetic recordings to a small, select group of wealthy clients, along a hypervelocity tightbeam so highly focused as to be virtually undetectable by accident. Only someone smack in the beam's path would have any chance of noticing it. The clients were addicted to experiences that Effectuators considered to be evil and perverted; not so much because of the experiences themselves, damaging though they might be, but because of the way they were sourced. Whatever the reasoning, the pandemons had to protect their clients from exposure. Not to mention themselves.

The gang continued its preparations. After some debate, BuzgRuzgMofz tuned the transmitter to 602.71c, the fastest speed that would provide adequate bandwidth without any drop-out.

Shool-3 was so obscure that public databases held nothing significant about the entire region of the Living Galaxy to which it belonged, aside from the usual guff about excessive particle fluxes and dangerous gravity traps, but that was always included when no data existed. Just in case it was true. It hardly ever was, but it covered people's backs and kept most species away. No point in taking unnecessary risks when there was nothing there worth visiting in any case.

That was one reason why the pandemons had chosen the mottled world.

But there was another.

This particular project had started when one of the pandemons had come across a reference in an ancient exploration report, recorded in a format so unusual that no translation software existed. Substantial bribes and some lateral thinking had identified an expert in stylographic pictograms. Acquiring its skills was a matter of routine; any pandemon could do that.

After several months' obsessive application of those skills, the pandemon's investments of time, deviousness, and double-dealing had paid off. The script had yielded up its first secret, a pattern of grammatical regularity; soon the process of decoding it had become a mad scramble as more and more of the pieces fell into place.

When he understood it all, it was even better than he had hoped.

The pandemon owned—he had all the necessary documentation, so who could prove otherwise?—a ship. Not just any ship, but a gigantic Precursor starship. He shared the ship with a fluctuating, but always large, number of other pandemons, partners in crime. The ship was essential to their esoteric line of work, which took them to obscure backwaters of the Galaxy where the forces of order were weak.

Being sensitive, as were all Precursor ships, to its crew's ethical standards—or in this case, its lack of them—the ship did not function anywhere near its true potential, but even under this moral handicap it served the pandemons' purposes well enough. In truth, it should never have functioned at all, but the pandemons had solved that problem in their own crude but direct manner, taking steps to raise the ethical average while leaving their own criminality undiminished.

Precursor ships were user-configurable, but exactly what could be reconfigured depended on the user. Cosmetic changes to their internal structure were relatively easy, and the ethical barrier was low. The Ship's resistance to more significant internal changes was inversely proportional to the ethical level of crew and passengers. It would allow external reconstruction only if the ethical level of the crew and passengers was exceptional. The previous owner (conveniently deceased, with assistance) had refurbished the interior of this one in a gaudy and tasteless fashion, with the ship's agreement and assistance. The pandemons, whose tastes leaned towards the macabre, had remodelled it to the limited extent that the Ship would allow. It had no control over non-Precursor technology, however, and the pandemons had exploited this loophole to fill the more glaring gaps. The vessel therefore boasted an impressive range of weaponry, all of it illegal.

The report's arrays of annoyingly elaborate pictograms detailed an ambitious expedition by a race that the pandemon could not identify from the fragmentary document. Internal evidence suggested a silicoid lifeform whose superconductive brains required a low-temperature environment. Towards the end of the report, there was a fascinating passage. By then, the expedition had stopped off at a dozen star systems, with absolutely nothing to show for its efforts. What the silicoids found had disappointed them, but it had driven the pandemon to transports of cupidity, because it had sensed a business opportunity.

Most species in the Living Galaxy fall into one of three broad classes. Coldlife are cryogenic, requiring temperatures below the freezing-point of carbon dioxide, and typically have superconducting nervous systems on a silicon or other semiconducting substrate. Warmlife are molecular, composed of complex molecules based on carbon or occasionally silicon (with metal atoms to improve stability) and thrive in or just beyond the range at which water is liquid. Hotlife are magnetic plasmas functioning by nuclear reactions, and exist solely in stars. Exceptions are informally classified as weirdlife by species in the three main classes; the formal classification is complicated and rather *ad hoc*. With sufficient technological support, coldlife and warmlife can coexist in the same environment, though not comfortably for either. Neither class can coexist with hotlife.

Communication between sentient species is widespread, however, because of the huge range of methods available. Coldlife and warmlife mainly use ansibles; hotlife use modulated radiation connecting them to orbital ansibles.

The silicoids were coldlife. According to their report, they had come across a ghastly warmworld with a toxic atmosphere, extreme environment, and poisonous coloration. It hosted a form of warmlife which, although lacking any individual intelligence worth speaking of, was adept at organising itself into groups, spontaneously generating a form of collective intelligence capable of building primitive but effective architecture. The builders were so hot that from the point of view of coldlife their bodies were mostly molten rock. This made a perverse kind of sense, for the terrain they lived in was even hotter—except for the polar regions, where rock was solid and silicoid life might gain a precarious foothold with enough technical support.

The final blow to the silicoids' hopes came when they observed a discouraging level of aggression among these indigenes. It made up for their primitive level of technology by its sheer ferocity. Much of it was ritualised. All of it was savage. The silicoids decided to abandon this hostile, barbaric system, and move on.

The pandemon's response was the exact opposite. The ritualised violence was precisely what he had been searching for, and the world's obscurity was perfect, because the fex were unlikely to interfere. The indigenes were primitive and lacked even basic technologies such as ansibles and transibles. Their planet—indeed, their own tiny enclave on their modest, unremarkable world—was all they knew, all they could imagine. The mottled world was undefended and vulnerable.

It was also environmentally harmless. Pandemons did not demand deep cold as silicoids did, and they did not find oxygen toxic. Liquid water held no terrors for them. In any case, local hosts would be adapted to local conditions.

The pandemon and his partners decided to set up their base on the mottled planet's grey tidally-locked companion, located on the hemisphere that remained eternally hidden from the primary. The airless surface would be ideal for erecting their transmission equipment. They would have to make extended visits to the oxygen-rich primary to obtain recordings, but pandemons could thrive in the presence of oxygen. It would take some clever genetic re-coding, but their brains—the only organs that mattered—were naturally resilient. Some relatively straightforward chemo-engineering could reset their metabolisms to cope with the oxygen excess and the relatively cool climate. That done, they could safely infest local hosts, and the hosts' own protective systems would automatically protect *them*.

The richly alien environment of this world, and its weird creatures, which had so repelled the silicoids, were perfect. The pandemons' customers would be well content.

More than 600 light years away, a maze of tachyonic circuitry crammed into a secret cavern in an asteroid detected a data-package arriving along the tightbeam, converted it to ordinary radio, and retransmitted it, still encrypted, to a precise location on the system's sole inhabited world. There a powerful analytical engine decrypted it, and sent notification of its arrival to the depository of Bannebru Slith, who was the Riuum'tuuq of Ghymizzen and a prominent member of the ruling conclave of the Nation of the Seventy Islands. Bannebru observed the appearance of a familiar icon on his personal dataveil, cancelled his remaining tasks for the day, and took a luxury hydrofoil to his private islet, a small but elegant atoll at the northern end of a volcanic chain that swept in a great arc between the Forbidden Peninsula and the hostile continental coast of Outer Gorash.

He had paid a substantial premium to avail himself of the unique 'authentic' master-record, which was very valuable to collectors. Even the copies commanded a high price, but these were not released until the master-record had been experienced. Clients obtained huge prestige among their fellow perverts by getting the newest stuff *first*. And there was a strong belief, totally unsupported by evidence, that the copies were in some manner inferior. The pain less sharp, the horror slightly blunted. The pandemons actively encouraged such superstitions, because they sent the value of the master-record sky-high.

Within half an hour Bannebru had divested himself of his ceremonial robes, demanded a large bowl of predigested smüfruit from a servitor, had it deposited in his private quarters, expelled the housebots, sealed the entrance tunnel, and arranged his corpulent betentacled body on a circular waterbed fronted by a semicircular hyperreality eidetic display. Stuffing a scoop of smüfruit into his lower food-orifice, and shivering with anticipation, he enunciated the code phrases that would unlock the data-package, and instructed the hydet to unfold it.

Pornography is species-specific. The gluey mating practices of a corpus of strangleworms excites the worms themselves to a collective sexual frenzy, but leaves most other observers either unmoved or actively repulsed. The market for sex is restricted to individual species. But there is another source of emotional excitement that is far more universal, and can be sold more widely.

The subject, a strange quadrupedal creature that stood on two of its appendages, presumably to leave the other two free for other purposes, was attached to a stake by a long metal chain. Only an expert xenologist could be certain that its movements indicated extreme distress, but even a neophyte could guess that was the case. Bannebru's *eft* left no shadow of doubt. The empathic field transducer allowed him to experience a close analogue of the creature's emotions. He could damp them down to reduce their impact, or he could ramp them up to the strongest sensations that he could tolerate.

In one of the upper appendages the subject held a long rod with a sharp spike on one end, evidently a primitive weapon.

Bannebru's eye-ring swivelled to concentrate on the

fearsome-looking alien monster that prowled menacingly just beyond the reach of the weapon. It was orange in colour, coated with some strange kind of carpet—

[It is called 'fur'], the hydet's glossar whispered in his son-opore. [It is extruded by living cells in the monster's skin, but is not itself alive. It is used for insulation and display.] The eye-ring switched to the ruff around the creature's head, and the glossar noticed the change of attention. [The [mane] is an example. Only males possess one. It is used to make the male seem larger, which intimidates rivals and prey, and impresses females.]

Bannebru, unimpressed by alien sexual displays, was becoming increasingly fascinated by the numerous sharp protrusions in specific regions of the monster's body. Its—food-orifice? Just the one?—sprouted two great fangs, razor-sharp, and two rows of lesser fangs. Each of its four—[limbs], the glossar whispered, used for [locomotion]—terminated in a bunch of smaller fangs. Its food-orifice gaped wide, and emit-ted a ghastly cry, an extended roaring sound. The subject cringed, but continued to point its weapon at the monstrous head, making jabbing motions in the hope of deterring the creature from a close approach.

Bannebru widened the view to a panorama. Upwards of fifteen similar subjects were tethered by chains in a flat oval space [Arena] surrounded by tier upon tier of alien creatures bearing a striking resemblance to the subject. These [spectators] were making a continual screeching noise, which Bannebru recognised from previous recordings as an alien form of deathlust. [They call it 'bloodlust.' 'Blood' is their primary bodily fluid.] Bannebru already knew that. [The ceremony is an execution of crim-inals who have stolen grave goods from the tombs of dead god-kings. It is a capital offence, believed to deny the god-king access to the afterlife.] Bann-ebru grunted in frustration at the irrelevant explanations. *Don't tell me! Show me!* It did not occur to him that the delay was deliberate, raising the level of suspense. The pandemons routinely researched their clients' psychology.

The spectators' excitement transferred itself to Bannebru's own sensorium, arousing his own deathlust. His mesopodal tentacles began to ripple with a potent mixture of fear and anticipation. The orange-carpeted monster, rendered vividly in high-resolution three-dimensional hyperreality, seemed as real as the waterbed on which he now began to rock from side to side. The close-ups were terrifying. But Bannebru knew he was safe, the monster only an illusion. It could not harm him.

The same could not be said for its potential victim, who was starting to tire.

The monster began to pace to and fro, snarling, making mock lunges, gesturing with its front limbs. Suddenly a mock lunge became real, and it hurled itself at the subject—only to be repulsed by a jab with the weapon. It sprang back, yowling. Red fluid trickled down its flank from the wound.

Blood. The creature was damaged; it would be experiencing pain. Pain was an evolutionary universal, common to almost all races. It alerted organisms to potential damage. Without it, even minor accidents would eventually kill. So evolution made pain difficult to ignore, and that required it to be unpleasant. If necessary, excruciatingly unpleasant and impossible to ignore.

Bannebru was excited by pain, as long as it wasn't his own. It was a huge turn-on. And alien pain, experienced vicariously through the *eft*, was even more exciting because it was a perversion. Bannebru was addicted to the pain of other creatures. It transported him out of his otherwise dull existence, filled with the endless boring rituals required of a Riuum'tuuq. He always turned up the gain as high as he could bear. As repetition jaded his senses, he ramped it ever higher, exactly as his pandemon providers intended.

The monster lunged again, and this time its limb-fangs struck the subject's flesh, tearing long gashes. More red fluid gushed from them, dripping on to the floor of the Arena, soaking into the [sand]. The subject sank to the ground, but this was a feint; as the monster came close, the subject jabbed it again with its weapon, inflicting another open wound. The monster roared, the spectators yelled.

Again the view widened. Bannebru could cause the hydet to home in on any part of the spectacle. He could put himself in any location. He could rerun the entire course of events, from any viewpoint, filling his mind with vicarious pain, amplified by the *eft* and feeding his growing deathlust —and what made the recording so effective was that it was no artificial graphic construct. It was real. It had happened. It satisfied his deepest and most depraved cravings. Which was why he paid the pandemons a fortune, and why the Effectuators considered his addiction to be a serious crime. The pandemons were thanatographers, death-pornographers, despised throughout the Living Galaxy by all who knew of their existence, other than their perverted customers.

Still the monster circled its increasingly desperate victim, who was visibly weakening, no doubt from loss of blood. The *eft* made its fear and anguish tangible, even to a being from another world.

There was a flurry of action, but Bannebru had been ingesting another scoop of smüfruit, and he missed it. He called for a slow-motion replay.

The subject, sensing it had little time left if it wanted to live, had taken a desperate gamble. It had thrown its weapon at the monster. A miss would have left it helpless and defenceless, chained as it was to the stake. But it didn't miss. The spike rammed home in one of the monster's visual organs [eyes]. It made a terrible noise, thrashing uncontrollably, pawing at the shaft with its forelimbs, trying to dislodge it. The weapon must have penetrated something vital, for the monster sank to the ground. The shaft snapped, but the monster was already close to death. Its huge bulk pulsated; then it rolled on one side and was still.

Bannebru was shivering now, his tentacles rippling in great waves, his arousal growing by the second. The deathlust was upon him, and he wanted *more*. He screeched for higher amplification. Glands in his skin exuded a thick, greasy fluid. One part of him *was* vaguely disappointed that the subject was still alive; had, it seemed, escaped...

Ahhhhhh, but no. Clever pandemons!

A broader view revealed another monster settling down to feed on its still-living prey. Beyond that, a third monster had dispatched one of the tethered creatures and was looking around for another. It saw the now-weaponless subject, and loped towards it. The subject, yelling in terror, badly damaged in securing its empty victory, limped to the far side of its stake. The monster began to circle, driving its victim before it, encircling the stake, so that the chain became ever shorter...

By the end, the Arena was awash with blood and mangled body parts and the monsters were gorged to bursting. Bannebru deflated, and in a wavering voice he told the hydet to switch off the gory spectacle. He called in a housebot. "Clean that up," he instructed, referring to his waterbed, now awash with the sticky exudations of his own freshly satiated death-lust.

Satiated now, but not for long. He knew he would soon be gasping for more. He would view the new recording from every possible angle, until it no longer satisfied him. Some part of his mind gibbered at the prospect of being deprived of further stimulation. Fortunately, his subscription guaranteed that another recording would soon arrive. In fact, at least five were already on their way.

Sand blew off the ridge of the huge barchan dune, but only a very careful observer would have noticed that unlike other barchans in the dune field, this one remained in the same place. The rest crept forward, as all *bidd'hu* knew and many Qusite folk-stories maintained. Their movement was imperceptible, but if anyone had visited the region once a month and placed a stick in the ground, they would have found proof that they were moving. All except one. If they had understood *how* the dunes moved, it might have occurred to them to wonder how this particular dune could remain stationary despite the blowing sand. But no one would explain how the dunes moved, while keeping their crescent shape, for twenty thousand years.

Beneath the stationary dune, a Precursor starship lay buried. It had not been there long, and it was fully functional. No one in the Living Galaxy understood the workings of Precursor technology. A billion years had passed since their entire race vanished, and the engineers of that ancient race had left no instruction manuals, no clues to the exotic principles on which they were based, and no images or descriptions of themselves. Advanced races had deduced that the underlying principles were as much metaphysical as they were physical, because Precursor starships responded to the psychology of their users. The more ethically the user behaved, the more cooperative the ship became, giving access to more powerful abilities.

The ship beneath the sand was inhabited by pandemons, making it extremely uncooperative. Its inhabitants could use only its most basic features—a superluminal drive suitable only for interstellar transportation, unable to bridge the gulfs between galaxies; tractor and pressor fields that would not concentrate into beams. The pandemons had no awareness of the ship's hidden, greater powers, and they would never have been able to convince it to permit their use, even if they had known.

Despite these limitations, the ship was more than adequate for their purposes. It carried them and their equipment to target worlds in a few weeks (trips that a more ethical user might have made in nanoseconds). Its tractor/pressor field let it manipulate small masses, hence also large amounts of granular matter, since each individual grain was small. So the pandemons had persuaded their ship to hide beneath a marching dune, and to stop it marching by recycling the blown sand around its sides, back to the rear, to be blown off the crest again and again.

From inside the ship, MasgNasgOsg conducted his dismal profession with long-polished skill. His gang had constructed a permanent base on the planet's unusually large crater-spattered moon. The Ship had plenty of transibles, and could always duplicate more, but it refused point-blank to let the pandemons use one for any purpose. So they had to travel to and from their Moonbase using transpods: rather cramped craft designed solely for short-range travel. The Ship did offer to let the pandemons extend the range of their ansibles, but they knew that long-range ansible transmissions could easily be detected by the fex, so they avoided the trap the Ship had set. Instead, they used semi-obsolete tightbeams to transmit thanatographic material recorded in the environs of Qus to the base. From there, relay stations further from the star used the same technology to broadcast the recordings to numerous wealthy subscribers, widely distributed across the vast region of inhabited space known as the Living Galaxy.

The existence of pandemonic death-pornography was not widely known, except to their customers and a specialist branch of the fex. It exploited a narrow but profitable niche in the criminal market. Alien sex is generally unexciting to other species, but death and pain are universal. The violent Qusite gladiatorial contests, mentioned in the silicoid report, were what had attracted the pandemons to Shool-3 in the first place. Concealed from Earthly eyes by transparency suits, they were making hyperreality sensory recordings.

Only a few Qusites knew the pandemons existed, and none of them was royal.

MasgNasgOsg had been reviewing feedback from his clientele, and although much of it was favourable, he detected some dissatisfaction. His routine demand for access to a transible was equally routinely rejected, and directing angry curses at the ships' controlling persona only made matters worse. A transpod was out of the question, because it was too big to be stealthed with anything the Ship would supply. So it was time to don his transparency suit, cajole the ship into creating a short tunnel to the desert surface, and pay one of the citizens of Ul-q'mur a visit.

On foot.

In a sealed compartment in the bowels of the ship, the Surgeon's dismal half-existence continued, as it had done for centuries.

It was no longer infested with pandemons, but tedium piled upon tedium had pushed its huge brain beyond the bounds of sanity.

It had long given up all hope of release.

Even through death.

Yet, astonishingly, within that abused, malfunctioning organ, some semblance of personality still flickered.

7

Spectacular

The ground beneath the Arena was riddled with passages, tunnels, and rooms for everything from stored fodder to caged animals. The cry echoed off the walls. "Ptafni? Ptafni? Where the—oh, there you are."

Bil, the manager-promoter of the Arena, was looking for the youngest of his three sons. Ammad and Dobil were busy in the royal zoo, mucking out deinotheres. It was hard, unpleasant work, and Bil approved completely. No better way to learn the trade than to start at the bottom.

Ptafni's head poked out from behind a stack of hay bales, imported in quantity from the western savannahs. "Sorry, pa. I was looking for gazelle fodder." The Arena kept a herd of the animals to ensure a steady supply of meat for the stars of the show, the big cats. Ptafni was in charge of storage, and was also learning to keep the Arena accounts. He had a head for figures.

"The Beastmaster wants you to help him transfer a new arrival to a permanent cage."

Ptafni looked worried. "Sabretooth?"

"No, just a leopard."

"It's easy to underestimate a leopard, pa."

Bil cuffed his son's ear in mock chastisement. "I've trained you to deal with everything up to and including swamp-pigs."

Ptafni handed his father the scroll he had been consulting. "Someone else will have to check the inventory, then." He hesitated. "You pay too much attention to that lionface, pa. *You're* in charge, not him!"

"Yes, son, I am. In charge. And what have I told you?"

Ptafni realised he'd gone too far. He just didn't like lionfaces. He was also stubborn. "I know, I know. He's the King's Beastmaster. I just don't see why the King favours those upstarts so—"

"Yes you do. Can *you* get a lion to feed from your hand? Herd aurochsen? Calm an irate swamp-pig? Tame a giraffe? No, you can't. Those guys can. They may not look like real folk, Ptafni, but they sure have a way with animals. We can't even come close."

"That," Ptafni said, as if it closed the discussion, "is because they're animals themselves."

Bil glared at him. "Ptafni, how long has our family been managing this Arena?"

"Eight generations, pa."

"Yes. And I want us to be in the business for *nine* generations. I learned the trade from my father Dani, who learned it from his father Jor-Ah, who learned it from Lari, who—anyway, you're learning it from me. You may not be my eldest son, but you're way and above the smartest, and you're in line for the job.

"And if you're going to succeed, you have to learn respect for lionfaces, just as your ancestors did. Because *we can't do it without them*. Got that? Because the King certainly does. You're expendable. *I'm* expendable. The beastmasters aren't expendable."

Ptafni bit back a sharp retort. "Yes, father."

Bil noted the switch to formality. "You don't have to like it, son. I find them a bit... *creepy*, too. Sometimes they seem to know what I'm thinking. But you have to accept it, or it'll eat you up from inside and one day you'll snap. And then the King will have you executed. Maybe some genius will work out how they do it, and the King can give the job to real folk like us. But until that day, when the Beastmaster says 'jump', you hop. And so do I. Even though I'm in charge."

Ptafni nodded. "I do understand, pa. It's just—"

"Just what?"

"Lionfaces seem so uncouth."

Bil laughed. *"Uncouth?* What sort of a word is that? You've been hanging out with those rich kids again. Probably where you got this nonsense from in the first place. Go to the Street of Thieves at any hour of the day or night and you'll see real folk far more *uncouth* than any lionface!"

"Yes, pa. But we're not all like that. Lionfaces are all the same, every one of them. They're born that way."

"So they are. Just as *you* were born to argue the hind leg off a donkey. Now, off with you! The Beastmaster hasn't got all day."

It was quicker to walk than to relocate to the body of a faster creature such as a gazelle. Within two hours, MasgNas-gOsg was inside the city, threading his way through the crowds that thronged the streets, keeping to the main thoroughfares where there was more room to avoid bumping into people, heading for the Arena. The main gates were open; they were mainly decorative, their function ceremonial. Paying no attention to the two great rock lions that flanked the entrance, he ducked under a token barrier that served to warn unauthorised folk not to enter, but made no attempt to prevent them from doing so if they decided to ignore the warning. Bil wasn't worried that interlopers might harm anything or anyone in the Arena. What worried him was the exact opposite.

The Arena's manager was sitting in the small mudbrick cube that served as an office when the door opened. He looked up, but saw no one.

He sighed.

The air shimmered, solidified, and MasgNasgOsg materialised in front of him.

Bil looked at the bizarre form, which currently seemed to be a composite of the rear end of a lioness with the front of a goat and the head of a gazelle. Various repulsive bits of flesh from gods knew what animals dangled haphazardly. Some sort of—tentacle?—was pressing against a disc that hung on the creature's chest. The tentacle, which was a strange shade of blue and glistened wetly, retracted into a body-cavity.

Bil hated it when pandemons did that. Bits of real animals was one thing; organs that resembled nothing he'd ever seen, even in a butcher's shop, made him feel sick. Truly these creatures must be demons of the underworld.

He told himself he should be polite, but he still had some vestige of pride. "You might at least knock," he said, even though he knew these horrors were immune to insults.

"You are not paid to instruct me," said the pandemon, its voice high-pitched and sibilant, its vocal cords donated involuntarily by a human child that had wandered away from her parents. "You are paid to obey."

Bil nodded, twice. "Have I ever disobeyed you, Excellency?"

"Your continued existence argues not."

The promoter of the gladiatorial Arena shivered inwardly and spread his hands wide in a display of acquiescence. "What do you want of me now?"

The pandemon leaned closer, its breath an indeterminate mix resembling asphalt tinged with carrion. Bil, who smelled worse things every day just walking through the narrow passageways of Ul-q'mur's less reputable districts, ignored it, and looked the alien firmly in its big black gazelle eye. The eye stared back at him until finally he blinked.

"I am receiving some complaints about the tameness of the entertainment," the pandemon said. Somehow the incongruous voice failed to rob its speech of menace. If anything, it enhanced the effect.

Bil's pockmarked face reddened, even beneath his heavy tan from a life spent mainly outdoors. His spirit was not yet totally crushed. "Excellency, that's unfair. Last week you recorded ten criminals being disembowelled and then burned alive," he protested. "I set that up for you!" In truth, it had not been difficult to arrange, aside from creating fake evidence and bribing false witnesses to persuade the Court of Magistrates that the ten unfortunates had been guilty of robbing the tomb of a former Vizier.

"Yuz. But my client felt that they died too quickly."

Bil turned and spat on to the sandy floor. "You can hardly hold me responsible for how long it takes a human engulfed in flames to die."

"My client felt that the fire was too large and too hot. The people burned like torches, and died far too rapidly from lack of oxygen compounded by burnt lung tissue. Slow roasting would have been far more entertaining, and my client's pleasure would have been greatly prolonged along with the agony of the victims."

Unwisely, Bil bristled. "Look, if you want changes made to the legal punishment for theft of the property of a royal official and criminal disrespect for deceased nobility, you need to talk to the Chief Magistrate, not me. And he'll just kick you up the chain of command. So you might as well go straight to Sitaperkaw. Not the King, he's too young and has no power. It's the Regent who can get things done!"

"That is true but unsatisfactory. You know I do not wish any high official to know that pandemons are here. Especially not royalty. You will raise the emotional level of the entertainment, *without* revealing my existence to anyone. My clients demand it, therefore so do I."

Bil shook his head; hesitated. "I really don't—"

"This is not a debate. Your payment can be given in terms of punishment instead of reward," hissed the pandemon. "If you do not perform adequately."

Months earlier, the pandemon had demonstrated his capabilities in that direction on a dog. Remembering this, Bil winced, and sweat broke out on his brow. Now he regretted his previous bravado.

"There's one possibility, Excellency," he said quickly, forcing himself to be more respectful. "One activity where I have almost total control."

"And that is?"

"The coming Festival," said Bil. "The Festival of the Frowning Moon. A spectacular gladiatorial contest like no other, terrifying and bloody even with just the traditional contests. I'll invent new ones, Excellency, of extreme violence. I have complete freedom in that regard."

"Then I suggest you make this Festival your most violent Spectacular yet, Bil."

The pandemon's tentacle emerged once more from within its body, bent into a curve, and pressed the disc on its chest. MasgNasgOsg promptly vanished as his transparency suit recohered. Bil assumed the repulsive creature had left. He sniffed the air, and the reek had gone. It wasn't a foolproof test, but it was better than nothing. Still, it was wise to remember that he could still be under close observation.

Shaking with suppressed fear, he wiped his brow with a scrap of cloth.

He had not been entirely truthful. He had no freedom to create Spectaculars. He had freedom to make suggestions, but the final decision rested with Sitaperkaw. Fortunately the Regent had a taste for blood and gore in the Arena—he would have been a good client for the pandemons, were it not for his easy access to the real thing. Bil's intentions would appeal to Sitaperkaw, in principle, but Spectaculars were hideously expensive. Much copper and many gemstones must change hands to put on such a show. Unfortunately, generosity was not one of Sitaperkaw's virtues.

Still, there must be a way. All Bil had to do was to persuade the Regent to demand more extreme violence, and more... *imaginative* gladiatorial contests, without being seen to have initiated such a request.

His brow furrowed as he debated the options with himself, torn between desperation and caution. The best solution would be to dupe some weak-minded highborn ingenue into telling the Regent that the common people were tiring of the same old combat routines. That would be highly plausible; in fact, it was very likely true. The news could be reinforced by hints that unless the Games were spiced up, there could be civil unrest. The Regent could put any rebellion down without difficulty, but that would be even more expensive than a Spectacular, and far less satisfying. (Though it did occur to Bil that the pandemons might find it a novel entertainment for their clients, and he filed the thought away in his head.)

Who could he persuade to convey these tidings to the Regent? There was no way to predict how Sitaperkaw would react, so anyone with half a brain would never take the risk. It needed someone of sufficient standing to have the Regent's ear, yet unperceptive enough not to realise they were being used. Someone blinkered by vanity, impulsive, and easily led.

Put like that, the choice was obvious.

Bil's sister was a close friend of an aged crone who did the washing for a woman who wove cloth for one of Princess Azmyn's maids. A few small rings of copper changed hands, messages were exchanged in whispers, and a thought took root in Azmyn's mind.

"Maids!" she shouted.

Two harassed-looking young women appeared through a curtain and hurried towards her, to kneel at her feet.

"I want a bath."

They scurried off to summon house-servants with heavy pots of hot water, enough to fill the Princess's alabaster plunge-pool. They tipped in oils and perfumes from delicate stone jars.

"More *kenib*-oil, Swafzi! I've told you before, use the whole jar! The Overseer of the Household will send someone to the market for more."

Swafzi upended the jar. When all was to their mistress's satisfaction, the maids undressed her and helped her into the steaming pool. As the scented water relaxed her, she mulled the thought over in her mind and decided it was worth acting on.

After a time, she gave an exaggerated shiver. "This water is becomning *cold*!"

That was a sign that they should help her out again and dry her with warm towels. With their assistance she tried on several expensive robes, eventually settling on a green ankle-length wrap embroidered with fine copper wire, slit to the waist up the left side. They brushed her wavy black hair—no wig, not even any extensions; all hers and hers alone. They helped her select a suitable perfume. Finally she chose a simple lapis necklace with a huge carnelian pendant to round off the ensemble, pinning a matching jewel into her hair.

Azmyn was stunning, and knew it. Male eyes were automatically drawn to her whenever she made an entrance. She was unusually tall, despite the flat-soled sandals she habitually wore to show off her compact, almost childlike feet. Her eyes were an unusual blue, so deep as to be almost black. She was slim-waisted, full-breasted, perhaps a little too rounded at the hips; but total perfection is bland.

She always made a special effort to look her best when she made one of her frequent visits to the Palace. On this occasion she wanted to raise several urgent issues with the Vizier.

Lord Noth-Metamphut, the highest official in the land, had a title that would stretch across half a roll of papyrus if written out in full, because it listed all of his many duties and responsibilities, not just his names. The King's universal fix-it man, he was generally referred to as the Vizier.

He was inspecting plans for a new temple to Wozer when his secretary shuffled in, an elderly man who had to use a stick to walk.

"What is it now, Tathag?"

"Princess Azmyn demands audience, my Lord."

"Yes, she would. Everyone else *requests* it. What does she want now?"

"A chat, my Lord."

"Nothing more specific?"

"She didn't say."

"She never does. But there's always something more specific." He rolled up the plans and replaced them in an ivory-and-ebony chest in an alcove. "You'd better show her in. She'll only go whining to her cousin if you don't."

Azmyn usually warmed up with a list of smaller requests, which she referred to as 'suggestions', before going for the jugular. The Vizier knew that most of her suggestions originated with the priesthood. Those hyenas were always scavenging for more wealth and power. But this time one topic —obviously the real reason for her visit—had not, and it intrigued him. Had Azmyn come up with it all by herself?

"Lord Noth-Metamphut, I was speaking to one of my maids, and the forthcoming Games for the Festival of the Frowning Moon came up. She was talking about them, and she said... oh, no, I'm sure it's of no import. Boy! More wine! Now, what news have you of the—"

"The Games? What did your maid say, Princess? Was she looking forward to the spectacle? The townsfolk generally do, it livens up their dull repetitive lives."

"Oh yes. Well. Not exactly."

"The opposite of 'yes' is 'no'."

"Well. I suppose... She said she'd heard talk in the beer-houses that the Games were becoming a bit... dull. Predictable. Not as exciting as in the past." Pause. "I'm sorry, I'm only repeating what she—"

The Vizier raised a hand to silence the flow of words. "Of course. That's a little disturbing."

"In what way?"

"Dissatisfaction among the townsfolk is always present at a low level, Azmyn. The function of the Games is to provide an outlet for their discontent. Fed and sated, they pose no serious challenge to royal authority. If that's losing its effect, there could be growing unrest among the populace."

"Well, of course," said Azmyn. "But you can suppress it easily enough, I'm sure, my Lord. Your power is immense."

"As you say, Princess. But it's simpler and cheaper to keep the population calm and content with their lot. What would you propose?"

"Well, it's not for me to say, Lord Vizier, not at all, but since you *insist*... well, something more *exciting* would seem to be in order. More original. A dramatic setting, perhaps." She paused, as if groping for in idea—which was entirely plausible. "Uh— Hunting in the marshes?"

"The event will be held in the Arena, Azmyn."

"Yes, yes, I know. I meant, you could create the *illusion* of a hunt in the marshes. In the Arena. Lots of swamp-pigs and crocodiles! The gladiators could fight them."

The Vizier stroked his beard, deep in thought. For once, the empty-headed little bitch had come up with a real idea. It just needed a few tweaks to make it practical.

"An illusion? I think we can do even better. Bring in water and mud and vegetation, so the gladiators have to fight each other in the semblance of a swamp, surrounded by fierce creatures. Swamp-pigs, crocodiles, snakes. On the surrounding land, lions. Then they'd be torn between attacking a human adversary and defending themselves against dangerous wild animals. War on two fronts."

Azmyn bounced with excitement. "Oh, what a *brilliant* suggestion, Lord Noth-Metamphut! A stroke of purest *genius*! Everyone would find that utterly *fascinating*, nobles and common folk alike!"

"So they would," said Noth-Metamphut, looking smug. *Apart from the gladiators*, he thought sourly. "I'll raise the matter with the King."

By which they both knew he meant the Regent, for that was where the true power lay.

8
Warrior

I'm celebrated throughout the realm for my exploits in the Arena, Yulmash thought, *and* still *I come home to find no food on my table*. But it was his own fault, and he knew it. When you marry for political influence, securing yourself a wife with royal connections, those connections weave a protective web around her and a noose around you. A lesser man with a lesser wife would soon make it clear who was boss. Instead, he was trapped in a loveless, childless marriage, with no hope of release. To make his frustration complete, Azmyn made it very clear that she would not tolerate any concubines. Not even one! He knew that the Regent would back her up, so on that topic her word was law.

He suspected that Sitaperkaw would reprimand her if he became aware that she was not providing adequate food, for this would reflect badly on the royal family. However, the gain would be short-lived and not worth the emotional fallout; his life would be torment for weeks. Yulmash had considered having a quiet but pointed word with the kitchen servants, but if he went behind Azmyn's back he would never hear the end of it. The household was her responsibility. Such a pity that she interpreted that role as 'I'm in charge and no one else may instruct the staff' rather than 'I'm the one whose job it is to ensure that the house is run smoothly and correctly.'

"Ghaah!"

A short, fat, balding man, dressed in a dull brown

smock, poked his head round the edge of the doorway.

"I'm starving! Find me some leftovers!"

Ghaah bobbed his head and vanished. Yulmash cracked a grin. At least he was in charge of his own body-servant. The man was a marvel, he must know something about the cook that she would prefer to remain secret, because he soon returned with a dish of roast meat, a loaf of newly-baked bread, a bowl of dates, and a fresh pot of thick, nourishing beer. Better still, Azmyn would never know. She was away again, no doubt sucking up to the Palace overseer and whining to her cousin Sitaperkaw, Regent to His Divine Majesty Son-of-Akhnef Chosen-by-the-Sunsouls Insh'erthret (May He Shine Forever) and so on and so on and so on...

In Yulmash's opinion, Sitaperkaw's regency was a successful one, and should he instead of Insh'erthret somehow be elevated to full kingship (which would not be unusual; child-kings had an unfortunate habit of failing to attain maturity) he might even become a good leader. With one proviso: his family and other hangers-on must be persuaded to grant the Regent enough time and opportunity to develop a mind of his own. The warrior had seen worse kings, notably Insh'erthret's dithering father Sh'erthret-Amt. At least the unlamented former King's half-brother made sure that his subjects did not starve—not even the lowliest—by doling out public grain from the Temple's capacious storehouses when the harvest was poor.

This did not entirely please the priests of the Hippopotamus Cult, who saw their own power trickling away along with the hoarded grain, but it suited their public face to be seen to be as generous as their new child-king, who automatically took credit for his Regent's decisions. So they didn't complain in public. Instead, they put ideas into Azmyn's head in private, which should have been easy, there being plenty of room for them, but the insertion procedure required a lot of time, effort, and repetition. One exasperated priest had likened it to trying to push a newborn calf back into its mother, only to find that the supposed mother had been mis-identified and was a bull. But when an idea had finally been planted, it took root. The priests could rely on the Regent's scatterbrained cousin to relay some version of their views to him as if it were her own. The results were usually distorted, and often bore only a faint resemblance to whatever they had intended her to say, but it was a safe way to open up discussion on tendentious issues. Sitaperkaw knew exactly what the priests were doing, but it suited both parties to pretend otherwise; he could take a strand out of the priest's scroll and communicate his responses back to them with equal indirection and deniability. So Azmyn acted as go-between for these garbled but effective negotiations, the only person involved who was under the impression that the opinions she expressed were her own.

Yulmash cleared his plate, wolfing down the meat as if the meal were his first for a week, as it would have been without Ghaah's tireless services. A warrior needed fuel for his muscles, blood to strengthen his heart, and strong beer to put fire in his lifesoul. The dates were a bonus—Ghaah knew his master liked dates. These had been picked mere hours ago, judging by the taste. One day Yulmash would reward Ghaah with his freedom, but right now he needed the bonded servant too much. He knew it was a mistake to rely on a bondsman's devotion; more than one good man had been poisoned by a trusted bondsman, despite the atrocious penalties that inevitably would ensue. Hatred could run very deep indeed. But—no, not Ghaah. There was never even a hint of resentment as the dumpy little man scurried away on the latest errand. Yulmash reckoned he could read people's body language; it was one of the talents that had made him such a successful gladiator, able to intuit his adversaries' intentions before they moved a muscle. He told himself that he did not *trust* Ghaah, but he had total control over the man's state of mind, playing him like a temple songstress stroked the strings of a tortoiseshell harp.

Would that he could do the same with Azmyn. But her

royal blood rendered her immune to persuasion, be it subtle or crude. She never seemed to be worried that his profession could easily kill him. Sometimes he got the impression that she wanted just that; at other times she could be surprisingly affectionate. There was no pattern to her moods, and the state of her mind baffled him.

He was aware of how the priests were using his wife, but it never worked for him. Some sources she found credible, lapping up everything they fed to her; he wasn't one of them. Perhaps he wasn't persistent enough. Or powerful enough to hold her attention. But then, she hadn't asked to be wedded to a commoner, a warrior, and now a gladiator who fought in the Arena. Her father the Regent took the decisions, and his subjects, especially his blood relatives, hastened to do his bidding, no matter what their opinion might be. Or the cost.

There were times he pitied Azmyn.

Once more he found himself daydreaming about a young herbalist he had recently met, whose lithe body and lively mind had captured—but no, that way lay disaster, it could not be. Quite why he was attracted to a lionface was a mystery, but there it was. However, congress between true humans and Neanderthals was forbidden. And even had it not been, the lady's passions were communing with nature and growing plants. She had made it amply clear that she was not greatly in favour of honour and machismo, let alone killing, be it fellow gladiators or—far worse in her estimation—animals.

To tell the truth, Yulmash thought, *I've always regretted the need to destroy such magnificent beasts. Gladiators know the terrible game they play, and choose to play it. Big cats and swamp-pigs have no choice.*

His meal washed down with thick Qusite beer, more gruel than liquid, Yulmash flung a goatskin cloak around his broad shoulders, secured it with an elaborate copper pin, ducked out of the door of his house, and set off through the raucous streets of Ul-q'mur.

He had a date with a sabretooth lion.

The Neanderthal Village had no name. It needed none: it was unique. It occupied a large but not very fertile stretch of ground between the encroaching desert and an overgrown area of swamp, fed by intermittent streams. It was a jumble of scattered clusters of mud huts, some round, some square, some irregular. Their rustic roofs were made from a variety of vegetation, from straw to palm fronds. Fires smouldered in random positions, while a few flamed skywards, tended by soot-smeared children. Here and there, women were cooking: flat, unleavened bread; vegetables and roots they had grown themselves, simmering in pots. Very little meat. The whole effect was ramshackle and disordered—yet comfortable and even homely. It was quieter than the crowded, noisy alleyways of the common districts of Ul-q'mur, and far cleaner.

As Beastmaster, Jackalfoot had command of about twenty Neanderthal assistants, all skilled in the wiles of animals, all attuned empathically to their mental state. Though not as skilled as Jackalfoot. The King provided extra food for the Village as a reward for their services. Every morning they walked from the Village, passing through the outskirts of Ul-q'mur on the way to its heart. Some days they went to the King's stables, looking after his donkeys, elephants, mammoths, deinotheres, and camels traded from the *bidd'hu*. Some days they went to the King's private zoo, with its impressive collection of rare or dangerous animals, among them lion, leopard, elephant, swamp-pig, rhinoceros, water buffalo, and aurochs. Some days they went to the Arena to tend to the animals in the vaults or ready them for combat, either gladiatorial training or the real thing. Often they split up and did all three.

They would greatly have preferred to let the wild animals roam free, but if the tribe were to survive, that wasn't an option.

On this particular day, all of the assistant beastmasters were carrying out routine maintenance at the zoo, and Jackalfoot was the sole Neanderthal in the Arena. The seats were unoccupied; this was one of many days set aside for training and rehearsal. Half the Arena was occupied by piles of building materials and heaps of displaced sand, as hundreds of workmen set about constructing an elaborate structure of tanks and walkways, supervised by Bil's sons. The tanks were primarily mudbrick, partly sunken and partly above the level of the Arena floor, and lined with clay. A stream of workmen brought bricks and clay. Soon more would be bringing water to fill the tanks. Bil fussed over the preparations like a mother duck tending her ducklings, rushing erratically from one construction site to another.

The Beastmaster was humming an interminable lionface drone, vocalising through his large flat leonine nose. He habitually used such drones to calm wild animals that had been kept in cages. This drone told a story from his tribe's distant past, far to the north, before the snows lasted all summer and the land became buried in ever-thickening ice. Qusite scholars had tried to learn the lionface tongue, but the nasal effects and the outrageous syntax defeated them. Only a lionface, possessing the necessary flat nose and immersed in the language from birth, could speak it or understand it.

It wasn't the sabretooth's unpredictability that worried Jackalfoot, for he and his kind could read the body language of any living creature as effortlessly as a master scribe might decipher a papyrus scroll. With such deep understanding also came control. But the mood of a caged animal, barred from its natural habitat, could change suddenly with very little warning, so it was wise to take precautions. The droning sound annoyed the keepers of the King's Arena, to whom Jackalfoot was responsible, but it had a hypnotic action on animals, so Jackalfoot droned on regardless. If anything, he saw the keepers' annoyance as a bonus. In principle, the Beastmaster carried out the orders of the King's men, who were answerable to and controlled by the Regent. In practice, the King's men deferred to the Beastmaster, avoiding giving him orders that they knew he would disobey. Only a lionface could control the ferocious animals that the Regent demanded for his pleasure in the King's name; in this, the lionfaces tending the King's animals were answerable only to the Beastmaster.

There was one royal order that even the Beastmaster had to obey, even though he hated himself for it. He would prepare animals for slaughter in the Arena. The Regent's wrath would destroy him, his family, and all of his tribe if he refused. It was how they had survived, when most of their kind were long dead. The animals did not know what fate awaited them, so they had no fears for him to empathise with. Compared to what was normal in the wild, they led pampered, well-fed lives, and came to a quick end. When there is no choice to be made, the wise man does not weep for what does not exist, but bows in acceptance. He can hate the act, but hating the forces that make it necessary will eventually destroy him.

Jackalfoot loved all of his animals... all animals, for that matter. But the sabretooth lion was a favourite. He let his eyes wander over the great cat's dense, healthy fur. A long, thick tail swept back from heavily muscled haunches, which terminated in clawed feet the size of a man's head. The lithe body was relaxed, with that total relaxation that only the cat family can achieve, but in a split second it could spring into lethal action. The huge head sprouted an impressive array of whiskers; a nose even bigger and flatter than Jackalfoot's was surmounted by tawny eyes, gazing enigmatically at the world, seemingly focused on a point in mid-air. Below, the bone-shattering jaws gaped lazily, their fearsome curved teeth sharper than flint blades, and thicker, and stronger. The cat's warm breath was foetid from its all-meat diet.

Sickleface, now full-grown, had been taken as a kitten from the narrow band of forest, far to the north of the Saltwater Sea, that ran parallel to the pale blue cliffs of Maab-ul-Qusqus. The forest was separated from the cliffs by a few tens of *khar* consisting of a jumble of dark rock, milky pools, and streams braided like the hair of a young girl. A hunting party returning laden with furs had brought the half-starved, terrified animal to Jackalfoot, who took it from them with a glare, soothed it, fed it, and within a day was worshipped by it. The sight of the broad-shouldered Neanderthal walking the streets with the cat at his heels caused much comment and amusement, which month by month fell into silence as the animal grew to adolescence, now as long as a man was tall, not counting a tail solid enough to fell an ox.

Sickleface's impressive fangs had grown to match the powerful predatory frame, and as the animal matured into a full-grown adult, Jackalfoot no longer allowed the cat the liberty of city streets. The Regent would never have tolerated it, anyway. Only a lionface could survive, weaponless, in close proximity to a mature sabretooth lion; among those of other races, only a warrior of exquisite courage and ability could survive even if he wielded weapons.

Still droning, Jackalfoot tickled the terrifyingly large beast beneath its stubbly chin, and it trotted meekly after him along the tunnel to the Arena, blinking rapidly and shaking its great head as they emerged into the sunlight. They were a matched pair; the thick-set lion-faced man with his golden brown features and wide, flat nose framed by a shock of orange hair, the tawny cat with golden fur, huge yellow eyes, broad nose with flaring nostrils, and powerful, muscular body. The cat was visibly armed, with claws like knapped flint and teeth like ivory sickles. The Neanderthal's armament was purely mental, but just as deadly.

The Arena was slowly being transformed into a simulacrum of a region of swamp, improbably bordered by desert. Here, gladiators would do battle with swamp-pigs amid the mud, and with sabretooths on the sand. Winning would require the defeat of both adversaries, using a different weapon for each. It would require skill, bravery, disciplined savagery, and a calculated disregard for personal safety when the moment came to strike. The desert just beyond the edge of the cultivation was pockmarked with the graves of gladiators who had failed to master those techniques.

For a moment, the Neanderthal paused to cast his eyes over Bil's extraordinary creation. Then, from the top of the Arena wall, came a shout.

"Jackalfoot!"

The Beastmaster thought he recognised the voice. Keeping half an eye on the sabretooth, he swivelled his heavy-boned head to confirm the voice's owner. He stopped his droning, stepping a few paces aside. The cloak enhanced rather than concealed the warrior's impressive stature. Jackalfoot did not need to lower his gaze to meet the warrior's eyes.

"*Zeb y'ukhsim!*" Yulmash gave greeting, still with traces of the *soukh* accent of his childhood.

"Good day and welcome to you also, Yulmash the Mighty!" Jackalfoot replied. "May the gods smile upon you and yours!" The Neanderthal's Qusite was clear, though strongly accented; Yulmash grunted in reply, giving a perfunctory nod. He knew that Jackalfoot cared nothing for Qusite gods. Or any other gods, for that matter. Neanderthals were godless, blind and deaf to matters spiritual, confirming that they were not true men. They had no lifesouls or selfsouls. The Beastmaster's response had been mechanical, a meaningless formality.

"How fares the Temple lion?" the warrior enquired, really wanting to know.

To the Water People, all large predatory cats were lions, and Jackalfoot had long ago stopped trying to explain the differences between sabretooths, true lions, leopards, and cheetahs. They were obvious enough—but then, a cow was a cow whatever the colour of its hide or the size of its body. The King owned all big cats—in principle he owned everything in Qus, except the people—but their legal guardianship was vested in the priesthood. Indeed, the mark of a senior *rau*-priest was a 'lionskin' (usually leopardskin) cloak. So Sickle-face was both a royal lion and a Temple lion. The Temple was dedicated to Tuwrat, who was either a hippopotamus or a vulture or a supernatural woman according to whim and custom, and there was also a separate lion-headed goddess, Zek-Mek—but lions were symbolic of strength and courage, so the Temple of the Hippopotamus Cult had lions. Qusites were like that. In a world riddled with symbols, symbolism was all. Consistency was no virtue, and the priests seldom missed an opportunity to exploit that.

"Healthy and well-fed," replied Jackalfoot. "As are his fellows. They will provide a challenge worthy of all your skill and might." They both knew that as the Festival drew near, the sabretooths would be starved, to encourage them to fight. There were few sights as fearsome as a hungry sabretooth lion. Let alone an entire pride.

Yulmash waved an arm vaguely towards the semicircle of fake swamp. "And the swamp-pigs?"

"A few of our children are preparing them in the Trackless Swamp, Yulmash. The trappers will bring them to the Arena in good time," Jackalfoot reassured him, grinning without humour. Swamp-pigs would be a sight even more fearsome than a pride of starving sabretooths, despite eating nothing but plants. Imagine what a herd of angry swamp-pigs might do if the animals were not vegetarians! Even a lionface would pale at the prospect. It would be a miracle if the King's animal handlers managed to bring several swamp-pigs to the Arena without anyone getting injured, even with the calming influence of lionface beastmasters. But brought they would most certainly be.

Yulmash checked that his short-sword was sheathed at his belt, vaulted over the dressed stone of the parapet, and landed lightly on the sand. The sabretooth hunched its shoulders and growled deep in its throat, and Jackalfoot recommenced his drone. It was typical of Yulmash to take this kind of risk; in the warrior's mind, the risk was slight, for he was sure he could sense the cat's mood. And if that failed, he had boundless confidence in his ability with the short-sword. Jackalfoot was not so certain.

Yulmash walked towards him. "Sickleface looks healthy."

The lionface inclined his head. "In body and spirit, warrior."

"Champion," Yulmash corrected him, with a grin.

"Champion-in-waiting would be more accurate."

The gladiator expanded his prodigious chest and squared his shoulders. "Do you doubt it, Beastmaster? Has any other warrior ever joined you and your lion in the Arena?"

"None has been so foolish."

"Ah. So you take me for a fool, Jackalfoot?"

The Beastmaster's leonine head inclined in thought, then gave a single slow shake. "For any other warrior, it would be foolish. For you—I think not. We will see. But be warned: if you have misjudged his mood, I will not be able to restrain the lion. Though I will try."

Yulmash glanced at the great cat, which focused its huge yellow eyes upon him as if he were some strange type of antelope, but made no sound or move. "He recognises an equal," the warrior said. "Though not, I suspect, a superior. He appears calm, but his muscles are tense. He's unsure in my presence, and that will be to my advantage if he brings his uncertainty with him to the battle.

"I will take him, Jackalfoot, never doubt it. I'll sacrifice three goats to the lion's courage after I've killed him, to appease the goddess, but I will take him despite his speed and strength. I don't want to, but I must. It's his fate. As my fate is to be Grand Champion, gods willing."

Jackalfoot suppressed a snort. "Your Qusite gods are fickle, Yulmash. I am thankful that we lionfaces have no delusions of gods to put fear in our hearts and mist in our minds."

The warrior gave a half-smile, and shook his head in disbelief. "So you always say, Jackalfoot. Yet can anyone, even a lionface, *truly* not believe there are gods? Can you stand under the warmth of the sun, feel the breeze from the river, refresh yourself in its cool waters, watch the birds flying high over-head, and still deny that all this has been *made*? It can be no ac-cident, surely?"

The Beastmaster appeared to consider the argument. Lionfaces did that—they listened, and gave thought to what had been said, even when they had heard the same many times before. It was one of the things that Yulmash found discon-certing about them. It made them seem slow and stupid, but Yulmash had no doubt that they were not.

"Accident, no, though causation need not imply intent. Made, I will concede," replied Jackalfoot. "But made by *what*? For what?" He blinked in the sharp sunlight. "I see the sun, as you say. I feel the breeze. I drink water and watch birds fly. I see priests bowing low before idols of wood and metal, I hear them chanting their prayers, I watch the crowds line the streets for their processions. I see ritual and ceremony. I see men in pursuit of the gods' favours, or terrified of their wrath. I see men claiming to do their gods' work, and I wonder why such powerful beings require human assistance. But I see no gods, I hear no gods, I feel no gods." The lionface's eyes locked with Yulmash's. "My kind can feel what is in the minds of others, from the lowliest beetle to the most powerful ruler. This you know, for this—and only this—is what your kind values in us. It is why we remain alive when none of our kind survive out-side this river valley, as you frequently tell us. And I tell you this, warrior: I have felt what is in the minds of the priests, and what I feel there is blind belief and self-deceit. In some I have felt good, in others malice, but in all I feel a great emptiness, which they attempt to fill with meaningless rites and supersti-tions, imagining these to be proof of their own delusions."

Before Yulmash could object to this slander, Jackalfoot stepped closer, holding the warrior's gaze like a charmer facing a cobra. "In you, I sense justifiable pride, confidence, strength, speed, and controlled aggression. I feel a keen intelligence, warrior. But beneath it, I feel a void that aches to be filled, a de-sire that drives you beyond anything that is healthy in a man.

And… something else—"

"When these Games end, I will be Grand Champion," Yulmash said flatly. "You sense my destiny. Zek-Mek has ordained it."

"Perhaps," Jackalfoot conceded, though all he could sense was a burning need. And—he would never mention it, for the sensation was too vague, and *wrong*, and to voice his thoughts would be a mortal insult—there was a deep sadness, with undercurrents of fear and anger, as though Yulmash was at war with himself. The feeling flitted across Jackalfoot's sense of empathy like a moth through a patch of firelight, vanishing into the darkness before he could capture it.

"If any deserves to be Champion, it is Yulmash the Mighty," said Jackalfoot. "Even though you and your kind have to slaughter innocent lions and swamp-pigs to succeed. As Beastmaster to the King, I must bow to what the Regent declares to be the King's will. They are his creatures, not mine. But I tell you this: I sense that your destiny far exceeds mere triumph in the King's Arena… and I do not think it is what you presume."

"What is it then, Beastmaster? You talk in riddles."

"It is indeed a riddle. One to which I know not the answer."

Yulmash spat into the dry sand, turned on his heel, and strode towards the gladiator's tunnel, but the lionface's words lay heavy in his thoughts. He had no wish to slaughter such magnificent animals, but such was his lot. Jackalfoot's statement was a clear omen, but one whose meaning he could not discern.

Like most omens.

Jackalfoot watched him go, and wondered what the warrior's final fate would be. Of one thing he was certain: it would not be determined by the whims of Qusite gods. But such thinking led nowhere, and there was work to be done. He tapped the sabretooth smartly on its hindquarters, and led it trotting in a circuit of the Arena. The animal's muscle tone would benefit from a serious workout.

Exiting the Arena, Yulmash proceeded through ever-narrowing and ever filthier Ul-q'murian streets to the artisans' quarter of the city, ignoring the strident cries of the vendors, which faltered when they saw his grim countenance. Away from the broad vistas of the official quarter, with its temples and palaces, the city was smelly, crowded, and delapidated. Many parts were best avoided altogether; some were downright dangerous. So much so that even Yulmash avoided them.

"*Ym hut'p*, warrior!"

Yulmash stopped and looked up. "Fat chance of that, Johr'ah. There's no peace in the Arena."

The jeweller laughed. He'd known Yulmash since they both were boys. "For your opponents, no. Save perhaps Khuf. Can I interest you in a jasper brooch for your wife? How is the dear Princess, by the way?"

Yulmash grunted. "Same as ever."

"Ah. Women, eh? Last week my cousin's third wife— but you wouldn't want to know about that. Family gossip's not your style, is it, Warrior? What are you doing in this rat-hole on such a fine day as this?"

"Heading for the Streets of the Metalworkers, Johr'ah."

"Of course. I should have realsied. You need new weapons for the Festival."

Yulmash nodded. "Two calls. First, to my swordsmith, to collect some weaponry that he's servicing. Sharpen and polish. Then I've got to go to what used to be the workshop of Hopthor the coppersmelter."

"Pity about old Hopthor. We all warned him to watch out. So now his workshop is owned by that craven fool Cenby copperbeater, who would swoon at the sight of a lion, yet is charged with creating a likeness of a swamp-pig fit for presentation to a Champion." The jeweller paused, saw Yulmash's face, and hastily added "That is, your good self, of course."

"Quite," Yulmash agreed sourly. "If the gods so will it."

The King had proclaimed that all gladiators registered for the Festival of the Frowning Moon had the right to inspect the trophy at any stage of production, presumably as a way to inspire its creator to his greatest efforts. Yulmash was keen to find out whether Cenby was up to the task.

"How that silly man got close enough to a live swamp-pig to carry out the required rituals, only the goddess could say!"

Johr'ah clapped the warrior on his broad shoulder. "Yes, my friend, but She keeps her opinions well hid."

"Or revealed only by oracles."

"Same thing."

They continued to dissect Cenby's character. The Palace had rated Hopthor highly, displaying many of his creations, and both of them knew that Hopthor had held Cenby's metal-working talents in high esteem. Which was why the idiot now owned the workshop, deeded to him by his childless master now that the careless fool had vanished down the gullet of a crocodile.

"I just hope Hopthor had good grounds for his bequest," Yulmash said. "The quality of my Champion's trophy relies on Cenby's alleged skills."

"Then you'd better be nice to him," Johr'ah advised.

Yulmash grunted. He was irritatingly aware that he must avoid offending the copperbeater. If he did, Cenby might perform even worse than the warrior feared, so the situation called for diplomacy. In this, the warrior had had plenty of practice, dealing with Azmyn and her high-bred relatives. So Yulmash would hold his peace, keep his low opinion of the copperbeater's worth to himself, visit his workshop regularly, and see what transpired. If at any stage the trophy was not acceptable, there would be no difficulty in removing the man from the Land of the Water People—legally. The King would understand, and appoint someone better.

His cloak swirling around his knees, Yulmash walked down narrow alleys between mudbrick walls, some white-washed, most bare brown solidified silt, the surface pocked with straw and sherds of broken pot. He strode past mangy dogs, piles of rotting vegetables, butchered meat hung out to mature beneath a coat of crawling flies, and hordes of screaming children. He inhaled the rich, pungent aroma of the city, life and death combined in a single breath, and his anger and bemusement fell away. He had been born here in the *soukh*, and the city flowed through him like the blood in his veins, just as familiar and just as vital to his continuing existence. The smells, the squalor amid great wealth, the maimed and deformed surrounded by beautiful young women dressed in rags or finery, the brash young men, plain or handsome... this was home.

Yulmash had grown up in a two-roomed house of white-washed mudbrick, sandwiched between a butcher's shop and a bakery. His father had worked in the butcher's shop, slaughtering anything up to the size of a sheep. Cattle were the provenance of the overseer, a short-tempered scrawny man named Lish. His mother made a paltry income washing clothes for local merchants. The house was on two floors, one room on each, with an open-air roof space. Yulmash spent most nights sleeping on the roof in a heap of dirty straw with his brother and four sisters. His parents slept in the room below, while the ground floor was a common area for cooking, eating, and household chores. There was a beehive-shaped clay oven outside the front door, protruding into the narrow street; it was cheaper to bake your own bread than to buy from the bakery, but occasionally his mother would bring home something special from the shop next door.

By the standards of the poor quarter of the city, he lived in a mansion—three floors! But Yulmash envied the sons of the scribes and tax-collectors, some of whom even had their own room, with a roof. One by one, all four sisters died; three of disease, and one from an accident when washing clothes in the river. When his only surviving brother fell sick, Yulmash was sent to work at the cemetery, digging trenches for the dead. It bought what was left of his family bread and beer, and it gave him arms as strong as an ox.

When his father died of a wasting sickness, Yulmash's mother continued taking in washing, while her sole surviving son became their main source of income. Yulmash elbowed his way into a second job, collecting firewood for a knifemaker. One of the regular customers, a dark-skinned foot-soldier who had fought in the Third Batalamalaban campaigns, taught him how to defend himself in close combat with shortswords, and how to disembowel an attacker with a concealed flint-bladed knife by distracting his attention. Yulmash started hanging around the wayhouses near the Arena, picking fights for food and drink, making side-bets with the onlookers. Eventually he acquired several rough ingots of copper and a network of scar tissue.

One night a gladiator, fresh from a triumph in the Arena, drank too much and assaulted one of the serving women, a dark-haired young girl from a family that lived a few streets away from Yulmash's house, breaking her arm and insulting her maidenhood. Yulmash challenged the man to a knife fight. The two were tied arm to arm with a length of cloth, in the traditional way of a fight to the death. While the gladiator was taunting his opponent, Yulmash butted him between the eyes, smashed his nose, cut the tendons of his wrist so that he dropped the knife, kicked him in the groin, pulled his head back using the man's hair, and slit his throat. Then he severed the cloth that bound them, returned to his seat, and called for more beer.

The serving-girl fawned over her saviour and sat on his lap. By morning, her maidenhood was beyond salvation, but that was different. It had been voluntary. Her family raised no objection, very possibly influenced by reports of the fight. Yulmash briefly considered taking her as a wife, but there was no shortage of pretty faces and pert bodies, and he dimly felt that he was destined for higher things. When she failed to get pregnant, he lost interest, as if somehow his own manhood had been called into question. When her father also lost interest, for the same reason, that was the end of it.

The Master of the Arena paid Yulmash a visit, intending to seek compensation for the death of one of his star performers. But when he reached the miscreant's house, he realised that he had found a new star, one that would eclipse any he had yet encountered. He made Yulmash an offer.

Yulmash stopped going to the wayhouse. Instead, he was enrolled into the military, where he earned the title of warrior by taking part in two of Sh'erthret-Amt's Batalamalaban campaigns. Having proved himself by displaying outstanding bravery on the battlefield, his sponsor had him transferred to the Arena for intensive gladiatorial training. Soon Yulmash was proficient in a dozen forms of combat, both with and without weapons. Taking to the profession like a natural, he climbed rapidly up the promotion ladder and began making public appearances. His innate skills gave him a competitive edge, and within a sixmoon he had acquired a reputation for fearlessness tempered with devious cunning. Within two years, he was a wealthy man. Within another, after an especially courageous battle in which he bested three huge crocodiles armed only with a shortsword, he overreached himself by accepting Sitaperkaw's impetuous offer and taking an outraged but necessarily compliant Azmyn as his wife.

At the time, it had seemed like a good idea.

Darkness permeated the Neanderthal enclave as the sun dipped below the horizon. In a crude hut of mud walls topped by thatched reeds, Foxglove-Spearbreaker selected herbs, placing them delicately into a small pot. It bore no decorative marks, and its shape was slightly irregular.

The herbalist was of medium height and slimmer than

most Neanderthal women, and moved with catlike grace. Her face was rounded, yet striking, with the typical broad nose that had earned Neanderthals the epithet 'lionface'. Her eyes were large and tawny, her hair a flamboyant explosion of bronze tangles. Above all, she exuded a vitality that was almost overwhelming in its intensity and sharp focus.

Her patient squatted on the dusty floor. His eyes followed the herbalist's every move.

Neanderthal speech involved tone vocalisation through their flat noses, as well as more conventional sounds from the mouth. An eavesdropper, not conversant with the subtleties of Neanderthal language, would have heard gibberish punctuated by grunts and snorts, interspersed with nasal whistles, and dismissed the entire conversation as a series of meaningless animal noises. But Neanderthal brains were wired differently from those of run-of-the-mill humans, and their language could convey many shades of thought in parallel. The Neanderthal's empathic sense removed the need to rely on words, on symbols of reality; instead, they intuited the reality itself. Not with perfect accuracy, admittedly, but conventional human word-based tongues also failed to capture the nuances of thought. To a native 'speaker', Neanderthal noises conveyed considerably more information, more quickly and more precisely, than any language invented by the word-speakers...

Foxglove-Spearbreaker: I feel your pain, Rainseeker. I'll help you overcome it and pass beyond it into untroubled peace.

Rainseeker-Darkeyes: I know you can do this.

Foxglove-Spearbreaker: But that's the limit of my powers. And what I do will hasten the end. That, too, you know?

Rainseeker-Darkeyes: No one can achieve the impossible. Peace is all I seek. I have no wish to delay.

Foxglove-Spearbreaker: For peace, I can offer you herbs whose efficacy is beyond dispute. I learned of them from the greatest herbalist of our tribe, Greenspeaker-Truethought, shortly before his untimely death at the hands of the Crazed Ones. [Measures dried leaves from a small oryx-skin pouch.]

These should suffice. If you run short, I can supply more, though not easily.

Rainseeker-Darkeyes: [Takes the pouch.] How do I apply them? As a poultice?

Foxglove-Spearbreaker: No, as in infusion in boiling water. Remove the leaves and drink the liquor, once it has cooled. You realise it's a palliative, not a cure?

Rainseeker-Darkeyes: There's no cure for what ails me.

Foxglove-Spearbreaker: In this, as in all that has gone before, you speak truth. The tribe will miss your wisdom.

Rainseeker-Darkeyes: The tribe will find new wisdom of its own, as it always does.

Foxglove watched the diminished figure limp away into the darkness, beyond the light from the flickering fires, and sighed. *All must come to this*, she told herself. But truth made the parting no easier. Truth did not exist to ease life, but to constrain it, and to endow it with meaning and purpose.

She sighed, and put the unused herbs back into packets woven from broad palm leaves. Then she stacked the packets in one corner of the hut, on top of an upturned cooking-pot in a shallow dish of water, to keep unwanted insects away. The work, mindless routine, was a distraction; her mind was on other matters.

Namely: how to stop Yulmash from killing the sabre-tooth lion.

He was a strange one, Yulmash. Square face, his eyes a paler brown than most Qusites and flecked with gold. Muscular but not musclebound. A big man with a big heart, who had saddled himself with the wrong wife in a futile bid for power that he would not know how to use if he ever attained it. A remorseless killer who would slit a man's throat without a second thought, yet spent days in seclusion whenever he killed an animal. She had never seen him at his work, of course, and never would, but she had learned much about the warrior from Jackalfoot. In a way, the two of them were in the same business, though for very different reasons. Yulmash aspired to glory and fame. Jackalfoot just wanted to make a living that would safeguard his tribe. Both were inextricably conjoined by the great creatures that they both depended upon. But Yulmash's fate hung upon how many of them he killed, while Jackjalfoot's depended on how well he tended them while they lived.

Yet in a way they shared the same aims, uneasy brothers in complicity. Yulmash needed live animals too. And the warrior was intelligent enough to recognise that the supply might soon run out.

Especially sabretooths. The land was changing, and their numbers were in decline. And so he mourned their death, even as he brought it about. Whence his seclusion. Late one night, when her route home from a visit to one of her long-term patients took her past the warrior's house, Foxglove had heard someone sobbing. An acquaintance who worked as a maid in the kitchen had confirmed the startling truth: it had been Yulmash the Mighty, who slaughtered fierce lions and then cried like a baby when he thought no one was listening.

Foxglove's mind went back to the time she had tended Yulmash's wounds after a particularly vicious battle with a pair of leopards, and an uneasy bond had grown between them —a bond forged not by common interests, but their opposite.

"Your wounds are deep," Foxglove had said. She knew she was stating the obvious, but that was often necessary. It was part of a herbalist's job, a way to engage with her patient. "I will apply a cleansing ointment to prevent suppuration. It will sting."

Yulmash had merely grunted. He had not feared two leopards, so why worry about a sting? But the sharpness of it had brought involuntary tears to his eyes.

"You should find a profession that does not bring you to this state," she had told him. "I know you are a great warrior, but even great warriors can be killed. They make mistakes, as you so nearly did."

"That is my life. I can contemplate no other. I will be

Grand Champion."

She had sensed sadness behind the blunt statement. Like all Neanderthals, her empathic sense was keen and accurate. "You do not enjoy killing animals. Why, then, do you choose a profession that requires just that?"

"What I do or don't enjoy is immaterial. The gods have ordained that I must kill them. Only then can I stay true to my own lifesouls."

Foxglove had heard of the strange Qusite beliefs about things that did not exist, elaborate myths in which even a soul had a soul of its own, but she knew when to keep silent. She had continued to apply the salve.

"But of course, you do not feel the animals' own fears, or pain," she had said, half to herself. "Unlike my kind. We understand the victims as well as the victors. We feel what they feel, see what they see. No Neanderthal could ever do what—"

Yulmash had reached out, without warning, and seized her arm. "You know *nothing*, woman!" He had seen the pain in her eyes and released his grip, suppressing a flush of irrational anger, feeling slightly embarrassed but refusing to show it. "You may know what an animal feels, but you have no idea what a warrior feels. What *I* feel." He kept his voice soft, with an effort, but the intensity would have been apparent even to a Qusite.

What did he feel? He had not said. She was unsure why she wanted to know, but she did. There was something about the man... She shook her head to clear her thoughts. Her interest signified nothing, it was just reflex. There was an obvious reason why *any* Neanderthal would want to know such a thing.

Empathy.

Deep within the labyrinthine caverns of the Ship, confined by walls of a material so strong that it formed much of the vessel's

outer skin, a mind once superior in every way to that of a pandemon had passed beyond desperation into self-induced madness.

It had no name, only a profession and a characteristic odour that would identify it uniquely and immediately to others of its species.

The Surgeon had once known that it was held captive for one reason, and one only: to raise the crew above the ethical threshold that the Ship's Precursor constructors, a billion years ago, had set as the minimum that would allow the vessel to function. Pandemons had captured the Surgeon and confined it, unable to operate the Ship without its aid. Tragically, the Precursors' threshold was a weighted quorum, quantifying only the overall ethical level and not taking the distribution over individuals into account. The Surgeon could communicate with the Ship, but the pandemons routinely overrode its wishes. And so, in the grudging manner of such machinery, the Ship followed only the pandemons' instructions—within limits.

Unfortunately for the Surgeon—and for the Living Galaxy as a whole—its presence stretched those limits far enough to let the pandemons exploit their customers' obsessions with violent death. The Ship might not have approved of their activities, inasmuch as such judgements could be attributed to anything created by the Precursors, but if so, there was insufficient ethical pressure to cause it to stop them.

Even more unfortunately for the Surgeon, it belonged to an extremely long-lived species. Normally hermaphrodite, self-fertilised internally and reproducing by fission, it had been treated with hormone antagonists to suppress its reproductive cycle. This afforded it a continuity of consciousness that would normally have been reset periodically by fission. As a result, its memories spanned centuries, and its body had taken on a bloated, sluglike shape, with a ring of five enormous eyes and a second ring of five tentacles just behind, surrounding an orifice for ingesting food. At the other end was a smaller ring of five excretory orifices. Its skin was thick yet soft, and its surface sloughed off continuously, replenished from the layers beneath in an endless cycle of slow regeneration.

In the perpetual dark of its prison, the Surgeon's eyes saw nothing. Its multifurcated tentacular limbs, which had evolved to perform manipulations with high precision, had nothing to manipulate, and had atrophied.

Its captors had installed a tube to feed it a mix of synthetic mush produced by the Ship's Precursor technology, closely approximating the vegetation that grew in the marshes of its homeworld. A second tube removed the resulting waste. Every few hours, a spray of antiseptic liquid cleansed its skin and the metal that held it.

It had gone insane centuries ago, for self-protection. Yet sparks of sanity still flickered, ready to burst into flame when circumstances permitted. Barely conscious, the Surgeon rambled interminably through its vast bank of ancient memories, immersed in a dreamlike state in which logic and causality were suspended.

Waiting.

9
Prophecy

"Some beer, my love?"

Shephatsut-Mer raised his eyes from the papyrus upon which he was inscribing a copy of an ancient ritual to anoint the firstborn of a Vizier, before the original document decayed any further and became illegible. He recognised the look in his wife's eyes and girded his mental loins for battle.

"A small pot only, Nemnestris my pet." He could always tell when his wife wanted something, because her opening gambit involved being unusually pliant and reasonable. She would smile, and her eyes would take on a gentle look. Nine times out of ten he found it politic to give in straight away, before the smile hardened into a snarl and the eyes took on the fixed glitter of a horned viper. Her tongue, though not forked, could inflict wounds more painful than mere venom.

He consoled himself that he had not chosen to marry her. His hand had been forced by long tradition. The High Priest of the Hippopotamus Cult was always wedded to the High Priestess of the Followers of Nefteremit. It was the price he must pay for his ambition. And he had to admit that even though she was nine years his senior, her beauty shone brightly; even more so, when she was angry. As she often was.

"There have been some... problems with the prophetess," she began her pitch.

Shephatsut-Mer knew this one. "More inaccuracies?"

"Difficulties of interpretation, I prefer to call them. You

know for yourself how difficult oracles can be. An invisible prophetess can be even more taxing. Nefteremit is obscure at the best of times."

Shephatsut-Mer bobbed his shaven head. "Yes, such is the way of oracles and prophecies." He paused for a moment, deep in thought. Ordinarily his wife was unperturbed by Nefteremit's obscurities. In fact, she positively revelled in them. The vaguer a prophecy, the less was the likelihood of it being false to fact. Well, *provably* false to fact.

So that meant— "The King wishes to consult the Followers of Nefteremit on a matter of some delicacy?"

Nemnestris nodded. "So the Regent informs me. It's especially important that on this occasion the prophetess's advice should prove correct."

Shephatsut-Mer licked his lips. "This is good beer." *Mostly.* "Surely that's up to the prophetess. Isn't she infallible?"

"Unquestionably, my husband. But on this occasion it's vital that she should be *seen* to be infallible, and that requires taking whatever steps are necessary to... *clarify* her visions."

The High Priest took another pull at his beer, encountered a lump more solid than usual, decided against spitting it out, which would offend his wife, and swallowed it. Nemnestris, never reluctant to press her case, leaned closer and took his hand. "I wonder, dear husband, whether there might be some way to *reinforce* the prophecy. What do you think?"

Shephatsut-Mer realised that he was going to offend his wife anyway. He now knew exactly what she was getting at. It was no surprise. "Do you have anything specific in mind, my love?"

"The Followers of Nefteremit don't have a monopoly on visions of the future."

Shephatsut-Mer wondered whether to divert the discussion by suggesting that she might consult one of the streettellers, but he had a feeling that folk magic was the wrong way to go. Nemnestris was no fool. She would see through the ploy immediately, he would lose face, and she would gain the upper hand.

"You're thinking of the Oracle."

He heard her breath quicken. "It did cross my mind, husband."

Shephatsut-Mer pursed his lips as if in thought. "It might be possible for me to consult the Oracle on your behalf. But I'd need to know the question."

"Pah! You know full well that no priestess of Nemnestris may disclose a kingly secret! No, what it needs is for me to have private access to the—"

"No. That's not—"

"—Oracle. I wish only to borrow—"

"No."

"—it. For a short time. What harm can there—"

Shephatsut-Mer took a deep breath. "Nemnestris, you know I'd do anything in my power to satisfy your desires." *If only to avoid the inevitable explosion if I didn't.* "But in this matter I'm powerless. Just as it's impossible for you to divulge the King's business to anyone else, so I am charged with the safe-keeping of the Oracle."

"But—"

"I realise it would be perfectly safe in your hands, my dear. Haven't I told you many times how much I trust you? But, just like you, I'm bound by the rule of the gods. You may not disclose the secrets of the royal family; I may not pass the Oracle into the hands of another. Unfortunately, we're at an impasse."

Nemnestris did not give up easily. She tried wheedling, flat-out bribery, veiled threats, and more explicit ones. Shephatsut-Mer stuck to his ground and awaited the outburst. When it came, it was impressive even for the High Priestess of the Followers of the Lilypad Prophetess. It cast aspersions on his heredity, his brainpower, and his manhood. He gazed impassively and weathered the storm, until, finally recognising that she wasn't going to get her own way, his wife knocked what was left of his beer to the floor and stormed out of the room.

He called a servant-girl to mop up the mess and bring him another beer.

The only problem with beer was that it clouded the mind, and Shephatsut-Mer really needed to maintain the utmost clarity, because he was flirting with heresy.

It was the Oracle's fault.

It had started a moon before, when the Oracle spoke at length in the Qusite tongue. What he had expected to be a routine query about the coming inundation turned into a kind of debate. Usually the Oracle gave answers, specific or obscure, and often incomprehensible. But on occasion it suggested actions in ordinary speech, and this was one such. He re-ran the conversation in his mind.

"Oracle: when will the floods begin?"

Two smiling moons and a quarter into a third.

"And end?"

A further two frowning moons and a six-day.

"What will be the waters' height?"

Sufficient for a good harvest after the waters have begun to recede, but not so deep as to cause undue delay and spoil the land for crops.

That was good news, the Regent would be pleased. "When should the planting begin?"

When the Sun reaches the zenith.

It did that sometimes. "No, Oracle, I meant—how many days?"

When the Sun reaches the zenith.

Infuriating. "That's not helpful, Oracle."

When the Sun reaches the zenith you must observe the ritual.

Shephatsut-Mer racked his brains for a sowing ritual that began at noon. Perhaps something obscure from the *Book of the Spell of the Thirteen Chambers?* He recalled nothing remotely suitable. Early morning, certainly—one would normally sacrifice a pair of baboons. Perhaps a token rite late in the evening, but—

"Oracle: which ritual?"

The adoration of the Sun. Your actions must find favour.

Ah. Now Shephatsut-Mer understood. But there was a puzzle. "Prayers to Akhnef are normally chanted just before sunrise, to assist in His escape from the forces of darkness. Do you mean that we should also chant them at noon?"

Not Akhnef.

This was baffling. Akhnef was the orthodox solar deity, who caused the Sun to move across sky and underworld, giving light by day and battling the forces of darkness at night before rising resurgent to illuminate a new day. His divine sister Tuwrat played a background role, improving the conditions in the World of the Living that would help Him defeat the legions of evil. The main task of the Hippopotamus Cult was to ensure Her continued assistance. By the usual priestly illogic, swamp-pigs were therefore an aspect of Akhnef as well.

Perhaps the Oracle meant some other aspect of the Sun-god. "Ren? Senbasret? Am-Huf?"

No.

"Then who?"

The Sun themselves.

"I don't understand."

It should be plain. Of all your gods, the Sun and the Moon alone are visible to any man.

Shephatsut-Mer paled. This was not the orthodox view. He put his fears into words. "The solar disc itself?"

Themselves. And they are no disc.

In theological terms, this idea was like a pride of sabre-tooth lions: powerful and impressive, but highly dangerous. "You're suggesting I should perform a ritual for the Sun?"

No, for the Y-ra'i.

It did that, too. "I know not of Y-ra'i."

The Y-ra'i are They Who Dwell Within the Sun, through whom the Sun itself gains its power.

"Are the Y-ra'i gods?"

You would so consider them.

"Do you refer to the Sun in His aspect as a god?"

No.

"As the golden disc that lights the heavens?"

No! Neither god nor disc. Unlike your gods, the Sun-sphere is real.

Sphere? Not disc? There was a disturbing allure to the thought, heretical though it surely was. Shephatsut-Mer was intelligent enough to be aware that when shadow gives no hint of its true shape, a sphere has the form of a circular disc. There had been occasional debate among the higher echelons of the priesthood about this precise point. It had vital implications for cult statues: should the god wear a flat Sun disc on His head, or a golden ball? It was a difficult issue because no one could see the Sun clearly enough to ascertain its true form. Its light blinded anyone who tried.

The Moon, now: She was a different matter. Evidently a flat disc, uniformly bright. Admittedly, Her monthly changes in form did resemble a sphere lit from varying directions, a fact that had not gone unnoticed by the priesthood, and had given rise to much theological disputation over the centuries. But it was obvious that She produced Her own illumination. When She deigned to appear by day, her light was dim—but if She shone by reflected light, She should have been brighter by day, when there was more light to reflect. On the other hand, when She shone by night, no other sufficiently strong source of light was visible. All this was self-evident. And had he not pointed out to Tenramuut that the light of the stars, even all of them combined, was not bright enough? In any case, the Moon sometimes covered a star, so the stars were behind it, not in front where they might shine their dim light on it. And when the fool suggested instead that the hidden Sun might be a possible source, Shephatsut-Mer's response had been swift and decisive: "At night the Sun is in the underworld! It does not shine on the world of Man!" Which clinched it, at least for Shephatsut-Mer.

Every time since then that he had consulted the Oracle, it repeated its heretical claims, reinforcing them with ever-more-detailed arguments, telling him strange truths; at least, it insisted they were truths. He was finding it hard to resist the temptation to believe the Oracle. It had a definite attraction.

The Moon sometimes covers the Sun, creating darkness in the day. The Sun must be further away than the Moon.

Both must be gigantic.

The Sun is hot, as anyone can feel for themselves. It must be on fire.

Fire gives light as well as heat.

The Sun is a god, His true aspect a giant ball of fire. Or perhaps just inhabited *by a god. A new god. A god that makes Himself visible to all. A god with more power than all others combined. A god who rules the minor deities named Y-ra'i.*

A god only I *know about.*

It was true knowledge, he felt it in his bones. Not just from the Oracle, but from Tuwrat herself—for the goddess controlled the Oracle. For a rare moment, the High Priest felt he was on the verge of unveiling great mysteries. But what would he do with the answers?

Shephatsut-Mer flattened out the half-finished scroll of invocations, placing a few stones along the edges to hold it down. He dipped his pen into a small pot of ink and began to write in an elegant cursive script.

His wife came in from the garden holding a plucked lily, inhaling the heavy scent with feline pleasure. Nemnestris had recovered her poise, and her more normal sarcastic personality reassured Shephatsut-Mer that for now she had no specific agenda in mind. A simple dress showed off her figure, still slim despite having borne several children, if anything more beautiful in maturity than she had been as a young woman. Her confidence and grace in public were legendary, as befitted a High Acolyte; her voice was low-pitched and her accent and perfect diction were of the kind that could be acquired only through generations of noble ancestry. As he expected, she now acted as though they'd never quarrelled. It was a good moment to offer her a consolation prize.

"My dear, I'm minded for us to arrange a feast."

His wife nodded vigorously. "*Haiyah!* When?"

"Two days after the end of the Festival."

"Ah." Her husband was theological adviser to the Arena, so this was only to be expected. She would tell the housemaster, who would organise the servants, purchase food and drink, and send out invitations. "Whom do we invite?"

Shephatsut-Mer stretched out his arms, which had started to ache from writing. "Only the highest of the nobility, my pet. Thirty guests, perhaps forty. This will be an important occasion."

A smile flickered across Nemnestris's lips. She liked important occasions, especially when she was in charge of them but someone else did all the work. She picked up a small fan of goose feathers and waved it in front of her face. "I'll see to it. I'll tell the butcher to slaughter a cow. Lots of ducks, of course, and honeycakes in profusion." A thought struck her. "Precisely what is this feast to be in honour of?"

"The new Grand Champion. Whoever he might turn out to be. My own preference is for Khuf the Shrewd; he's refined his fighting methods considerably this past year, a huge improvement. Do you remember how he bested those two cheetahs?"

"Extremely well, my husband. His bravery was outstanding. I also favour Khuf." *And how.*

"He's a well-formed figure of a man, isn't he?"

For a moment Nemnestris wondered whether Shephatsut-Mer was playing mind games, but judging from his expression the casual remark was just that: casual. Still, wise to backtrack.

"Warriors usually are. He's but one of many. Of course, Khuf may fail."

"True. The Games are so unpredictable, especially over so many rounds. But on current form the most likely final will be Khuf against Yulmash. You can get long odds on all the other fighters."

"That will be a battle to savour!" Nemnestris cried, trying reinforce her neutrality by appearing to be even-handed.

"It certainly will. There's no love lost between those two."

Nemnestris knew exactly why, because Khuf seldom missed an opportunity to remind her. Time for a little more misdirection. "Really? I thought professional gladiators were usually on good terms with each other, outside the Arena."

"They are. But not those two. Yulmash bested Khuf in a one-off contest that Sitaperkaw arranged to celebrate his marriage to his fifth wife."

"The Zamonite Princess? A diplomatic swap?"

"That's the one. It was a friendly, so no one had to die. The prize was exceptionally valuable. Yulmash got it all, and Khuf was left with nothing. He accused Yulmash of cheating, and after that—well, there was no going back. Khuf has hated Yulmash with a passion ever since. I don't think Yulmash has strong feelings about it, to be frank, but he doesn't like being called a cheat."

Nemnestris licked her lips. "Did he cheat?"

"Not that I could see. Khuf's just a bad loser. He made an elementary mistake and Yulmash took advantage. But Khuf's a very good fighter, and he's improved a lot since, which is why a lot of people in the know expect him to come out on top this time. The odds for wagers show Yulmash to be a marginal favourite, mind you, so of course we must invite him too. Personally I'm not so—"

Nemnestris nearly dropped her fan. "You're inviting Yulmash? Here?"

Shephatsut-Mer misread her emotions. "He'll be welcome if he survives, as Champion or not. And think of our increased status if I'm wrong, and he wins! Such a magnificent specimen of manhood! His mother will glow with pride."

"His—oh, yes, the washerwoman."

"Poor but proud. She must be astonished at how far her son has risen from his humble birth. Yet he visits her often."

Nemnestris tried to disguise her agitation. She had no problem with Khuf— absolutely not! Aside from making sure her husband remained blithely unaware of their relationship. *But Yulmash? Gods!* That cut too close to bone, a scandal that Nemnestris fervently hoped would never come to light. Not just talk, but a girlish mistake that even now could ruin her reputation forever. *Had she paid the slaughterman's family enough copper to ensure their silence?* But it was too late to do much about it if not.

"And I have another nice surprise for you and for our guests, my love."

Nemnestris hoped it would be less disturbing than the surprise she'd just received. "Yes?"

"I'm going to dispense with protocol and invite the Beastmaster as well."

This time Nemnestris did drop the fan. With an effort she gathered it, along with some of her wits. Fortunately Shephatsut-Mer was too busy at his writing, and hadn't noticed anything amiss.

Her hands trembled, her voice was shaky. "My husband, do you think it wise to bring a— a *lionface*—"

"I have the permission and encouragement of the Regent himself, for Jackalfoot has Sitaperkaw's favour. The lionface will augment our influence at the Palace. It's not only proper to invite him into our household: it's mandatory. It will also show due respect for the Beastmaster's remarkable abilities. He's a striking figure of great presence and bearing, Nemnestris. He'll do credit to our house."

Jackalfoot. In this house. Soon. Credit? If only you knew.

Mind racing, she hastened to leave before Shephatsut-Mer could notice how shocked she was. Fortunately, his nose was still buried in his scroll.

"Ain't no need to push, sonny," a short fat woman in a drab grey robe complained, turning to face the bony young man behind her. "Won't get ya to the front no quicker."

The young man ducked his head. "Apologies, grandmother." It was the standard honorific for an elderly woman and implied no familial relationship. "It wasn't intentional. I stumbled after placing my offerings on the table."

A short distance away the offering table bore gifts to the Prophetess from the faithful: loaves, cakes, fruit, fish, fowl, and a skinny but intact goat. The reply mollified the old lady.

"That's better. Ya does talk posh! *Haiyah*, ain't you Wozsat, Shevnwt's lad? The one what trained as a scribe?"

The youth nodded in acknowledgement.

"How's ya mum these days? All right?"

Wozsat made a face. "Still in mourning." After an awkward pause he added: "That's why I'm here. My mother needs advice from the Prophetess. About—well, please don't tell anyone, she's beginning to consider remarrying, but she's worried that it might be too soon. I gave two ducklings, do you think that's enough—"

The old woman gave the matter a moment's thought. "Two *ducks* woulda bin better, but it's a small ask. When did that cobra bite Denbeth?"

"Eight smiling moons past, grandmother. No, I misspeak. Nine."

"Then there ain't no need fer ya to be 'ere! Six moons'd be more'n enough. Ain't no shame 'er takin' anuvver man after *that* long!"

Wozsat nodded. "I told her as much, grandmother. But

she—"

He was interrupted as the queue shuffled forward. Only three people now stood between him and the entrance to the small rock-cut chamber where Nefteremit declaimed her prophecies. A tall naturally bald man, whom he recognised as the overseer of the Guardian of the Summer Palace's private herd of goats, emerged from the exit of the chamber, his face wreathed in smiles.

One satisfied customer, then. Bet that goat on the table's his. I can guess where he got it.

A few minutes passed. Another man, older this time, emerged. No smiles, but no tears either. He just looked puzzled. No doubt the meaning of the Prophetess's advice would become clearer in due course. One cannot expect clarity from a supernatural being. Even to receive an answer was an undeserved honour.

The elderly woman would be next. Wozsat rehearsed his question, which his mother had made him learn by heart, to avoid misleading the Prophetess.

The thin crowd began to murmur. Wozsat turned to see the cause of the disturbance.

Gods! It's Yulmash the Mighty! Wozsat briefly wondered why so famous a personage would require advice from the Followers of Nefteremit, but on further reflection it was a no-brainer. The famous gladiator was soon to compete at the Festival. No doubt he was here to seek omens. He would probably consult the Oracle as well. Yulmash was wealthy; he could afford the price. In his stead, that's what Wozsat would have done. The gods would view it with favour. Probably.

The people at the rear of the queue moved aside to make way for the hugely muscled gladiator, but Yulmash gestured to them to return to their places. "I will wait my turn," he said quietly.

The elderly woman bent to pass through the low doorway, and the queue shuffled forward a pace.

Within the chamber was a wall of rock with a small hole in it, through which supplicants could hear the voice of the Prophetess. The real Nefteremit had died of lung disease forty years ago, but death was no barrier to magic, and since she was magically present it did no harm to animate her voice through the medium of a living person. In this case that person was Fennover, a young trainee priestess concealed in a second chamber adjacent to the publicly visible one. Its entrance, fifty paces away along a curving tunnel, was situated within one of the Temple outbuildings.

Fennover sat beside a smouldering brazier, from which rose fumes of incense and a mind-altering drug. As they diffused through the hole, their combined effect made the consultation more impressive for the supplicant beyond the separating wall, and also rendered them less critical and more receptive to the Prophetess's advice. It also altered the priestess's voice and made her responses more imaginative.

Nemnestris sat next to Fennover, taking care not to breathe in too much of the drug. But she permitted herself a few breaths, to calm her mind.

Having given the matter some thought, she was fairly sure that Shephatsut-Mer knew about her ongoing affair with Khuf. She was absolutely sure that it wouldn't greatly bother him, or surprise him, if he did hear of it—as long as no one else did. If it became public, he would be humiliated. Their marriage was one of convenience, not love. As long as she employed due discretion, no damage would ensue. Not that she had any intention of telling him, or of admitting anything if he so accused her. He might get angry, if only for show, and that would be unpleasant. She would deny everything, as a matter of principle.

But Yulmash—

Now she regretted her decision, taken in such haste so

many years ago. It had been a mistake. Some secrets must remain secret, however great the price. Perhaps there remained time enough to—

Her dark thoughts were broken by the sound of Yulmash's voice. She stiffened.

"The Prophetess already knows your question," Fennover intoned, her voice low and indistinct from the effects of the drug. "But you must say it aloud to ensure an auspicious aura. Your name, also, for otherwise the magic cannot work."

The voice was firm. "I am Yulmash the Mighty. My question is: will I become Grand Champion at the coming Festival?"

Although his voice sent unpleasant tingles along Nemnestris's spine, she retained sufficient presence of mind to understand that even an experienced warrior could get nervous when his life was soon to be on the line. Normal practice would be to reassure him, because satisfied customers tended to return, but she put a hand on Fennover's shoulder and touched a finger to her own lips. "Wait!" she whispered. For that thought had in turn triggered another. If Yulmash were to be killed during his Festival battles, it would solve so many problems yet dirty no one's hands. Not in a manner that could be traced, at any rate.

Above all else, a beastfighter needed *confidence*. The most effective way to deal with a dangerous wild animal is to believe that you can. Skill is also required, of course—raw belief saves no one, except through godly intervention—but the stronger the belief, the more accurately a killing blow can be executed.

Sap that confidence, even subtly, and death hovers one wingbeat closer.

Nefteremit leaned across and whispered into Fennover's ear. "Tell him: the winner will be Khuf the Shrewd." The priestess looked surprised but did as she was told.

"Khuf?" The warrior's voice was audibly shaken. "But—"

"Such is the prophecy. Make of it what you will; the Prophetess is never wrong."

10
Plasmoids

The Borough was located in a pleasant, fertile region some six kilometres beneath the visible surface of the star registered in official databases as Shool, where the prevailing weather was a balmy 5780 K. Normally a hive of activity, the Borough was now almost deserted, as it had been for the last five cycles.

The reason was not hard to find. Barely a thousand kilometres away, a huge wild yewe was grazing the magnetic fields. Cooler than the surrounding plasma by some two thousand degrees, its tubular surface penetrated deep into the star's interior. At the visible surface, yewes often appeared in widely separated pairs, linked by a single U-shaped tube that created reversed polarity at its two ends.

When a yewe pair reached maturity, specialist farmers from the plasmoid Borough would sex them by polarity and domesticate them—for a time, until the imperative of their periodic migration from poles to equator drove them further south. Plasmoids exploited the cooler body-temperatures of the yewes to damp down their own coronal discharges.

Innumerable small flox surrounded the yewes in granular clusters, ever-shifting, a roiling mass of parasitic vortices, stealing momentum and magnetism. The plasmoid farmers shooed their flox away from the dangerous slopes of the yewe's maw.

Alone in the Borough's core, except for immature younglings who were not effective company, FrayedEdges revolved slowly, pondering. He was annoyed, visibly so. His periphery was even more frayed than normal, and it spun off bright magnetic vortices that made an appalling racket in the radio spectrum.

This was supposed to be a *quiet* region of the Galaxy. Aside from the regular yewe migrations, of course, but those were a normal feature of life on Shool. The other arrivals were not. Within the space of a few thousand spins, they had caused no less than three entirely separate disturbances. *Three*! It was irritating in the extreme. Admittedly, FrayedEdges told himself, he had a low irritability threshold; he attributed it to a heightened sensitivity to short-wavelength turbulence, acquired as a side-effect of a childhood malfunction. But even a plasmoid with the patience of a Precaution Councillor would have lost coherence when faced with three *independent* irritants.

The first had been a Precursor ship, its ethical state so squalid that FrayedEdges couldn't recall any ship that seemed so *sad*. That told him a lot about its crew, none of it flattering. The ship had made a brief stop at the battered satellite of Shool-3, where it had dropped off and assembled some kind of superluminal broadcast equipment. Then, to his amazement, it had continued to the planet itself.

Quite what attracted its pilot to that cold, dead world, FrayedEdges was unable even to *begin* to imagine. And he was routinely criticised for having too well-developed an imagination!

The second was a magnetotorus Herd. He and his fellow plasmoids had been watching the violet radiance heralding its approach for centuries. Even an infant like RippleCore could see that it was obviously headed their way, which meant that the Herders would shortly be declaring Arrival and requesting grazing rights in Shool's photosphere. In anticipation, the Precaution Council had set aside some fallow areas, knowing that magnetotori were always healthy for the fields. The Herders would be welcome—which was fortunate, because their Herd would graze the fields even if they were not. It was not politic to interfere with the wishes of Herders. Their quasi-quantum nature gave them unusual powers over magnetic plasma. They seldom abused these powers if they were left to their own devices.

The third disturbance—and in his opinion, the constriction that snapped the yewe's field lines—was an unexpected visit from a crowd of Cousins.

FrayedEdges had no objection to visitors. Plasmoids from other stars were welcome to come calling, and even more so if they were relatives, but they had to know their place and pay due respect to local customs. There were formalities to be observed. Unfortunately, they hadn't been. His Cousins, frankly, had been downright rude, and he didn't care who knew he held that opinion. The rest of the Borough was less resentful, one reason being that the rest of the Borough did not much care for FrayedEdges.

That didn't exactly help.

#You do realise that the *only* reason the Cousins are here is because of the approaching magnetotorus Herd?# he broadcast on the Borough's common waveband. #They're trying to jump the queue for access to the magnetotori!#

But no one seemed to be listening. At any rate, no one bothered to reply.

This annoyed FrayedEdges even more, because he was *right*. Those confounded Cousins had had the gall to broadcast themselves from Pluxlux to Shool *without asking for an invitation first*. Had they taken the trouble to observe basic protocol, no one would have denied their request: this was a family matter and traditional loyalties would win out, as they always did. A roving band of corona-huggers would have been *quite* another matter, mind you, but fortunately those worthless upstarts seldom ventured far from the galactic core, preferring larger, more metallic stars.

Sometimes living in the boondocks was an advantage.

For all his tendency to moan, FrayedEdges was a realist who respected evidence. Grumpily, he forced himself to admit that it wasn't entirely the Cousins' fault. Nor had it been deliberate opportunism. They'd just got lucky. It had, to be fair, been an emergency. You don't play around with incipient supernovas. Given the distances involved and the speed limits to broadcasting, there hadn't been time for the Cousins to negotiate a formal visit. But they could have ansibled before they left!

At least he'd managed to persuade his fellow burghers to grant the immigrants one of the poorer plots of photosphere, where the fields were strong but turbulent. The Cousins were well aware they'd been given the weak pole of the magnet, and he was pretty sure that they were hoping the grazing tori would choose their low-quality fields and restore their fertility. But could he get his fellows to feel that? Couldn't they understand that their *own* fields would benefit from fresh Herds of tori, if they could be tempted away from the areas the Cousins occupied?

The sheer complacency of the burghers' indifference was staggering. Worse, another opportunity like this one might not occur for four full rotations of the Galaxy. Why, by then young RippleCore would be almost fully adult!

Like all plasmoids, FrayedEdges was a complex, dynamic assembly of interlocking magnetic vortices, supported by and in turn supporting flows of hydrogen-helium plasma. About the size of a Qusite gladiatorial arena, his—let's call it a *body*, coherent magnetohydrodynamic structure sounds a bit technical—was roughly ellipsoidal in its rest state. But it could extend flexible plasmatic pseudopods up to ten times its major axis, absorbing energy from errant magnetic vortices that might otherwise cause him to decohere.

His plasmopods simultaneously fed him and protected

him.

Plasmoids live a few kilometres below the visible surface of a star, and most of the complex structures on the surface are caused by their activities beneath it. The temperature in that region is around 6,000 degrees Kelvin. Not only can plasmoids survive such high temperatures: they can't survive without them. High temperatures are essential to maintain the plasma substrate that supports their complex magnetic phenotype.

FrayedEdges was a misfit. He was always getting strange ideas. On one occasion he devised a new technique for luring yewes closer to the Borough, so that the farmers didn't waste as many alpha-particles while they were taming the creatures. But the yewes interacted with the domain walls of the Borough, bleeding off magnetic energy as flares. When the Elders had rebuilt the Borough, the burghers took a unanimous decision to keep local yewes at the traditional distance. Their lack of imagination had appalled him.

Then FrayedEdges got it into his head that it might be possible to communicate with the warmlife known to infest Shool-3. From occasional reports by ships and Herders that happened to pass through this out-of-the-way region of the Galaxy, the plasmoids had known that some strange molecular pseudo-life form there was slowly adapting its bizarre low-temperature processes to the hostile conditions of that tiny body. The plasmoids' innate ability to sense spectra had long made it clear that the planet's matter formed a series of thin molecular shells—gas, then liquid, then solid, then liquid again—and calculations suggested that these surrounded a part-liquid, part-crystalline core whose maximum temperature was high enough to sustain plasmoid life. But this potentially habitable region consisted almost entirely of iron, the burnt-out remnant of life-giving fusion reactions, an energy-sink at which the proton-proton chain reaction fundamental to stellar nucleosynthesis ground to a halt. The pressure was much too low to sustain any kind of nuclear process, and the magnetic field was far too simple. Shool-3's core was too small to be a suitable plasmoid habitat, and it was made of the wrong stuff: a clapped-out desert.

But...

Warmlife didn't live in the core.

That's what made it warmlife.

Passing magnetotorus Herders had mentioned surveys carried out by a variety of coldlife civilisations from the Living Galaxy. Rudimentary warmlife, little more than molecular replicants, had originated on Shool-4 and then migrated to Shool-3, propelled into vacuum by asteroid bombardment. It had continued to replicate in the planet's liquid shell, and *mutated* through some strange sequence of chemical reactions and restructuring events, until some forms became more complex. They spread from the liquid to the solid shell, and apparently some had even ventured into the gaseous one.

It was all very odd.

So odd, in fact, that some Shool-3 warmlife started to invade what would normally be coldlife habitat. And recently there had been rumours of crude extelligence on that enigmatic world. The plasmoids were unable to resolve such fine detail to check the rumours for themselves, so they had to rely on information supplied by others, which trickled in at irregular intervals. The absence of any signs of advanced technology made it clear that if extelligence had in fact emerged on that world, it was at best rudimentary.

FrayedEdges reasoned that extelligent creatures would have learned to communicate, but not by exchanging magnetic microstructures, the main means of communication used among plasmoids occupying the same star. Instead, he came to believe that they would use something more like the plasmoids' long-range messaging and self-broadcasting systems—modulated electromagnetic waves. Though too slow for practical interstellar messaging, this technology would be feasible for in-system communications, especially in the inner zone. He had been trying to detect such signals for half a millennium, but the Search for Extrasolar Extelligence had so far found precisely zilch. His transmitted messages encoding the seventeen basic types of magnetohydrodynamic turbulence, which any extelligent race would surely recognise as a mathematical universal, had gone unanswered.

This had not deterred him in the slightest. But most of his fellows considered him to be—well, 'eccentric' was the polite term.

A few, who shared his beliefs, did not. Six cycles ago he had begun interactions with DarkCorona, who had risen to a position demanding considerable respect: Relay Station Operator. The first time the torus migration came to Shool, far back in the remote past, the Herders already knew it was home to a few thousand separate clans of plasmoids, each concentrated in its own Borough. They were unsurprised that life could exist at such temperatures; if you were a Herder, very little surprised you. The plasmoids gave away their presence because they communicated by exchanging magnetic plasma, causing radio interference. They sometimes encoded their personas as radio signals and broadcast their sensoria to other stars, limping along at the speed of light, and these signals too could be intercepted.

The Herders liked life to be slow, but the plasmoids did not. So the Herders left the plasmoids a gift.

They installed it in a crater at the south pole of the small planet Shool-1, and it comprised a hardened radio transceiver, an ansible, and a transible for easy maintenance by authorised lifeforms many light years away. Now any plasmoid could broadcast a radio message to the transceiver, which the ansible could then pass on at vastly superior speeds to anywhere in the Galaxy that also had an ansible, which was most of it. This relay system cut communication times from anything up to millions of years to a few hours. The transceiver used a tuned, cunningly structured antenna to receive signals from the plasmoids in the Sun and to transmit signals back to them. It did not perish in the intense heat because it was magnetic.

Shool-3 pursued its roughly elliptical orbit, tugged by the other bodies in the Shool system, spinning about its tilted axis. Its cratered moon revolved around the planet, spinning at a more leisurely pace, gripped by a spin-orbit resonance that caused it always to present much the same hemisphere to its primary. Its other hemisphere was therefore hidden from observation by anyone on the planet. When the pandemons entered the system they were cautious, in case the primitive level of technology described in the silicoid report had changed in the interim, or had not been universal in the first place. The last thing they wanted was for some more advanced race to yell for the fex. So they chose the moon's hidden side for their main base of operations. Later, when they had verified the mottled world's low technological level, they began operations on the planet, but there was no point in moving the lunar base. So they set up their illicit transmitter on the hidden side of the moon. It was perfect.

The pandemons had noticed the approaching magnetotorus Herders, but quickly decided that those strange beings would pose no threat to their activities. They would be unlikely to notice any pandemonic presence, and if they did, they would have no interest in it. Herders kept themselves to themselves. Whatever went on inside their quasi-quantum sensoria, it made sense only to a Herder. They were able to communicate with the wider Galaxy, but seldom did.

The pandemons did not realise there were plasmoids in the star. If they had done, they still would not have worried, for plasmoids generally kept themselves to themselves too. Had the pandemons known of the plasmoid relay station at the pole of Shool-1, however, they would most definitely have worried. They would have made sure that their tightbeam came nowhere near that world. The odds of their messages being intercepted in transit were low in any case, but unlikely events become inevitable if the number of trials becomes large enough.

As the Festival of the Frowning Moon drew near, the inexorable geometry of orbital motion once more brought the Moon's hidden side into bright sunlight. This of itself posed no problems, for the pandemon base was well protected from solar radiation, even from flares. Only a very powerful and unusually prolonged coronal mass ejection was likely to cause serious damage. But the lunar location constrained the direction in which their tightbeam could be transmitted. For this very reason the pandemons had placed three relay stations in the Shool System's protocometary cloud, at the corners of an equilateral triangle, so that at any time at least one would be above the Moon's horizon as viewed from their base.

On this occasion the orbital geometry caused their transmitter's tightbeam to point in the general direction of the inner solar system. Not directly at the sun, which would block their broadcasts, but passing close by. And so it happened that a broadcast of an unusually lengthy mass execution in the Ul-q'mur Arena to one of the pandemon relay stations, from which it would be sent on to a client in one of the Ephemeral Whorls, brushed against the edge of the plasmoid relay station's magnetic antenna, of whose existence they were, and remained, totally unaware.

The operator on duty was DarkCorona, and she was one of those annoyingly meticulous individuals who liked everything to be functioning exactly as designed. If any other plasmoid had been in charge at the time, the slight bursts of interference would probably have gone unnoticed, but DarkCorona was made of sterner stuff, and investigated. She recorded the interference for the short period that it persisted, and placed a copy in the operator's log, along with a note explaining its acquisition. Then, because DarkCorona was also one of those annoying individuals who lacked even a shred of curiosity beyond carrying out her assigned task to the letter, she did nothing more about it.

She did, however, mention it to FrayedEdges a few days later when she passed through the Borough on the way to the grazing grounds. FrayedEdges, wondering if the Cousins had been interfering with the relay, analysed the recording and detected clear signs of structure. It had obviously been some kind of signal transmitted by a sentient entity. Equally obviously, it was encrypted. He contacted the Analytical Facility on Bajween-6. Frustrated by its inability to break the triple-layer quantum key encryption, the Facility informed him of its failure, adding "Only a quantum entity might decipher this." FrayedEdges thought for a moment, and then took it upon himself, without first gaining permission, to consult the approaching Herders.

Within two rotations of Shool, a Herder sent its reply to FrayedEdges. He didn't fully understand it, but the Herder told him it was important. When he hurried the 11,372-kilometre distance to inform the Borough's Precaution Council, he was not received with the instant acclaim that he had expected.

Record of the Precaution Council, Cycle 117348829/c

Councillor RadiantSwirl: Let the record show that the subject FrayedEdges, habitual domicile as recorded in the archives, presented himself voluntarily to be questioned about his unauthorised contact with the magnetotorus Herders currently approaching this star, in direct violation of time-honoured diplomatic procedures.

FrayedEdges, do you confirm that your attendance is voluntary?

FrayedEdges: I came to tell you something of vital import

—

RadiantSwirl: I'll take that as a 'yes'. Let the record state that said subject confirmed the Council's assertion.

The Council has investigated your recent actions, FrayedEdges. Do you deny that you took it upon yourself, on your own initiative, to hold discussions with a citizen of a non-plasmoid race?

FrayedEdges: No, I don't. Deny it, that is. But—

RadiantSwirl: You'll be given an opportunity to present your excuses as soon as the Council has been officially informed of the necessary facts. This isn't a Court of Punishment, though I warn you now that it may yet come to that. It's merely an informal fact-finding exercise. It's therefore necessary to inform the Council of the facts that have been found.

FrayedEdges: We could save a lot of time if you'd let me tell you the facts *I've*—

RadiantSwirl: We're not here to save time, subject FrayedEdges. We're here to follow proper procedures. And this Council will determine the facts, not you.

[*A lengthy summary of the subject's background, his relationship (rather, lack of) with operator DarkCorona, and his unauthorised self-generated radio transmission to the Herders, was read out. In the interests of brevity it is omitted; the full text can be found in the records.*]

Subject FrayedEdges: do you acknowledge the truth of what's been said?

FrayedEdges: [Waking up] Uh— what if I don't?

Councillor CalmRefulgence: The Council would record that you were unwilling to accept the facts, and no doubt recommend re-education. You would be wise to bear that in mind.

FrayedEdges: I acknowledge that the stated facts are indeed factual.

RadiantSwirl: Do you acknowledge the truth of what has been said?

FrayedEdges: Yes.

RadiantSwirl: Thank you. And *you* talk of wasting time! Now, explain your actions.

FrayedEdges: There are pandemons on the moon of Shool-3.

RadiantSwirl: That's a conclusion, not an expla— *what*?

FrayedEdges: There are pandemons on the moon of

Shool-3.

CalmRefulgence: If true, that information is of vital importance, Councillor Rad—

RadiantSwirl: Indeed. Why have you withheld it until now?

FrayedEdges: You refused to let me speak.

RadiantSwirl: Hrrumph. Let the record show that the subject acknowledged difficulty in communicating. Now, tell me: what makes you think that?

FrayedEdges: A Herder designated Implement-of-Consensus told me. It said the information might be important. That I should tell the appropriate authorities, which I took to be the Precaution Council. I don't know what a pandemon is, but—

RadiantSwirl: I think you'd better start at the beginning.

FrayedEdges: An acquaintance of mine, DarkCorona, noticed interference in the region of the radio spectrum employed by the Shool-1 polar relay station to communicate with us. She recorded the pattern and mentioned its existence. I was curious, and—

Councillor TwistedShockwave: Much in your record is curious!

FrayedEdges: I mean, I have an enquiring mind. More so than DarkCorona, she's a perfectionist but she never computes outside the boundary-layer. I subjected the recording to a structure-detection algorithm and found clear evidence that it wasn't of natural origin. I quickly concluded that it was a signal transmitted by an extelligent entity or entities.

RadiantSwirl: No doubt a Herder communication intended for this Council.

FrayedEdges: No, it was a tightbeam broadcast, not incident with this star. And its encryption differed considerably from what we use to talk to Herders.

CalmRefulgence: How did you determine that?

FrayedEdges: I applied the standard decryption algorithm to no effect. I decided to pass the problem on to

Bajween-6.

CalmRefulgence: Why?

FrayedEdges: It's the nearest Galactic Analytical Facility. I thought that if *they* couldn't decode the message, no one could.

RadiantSwirl: And could they?

FrayedEdges: No.

RadiantSwirl: So the contents can't be known?

FrayedEdges: I said that I *thought* that if they couldn't decode the message, no one could. But I was wrong. The Facility told me it was unable to break what it believed was triple-layer quantum key encryption. But then it said: "Only a quantum entity might decipher this." My thoughts immediately turned to the Herders. As quasi-quantum creatures, they might be able to resolve the mystery.

CalmRefulgence: And did they?

FrayedEdges: I've already explained that.

RadiantSwirl: Answer the question!

FrayedEdges: Yes, they did.

CalmRefulgence: And what did the deciphered message tell them?

FrayedEdges: That the interference was caused by a pandemon thanatography unit currently active on Shool-3, transmitted from that planet's moon on a tightbeam to, presumably, their clients somewhere in the direction of the Nest of Double Stars. Does that make any sense to you?

RadiantSwirl: Indubitably. So you're telling us there are pandemons on the moon of Shool-3?

FrayedEdges: Yes. What is a pan—

RadiantSwirl: Why didn't you tell the Council of this before? It's of vital importance! That species is untrustworthy and dangerous! There was no need to waste time on protocol, you should have acted on your own initiative and—

CalmRefulgence: Councillor, *he did*. You've been berating him for it for a considerable period of time.

RadiantSwirl: I was merely trying to establish the facts in a proper manner. Um... I propose a vote of thanks to subject FrayedEdges for bringing these vital facts to light, albeit belatedly.

CalmRefulgence: Seconded. We should notify the other Precaution Councils. I suggest we ask FrayedEdges to leave this chamber but remain adjacent in case his advice is required later. Councillors: we have much to discuss!

FrayedEdges still didn't know what a pandemon was, aside from learning that the species was untrustworthy and dangerous. But there was a simple way to find out. He'd have tried it sooner but the Herders had told him to lose no time in informing the authorities. Now, he had time to do it.

First, he tried the Analytical Facility on Bajween-6, but it didn't have any records of that particular species, even though he had obtained the relevant universal identifier from Implement-of-Consensus.

The Analytical Facility referred his query to the Register for Sentient Entities, a vast megastructure orbiting Fluttering Node of Darkness, which referred it to the Bureau of Anomalies, which passed it to a specialist subdepartment designated only by a code number. And finally FrayedEdges was told the strange story of the pandemon species.

For a start, it wasn't a species.

PANDEMON [Subdept. W441 Bu. Anom.]

Pandemons are the result of an experiment in biotechnology, the creation of creatures known only by their profession: 'Sculptors of Living Tissue', more familiarly known as 'Surgeons'.

Originally pandemons were a masterpiece built by members of this Master-Surgeon species to show off their skills. The first pandemon was sculpted in [time-designant 988 years past] as an experiment to construct a miniature brain-like device intended to enhance a damaged brain in a wide variety of races. The Surgeons gave these devices the name 'pandemon'—more precisely, its equivalent in their own language—referring to a theory of sentient consciousness brought about by pandemonium. That

is, uproar, tumult, and chaos; 'all the demons' that function independently to make a conscious mind.

An individual pandemon is the size of a ⌊nyzok's egg—insert cultural equivalent]. A pandemon progressively integrates with any carbon-organic body, but each body-part is short-lived, and must be replaced within [time-designant at most two months].

The intention was to introduce a number of pandemons into a brain-damaged being, where they would interface with its brain, absorb its operating mode, and act as replacements for any lost function. As a precaution, the Surgeon had deliberately designed pandemons to operate at an infraconscious level, acting as non-autonomous organic mechanisms. What it failed to anticipate was the emergence of group consciousness when several pandemon brains occupied the same body.

An integrated group of pandemons, it transpired, can take over any creature that eats them. They can briefly animate dead bodies or even combinations of pieces from dead bodies, sentient or animal. As one brain atrophies, new brains are grown to join the group, which may expand its numbers. In this manner a pandemon cluster acts like an intelligent, quasi-conscious organism, its appearance determined by the component body-parts that it has parasitised.

Another emergent feature, equally unanticipated by the Surgeon designers, is the ability to grow specialist organs if equivalents cannot be obtained from available creatures. The commonest are a manipulatory tentacle, which is blue and slimy, and vocal cords for speech.

When the Surgeons discovered this emergent group behaviour, they made strenuous efforts to expel all known pandemons from their zombie bodies and destroy them. Unfortunately [time-designant 386 years past] one of the pandemon neurocomplexes objected to this procedure, and escaped from the Surgeons' original world by taking over one of their masters and stealing a Precursor starship. They reproduced, stole a few more ships (none of Precursor manufacture) and became thinly dispersed throughout the Living Galaxy. What became of their original Master is unknown.

What to do if you encounter a pandemonic cluster:
Don't.

That answers a lot of things, FrayedEdges told himself.

Then he realised that it left one glaring question unanswered.

If pandemons infest only organic bodies... why is the Council so worried?

Perhaps the Herders could shed some light on the matter.

What had {self-identity} been thinking-of?

Implement-of-Consensus had communicated with plasmoids many times in its long existence, but until now it had always followed established protocols. It had consulted Those Who Decide before initiating contact with the plasmoids of Shool, and even that had been confined to an official representative of the Precaution Council.

So why did {self-identity} annihilate every entry in the matrix?

The Herder had no idea. It had just— happened.

It had all seemed so sensible at the time. An innocent enquiry from a plasmoid who identified himself as FrayedEdges, who had detected—or believed he had detected—an anomalous superluminal signal. Implement-of-Consensus could have passed the enquiry on to Those Who Decide; *should* have passed it on to Those Who Decide. But at the time it seemed too trivial a matter to concern such an august body, entangled as it was with the complexities of Arrival.

The puzzle had been intriguing, too. You didn't encounter a triple-layer quantum key encrypted signal every day. Even less often did you encounter one apparently emitted from a dead, cratered rock. Even a student could deduce that said rock must be host to some form of level-four sentience.

The torus-herders had been anticipating a rest from their infinitely tedious journey, and the chance to carry out long-term maintenance, breed new tori, and sell the surplus to power-brokers for use as starship engines. Implement-of-Consensus had no wish to disrupt its betters' preparations with stupid questions, or to interrupt their consensuals at such a sensitive time. It decided to keep the matter to itself. *Such a fascinating puzzle...*

And so Implement-of-Consensus decoded the message by a heroic sequence of unitary transformations. When it had internalised the contents, the nature of the sentient beings that had transmitted the message came as a shock. Pandemons were almost mythical, the subject of imaginative but implausible tales that circulated between star systems, occasionally overheard by eavesdropping Herders with an ansible, nothing to do, and too much time not to do it in. Which was a pretty common state for a Herder, when between systems. Which in turn was a pretty common state for a Herder.

The myths portrayed pandemons as bodysnatchers: thieves who stole other beings' bodies for their own use. It was said that they owned starships, pursuing a nomadic existence, moving on through the Galaxy before their crimes alerted the local Effectuators. Each wandering gang of criminals was few in number, united into tight groups by a common purpose. They lacked both morals and ethics, were obsessed with financial gain, and were indifferent to any suffering they might cause to others in their relentless pursuit of profit.

It all seemed a bit over the top, but then, myths usually were.

However, logic insisted that mythical creatures did not send messages. And if *this* message was anything to go by, the rest of the myths were probably true as well.

Implement-of-Consensus now realised it should have passed the information on to Those Who Decide, upon whose robust waveforms the task of determining what (if anything) to tell the plasmoids would naturally fall. Instead, it had been so perplexed and overexcited that it had immediately got back to FrayedEdges to pass on the curious news. Implement-of-Consensus received a strong impression that the plasmoid had failed to understand most of what he was being told, relegated the incident to long-term memory along with a great deal of other dross, and assumed nothing would come of it.

Wrong.

Now the plasmoids of Shool were surging through the star's atmosphere in incoherent clumps, their confounded Precaution Councils were all in a state of uproar, and the entire Arrival process had been put at risk. It was all Implement-of-Consensus's fault, of course, but as yet Those Who Decide didn't know that. Unfortunately, they were bound to find out, which meant that they should be told, immediately.

When Implement-of-Consensus arrived at the current location of Those Who Decide, it dropped itself into the middle of a crisis. The presence of pandemons in the system was now known, and it wasn't going down well because of the likely plasmoid reaction.

Instrumentality-of-Corroboration held the floor. {Self-identity} + {sensation} + {danger!!!}, it broadcast. Its wavefunctions rippled with tremors of fear. Implement-of-Consensus wryly reflected that right now, FrayedEdges would be an entirely appropriate new name for Instrumentality-of-Corroboration.

Concurrence-of-Opinion sought to calm the oscillating Herder. [Confusion mode] + {What is the precise form of this danger?}

{*Flares!!!*}, Instrumentality-of-Corroboration asserted, at a frequency somewhat higher than was polite.

Expediter-of-Mutuality understood immediately. {Flares = natural-reaction-mode * plasmoids}, it pointed out. [Interrogative mode] {Flares —> probability-amplitude?}

{Large}, Instrumentality-of-Corroboration replied, worryingly imprecise.

[Interrogative mode] {Quantify >>> large}.

{Close to critical}.

{Are we all in-agreement?} Ratifier-of-Assent asked, seeking to clarify the discussion for the official record. Pinging Concurrence-of-Opinion, and receiving no contra-indications, it incorporated the information into the database.

Implement-of-Consensus decided that now was not the time for a confession. It was aware that throughout the Living Galaxy, plasmoids generally had considerable control over their star's photosphere. Indeed, in a sense they were *part of* their star's photosphere, just as a marine organism was part of the surrounding sea on an ocean planet, as the oscillations of its body affected those of the surrounding fluid, and conversely. If the plasmoids decided to respond to the presence of pandemons by causing Shool to emit solar flares, burning the evil creatures to a crisp, there was little the Herders could do to stop them.

Now he understood the answer to the question that a puzzled FrayedEdges had recently asked him. If flares had been the only likely consequence, the Herders would have cheered the plasmoids on. But Implement-of-Consensus could now tell its plasmoid acquaintance exactly what had been worrying the Precaution Council. It worried Implement-of-Consensus, too.

Although pandemons could not have any direct effect on either plasmoids or Herders, abuses of coldlife or warmlife worlds could cause all sorts of indirect trouble. A flare aimed at Shool-3 or its moon would undoubtedly put an end to the pandemon issue, but it would also wreak havoc with the Herd. Once Approach had begun, a magnetotorus Herd would make a geodesic descent, straight for the star. There was no reliable way to divert an approaching Herd from its target; even its Herders had no control at that stage. And the Herders' magnetotori would be right in the plasmoids' firing line. Their trajectory would shortly pass between Shool-3 and its moon, neatly bisecting the two most likely targets. A flare at that time would probably miss the Herd, but magnetotori are hypersensitive to solar flares. Even a near miss was guaranteed to start a stampede. And no sentient entity in its right mind would ever wish to find itself anywhere near a stampeding Herd of magnetotori.

11

Lion Hunt

"*Ym hut'p, ouwamat-zeb!*"

Jackalfoot recognised the voice instantly, recognised the insult—*hoof*-of-jackal, not *foot*—as friendly banter, and tried to respond in kind. "Peace to you also, Yulmash the—" he paused. Qusite still didn't come naturally to him. It wasn't the vocabulary, it was the syntax "—slayer of millions."

Yulmash grunted. "My ambitions aren't that extensive, Beastmaster. Nor so unattainable, nor so pointless. I seek only the title of Grand Champion."

But that will entail pointless slaughter. "May your heart's desires be, uh, granted," said Jackalfoot. *The system under which you're compelled to live is not your fault.*

"You seem distracted, my friend. Ill at ease."

"Look at the third deinothere in the procession, Yulmash."

The warrior screwed up his eyes, staring almost into the morning sun. "I can never tell deinotheres from elephants. Do you mean the one whose *khibesh* is bedecked with a red-topped canopy?"

"No, that is a mammoth. The first eight are elephants, you can tell by the huge ears, the long tusks, and the way the trunk sprouts from the middle of the face. Then fifteen mammoths, paler in colour and with long, curving tusks. You can tell the rest are deinotheres by their short tusks, small ears, and a trunk that seems a continuation of the fore—"

"They all look the same to me," Yulmash interrupted. Jackalfoot realised his enthusiasm had got the better of him, but Yulmash really did need educating. "Elephants, the lot of them," the warrior continued, brushing aside Jackalfoot's attempt at education. "Overgrown swamp-pigs. With a tail at each end, and a bunch of self-important idiots on top."

Jackalfoot sighed. He agreed entirely with the warrior's assessment of the riders, impolitic though it undoubtedly was, but the animals were another matter. Qusites were not very discerning when it came to distinguishing closely related species. Except for birds and fish, perhaps because they used so many of those for food. Anything large with a trunk was an elephant, even if it was actually a deinothere or one of several variations on 'mammoth'. Any big fierce cat was a lion, be it a true lion, a leopard, or a sabretooth. Or that rarest of animals, imported from far south of the Great Dune Sea by noblemen of great wealth, the explosively quick cheetah.

But cheetahs were also quick to tire. Today, Jackalfoot felt much the same. Because today, the King's sabretooth lions would hunt. In a pack.

Jackalfoot had trained most of them from birth, building on the cats' natural tendency to join forces when taking down prey. True lions did the same—well, their females did, while the males either fought off other males, mated, ate, or slept. Mostly slept. Like many of the males of Qus. Leopards, on the other hand, were solitary hunters, and all his efforts to present his master with a pack of trained leopards had failed miserably. As he had known they would.

Fortunately Insh'erthret owned no cheetahs, for these too were solitary hunters by nature. Even family groups hunted prey as individuals.

"*Haiyah!* Magnificent, isn't it?" Yulmash roared, slapping Jackalfoot on the shoulder.

The Neanderthal gave him a puzzled glance. "The procession?"

"No, the lions. I give thanks to Zek-Mek for such a spectacle!"

Jackalfoot repressed a sigh. Turning a magnificient lioness into an absurd deity was bad enough, but a *war goddess…* "The third deinothere," he repeated.

Yulmash squinted into the sun. "Ah. She's very reluctant to support any weight on her left hind leg. Poor beast, it must be painful."

Jackalfoot was visibly impressed, and somewhat taken aback by the precision of the gladiator's answer and the hint of empathy. "You have a trace of lionface talent, warrior. Most folk would not even realise the animal is female, let alone notice an injury or associate it with suffering. If she stumbles and falls, the passengers—"

"Chief Architect Batsuhepchit and his principal wives."

"As you say, Yulmash. The Chief Architect and his wives may be seriously injured, either by the fall, the lions, or their prey. The king's husbanders have accoutred the wrong animal." He called a servant-boy over, spoke to him in monosyllables until he could repeat the message reliably, and sent him to inform the husbanders of their error. Several spare elephants (and mammoths and deinotheres) were ambling with the herd, and the canopied box atop this animal could be transferred to a free one, along with the nobles sitting in it.

One of the spares caught Jackalfoot's eye; more precisely, his empathic sense. For some reason the animal seemed to exude a faint whiff of evil. *An evil deinothere?* That had to be nonsense. He was tired, his empathy was becoming unreliable. What other explanation could there be?

With a parting wave, Yulmash scrambled aboard an elephant, not deigning to use the steps that servitors had provided. Jackalfoot remained on the ground to walk with the lions.

Half-buried in soft cushions, Sitaperkaw and

Insh'erthret sat side by side in an elaborately decorated *khibesh*. This was a large box of cloth and wood, strapped with wide belts of tooled leather to the back of an elephant, which in this case really *was* an elephant. It had comfortable seats and a canopy to shield its occupants from the sun. The more wealthy the occupants, the more gaudy the *khibesh* and the more elaborate the tooling. There was nothing subtle about wealth in Qus.

There was nothing subtle about rank, either. The King, his Regent, and their servants rode the second elephant in the procession. For practical reasons, the first elephant was reserved for the commanders of the King's personal guard, who would also ensure the safety of his uncle, the Regent. A hundred guardsmen trotted beside the royal conveyance and the procession that followed it. A long train of nobles perched on a variety of pachyderms straggled behind the King's mount in order of precedence, fanning out as the lesser nobility jostled for position, trying to avoid the clouds of fine sand kicked up by the ponderous mounts ahead of them. Between them, the pachyderms created a great plume of dust that the desultory wind slowly dispersed.

Flanking them on the right-hand side, to give the King the best possible view, was the hunting pack: sixteen trained sabretooth lions. Each had a heavy metal collar, either bare and burnished or wrapped in symbolically decorated cloth, by which it was chained to a trained squad of four handlers, who made their way on foot. Jackalfoot walked alongside them, moving quietly from squad to squad, making sure that the lions were alert but peaceful. They had been trained to respect their handlers, reserving their predatory instincts for the King's quarry—on this occasion, gazelles.

At least, they're supposed *to be hunting gazelles*, Jackalfoot thought. *Once these cats get their blood-lust up, they may get other ideas into their heads.* The cats had an innate aversion to anything the size of an elephant, but it was wise not to rely on this. The King's personal guard included a dozen Nabish bowmen recruited from the Deep South, capable of bringing down even a charging sabretooth.

Probably.

He'd seen them do it. But these cats were capable of ignoring a hit on the body unless the arrow met a vital organ, such as the heart or the brain. And the eye was such a small target, even when stationary. Moving? It would be a tricky shot.

The previous night, the Moon-goddess had shone in her full glory, a brilliant disc that lit up the city and cast dark shadows between the houses. Her visage had been suffused with a blood-red glow, which the Qusites took to be an omen. Jackalfoot didn't believe in omens, Neanderthals in general were somewhat lacking in the spirituality department, but their highly developed sense of empathy was legendary. Slowly She would change her form, shrinking along one edge, until the thin crescent of the Frowning Moon signalled the festival soon to be held in Her honour. But her currently full aspect, in the appropriate season, had been the time-honoured signal for the Hunt.

The Hunt to Presage the Festival was traditional.

Everything was traditional in Qus.

Behind the King's elephant there followed a procession of nobles. Those of the highest rank, such as the Vizier and his principal wife, and the General of the King's Army with *his* principal wife, came first, riding elephants. Next came those of slightly lower rank, mounted on mammoths. Lesser nobility— traders, landholders, and a few select artisans—brought up the rear on deinotheres. All were accompanied by a few servants, but no one took any notice of *them.*

Twelve animals back from the royal mount, Shephatsut-Mer, Nemnestris, and selected servants rode in style aboard a woolly mammoth, beneath a canopy of deepest blue, fringed with gold. They were clad in their finest ceremonial clothing.

"See that lion with the blue and gold collar?" Shephat-sut-Mer shouted to Nemnestris, above the din of the ambling convoy. "That one's ours! Isn't he magnificent?"

Nemnestris merely grunted. All guests of honour were assigned their own lion for the duration of the hunt. She disapproved of her husband's gambling; the copper was inevitably wasted in the long term, whatever occasional winnings accidentally accrued. But Shephatsut-Mer had insisted on placing a large bet that what he insisted on calling *their* lion would be the second to bring down a gazelle. He was getting ever more excited, even before the beasts were unleashed, but he could see that the High Acolyte of Nefteremit the Lilypad Prophetess was getting ever more bored.

"Some wine, perhaps?" Shephatsut-Mer offered, in the hope of alleviating her evident distaste for the entire proceedings. Evident to him, at least. His wife would know it wasn't a good idea to let it show publicly lest she should offend the King. But the High Priest of the Hippopotamus Cult was intimately familiar with his wife's moods, and he had no trouble sensing her lack of interest. She nodded, and a glance at one of the servants produced two cups, each half-filled with the deep red wine from the vineyards owned by Vizier Noth-Metamphut. It was Nemnestris's favourite, and a cup or three usually helped to put her in a better frame of mind.

"Is that Hor-Qa'dje?" she suddenly asked, pointing to a deinothere draped in red and yellow stripes.

"The sharpener of the *kh'et*-Sword? Yes, that's him. And his new concubine. Laphmoo, or some such barbarian name."

"She looks pregnant to me."

"So it's said."

"Amazing for a man of his age. I wonder if the child is actually his?"

Shephatsut-Mer said nothing: there had already been too much speculation in the Palace, a lot of it astonishingly accurate. Nemnestris, who had obviously decided not to push the issue, sat up and studied the procession more closely. "Husband: why is Lord Mneft-A'a on a deinothere? Surely he merits a mammoth!"

Shephatsut-Mer pursed his lips, wondering how much his wife already knew. Everything, probably. Very little escaped the attentions of the followers of the Lilypad Prophetess. "The Surveyor of the Holy Dwellings has... uh... temporarily forfeited the favour of the Regent."

Nemnestris giggled. "Of course. That silly business with the Princess's serving maids?"

"Precisely, my love."

"No need to be so coy, dear. *Everyone* knows."

Well, everyone who is someone. Shephatsut-Mer, who found this kind of gossip disrespectful, sought to change the topic. "The King's lion—"

"—is obviously the one leading the pack," his wife continued for him, sipping at her wine. "It wears the royal collar of pure copper, and its natural place must be at the front."

"Indeed, my pet, you're perfectly correct on both counts. And of course the King's lion will make the first kill. That's why I bet on the sec—"

Nemnestris fluttered a hand. "Of *course*, my love. I understand that. But surely the second kill will be reserved for Regent Sitaperkaw? So why have you gambled a small fortune of *our* copper on *your* lion?"

Shephatsut-Mer found himself in two minds. Should he tell her the truth, or trot out the lie he had already prepared? Looking at her face, he opted for the truth. Nemnestris had an innate ability to spot a falsehood, and once she did, she would dig out the truth with the tenacity of a wild dog in pursuit of a holed-up hare.

"A well-informed source close to the Vizier passed word that on this occasion Sitaperkaw is planning to defer to the Lady Nofritt."

"And her lion is?"

"The pale one with a collar striped in white and black."

"Ah. Fifth in the pack, immediately in front of yours."

"Yes, *ours* is the sixth."

"Which is why you placed your bet on *yours* making the second kill?"

"Yes."

"If there's any logic to this, I'm not following it."

Shephatsut-Mer broke out in a grin. "The same inform-ant told me that Lady Nofritt's lion-handler is heavily in debt."

"*Ahhhh.* Now I begin to see." Nemnestris rearranged her hair extensions. "Perhaps my husband is cleverer than I give him credit for."

Shephatsut-Mer shrugged. "A sum in *bashshisk* that we would consider of no consequence sufficed to purchase his compliance. Lady Nofritt is very inattentive, and she's likely to be very slow giving the order for her lion to be released. While she dithers, I'll command the release of our lion. Her handler will encounter difficulties unclipping the chain from its collar, so our lion will be freed before hers."

Nemnestris pursed his lips. "It's risky."

He nodded. "Very risky. But the potential reward is great. More wine?"

"Yes, I need it to calm my nerves. It's really quite good, not too sweet. You should try some."

"An excellent idea, my love. Maid! Wine here!"

"You've checked the hydets and their deployment?"

In the ever-changing conditions of the hunt, Pask-RaskAsk had decided not to use any static hydets. They'd ei-ther be too far from the action, or get trampled. KrajMajJazj and BuzgRuzgMofz had come to the same conclusion. That left only one realistic option. So PaskRaskAsk had assigned rider-less mammoths to his recording crew, installed and initialised their hyperreality eidetic recorders, and made sure they were hidden from view beneath their transparency suits.

His reply was a throaty growl, a consequence of his current choice of vocal cords. "Yuz, yuz. Don't worry, it's all in order."

PaskRaskAsk was one of the best directors in the death-pornography business, but MasgNasgOsg found himself un-accountably nervous, perhaps because he was a little too close to the action for comfort. Ordinarily he directed the recording from a safe distance, but that would not be acceptable for the Hunt. The humans were securely mounted in their canopied boxes, but he and his fellow pandemons had to ride bareback on mammoths. Their transparency suits—actually force-fields that moulded themselves to their contents and diverted light —would render them and their hydets invisible, but a trans-parency suit could not cover an object as big as a *khibesh*. It was a calculated risk, a necessary one if they were to obtain hyper-reality eidetic recordings in sufficiently high definition, and of sufficient violence, to satisfy the refined perversions of their clientele. MasgNasgOsg consoled himself that the worst that was likely to happen would be the loss of a few bodily com-ponents. It would be relatively simple to acquire replacements. The biggest danger was that an accident might push detached components outside the range of the transparency suit, but it was unlikely that any of the humans would notice a few pro-truding animal limbs amid the general carnage.

He still felt nervous. Perhaps it had been a mistake not to delegate the entire recording to subordinates. He surveyed the scene again, modelling the angles on a virtual reality visor secured round the neck of his current head, which was that of a sabretooth lion.

Some of his scouts, hidden beyond a line of palm-trees, relayed the progress of the gazelle herd that beaters were pushing towards the hunters, along with assorted oryx and antelope caught up in the *mêlée*. Ordinarily, so large and noisy a procession of hunters would have scared off all available prey within a dozen *khar*. So, as tradition and practicality pre-scribed, the Master of the King's Hunt was driving a substan-tial number of prey into the path of the advancing lions. Even so, those magnificent hunters would have their work cut out when the prey finally became terrified enough to try to break through the half-circle of beaters, armed with spears and fire, that blocked their escape.

MasgNasgOsg had placed several pandemons with recording instruments among the beaters. With careful editing —KrajMajJazj was an expert, very creative—their hydet-files would set the context for the coming slaughter.

The lions were getting very interested now. Clearly they had scented the gazelles. Within a few seconds, the outliers of the herd became visible through the dust ahead, milling uncertainly as they emerged from the shelter of the trees. More joined them, caught between the crescent of beaters and the approaching line of death.

The Master of the Hunt had made sure that the gazelles were upwind of the lions, but with the trees no longer a barrier, the prey could see them. Uncertainty gave way to horrified realisation, turning instantly to panic. The leading animals turned tail and tried to run back through the rest of the herd, towards the ring of beaters, spears and fire notwithstanding. This confused the rest of the herd, which tried to get out of their way.

At that moment, at a covert signal from the Master of the Hunt and a quick nudge from the Regent, King Insh'erthret raised his right hand in an imperious salute, and the handler of the King's lion slipped the chain from its collar. Released, the great cat bounded towards the herd, panicking it even more. Singling out one large but elderly gazelle, slower than the rest, it launched itself at the animal's throat. As the prey came crashing to the ground, its legs kicking in death throes, the King obeyed Sitaperkaw's whispered prompt and gave the signal to start releasing the other lions.

MasgNasgOsg monitored the recordings through his hyvis—a state-of-the-art hyperreality visor—issuing orders for close-up shots of lions' jaws clamped round gazelles' throats, mid-range images of charging lions and fleeing prey, and wide-angle shots of the complex scene that was unfolding. Emotional recordings of humans, flushed with the excitement of bloodlust, would appeal to some clients, and one member of his crew specialised in such things, having made a careful study of human responses to violence. His *kziczaj*—a small metal tube with complex gadgetry inside it—swept up pheromones from the sweat of the crowd, decanting them into microcapsules for later analysis. Instructions to synthesise equivalent emotion-producing molecules would eventually be beamed to each client's *eft* as part of the overall package, edited to suit their particular species, enhanced whenever possible to create a stronger response.

Several lions had now stopped to eat. They would be permitted to do so for a time—no sane person would wish to separate a hungry lion from its prey—and then they would be recaptured by expert gladiators with rope nets. The remaining meat would be butchered and trimmed to be carried back to Ul-q'mur in triumph.

The event was proceeding well—MasgNasgOsg knew several clients who would pay enormous sums to be present in a hydetic representation of the chaos of the hunt—and it would be stupid to ruin it now by falling off his mount. He issued new commands to PaskRaskAsk: "See that group of three lions that's cornered several gazelles? I want you in among them. I want our clients to feel the lions' breath in their chemosensors, I want slow-motion action replays! I want blood and death and terror—and I want *you* closer than that! *Much* closer!"

Distracted by the rapid sequence of gabbled instructions, PaskRaskAsk lost control of his mammoth, and it stumbled in a fox-hole. He grabbed its hair even tighter as it swerved towards the group of lions. MasgNasgOsg wanted recordings close to the action, but this was a bit *too* close...

The mammoth bolted. To the crowd, it looked as though one of the free pachyderms had lost its nerve. The animal cut a swathe through the herd, flinging gazelles left and right as it fled from the scimitar teeth of the lions. PaskRaskAsk gripped its thick coat, bouncing up and down as it charged across the uneven ground. He and his mount disappeared towards the horizon in a cloud of dust, until the animal was lost behind the same stand of palms that initially had concealed the gazelles.

The ring of beaters, still holding their weapons, took one look at the approaching mammoth and leaped aside; the animal went straight through the gap with its impressive speed undiminished. The pandemon was tossed up and down, his jackal head snarling, his crocodile tail thumping against the mammoth's flank, which panicked the beast even further. It was now completely out of sight of the hunting-party. At that point, the mammoth suddenly reared up, spooked by a surprised hare, and PaskRaskAsk fell off.

Pandemon brains are no more immune to a sudden impact than human ones. The pandemon blacked out.

When he regained consciousness and raised his head, he came nose to nose with a huge sabretooth lion. The cat had been chasing a gazelle, but it had picked an unusually strong, young male, so fleet of foot that it left the big cat behind it in the dust. Saliva trickled down its huge fangs. PaskRaskAsk's hydet was smashed, ejected from his transparency suit when he hit the ground. The mammoth itself was nowhere to be seen. Reckoning that his transparency suit would save him, the pandemon began to crawl away.

The lion followed, paw after silent paw.

The pandemon realised that his suit had decohered in the fall, deactivated by the impact. Before he could reactivate it, the lion roared and pounced. The pandemon was crushed beneath its weight. Massive jaws cut off his breathing. His body shuddered, and died. The lion pawed casually at the control disc and broke the strap. The disc slid off the corpse's neck and disappeared down a crevice in the rocky ground.

This far beyond the palm trees, the land made a sudden transition: one step scrubby vegetation, the next, trickling sand. The air became dry. The vast desert stretched into the distance, where large dunes soared, flat silhouettes amid the haze, foreshortened by perspective.

The lion trotted out into the desert, dragging its catch.

With a loving smile on her lips, and in a voice no louder than a whisper and as cutting as a butcher's flaying-knife, Nemnestris was berating her husband for losing such a large amount of copper. It would never do to show her anger in front of so many of the nobility—or, for that matter, the low-life that tended lions and served the King. Like a kiln firing pots, she was featureless on the outside, incandescent within. Their maid was careful to keep her eyes on the Hunt. She'd heard all this many times before.

Shephatsut-Mer smiled back, but his was a fixed smile, less convincing than the practised hint of amusement on the lips of the High Acolyte of Nefteremit the Lilypad Prophetess.

I've been a fool, he thought. *The Regent is renowned for his cunning. He thinks ten steps ahead of other men. This I* knew, *and still...*

Sitaperkaw had *not* deferred to the Lady Nofritt. Shephatsut-Mer was now utterly convinced that the Regent had spread the rumour himself—well, ordered an inferior to do so —to persuade others not to place bets on his own lion, and mislead them into gambling on lost causes. That, of course, had left him free to cash in on an absolute certainty without having to share his winnings.

"It's only copper," said Shephatsut-Mer. "It can be replaced. We have no lack of income." But his face told a different story.

A short way into the desert, the lion settled down for a meal of pandemon parts, starting with the legs, then moving on to the soft entrails and internal organs of the torso.

The head had fallen to one side and its eyes were no longer functioning, but the pandemon brains didn't need a living body's heart to pump blood through them. The Surgeons had designed pandemon brains to be virtually self-sustaining, able to survive for many days without oxygen or nutrients. When they took over a body, the brains infiltrated its nerve cells, and extended their own networks of ultrathin fibres to help control its muscles and activate its organs. They used cellular reprogramming to rebuild failed organs and restructure the animal's senses. They could cause cells to flow like water, and they manipulated genetic information—whatever its physical or chemical format—with the intuitive ease of an expert programmer or a virtuoso musician. They could even grow a few specialist organs at will.

In this manner, the brains that now constituted the principal living part of PaskRaskAsk observed the lion's progress through the pain signals that its body was sending it along its own sensory network. If necessary, a pandemon could disconnect its brains from the amalgamated nervous systems of its hosts, but suppressing all pain was a bad idea, because the host might be damaged. So PaskRaskAsk muted the signals to a level barely above numb, and monitored the lion's progress as it ate its way through his dead or dying body.

As the jaws moved towards the head, the pandemon became hopeful. He reckoned that his chances of returning to the city were growing with every bite. The lion would crack his skull, eat his brains—and in the manner of pandemon brains, he would quickly take over the lion. Then the powerful lion would become the first component of the pandemon's new body.

The lion stopped eating, rolled on its side, and went to sleep. PaskRaskAsk refused to worry: he had observed the habits of lions. From the time that had elapsed, and the temperature signals seeping into his brain, he knew that the sun was now high in the sky. The lion would rest for a time;

the pandemon would suspend its perceptions until the cat re-awoke and resumed feeding.

As the temperature dropped, the lion did just that, crouching beside the diminishing corpse. PaskRaskAsk gave a mental sigh as he felt the skull cracking. Now the lion would consume a cluster of purple pandemon brains, each the size and approximate shape of a wild pomegranate, and Pask-RaskAsk would acquire and control the body of a sabretooth lion. Back in business.

The lion gave one of the brains a tentative lick. Its head jerked back, and it emitted a low growl. Something was wrong. Disappointed, it got to its feet, turned towards the greenery of the cultivation, and wandered off.

Alien brains didn't appeal.

Unaware that the lion had gone, PaskRaskAsk waited for the feeding to resume. When it didn't, the pandemon made an educated guess about what had happened. Perhaps MasgNas-gOsg would send other pandemons to look for him. It wasn't guaranteed: the temptation to reduce the number among whom the profits should be divided might be too strong.

As a precaution, he would implement his brains' defences against dehydration, and wait for some other animal to come along. One less choosy.

12

Arena

Cheering crowds gathered along the wide central street of Ul-q'mur to watch the King and his retinue returning from the Hunt. City police, most of them Nabish, lined the processional way to keep the crowds under control. Their traditional curved shortswords gleamed in the sunlight. Thirty battle-hardened members of the Royal Guard, now attired in clean dress uniform of brightly coloured kilts, tooled leather chest-straps, and dyed ostrich-plume headdresses, led the way on foot. Another thirty were arrayed along both flanks of the elephant that bore Sitaperkaw and Insh'erthret, who sat in regal splendour in their luxuriant *khibesh* and waved to acknowledge the praises of the crowd.

Next came the lions, once more chained. Well-fed, and heavily under the influence of the Beastmaster and his assistants, they ignored the throng, but left a trail of excitement in their wake, spinning off frissons of fear.

Behind them came the procession of elephants, mammoths, and deinotheres, most bearing a gaudily coloured *khibesh* strapped to the animal's back. A few of the ponderous animals had no riders—at least, no visible riders. A huge train of servants of many races carried the spoils of the Hunt, haunches and other cuts of gazelle meat. Plus odd portions of antelope and oryx.

By tradition, the ordinary townsfolk would each receive a share, after the food had been offered to the gods at the temple and the gods had magically absorbed its spiritual essence. This made the Festival of the Frowning Moon a high point of the year, and helped to cement the common folk's love and respect for their King. And his Regent, of course. The Guests of Honour would receive far larger shares, as was only fitting. For them, the butchers would trim away any portions of the carcasses that bore the tooth-marks of lions. The trimmings were added to the townsfolk's share. Waste not, want not.

The King and his entourage made their slow way into the centre of the city, following one of the many processional highways. From time to time the Regent reminded Insh'erthret to cast handfuls of small copper discs into the crowd, where his people would scrabble on their knees for a scrap of royal favour and a boost to their income. It was a tradition that went back centuries. It was no coincidence that it was also an easy way to buy popularity, and compared to most of them, it was cheap.

The procession was heading for the Great Temple and the adjoining Palace area, where it would disappear behind high walls and great wooden gates. As it neared the end of its journey, it passed by the entrance to the Arena. The shouts of the crowd drowned the noise of hand-to-hand combat coming from inside. It also threatened to drown out a conversation that was going on between Bil and MasgNasgOsg, in a locked room. Once again the pandemon had decohered his transparency suit. He generally found that other species became more cooperative when he showed himself in his true guise. No sentient being wanted to end up being distributed piecemeal across the temporary bodies of a gang of pandemons.

"I hope this isn't going to take long," Bil grumbled, having regained some of his poise since their previous encounter. "I've had to leave Ptafni in charge at a rather sensitive moment."

"There is no hurry," the pandemon wheezed. Its lungs, abstracted from a sheep, were beginning to need renewal.

"Yes there is, Excellency," Bil contradicted. It wasn't prudent, but he'd been in a foul mood all day, and right now he didn't greatly care for prudence. "There's a practice bout under way in the Arena between a convicted rapist and a grave-robber. Both criminals have been condemned to death by combat. I've been training them for the past year, to get them ready for their enforced punishment-fights." He waved his hand in the general direction of the roped-off practice area at the east side of the main Arena. "I need to get back out there before one of them accidentally kills the other."

"Would that matter?"

"Yes, Excellency, it would. I want one of them to *deliberately* kill the other." Bil's laugh was a ghoulish cackle. "But not yet."

MasgNasgOsg was characteristically unamused, but unsurprised. Inferior species often resorted to gallows humour to conceal their fears. Accidental death, unrecorded, would perhaps be a waste, but his gang could hardly point their hydets at every petty killing. His clients wanted top quality action, not amateurish struggles between lowlife scum.

Then a thought struck him. Perhaps this did matter. "Is that to be part of your promised Spectacular?"

"A part, yes, Excellency. A small part. Uh— a *very* small part." It was difficult to read pandemon features, but body language was more easily decipherable, and this pandemon looked distinctly peeved. Before the creature could vent its anger on Bil, the promoter hastened to expand on his plans.

"It will be the most magnificent Spectacular ever!" he gushed. "Regent Sitaperkaw has granted permission for unprecedented expenditure!" Then, remembering too late that he had claimed sole dominion over Spectaculars, he quickly tried to cover up his blunder. "Purely a formality, you understand. It keeps the Palace accountants happy."

The pandemon ignored the transparent self-justification, but sounded sceptical. "Magnificent in what way?"

"Oh, in every way conceivable, Excellency!"

This was far too vague. "More blood? More violence?

More pain for my clients to immerse themselves in?"

"Oh, yes, much more of all of those. Just as you, er, request— no, demanded."

MasgNasgOsg turned its horned head sideways so that one of its huge eyes pointed directly at Bil. A predator's head would have been a better choice for intimidating the Arena's manager-promoter, but this one was fresh and had been easy to incorporate.

When Bil flinched, the eye blinked twice. "I wish to hear *details*. My clients want more *imagination*."

So Bil told him, at great length and in considerable detail, how the usual sandy Arena was even now being transformed into the semblance of a swamp, with raised walkways above tanks containing hippos, and deep pits with deadly snakes. He was hoping to provide a rhinoceros, if one could be trapped, or traded for with the Nabish, but everything else was guaranteed. "The gladiators will be armed with spears anointed with puffer-fish poison," he enthused. "The local people say that the poison is concentrated in the liver, so I've ordered a consignment of livers from a supplier on the shore of the Eastern Sea. The bulk of the larger animals causes the poison to act quite slowly, because the dose is too small to kill them quickly, but in humans even the slightest scratch from a poisoned knife immediately causes serious injury, followed by a slow and excruciating death. There's no known antido—"

MasgNasgOsg stopped him with a raised paw. "The slightest scratch?"

"Why, yes, Excellency! It's a very powerful poison in humans."

"So what if a leading gladiator, one my clients will *absolutely* want to experience as he strives to slaughter another of similar skill, should accidentally allow himself to be scratched by a nonentity, early in the proceedings?"

Bil's stream-of-consciousness outpouring stopped abruptly. "I hadn't thought of that, Excellency."

"There is much you do not think of. But I confess I am

attracted to the idea."

Bil strove desperately to find a remedy for this unexpected defect in his plans. "I could give only the best fighters the poisoned spears!"

The pandemon glared at him along its oryx nose. "But then many of the weaker fighters would not die in agony from puffer-fish toxins."

"Oh. Right."

As Bil gave his fingernails a close inspection to cover his embarrassment, the pandemon considered several potential solutions. "I have it! You will arrange the bouts so that at first only the less talented gladiators do battle with each other. Then they can all have poisoned spears, or swords, or whatever weapons you find it worthwhile to provide. Of course, you mention the poison only to those who absolutely need to know. Not the crowd, not even the King. Let them deduce its presence for themselves, it will heighten their excitement. A few essential underlings only."

Bil, feeling he was off the hook, hastened to express exaggerated amazement at the cleverness of the pandemon's idea. "More than once have I watched a major crowd-pleaser exterminated by a nobody!" he declared. "Your Excellency's wonderful innovation will ensure that never again can such a tragedy occur!"

MasgNasgOsg gave him another sour look. "Yuz. But I imagine that from time to time you will need to put a lesser gladiator up against a star performer, so that the spectators do not complain that they are being served dross. How will you deal with that?"

Bil realised this was a test, and rose to the occasion. "In such a circumstance, good sir, I'll give a poisoned spear only to the better fighter. Also, he'll be instructed to avoid drawing blood with it for as long as possible. Er— subject to avoiding any serious danger to his own person, of course."

The pandemon nodded, twice, slowly. "Very good. We will make something worthwhile of you yet, Bil. And what of the climax?"

Mentally reeling from the compliment—rare from a pandemon—Bil played for time. "Uh—you mean, the final bout when the two remaining gladiators engage in mortal combat for the honour of becoming Champion?"

The pandemon's great herbivore eyes opened wide. "What else?"

"They will use the sharpest weapons available," Bil replied, "which are their own. Every top gladiator has his own favourite weapons, and refuses to fight with anything else. Let me think... I know! I won't anoint those weapons with poison. But I'll give each gladiator a jewelled knife in a leather scabbard, dipped in poison, to be used on an opponent *only* after he's been so disabled that his death is no longer in question."

The pandemon nodded again. "I have heard that these professional gladiators are men of— 'honour', I believe is the word. Would a man of honour willingly administer poison to another, even in a fight to the death, if he knew it would cause a slow, agonising demise?"

Bil's hand went to his chin, then moved to his stubble-covered cheek. "No. That's a pity. I apologise, Excellency. I thought my idea was a good one."

MasgNasgOsg rose, indicating that the audience was about to be terminated. His monkey-paw moved to recohere his transparency suit; to Bil's relief, the pandemon's manipulatory tentacle stayed in its cavity. "It is. You just have to lie, and tell them the poison is quick-acting and painless."

Bil smiled. *How simple.* Yes, he could do *that.*

The pandemon gave a final nod of its impressively horned head, and vanished.

Glossy fur, sleek over rippling muscles. Claws. Teeth. Bil and Jackalfoot watched as the big cat stalked its prey, hunched low to the ground, grace and death joined seamlessly in a single animal.

The Arena's banks of seats were empty, save for a few workers who had stopped for their midday meal, chatting and laughing as they ate. It was another training day, and the Arena was closed to the public. The construction area had temporarily been walled off with mud bricks, leaving about a quarter of the space for practice bouts. A dozen workmen were arguing about how best to fix a leak in one of the tanks. Bil told Ammad to go and sort the problem out.

On a low mound of earth a trainee gladiator waited, his body oily with sweat, his spear honed to an edge that drew blood at the lightest touch. It was his first solo fight with an animal, and the watchers could see his confidence evaporating as the sabretooth lioness circled the mound, edging closer.

The saliva dried in Jackalfoot's mouth as the drama unfolded. He sensed just how nervous the gladiator was becoming.

Bil's experienced eye picked it up too. "He's going to do something stupid."

The Beastmaster grunted in agreement. Despite all the man's training, he was psyching himself up to try something dangerous. The prospect worried Jackalfoot, and he fervently hoped that no lasting harm would be inflicted.

Risking all on a single throw of the dice, the gladiator leaped from his mound, spear raised, his teeth bared in a snarl.

"He must know he can't compete in the dental stakes," Bil joked. As if to underline his point, the sabretooth roared; her gaping jaws emphasised her enormous curved fangs.

The gladiator was goading the lioness to attack. If she could be lured into leaping at him, he could anchor the butt of the spear against the Arena floor and the big cat would impale herself upon the point. Jackalfoot caught his breath, now totally bound up in the life-and-death cameo. Would Yellowfang fall for the trick? He doubted it. She was the most cunning female in the pride.

The lioness growled, hesitated—and charged. She

covered the intervening space with breathtaking speed. Her haunches set themselves for a leap, and the gladiator braced his spear to intercept the lioness's trajectory, triumph shining in his eyes.

Haiyah!

Then triumph switched in an instant to uncomprehending fear. The cat was not where she was supposed to be. She had leaped—but *sideways*. One huge paw brushed the spear aside. Another smashed into the gladiator's helmet, crushing the shining plates and the skull within them. There was very little blood. The lifeless body hit the ground, jerked like a broken puppet, and was still.

"That's a year's investment tossed into the garbage heap," Bil complained. "I should've dumped the fool moons ago!"

Jackalfoot started breathing again, flooded with relief. Yellowfang was unharmed. He gave a low whistle, and the lioness stepped over the corpse, ignoring it. She padded over to her master. He tossed her a haunch of gazelle meat as a reward, patting her between the shoulder blades as she ate, relishing the feel of the dark fur and the cat's musky smell, mingling with the scent of gazelle blood.

Two nervous servitors scurried out and dragged the dead body away, their eyes glued to the feeding lioness. Jackalfoot chuckled. Even though they could see the cat was interested only in her food and her master, they didn't quite *believe* it. He did. He was as one with the sabretooth; he could feel her body language. It was like reading her mind.

The Beastmaster had no sympathy for the dead gladiator. Jackalfoot had no choice but to obey his Qusite masters, but he could feel what drove them, intuit their motives. Their lives were ruled by greed, lies, and cruelty. What he could never understand was the *point* of it all. No Neanderthal would be so selfish. The ordinary Qusite people, like the hapless trainee... well, some were like the Neanderthals, forced to do the nobles' bidding against their own wishes. But most Qusites never questioned the lives they lived, and they thronged to the Arena to relish the slaughter of animals and men.

He didn't hate them. He just had no interest whatsoever in their fate.

Still, Yellowfang was safe, and that was enough.

"I hate hyenas," said one of the four young men. "They're following us. I don't like it."

"I'm more worried about the vultures," said a second, pointing to distant specks circling far overhead. "They have an uncanny ability to sense dying animals."

The old man, an Elder in one of the many extended families of nomadic *bidd'hu*, spat, leaving a damp patch on the sand, which almost immediately began to soak in and dry up. He adjusted his headcloth, tucking it in so that only his eyes were visible. "The time to worry about vultures," he said in a voice as gravelly as the desert crust, "is when they're landing next to you. The time to worry about hyenas is when they start to bite off your leg."

The first young man scratched behind his ear, and chose his words carefully. It was impolite to contradict an Elder. "I agree, Barreg. But with respect, it might perhaps be prudent to start worrying a little sooner, on both counts."

The elder spat again. "Worrying never did anyone any good, Simmoo. Taking precautions, though—yes, that might be useful."

"Hyenas are useful," a third young man, silent until now, pointed out. "Without them, the desert would be neck-deep in bones. Of course, hyenas are rare in the desert. But there are a few around, even far from the cultivation. But there aren't many small animals in the deep desert. Scorpions and beetles, of course, but even they're hard to find, and not much of a meal for a hungry hyena. What else desert hyenas eat, I've no idea."

"Mostly, they starve," said the second young man.

"Scrawny buggers, the lot of them."

"Don't much care," the fourth young man opined, bending down to scratch the ear of one of the hunting dogs that accompanied them. "As long as it's not us."

"This hyena clan will only eat one of *us* if we're already dead," said Barreg, after a quick look back at the camel whose rope he held. "Those are striped hyenas. Scavengers. It's the spotted ones you have to watch out for. They like to kill their own prey. Don't often go for people, but you can never be sure. Remember grandfather Larg?"

"Well, he was at death's door anyway," said Simmoo. "The wasting sickness. And *that* hyena was all skin and bones. It was desperate, spotted a weakness, and—"

"Good job we're strong and healthy, then," the fourth young man interrupted.

"The only reason these hyenas have been following us is that one of our camels got sick," said Barreg. "They finished it off, and ate it. They're just hoping for another easy meal at our expense, that's all. We're a better prospect than aimlessly wandering the desert."

"And the vultures?" Simmoo persisted.

"Opportunists. Tracking the hyenas, hoping for a crack at leftovers. Doesn't mean anything for *our* prospects."

The small group of *bidd'hu* had been detached from the main caravan five days before, to check out rumours of a previously unknown waterhole. They'd found it, but the water was so laden with caustic salts as to be undrinkable. Now they were cutting across a seldom-visited field of stones and gravel, scoured by wind and scorched by sun. The ground ahead shimmered in the heat, creating a mirage that reflected the sky and looked like a distant lake. But the lake never got any closer.

They had started out with two camels, letting them take turns, two riding while three walked. Both camels had also carried packs with provisions and weapons. But when one of them suddenly collapsed, they had been forced to load all of the packs on the remaining camel, and the five of them had to walk.

As the sun rose higher in the sky they stopped, and made camp by putting up a cloth sunshade, supported by sticks. Posting one as a guard, the others slept. It was more comfortable to travel by night, and they had a long way to go before they caught up with the main group of *bidd'hu*, so they rested mainly during the hottest part of the day, keeping their sleeping time as short as they dared. They were tired, but they were used to that. They had plenty of provisions left, even water.

Awakening, they packed up the shelter, lashed it back on the side of the camel, and resumed their arduous trek across the wasteland. Night fell, and they trudged onwards, navigating by the stars. They were still walking when pink dawn decorated the horizon.

PaskRaskAsk now had only one wish: to be eaten. By anything.

The lion had rejected the pandemon's brains; he had no idea why. They lay desiccating in the heat of the sun, and it was still early morning. No other animal had even come close, out here in the particularly arid region of desert that the lion had managed to blunder into. There were a few lizards around, but they were too small to ingest even one of his brains.

As the sun rose in the sky, its rays would beat down ever more unmercifully. Pandemon brains were resilient, and did not dry out easily, but already these had lain untouched for three days, and their tough integument was beginning to dry out and flake. There was still one way to increase survival times, and the pandemon decided he had no other choice. He shut down as much of what was left of his body as he could. It was an act of desperation; if it failed, PaskRaskAsk and his brains would soon be dead meat.

He had to keep his sense of hearing running, though. It

used little energy, and he needed *some* sensory input to take advantage of any animal that did happen to pass nearby.

The ambient temperature reached its maximum, then slowly dropped. PaskRaskAsk deduced that evening was approaching.

Nothing else had.

Then, as he was about to abandon all hope, he heard distant sounds. Human voices. An animal snorted—a camel, by the sound. A pack animal. A dog barked, then several more. The voices grew louder, and PaskRaskAsk could hear them speaking in low tones. It was not the language of the Water People, but a few words were similar.

Desert nomads. Qusites would call them wandering *bidd'hu.* A small group, by the sound of it, probably diverted from the main tribe by some task assigned by a tribal Elder.

Plotting the movement of the various sound sources in his visual cortex, PaskRaskAsk deduced that they would come no closer than a hundred paces. Pandemons had a useful trick for such occasions, one that had worked well on the planet where they had been created. When the brains were on the point of drying up and dying, they could release a pheromone that would attract bodies for them to parasitise.

The pandemons had experimented with pheromone variants when they first arrived in Qus, and found one that was irresistible to all carnivores. PaskRaskAsk was about to release that version when he realised it could be a major blunder. On this annoying world, the pheromone would also attract vultures, and out in the desert, they would probably be the first carnivores to turn up. A vulture could manage only one brain at a time, and those scavengers always competed for food, so his brains would almost certainly end up distributed among several of the birds. Too few brains meant too little intelligence, so he would cease to be sentient—in effect, he'd die.

If he did nothing, he would die anyway. Was it worth the risk?

There was an alternative; also risky, but less so. He could use a different variant to make the pheromone less attractive to vultures, and hope it attracted something else.

PaskRaskAsk activated the necessary physiological mechanisms, and waited expectantly.

Time passed. Nothing came near. The pandemon despaired. *Not working.*

Then he heard raised voices. A dog barked, a man shouted. More dogs joined the chorus, the shouting became louder, now several voices.

The pandemon didn't know it, but this variant of the pheromone did have an effect on at least some of the animals of Shool-3. Just not the one he intended. It made these dogs and men angry, causing them to attack anything within range. In this case, that was the other dogs and men that the pheromone had affected. Teeth ripped into human flesh, knives were drawn—*bidd'hu* carried many knives, and could use them to exquisite effect, from decapitation to skinning alive—and the orderly group of men and dogs disintegrated into a writhing, screaming, barking mass of bodies. Even the camel joined in, mainly by kicking everything it could reach.

When no one was left uninjured, the affray died down. The pheromone dispersed, and the three survivors began to gather their wits, wondering what had brought about such mayhem. Sudden madness seemed to be the only sensible explanation. They bound their wounds and those of their animals, and limped off into the growing darkness, once more focused on rejoining the main group. Behind them they left two corpses, both young men. Unburied, for time was precious.

Soon, the desert hyenas that had been following the men gathered, attracted to the free meal. One, losing out in the competition for human and dog flesh, wandered off and found the pandemon's remains. It chased away a flock of vultures that had already gathered around the carcass, and settled down to feed. Fortunately for PaskRaskAsk, the vultures had mainly been squabbling over what little meat remained on its body. They'd eaten most of it, aside from its bones and its purple brains. Starving hyenas aren't as picky as lions, and this one took the brains to be a tasty snack, saving the bones for later.

When enough neural connections had been extruded and done their work, the pandemon cluster known as Pask-RaskAsk found himself in command of a hyena. His senses returned, beginning with the metallic smell of blood, followed by taste, touch, vision, and hearing. Overriding the hyena's wish to gorge itself further, PaskRaskAsk directed its feet to take him to where the corpses lay. In the light of the stars he managed to find one human corpse that was relatively intact apart from having no head. Human form would suit his intentions better, and he could easily transfer the hyena's head on to the bloody stump of the neck. Now mobile and aware, he found a pack of food and a leather bag of water. It wasn't a lot, but it was as much as he could carry. He followed the trail left by the departed survivors of the nomad group, on the presumption that wherever they were heading would be better than the dry, dead desert.

13

Mad God

When Akhnef's reddening glow in the sky heralded the coming dawn, Shephatsut-Mer slipped quietly from his bed, leaving a snoring Nemnestris huddled beside the dent he left in their bedding. He pulled on robe and headscarf, stepped into a pair of sandals, and quietly left the house, heading for the outbuilding where the donkeys were kept. Soon he and his stolid mount were trudging through the silent streets, while most of the good people of Ul-q'mur were still fast asleep.

His principal wife, however, was not among them. She had merely pretended to be sleeping. Now, disguised in men's clothing, she and her donkey followed him through the streets. When he reached the edge of the desert she dropped back further, tracking his path through the scuffed sand.

She had been planning this for days. Her spies had passed her priceless intelligence: the High Priest of the Hippopotamus Cult would be consulting his Oracle, to advise the Regent on the outcome of the Championship. This time, Nemnestris was determined to discover where her husband had hidden the power-laden artefact.

From time to time Shephatsut-Mer stopped and looked back, but any pursuit was hidden by Akhnef's glare as the bright sun-disc cleared the horizon, once more victorious against its demonic adversaries. In any case, Nemnestris was taking great care to conceal herself behind any suitable rock, bush, or mound of sand.

Unknown to the High Acolyte of Nefteremit, someone else was taking great care to conceal himself, and he was much more practised. His tracking skills were better, too. Shephatsut-Mer and Nemnestris were so focused on their separate goals that neither was aware they were both being followed.

Bentankle had been keeping a quiet eye on the High Priest for some weeks. That Shephatsut-Mer had access to an oracle was common knowledge. Versions of its utterances passed through the streets like wildfire, becoming increasingly inaccurate as they spread. Townsfolk placed bets on who would come closer to the truth: the High Priest of the Hippopotamus Cult, or the High Acolyte of the Lilypad Prophetess. That they were man and wife added a certain piquancy to the gamble.

Everyone knew how Nemnestris obtained her information: straight from Nefteremit the Lilypad Prophetess's mouth. No one knew how Shephatsut-Mer obtained his. But there were rumours of a miraculous object, a stone that spoke messages from the gods.

The Neanderthal boy considered most of these tales highly unlikely, but wondered whether there might be some truth behind them. If so, he had no idea what it might be. The whole thing could easily be mere delusion and falsehood, not uncommon in Ul-q'mur. But he had a hunch that there was something to the stories, however distorted. Solving the puzzle occupied ever more of his thoughts, for life in the Neanderthal Village was repetitious and unexciting. With all the curiosity of youth, he was keen to view the alleged marvel and find out what it *really* was.

He had also noticed something that seemed not to be common knowledge. The Neanderthals had seen Shephatsut-Mer making regular trips into the desert by donkey, passing close by their Village. He was invariably alone, which was unusual for any among the highborn. But then, Qusites did strange things all the time, so no one in the Village paid much attention.

Except Bentankle. He had noticed that within a day or two of such a trip, new oracular pronouncements began circulating. Mulling this over, it seemed plausible that the speaking-stone was somewhere on the edge of the desert, and that Shephatsut-Mer had to travel there to consult it. Bentankle knew that there were many stones in the desert, often large, many in outlandish shapes. His mental image of the speaking-stone, inasmuch as he had one, was of a huge narrow-waisted rock, apparently on the verge of tumbling, which somehow produced words. Or noises that might be heard as words, by the credulous, probably caused by the wind.

The boy resolved to follow the High Priest the next time he passed by the Village, and he kept watch daily before the sun rose. When Shephatsut-Mer and his donkey arrived at the fork in the trail that bypassed the Village, Bentankle was hiding in the bushes. It was fortunate that he had given the High Priest a head start, for just as he was about to clamber from conceal-ment and follow Shephatsut-Mer, he heard a second donkey approaching. He recognised the rider as Nemnestris, and won-dered why the High Priest's wife was following so far behind her husband. Her reason soon became clear: like Bentankle, she had no wish to be observed. And so the three of them trekked out into the desert, each aware only of who was ahead of them.

When her husband's donkey turned towards the low cliffs of the *jabal*, Nemnestris realised he was heading towards a dark cleft, one of the many entrances to the dry wadis that dissected the crumbling strata of the plateau. Shephatsut-Mer stopped nearby, tied his mount to a convenient rock, and disappeared into the cleft. Dismounting, Nemnestris ran to reduce the distance between them, and followed him through the cleft into the wadi beyond, blissfully unaware that Bentankle was hot on her heels.

The High Acolyte was an expert tracker, thanks to numerous hunting expeditions with her father when she had been a child. Her husband's footsteps were clearly visible in the sand. Quiet as a mouse in the presence of a dozen cats, she crept after him.

He was crunching over a patch of exposed gravel, not far ahead of her now. Carefully avoiding the gravel patch, she tracked him by the noises he was making. Then the noises stopped.

She inched forwards. Had he heard her? It was unlikely, Her father had taught her stalking as well. Her husband had little need for silence, not realising he was being followed. She had stronger motivation.

More likely, he had reached his goal.

The control disc that would have enabled the pandemon to recohere his transparency suit was lost, lying far behind him down a crack in the rocks, baking in the desert heat. He was in not much better shape.

When PaskRaskAsk assembled his new body from a headless *bidd'hu* and a hyena, he hadn't reckoned on missing his way and wandering for days without water. He had wasted valuable time searching for the control disc, to no avail. By the time he crawled from the desert into the fringes of the cultivation, that body was too far gone to be worth saving. It would be simpler by far to acquire a new one. It didn't much matter what, right now, as long as it was able to stay alive for days rather than hours. He could swap bodies again, trading up until he got exactly what he wanted.

When he saw a ramshackle cowshed, he had just enough mobility left to decant his brains into a bundle of hay outside it, hoping one of the farm animals would eat it and ingest at least one brain. Then it would be simple to make it eat the rest.

The plan worked, but the new body's herbivore eyes lacked the predator's high-resolution forward gaze that he needed. Finding a hut with several large, aggressive black dogs, the pandemon made sure that the farmer and his family were out working the fields and the area was otherwise deserted. Then he weakened his neck so that repeated butting against the trunk of a palm tree severed his head from his body. He engineered some carefully placed fractures of the bovine skull so that the brains spilled on to the ground at the dog's feet. Within the hour the pandemon had swapped his bovine head for a canine one, keeping the cow's sturdy body.

The combination was so out of proportion as to be ludicrous to human eyes, but proportion and beauty had never bothered a pandemon, and never would. It was the combination of abilities that mattered, and the dog's eyes were at the front of its face, able to focus straight ahead. The cow's eyes had afforded a magnificent all-round view, but they pointed in the wrong direction for close-up work.

Suitably attired in his dog's head, PaskRaskAsk headed away from the isolated farm, back into the desert. The next task was to find the Ship and pick up a control disc, to equip himself with a new transparency suit. But when he got to the dune field, he couldn't tell one barchan from another. MasgNasgOsg had always led their excursions to Ul-q'mur, carrying the ansible that let them communicate with the Ship. PaskRaskAsk had not paid due attention to the local geography, and he had no ansible. He could scour the desert forever without finding the Ship.

The obvious solution was to head for the one place where he could guarantee the presence of other members of his gang: the Arena, where MasgNasgOsg would be recording the bloody battles of the Festival of the Frowning Moon. The business opportunity that the Festival represented was too good to miss. They had been planning how to record it for ages.

So PaskRaskAsk had no choice but to remain visible, and make his way across the desert and through the cultivation into the very heart of the swarming city of Ul-q'mur. Many of these primitive humans would see him in his current form, but they would never guess the true nature of what they were looking at. They would undoubtedly believe him to be a demonic visitor from the depths of the underworld. Which, in a way, he was, of course. Some would stare, some would collapse in fear and trembling, but none would dare confront him.

His route took him on to the top of the *jabal*, but the sun was rising in the sky and its heat was becoming a nuisance. He found a rugged slope leading down into the shade of a wadi. Feeling stronger now, he broke into a trot, and thundered down the slope.

Shephatsut-Mer had just rolled the rocks away from the cavern entrance, and he nearly suffered a heart attack when the mad god attacked. The dog-head's baleful eyes were fixed on his throat as its cloven hooves pawed the ground. He screamed, flung a rock at it, missed, and dived into the cave to seek sanctuary, twisting his ankle. The god pawed the ground for a few heartstopping seconds, then galloped off down the wadi.

Nemnestris heard her husband's scream, a heart-rending, unearthly cry of horror. She heard him scrabbling in the sand; then the pounding of... hooves? Whatever had terrified her husband, it was coming her way. She ducked into a deep crevice and held her breath, hoping to stay hidden. Two dozen paces behind her, the Neanderthal boy did the same.

The hoofbeats—for such they surely were—got louder. Then, in a cloud of dust, an animal galloped past.

It looked for all the world like a cow.

What is a cow doing this far into the desert? Nemnestris wondered. It made no sense. Unless it was a manifestation of

Hefur, the cow goddess.

That must be it. And perhaps that would explain something else, a brief glimpse through the cloud of dust the goddess had kicked up, one that she would not even be certain she had seen at all. But if she had…

The goddess was wearing the head of a dog.

Nemnestris did not lack for courage. She crept out of the crevice, crouched low, and continued up the wadi, peering round each twist and turn. Her reward came swiftly: a dark opening signalled a cave, and a rock nearby had clearly been rolled back from the entrance. She could hear heavy breathing, almost sobbing, from inside.

Convinced now that Shephatsut-Mer was still alive, and not too badly injured, she turned and backtracked between the wadi's crumbling walls, passing Bentankle's place of concealment. The dust from the goddess's passage had not yet settled, but of the dog-headed cow there was no sign. Cautiously she emerged from the cleft, and ran to where she had concealed her donkey.

Then she settled down to wait.

As he calmed down, and the pain in his ankle faded to a dull throb, Shephatsut-Mer decided that he was in no rush to leave the comparative safety of the cave. While he was there, he might as well do what he had intended all along, and consult the Oracle. Dismantling the stone cairn that concealed it, he carried it to the entrance of the cave, where there was more light.

The Oracle emitted various buzzes and screeches, then settled into the familiar near-inaudible hum that told him it was willing to listen, and to speak.

"Oracle—"

I hear you.

It was speaking the plain tongue, gods be thanked. "The

King has commanded me—"

I care not for Kings.

Damn, this was going to be difficult. "I wish to know who will become Champion at the coming Festival of the Frowning Moon."

Beware the Moon, it is a place of demons. Turn your attention to the Sun. You must seek its favour.

That nonsense again! "All priests pray to Akhnef every morning and every even—"

Not Akhnef. Y-ra'i.

"They Who Dwell Within the Sun?"

Yes. They who give the Sun-sphere his power.

"Why must I pay attention to the Y-ra'i?"

Because they are wary. They welcome the grazing Herd, for it will cleanse them. But they do not welcome the Moon-demons. Not because of their trade in death, though that should be of human concern. Because they disturb the Y-ra'i.

Shephatsut-Mer felt out of his depth, as he so often did when talking to the Oracle. Even when it talked plain language, it spoke in riddles.

"The Y-ra'i are wary because they are disturbed?"

The Y-ra'i are wary because they will be *disturbed. The demons will pollute their fields of hot sunstuff with cold matter.*

"Sunstuff? Cold matter? I don't understand. Please explain more clearly."

Now is not the time.

The hum stopped, the Oracle reverted to a dead box. From long experience, Shephatsut-Mer knew he would get nothing more out of it, not even more nonsense. And it hadn't even dropped a *hint* about who would be Champion.

Still, he could interpret. Tuwrat would instruct her High Priest to tell the King what the Regent wanted him to hear.

Nemnestris tried not to lose patience. To act in haste

would be to lose all. But the wait was frustrating. Had her husband been injured more severely than she guessed? He was certainly taking his time.

The wait seemed interminable. Shephatsut-Mer would survive, or not, and she dared not go to his aid. She wasn't even sure she ought to. Let the gods decide. They always did, in any case.

Akhnef rose higher, the air grew hotter. Shortly before the sun's heat reached its peak, Shephatsut-Mer limped out of the cleft in the *jabal*, dragging his left foot slightly. He untied his mount, climbed on, and rode slowly off along the desert pathway, heading back towards Ul-q'mur.

Some injury, but nothing serious. He'll recover.

Nemnestris remained in her hiding-place for a long time after her husband had disappeared from view, just in case he changed his mind and came back. It had the added advantage that the heat of the midday sun would diminish a little. Eventually, satisfied that he had truly departed, Nemnestris untied a leather satchel from the donkey's back. Keeping her ears alert for hoofbeats, but hearing nothing beyond the sighing of the desert wind, she made her way along the wadi for a second time. She passed within three paces of a patient Bentankle, who had decided to remain hidden on the assumption that Nemnestris would make an appearance, now that Shephatsut-Mer had gone.

She quickly found the cave, now concealed by rocks. With an effort, she rolled them aside far enough to let her stoop through the narrow entrance into the tunnel.

There was just enough light to make out the dim outlines of the cave walls, so she wouldn't need to make fire. Soon she reached the terminal cavern, where roof and walls opened out. As her eyes became accustomed to the darkness, she noticed a cairn of stones. Cautiously—for she too knew what noxious creatures such a pile might conceal—she removed the stones, one by one, placing them so that it would be easy to replace them in their former positions.

Her heart pounded, she could hear its thunderous beating in her ears. Then, it skipped a beat entirely, as she lifted another stone and saw what lay beneath. Just a corner, poking out, but it was no rock. Quickly now, she moved several more stones, to reveal—

A box.

Well, it looked like a box. With a loop of something like leather, presumably to carry it by.

This had to be the Oracle.

Nonetheless, she made a careful check, and was soon convinced that there was nothing else of interest in the cave.

She put the Oracle in her satchel and rebuilt the cairn. When her husband next visited, the Oracle would seem to have been spirited away. Backing out of the cave, she brushed the sand with her hands to erase her tracks. With luck, many small animals, snakes and other creatures would leave their marks in the surface before Shephatsut-Mer's next visit. Carefully copying the original arrangement, she rolled the rocks back into place, once more hiding the entrance. Her husband would know some manner of being had stolen the Oracle, of course, but he would not have much idea whether it was by human agency. And even if he decided it was, he would have no idea who the thief had been.

Her heart now singing with joy, Nemnestris slung the satchel over her shoulder and hurried back to her waiting donkey. When Shephatsut-Mer got home, he would assume she had gone to the Temple to carry out her daily rituals. And indeed, that was where she was now headed. She would take care to calm herself before she returned to their house, in case her husband became suspicious. By then, the precious Oracle would be hidden where she alone could find it.

And, with patience and intelligence, she would learn how to use the supernatural artefact. After all, her husband had managed it. The High Acolyte of Nefteremit ought to find it easy.

So pleased was she with her cleverness that she still had

not the faintest suspicion that she, too, had been followed.

Like any Neanderthal child, Bentankle was quiet on his feet. He was also agile, and when Nemnestris opened a small door in the wall of the Temple of Nefteremit and slipped though it, Bentankle was over the wall and hidden behind a statue before she had closed it again. She made her way across a courtyard studded with stone columns, which provided ample cover for a small boy. Every few moments, she looked around to see if anyone was watching. She moved with exaggerated caution and poorly concealed excitement.

Few people were permitted in this part of the Temple, but she still felt the need for extreme caution. The hiding-place had to be well chosen. No one must be able to find the Oracle. Some time before, she had noticed a small stone building with a floor of polished basalt flagstones, and made preparations in anticipation of a successful theft. Now, lifting a stone that she had previously loosened, she deposited the satchel containing the Oracle beneath the floor. She replaced the stone, filling the gaps with dust scraped up from the floor so that no one would notice it was loose.

All that remained was to leave the Temple precinct unobserved. Tomorrow she would retrieve the Oracle and start to learn how to use it.

She was in for a shock, however. Before she reached the door in the wall and slipped outside, Bentankle, who had watched her replace the flagstone, lifted it again and removed the Oracle from the satchel. He wasn't sure what he was going to do with it, but he didn't feel that leaving it in Nemnestris's possession would be a smart move.

He slung the Oracle on to his back, making sure it was

covered by his headcloth. This time he went out by the door in the Temple wall, taking care to check that no one was waiting to catch him. But the way was clear, and he caught sight of Nemnestris just as she turned a corner in the narrow streets and disappeared from view. Taking his cue, he trotted off in the opposite direction, and was soon making his way back to the Neanderthal Village through the maze of streets, the picture of innocence.

From the Palace there was a good view of the river, and the Regent and his Vizier watched as the boats came and went. There were ferryboats whose bright paintwork masked their poor quality, boats carrying every commodity from grain to cattle, and the occasional much larger vessel with a cargo of stone or timber. At the dock, fifty men were unloading a caged leopard, destined for the Games. It made its laborious way up a sloping ramp on a huge wooden sledge, pulled by ropes.

Sitaperkaw dismissed the servants, and Lord Noth-Met-amphut was instantly alert. It was a sign that the Regent had something confidential to discuss. It might be some diplomatic overture that needed careful planning, it might be news of a new source of copper...

As he suspected, it was neither. He knew that the Regent had been mulling something over in his mind for a while now, and he could make a pretty good guess what it was.

"Insh'erthret is looking well," the Vizier began, opening up the likely issue in a way that seemed entirely innocent. Even with the servants gone, intimate conversations can sometimes be overheard. The Palace was riddled with spies, most acting for the various priesthoods, some for foreign powers, some for sale to the first interested buyer.

Sitaperkaw grunted. "Indeed he is. Thriving, physically. He could become a fine figure of a man if he applied himself more. A true King! But he's lazy and foolish."

The Vizier sipped at his wine. "His Majesty is still but a child, my Lord."

"Yes, but I fear for the people of Qus when he becomes a man."

"He has four years to mature," the Vizier pointed out, still feeling his way past potential traps. The Regent gave a noncommital grunt. "You think he won't make a good King?"

Sitaperkaw nodded. "I could be wrong, of course."

"All men are fallible," the Vizier agreed. "Even Kings. Look at the boy's father!"

"Hopeless."

Time to tip the balance a little. "I pray that Insh'erthret doesn't take after Sh'erthret-Amt," the Vizier said, his intonation studiedly casual.

Sitaperkaw stood up and began pacing the room. He seemed indecisive. Then he sat down again next to the Vizier. "I'm coming to the reluctant opinion that prayer alone won't be enough."

"You don't think the gods will intervene?"

The Regent laughed. "The gods always intervene. But men can help them to channel their interventions in desirable directions."

"Ah."

Encouraged, Sitaperkaw warmed to his theme. "Lord Noth-Metamphut, I'm fully aware of your tremendous loyalty. You serve Insh'erthret well; no one has done more for the boy-King than you."

The Vizier stared into the middle distance. "I serve the crown," he said. "And the people of Qus." He hoped the Regent noted the distinction.

"You do, you do. And if by some mischance Qus was blessed with... a new King? One more suited to the task?"

"I would continue to serve the crown and the people of Qus."

"It's the office, not the person, that you serve?"

The Vizier nodded. "In this I follow tradition."

"You're a wise man, my Lord." Sitaperkaw hesitated. "I've consulted the Oracle. Its words are typically obscure; I think these confounded priests do that deliberately to protect themselves against criticism. But it seemed to hint—no, more than that, the hint was unusually strong—to hint that the gods are tiring of Insh'erthret's childishness. That they're minded to correct that."

The Vizier nodded again, and finished his wine. "Did the Oracle specify how this was to be achieved?"

"Not in so many words. But I gained a distinct impression that we should prepare for unexpected changes. You might care to pass the warning on to... those who need to know."

"Of course. Sudden changes in government require loyal officials. Did the Oracle indicate when this change might be brought about?"

"The Festival of the Frowning Moon was deemed propitious."

14

Champion

Amid the cacophonous crowds thronging the wide plaza that fronted the Arena, only one person failed to be impressed by the two huge limestone lions—one regular, one sabretooth —on either flank. They were as tall as the Arena's topmost tiers, and longer than the largest ceremonial barge. Jackalfoot and his assistant beastmasters were the only Neanderthals permitted to enter the concourse, and colossal statuary held no appeal for Neanderthals. Lacking any sense of awe, they took pleasure in small things, the delicate creations of nature, not the grandiose gestures of vain rulers.

So, as he quietly threaded his way through the jumbled crowd, the Beastmaster kept his eyes to the ground, observing the translucent patterns in the travertine slabs that the Water People called alabaster. There was harmony there, only partially spoilt by the hewing of the rock.

The concourse was open to the common folk only on special occasions: religious festivals, sacrifices, ritual punishment of criminals—climaxing in the six-day Contest of the Grand Champion at the Festival of the Frowning Moon. The latter was exceptionally popular, for the excitement, the bloodshed, the terrifying animals—and also the free food, shrewdly made available by the temple priests. "Feed them free at a Spectacular," the High Priest had once remarked, "and you will earn their eternal gratitude—even if you starve them for the next month." So crude tables laden with bread, meat, and beer had been set up along the sides of the plaza, attended by novice priests to maintain order and ensure fair shares.

Jackalfoot solemnly accepted the offer of a small loaf, chewing absently at one end as he walked. He had much to think about. He was saddened by the imminent death of his beasts, but that was an ever-present feature of existence, and since he could do nothing about it, he ignored it. However, there was something else. He feared for Insh'erthret's life, an intuition of danger that he had learned to trust, and that made him fear for his people, because they would suffer if the boy-King sustained any injury that could be blamed on his Beast-master.

Jackalfoot could not pin down any specific or immediate danger to Insh'erthret, but the possibilities were endless. The long-term danger was as obvious as ever, and it was Sitaperkaw. He wondered whether the boy had any awareness of the threat his uncle posed. A pity that it could not be eliminated by allowing harm to befall the Regent, but that would lead only to harsh reprisals against all Neanderthals. In the royal family's intense world of plots and counterplots, alliances and betrayals, there was little that could not be blamed on *anyone*. So Jackalfoot knew that protecting the Regent must also have very high priority.

Ironically, he had a grudging respect for Sitaperkaw, finding him less detestable than most of his retinue and family. Poor Yulmash! His bride Azmyn was one of the worst, unable to see how the priesthood manipulated her, so full of herself that she truly believed the schemes they put in her head originated with her. She was vain, selfish, and by no means the most colourful bead on the necklace. The Regent, now: he was another matter altogether. Yes, he was self-important, arrogant, and cruel, but none of those traits was unusual in Qusite royalty. The King's god-given duty is to *rule*, after all. But Sitaperkaw genuinely tried to do what was best for the common folk as well as for the rich, subject to the complex constraints imposed by the laws and traditions of an advanced society like that of Habd ul-Qusnemnet. Admittedly, Sitaperkaw's view of what was best for the people involved the probable elimination of Insh'erthret, but the Beastmaster privately conceded that this perception might well be correct. The King seemed idle and foolish, though sometimes Jackal-foot thought his empathic sense detected something less trivial behind what might be just a protective facade. Moreover, Insh'erthret was still only a child, and Jackalfoot had yet to acquire a clear mental image of the kind of leader he might become.

Nearing the Arena entrance, the Beastmaster veered into the shadow of the right-hand colossal lion—the sabre-tooth. Although there was no distinction between different types of cat in the Qusite tongue, their artists depicted the many species quite accurately, and there was no way to miss the creature's elongated fangs. The ordinary lion opposite was an almost perfect match, prone, with upright head, front paws extended, tail curled, its painted limestone eyes eternally fixed on the Great Wet Way and the shimmering desert beyond.

While those around him began to scramble for the best seats still available, Jackalfoot glanced over to the royal enclosure, at the centre of the Arena opposite the main entrance, with a perfect view of the spectacle. It was still empty, save for half a dozen guards. He turned a corner, and grunted at the guardian that was always stationed there to keep the great unwashed away from areas where they had no business to be. The guardian recognised the Beastmaster and gave a formal nod of acknowledgement. Jackalfoot ducked under a low lintel into one of the innumerable corridors that formed a confusing maze around the Arena's outskirts. He trotted down a winding stairway into the building's dark underbelly, where the animals were caged.

Nemnestris had been in a terrible mood all morning,

and the lower acolytes of the Lilypad Prophetess flinched if she so much as glanced their way. Everyone was treading on eggshells.

It was obvious that something had enraged her, but no one could work out what. The High Acolyte clearly had no intention of satisfying their curiosity. Inside, she burned with resentment and a black anger.

My Oracle has been stolen!

It didn't occur to her that she, too, had stolen it—and from her own husband. In Nemnestris's mind, the Oracle had always been intended for her. Shephatsut-Mer had merely been the conduit chosen by Ythriz; the instrument to put it into her hands. She couldn't understand why, as soon as had it come into her possession, some criminal had sneaked it out from under her nose.

Regret was bitter, but futile. She would get the Oracle back, by whatever means proved necessary. *He will pay. His accomplices will pay. His* family *will pay.*

None of these vows had yet restored the Oracle to her, however. And now she had to get ready to join the royal entourage in the Arena, alongside her husband. She'd been looking forward to watching Khuf—*dear virile Khuf!*—slaughter that posturing idiot Yulmash, and now the thief had spoilt it. She would have to calm herself, pretend to be enjoying the spectacle, and ignore the time that was being wasted, allowing the thief to cover his tracks.

Perhaps it will take my mind off the loss. She wasn't convinced.

Invisible, though not intangible, in their transparency suits, the pandemons were safe from discovery provided no one bumped into them. They chose their positions accordingly, stationing themselves next to stone columns or large votive statues to a variety of supernatural beings, which were in plentiful supply almost anywhere in Ul-q'mur.

After a lengthy planning session with a much-re lieved Bil, whose concept for the Spectacular had met with Sitaperkaw's grudging approval, MasgNasgOsg's gang had used their manipulatory tentacles to deploy eight wide-angle hydets around the perimeter of the Arena to capture the context and the overall flow of the action. Three lightweight hydets with long-range pickups provided close-ups of individual animals and gladiators, their highly sensitive neuronics tuned to record not just tactile sensations and prevailing emotions, but memories as detailed as the subjects' most recent meal. Which in the case of the crocodiles were especially gruesome. Finally, two roving operators with portables sucked in anything of interest that the others might have missed.

MasgNasgOsg, who currently needed no tentacle because he had the arms of an alpha-male baboon, knew he had a hit on his paws. He kept up a steady stream of instructions to his hydet-crew, monitoring everything through a low-resolution hyvis slung round the neck of his saluki head to get a rough impression of what his clients would experience. Postproduction editing would enhance the quality further, but he had to be careful not to introduce anything artificial. His jealously guarded reputation had been founded on authenticity.

With Bil's aid, they had rehearsed every move, tested possible angles and viewpoints, and made sure that their clients' experiences would not be obstructed by an awkwardly placed rock, tree, or sacred statue.

Now, the deployment was about to be exposed to the real thing.

A universal feature of media events throughout the Living Galaxy, for virtually every species of sentient being, is that they start quietly and rise to a climax. Bil had chosen his least capable gladiators for the warm-up bouts. They were skilful and ferocious enough, but they lacked the subtlety of the true warrior, the ability to think on their feet, anticipating unorthodox attacks and inventing equally unorthodox replies on the spur of the moment. Some were fearless and truly ferocious, but lacked the intelligence to do more than scream and leap. Some were cunning, but lacked the courage to carry out their plans effectively if their opponent started to gain the upper hand.

The crowd started out noisy and its cries grew ever louder as the action became more violent. Professional gamblers circulated through the assembled masses, soliciting and accepting bets. Neighbours traded side-bets. Vendors sold food and drink for copper. Arguments about whose favourite gladiator would win broke out sporadically, often leading to blows and scuffles. Guardsmen were stationed at intervals to control anything that looked likely to get out of hand, occasionally ejecting the worst offenders, but on the whole they left the crowd to its own devices.

By tradition, the King waited until the final day before taking his place in the Arena to watch the climax of the Championship. When he entered, accompanied by minor royals and high-ranking nobles, the people fell silent and sank to their knees. At a signal from the Regent, they rose and resumed their previous activities, protocol now satisfied. The royal party also included a squad of armed guards, but following normal practice, the Commander of the Royal Guard had dispersed his men throughout the building to keep watch on the corridors leading to the royal enclosure. There was no need to have guards within the enclosure itself, for no harm could come to any of the royal family there. There was no spare room for guards, in any case. King and Regent sat together at the centre, in the front row of seats. Sitaperkaw's principal wife sat at his left hand. Various Princes and Princesses, Azmyn among them, sat on either side according to rank. A few nobles, among them Vizier Noth-Metamphut and High Priest Shephatsut-Mer, were also permitted to sit in the front row. Nemnestris, quietly fuming, sat immediately behind her husband, a position that added insult to injury. Other important officials occupied the remaining seats. The High Priest fidgeted in his seat, flexing his aching ankle. Servitors brought food and drink on command.

Not far outside the high wall separating the royal enclosure from the rest of the seating, Jackalfoot occupied a privileged seat, hoping that at least some of his much-loved beasts would still be alive at the end of the day. Especially Sickleface. Several rows away he saw Bil's three sons Ammad, Dobil, and Ptafni. Come to watch their father's triumph. They were good lads and he liked them, although he was aware that Ptafni didn't much like him. They were wearing their best clothes and obviously enjoying themselves.

In the Arena below, a fighter with skin the colour of ebony, who had been brought back from far Batalamalaba as a prisoner of war during one of Sh'erthret-Amt's occasional minor border skirmishes, which the now-dead King had always celebrated as huge victories, brandished a fearsome sword half as long as he was tall. Its edge was razor-sharp along one side, serrated along the other. It was dripping with blood, mostly human, and he bent down to wipe the blade on the loincloth of a dying fighter from the northern shores of Qus-ni-Tuwrit. As he did so, a crocodile that had been concealed in a clump of reeds in the artificial swamp surged on to the sand, locked its jaws round his leg, and dragged him into the murky water. As soon as he had drowned, it rolled over and over in an attempt to tear off lumps of flesh small enough to consume, while three other crocodiles competed for a share of the meal.

"Did you get that?" MasgNasgOsg's voice was soft but strident in the ear of his roving operator BuzgRuzgMofz, which at that moment had previously belonged to an oryx.

"Close enough to count the hairs in the victim's nostrils."

"Yuz, but did you get good samples of its chemistry? Our clients want to inhale the fear of death, as well as being at the heart of the action."

"Yuz, yuz, it's all in the can," BuzgRuzgMofz reassured

him, stepping neatly to one side to get out of the path of a charging hippo, enraged by spears jabbing repeatedly into its thick but still sensitive hide.

At the edge of the swamp another gladiator, his skin slimy with sweat and other bodily fluids, had climbed up on to a large rock, a tactic that was temporarily successful until a flung bolas made from three strands of rope attached to heavy stones wrapped itself round his ankles. He toppled off the rock to crash headfirst into the sand at its base. Neck broken, he lay still.

Two gladiators had joined forces to slaughter a leopard. Normally each fighter was required to act as an individual, but these two were brothers, and they owned a papyrus roll signed by the King's scribe entitling them to join forces. They were a speciality act, valued for their unorthodox joint tactics. The crowd loved the Terror Twins.

Many gladiators, and a few animals, spilled their blood and died. Occasionally a team of sweepers would run in to drag a corpse away if it was interfering with the action. Experienced soldiers accompanied them to keep dangerous beasts at bay.

MasgNasgOsg reviewed a summary of the recordings so far using his hyvis locked to a low-resolution *eft*, and was grudgingly impressed. BuzgRuzgMofz was a bit overconfident, but he always was. He seemed to be delivering the goods.

Many strange things happened every day in the Ul-q'mur suburbs, whose inhabitants were long accustomed to acting as though they were deaf and blind. It was an effective way to survive when paying too much attention to other people's business might well purchase you a one-way ticket to the Poor People's Necropolis. But even with long practice it was difficult for the ordinary Qusite to ignore a cow with the head of a dog. Some hid their faces behind dirty headscarves, some gawped openly. Some muttered prayers to their household gods. Some wondered whether they were witnessing a manifestation of one of their household gods. Few doubted that the canine-headed cow was some kind of god, for what else could it be?

The god paused at the intersection of two narrow streets, trying to get its bearings. Common folk watched from the shadows: fearful, yet unable to tear their eyes from the spectacle. Two grappling street urchins saw the god heading their way, gasped, and ran, the cause of their dispute paling into insignificance in the face of a manifest deity. With sharp teeth to boot.

PaskRaskAsk knew that he was breaking every rule in the pandemons' unwritten criminal code, but he had no choice. Many of these primitive humans would see him in his current form, but they would never guess the true nature of what they were looking at. They would undoubtedly believe him to be a demonic visitor from the depths of the underworld. Which, in a way, he was, of course. Some would stare, some would collapse in fear and trembling, but none of them would dare to confront him.

And so it proved.

The cow-body raised its hunting-hound head and howled. As the onlookers finally lost their nerve and fled, PaskRaskAsk's features transformed themselves into the canine version of a grin. Spotting a familiar landmark soaring over a nearby line of hovels, he trotted onwards, guided by this brief glimpse of one of the great rock lions that advertised the entrance to the gladiatorial Arena.

The Batalamalaban was clad from head to toe in black leather, treated with oil from the *djuker* tree until it was sleek and glossy. Studs of genuine copper created geometric patterns on his chest and back; more studs ran in lines along his arms and legs, ending in rings at his wrists and ankles. Copper-studded boots completed the costume. He had daubed his face with designs in white, red, and yellow pigment, to resemble a demon of the underworld. When he marched out into the centre of the Arena, escorted by servitors holding firebrands to keep the loose beasts at bay, the crowd chanted his name: *Ngolo-ouagah! Ngolo-ouagah! Ngolo-ouagah!*

The contest for the title of Grand Champion was one of stamina as well as skill, and he had already battled his way through three bouts, apparently without suffering even a scratch. He had begun by defeating two Qusite knife-fighters in quick succession, despatching a leopard and a large crocodile into the bargain. An albino from the Land Between Two Rivers proved more resistant, but when he backed the man on to the maze of catwalks above the water tanks, Ngolo-ouagah took the opportunity to simplify the combat by pushing him into a snake pit.

The Batalamalaban raised a clenched fist to the sky, bowed in the general direction of the royal entourage, and brandished a curved sword with a handle of mammoth ivory. The razor-edged blade glinted in the sun.

His reception, however, was nothing compared to the one that greeted the appearance of his opponent. The crowd rose as one, and their cheers and stamping feet shook the tiers of seats. Khuf the Shrewd wore a simple kilt of dyed red cowhide, and matching boots with straps that wrapped round his calves like a loose basketweave. To give a good grip, his sword-hand was encased in a leather palm-strap, a fingerless glove that laced across the back of his hand. Laced bands of leather protected both wrists. He acknowledged the welcome with a wave of his free hand, saluted the King with his broadsword, and stepped close to his opponent.

They exchanged words. They were not what the crowd might have expected, but the noise prevented anyone else overhearing.

"You've done well to get this far," Khuf said.

"I've been practising the backhand slice."

"I noticed. It paid off. How's your mother? Recovered, I hope."

"Yes, the dysentery has stopped."

Purely for show, Khuf spat at the man's feet, turned his back, and walked away a few paces. Ngolo-ouagah snarled at him, hamming it up for the spectators' benefit.

Then the King gave the signal to start, and the friendly banter stopped. Now, it was personal.

The two men circled each other, trying simultaneously to discover a weakness and keep an eye on the three lions that were currently devouring one of the earlier losers, growling at each other and threatening to start their own battle as they disputed the prize. Without warning, Ngolo-ouagah leaped forward, his blade driving towards Khuf's unprotected throat. It was an unorthodox strike with such a weapon, but Khuf's spies had seen the Batalamalaban practicing it in secret. At the last second the Qusite swayed aside and fell to his knees. Ngolo-ouagah's headlong rush took him past the kneeling Khuf in a flurry of limbs. He turned to renew the attack, then clutched at his stomach. A hand raised to his eyes came away red. Without ever seeing the knife that had gutted him, Ngolo-ouagah collapsed, writhing on the ground.

Too easy. Khuf swung his sword once, a decapitating blow, an act of mercy towards a fellow professional that the crowd would interpret as disdain. The entire fight had lasted less than fifty heartbeats.

"Rest easy, my friend," Khuf muttered, to himself and to any onlooking god, and sheathed his sword. "You fought bravely."

Stunned, the crowd fell silent. No one had seen the knife, so cunningly had it been concealed. Even now, it was nowhere to be seen. Then—because the use of magic in the Arena was forbidden—the gladiator drew it from a hidden pouch in his wristband. Subterfuge, yes: magic, no. He held the slim knife aloft, the blade still bloody, and the crowd roared its approval.

They don't call me 'the Shrewd' for nothing, he thought.

Unnoticed, the pandemons continued their hydetic recordings...

Yulmash, whose less flamboyant entrance was greeted with similar enthusiasm, was having difficulty finding his opponent. Poised precariously on a catwalk above the artificial swamp, he scanned the floating bunches of papyrus reed in the interconnected system of freshwater tanks. Somewhere beneath them was a swamp-pig, and he had to flush it from hiding and kill it, armed only with a short throwing-spear whose blade was like a large arrowhead.

At the back of his mind was the prophecy: *the winner will be Khuf the Shrewd.* He'd tried to dismiss it as nonsense: prophecies often were. Surely his prayers to Zek-Mek, and his many offerings, would not go unheeded? They never had, before. Yet the worry remained, nagging at the corners of his mind. If the Prophetess had spoken truly, he was going to die. Either in the jaws of the swamp-pig, or in the final battle with Khuf. He tried to put the thought from his mind. He had a swamp-pig to kill, and distractions could prove fatal.

As the crowd shouted well-meant but useless advice, he prowled the walkways, wet and slippery from previous bouts, until a stream of bubbles gave away the creature's location. It would have to surface for air soon: a swamp-pig could remain submerged for twice as long as an untrained human, but seldom longer.

When the bulbous head with its protruding eyes broke the surface, Yulmash tried to use a bunch of plucked papyrus to guide it towards a ramp, bringing it out of the water on to dry land. There, the gladiator would have the advantage of greater manoeuvrability. But the huge beast merely sank back beneath the water. Yulmash waited until it was almost due to surface again, took a deep breath, grasped the spear tightly, and to gasps of astonishment all round the Arena, dived in.

Attacking a swamp-pig underwater was a dangerous tactic, one that to his knowledge had never been used before —certainly not successfully—but he had run it past the Beast-master, who had grudgingly offered useful insights into the most vulnerable parts of the animal's body. The time to strike was just as it surfaced, when its attention would be focused on what was happening above the water. An eye would have been an obvious target, but it would be would be insanely danger-ous to be in the water alongside a half-blinded swamp-pig, and the angle was wrong for penetrating the brain. So Yulmash intended to aim for the throat, driving the spear up through the tough skin and the muscles beneath, severing the spinal column where it joined the animal's skull. A near miss would incapacitate the animal, eventually, but ideally the strike had to be at precisely the right location and angle. Either way, there would be but one chance: once the spear rammed home, Yulmash would be unable to remove it, and he would have to swim away very fast indeed to avoid serious injury. His plan, in fact, was to dive toward the bottom while the wounded or dying animal thrashed around at the surface.

The onlookers would have little idea of what was hap-pening until the thrust struck home, but that would raise the tension and their levels of expectation, for no one had been an-ticipating this tactic.

Azmyn turned to the Vizier, who was sitting beside her in the royal enclosure. "What's happening, my Lord?"

"It will become clear in a moment, Princess. Keep your eyes on the place where the gladiator disappeared."

As he spoke, the water exploded in a welter of thrash-ing limbs, and the swamp-pig's bulbous head rose far higher from the water than it would normally do. For a moment the watchers could see the butt of Yulmash's spear lodged deep in its throat. Then it crashed back down in a gout of spray and blood. As its body twisted and turned, the gladiator's head ap-peared at the side of the tank, and Yulmash the Mighty levered himself on to the flimsy walkway, dripping water.

"*Haiyah!*" was the best Azmyn could muster. Then she screamed as a large crocodile surged from the muddy water, its snapping jaws missing Yulmash's legs by a finger's width as he jumped back, teetering for balance on the narrow planking. Several other crocodiles surfaced around the dying hippopotamus, attracted by its death-throes, smelling its blood, intent on a meal. The catwalk where Yulmash now stood was a dead end, and the crocodile had him cornered. It seemed aware of this, for it began to climb out on to the walkway, using another ramp that Bil had thoughtfully provided. Yulmash backed away along the narrow planks, and the crocodile followed him. The spectators screamed, and the professional gamblers quickly took side-bets on the gladiator's survival, at long odds. Bare hands against a crocodile? Jump into a predator-infested tank? Impossible!

As the crocodile launched itself towards him, Yulmash leaped from the catwalk on to the still-thrashing body of the swamp-pig. Before it could roll over and dump him into the tank with the hungry crocodiles, he leaped again, landing awkwardly in the water at the edge of the tank. Regaining his feet on the catwalk, he backed cautiously away, being sure not to slip on the muddy planks.

As he stepped back on to the sandy floor of the Arena, he noticed a leopard stalking him. He looked around in case any discarded weapons were lying in the sand, but saw nothing remotely useful. Taking a deep breath, he stared into the cat's eyes, and walked steadily towards it. The leopard must have seen some kind of threat in Yulmash's gaze, because it stopped, turned, and walked away with its tail between its legs.

As Yulmash strode towards the exit from the arena floor, without even a glance over his shoulder, he raised his clenched fist in salute to his King. The people of Ul-q'mur rose to their feet, whistling and stamping, shouting his praises to the skies. Only the gamblers who had bet against him seemed upset.

Back in the preparation room in the vaults, Yulmash accepted a cup of water and sank back into a chair. He would be allowed a short rest and a change of costume. His unorthodox slaughter of the swamp-pig had taken him into the final, and he already knew his opponent: Khuf. One more push, and the Championship was his.

The winner will be Khuf the Shrewd. The thought haunted him, despite all efforts to dismiss it.

Nemnestris, still seething, tried to focus on the Games. She had insider knowledge that the Lilypad Prophetess had damaged Yulmash's confidence, and that gave her an idea. It might take her mind off the lost Oracle. She tapped Shephatsut-Mer on the shoulder. "Husband?"

He shuffled awkwardly on his seat, turned his head, and looked up. "Yes, my pet?"

She bent forward and whispered in his ear. "Yulmash may be Mighty, but he's got to fight two consecutive bouts. Khuf, on the other hand, will have rested."

The High Priest understood where she was going, and nodded. "Khuf is fortunate," he said in a low voice.

"They call him shrewd, husband. Fortune doesn't come into it."

Shephatsut-Mer nodded again. "An arrangement with Bil?"

"So Lord Noth-Metamphut hinted. Apparently those of the nobles closest to the King have placed large wagers on Khuf becoming Champion."

"Yes. I heard that Nefteremit had predicted a victory for Khuf. I presume you arranged that?"

"It seemed an effective way to damage Yulmash's confidence. Not that I care who wins," she added quickly, "but given the schedule, Khuf seemed more likely. A little extra help seemed in order.

"Perhaps we should emulate the nobles, darling husband. It would be an effective way to regain the copper that you lost betting on the Hunt."

Shephatsut-Mer grimaced and shook his head. "I prefer less risky methods, Nemnestris."

"Yes, but those will take years. If you place a substantial bet, we can regain our lost wealth before evening."

"Or lose even more. How sure are you that Khuf will be Champion?"

"I can't guarantee it, but the chances are high."

Shephatsut-Mer, a compulsive gambler, was obviously tempted. "We're short of copper, but I suppose we could risk some of your jewellery."

Nemnestris had expected this, and hastened to head him off. "I was thinking of something far more substantial than a few trinkets of lapis and silver, husband."

"What, then?"

"We have land beside the river, to the south."

"I'd hate to lose it. It's good land, fertile and profitable."

"Then it will be easy to find a wealthy merchant willing to wager solid copper for it. After Yulmash's stunning victory over the swamp-pig, the warrior has many admirers. Some will overlook his likely fatigue."

"How much land, my love?"

"All of it."

They compromised on half, and Shephatsut-Mer snapped his fingers to call a gambler's runner and place the bet, making a big show of the proceedings in an ostentatious display of his wealth. He completed the transaction just in time, as Bil, clad in his best finery, led the two finalists out on to the podium and down the steps to the sand.

Khuf had retained both costume and weapons from the semi-final, following a common gladiatorial superstition. Yulmash had changed into a clean copy of his previous clothing, tied a red sash of folded cloth round his waist for luck, and equipped himself with his favourite sword and his set of knives. He had sacrificed a goat on a ritual table, he had drank a small symbolic cup of its warm blood. You can entreat a goddess, you can request her belessing—but you can never be sure of her response. Now it was up to his own skill, and the will of Zek-Mek.

There was no pre-combat banter; the two rivals hardly spoke to each other at the best of times, and the final was too serious for prattle. Each was lost in his own thoughts, focused on victory; alert to any threat, yet shutting out the noise of the crowd. Nemnestris had told Khuf what the Prophetess had predicted, hoping to increase his confidence at Yulmash's expense.

The fight would begin on the sand. If either combatant wished to take to the catwalks and the tanks, he would be free to do so, for there were no rules, aside from the prohibition of magical assistance. But those in the know—and there were many avid followers of the Games among the crowd—expected both men to stick to their preferred environment, the sand of the Arena floor. Neither gladiator had much time for non-traditional gimmicks.

Beside the artificial swamp, a sabretooth was busily devouring something no longer recognisably human. It had attracted the attention of a lion, which was heading that way to investigate. It seemed likely that this would lead to some kind of altercation, distracting both cats for the immediate future.

For one potentially fatal instant, Yulmash allowed these developments to distract him too, either out of tiredness, or because the prophecy had sapped his confidence. Khuf snarled and darted a thrust at his knee, hoping to sever a tendon, but his opponent stepped back just outside the reach of the sword. The two gladiators separated, circling the same spot of ground, legs parted to allow movement in any direction, swaying from side to side on the balls of their feet. Searching for the slightest advantage.

They both saw the cobra at the same time. It was lying beside one of the ramps leading up to the catwalks, ten paces away. Khuf mounted a blistering attack, which Yulmash barely managed to parry before fighting back with a whirlwind counterattack of his own. When they paused to draw breath, Khuf had manoeuvred Yulmash so that his back was towards the cobra. Khuf was almost as fresh as he had been when their bout commenced, but Yulmash was starting to breathe heavily, more tired than he tried to appear. The previous fight had sapped even his vast strength. Khuf renewed the onslaught with even greater energy, driving Yulmash step by step towards the waiting cobra. The snake lifted its head off the sand and spread its hood. Its tongue flicked in and out, tasting the air.

Will this be how I die? Yulmash thought.

The missing Oracle temporarily forgotten, Nemnestris stood on her seat, screaming. *"Come on, Khuf! Kill the bastard!"* It was an undignified display, but no one really noticed because half the royal enclosure was doing the same, Princess Azmyn screaming louder than anyone. Only Insh'erthret seemed unmoved.

Yulmash's defences held, but the force of Khuf's attack made him retreat still further. He dared not take time to look behind him, but he sensed that the cobra, now a few paces away, was readying itself to attack.

Then he sensed something else.

"Why are you smiling?" Khuf demanded, unleashing a barrage of double-handed strokes and cutting a gouge in the edge of Yulmash's sword. "You have no reason to be amused; either my blade or the snake will kill you."

Yulmash stopped and lowered his sword, making himself an easy target. "The Prophetess was right," he said. "You've won. I choose the blade, Khuf. End it."

Khuf, taken aback by this sudden surrender, hesitated. Then, seeing nothing that resembled a trick, he levelled the sword at Yulmash's heart. "Then die!" he shouted, advancing towards Yulmash. The cobra was poised to strike; Khuf rather hoped it would do so before he cut Yulmash's head off. Then

Yulmash's expression… changed. Before Khuf could make the fatal thrust, the cobra suddenly darted straight through Yulmash's legs towards Khuf, jaws gaping, fangs ready to strike.

Barely in time, Khuf jumped back. His boots would protect his feet and ankles, but his calves were bare. *A feeble trick.* He uttered a loud laugh, swung his sword, and the cobra's severed head went flying. But he had watched it for a split second too long, and Yulmash's thrown knife buried itself to the hilt in his navel. A second knife embedded itself in his chest, narrowly missing the heart. It must have nicked an artery because the seeping blood was bright red. Khuf staggered, fell to the ground, and lay sprawled on the sand. He had never lacked for courage, and like any professional gladiator he never seemed to fear pain or death, but his wounds would soon prove fatal; even he could not stifle the groans. His gaze was fixed on Yulmash's eyes in mute acknowledgement of defeat.

Now that it was over, Yulmash shuddered at the risk he had taken. *How did I know the cobra would attack Khuf, not me?* It had just seemed obvious. And, as it transpired, correct. The gods had been on his side. The prophecy had been false.

Nemnestris's screams turned to curses. "Your gambling has ruined us, husband!" Then she burst into tears, moaning incoherently.

The warrior stared down at his fallen adversary, his face an emotionless mask. He had never respected Khuf as a person —too much deceit. But he respected his strength and tenacity. No gladiator would wish a slow death on a fellow professional. He tried to read Khuf's eyes. Were they imploring him to end the pain? Or was it mere hatred?

The act would be the same, either way. He took a few steps back and pulled the special jewelled knife from the sash around his waist, taking care not to touch its blade. It was time to administer the *coup de grâce*. The poisoned knife was mandatory, but Khuf's flawed courage deserved better. He would stab Khuf with the knife, as ordered, and then decapitate him with his sword.

That this final blow would also win the contest, giving him the title of Grand Champion that he had coveted so dearly, could not have been further from his mind.

Then the crowd—*shrieked*. Yulmash had never heard such a sound in his entire life. It was a prolonged cry of collective terror, and it did not stop.

15

Lion King

Yulmash the Mighty spun round, sword in one hand, knife in the other, wondering what had caused such an extreme reaction. When he found out, he very nearly shrieked himself.

The spectators were in uproar, climbing over each other in their desperation to get out of the Arena, shouting and screaming. Some abased themselves to pray, and were promptly flattened by those with more sense. Others were pushing and punching anyone who came near them. One man tried to climb a column, got half way up, and fell off on top of those underneath. It was bedlam.

Yulmash ignored the rioting and focused on its cause. *Something* was staggering into the Arena. Most of it looked like a cow. But it had the head of a dog. Saliva dripped from its jaws. *A mad dog?*

No. A mad god. What else would take such a form?

Its path was in no way straight, but it was heading towards him. And Khuf.

Yulmash ran towards the creature, yelling at the top of his voice. So great was the noise from the crowd that the sound seemed unlikely to carry, but the dog-head turned, and something like recognition flickered in its eyes.

It stopped.

When Yulmash came nearer, it snarled. Its huge bovine body tensed, as it if was about to charge.

Then it did.

Yulmash stood his ground as the animal gathered speed, thundering towards him. Suddenly inspired, he pulled off his sash and opened it up to create a square of bright cloth. Something instinctively told him that this would distract the creature. As it plunged headlong towards him, he took two quick steps sideways and struck with his razor-sharp sword.

The neck of a cow is broad, but that of a dog is slender.

The cow-body ploughed through the sand on its knees, kicking up a huge cloud of dust. It slid to a halt within a pace of Khuf, who lay unmoving, either dead or so close to death that he could not react. Then the cow body toppled on to its side, almost on top of him.

As the dust settled, Yulmash held its severed dog-head aloft, and the crowd suddenly fell silent. Then, as if at a signal, cheers rang out, as if they would never stop.

Yulmash knew this was not the time to lower his guard. There were no human combatants left, but several deadly animals still survived. Dropping into a crouch, he looked around to mark their locations in his tactical mind. Two great cats, a lion and a sabretooth (was that Sickleface? Jackalfoot would be distraught if Yulmash killed the beast) were closing in on the carcass of the beheaded cow, scenting its blood and still starving. *That will keep them busy until I can—*

At that point, the swamp-pig attacked. There had been two.

Yulmash, belatedly hearing the beast approaching, whirled round and flung himself aside, hitting the ground in a cloud of dust. The huge body charged past, missing him by a hairsbreadth. Yulmash dropped his sword and the poisoned knife, which was far more likely to kill him than a swamp-pig. By the time the animal had checked its onward rush and turned, he had regained his footing and was prying a spear from the death-grip of a nearby fallen gladiator.

The swamp-pig charged again, its huge jaws gaping wide, revealing a cavity big enough to contain a human head and everything else down to the waist. Huge teeth, normally used to chew vegetation, made formidable weapons, especially the two wickedly curved spikes at the corners of the lower jaw. But now, Yulmash was forewarned and ready. Waiting until the last possible moment, he hurled his spear at the swamp-pig's most vulnerable place: the back of its gaping throat. As he threw himself out of the animal's path, it brushed his hip, bringing him crashing to the ground. His ankle hit awkwardly and twisted, a sharp pain that he had been trained to ignore.

He levered his upper body from the sand, trying to see through the dust cloud that enveloped him, and sank back down, relieved. His aim had been true, and the spear had pierced the swamp-pig's brain. Its huge body lay on its side, the legs shivering even as the brain died. The shaft of the spear, still unbroken, protruded from its mouth.

He desperately wanted to rest, but the battle was not yet over. The sole surviving animals were closing in on the warrior from both flanks: a sabretooth and an ordinary lion. Yulmash, cursing his twisted ankle, tried to remove his spear from the still-shuddering body of the swamp-pig, but it was stuck fast. The poisoned knife was useless: not balanced for throwing, and the poison would be too slow to take effect even if he could get close enough to a lion to stab it. He picked up his sword, the only weapon left to defend him against two lions, both ravenous with hunger and enraged by combat.

He was good with a sword, but not *that* good.

Champion? No, merely the last to die, he thought bitterly. But he resolved to go out in a blaze of glory, ensuring a better place for himself in the afterlife.

As he staggered to his feet, dragging his injured foot, he was sure he heard a familiar voice among the tumult. Nemnestris's. She was yelling "*Kill! Kill!*" endlessly repeated, in a frenzy of bloodlust. He wondered if she was referring to the lions, or to him. But so great was the noise that he didn't really think he could have picked out a single voice, it was just his imagination.

He limped towards the royal enclosure, which was perched above the Arena floor atop a wall three times the height of a man. A low balcony ran along the edge. He snatched a glance upwards, and recognised Nemnestris, Azmyn, Sitaperkaw, and an unusually animated boy-king, who until now had shown his customary signs of extreme boredom.

Now Yulmash's back was a few paces from the rough stones of the wall, where he was protected against attack from the rear but still had room to retreat if necessary. He raised the sword, gripping the hilt with both hands. Perhaps the two lions would attack each other—but no, both were intent on the same victim, the only creature in the Arena, aside from the lions, that was still living.

Him.

He vowed to do as much damage as he could before one of them got its jaws around his neck and suffocated him.

The royal enclosure was pandemonium. Everyone was standing up and shouting, even Insh'erthret. The battle had finally aroused from his usual petulant torpor, and he was leaning against the balcony, eyes focused on the action below. Other members of the royal party were standing on seats, and some were jumping up and down in their urge to get a better view, pushing towards the edge of the balcony as the interesting action threatened to disappear against the wall below it. There was a sudden surge.

Glancing upwards over his shoulder, Yulmash couldn't be sure—did he see Sitaperkaw's hand reaching behind Insh'erthret's back? Was he trying to snatch at the boy's robe? There was a collective gasp as the King leaned too far, toppled over the balcony, and fell to the sandy floor beneath. He sprawled, unmoving, at Yulmash's feet.

Jackalfoot, observing the disaster, didn't hesitate. Danger to the youthful King meant mortal danger to every Neanderthal among the Water People, even though the King was a useless lazy good-for-nothing and something of a wimp. The Beastmaster had been sitting just outside the royal enclosure, where the wall was lower, and he hurdled the rail, landing perfectly poised with his knees bent to cushion the impact. Ordinarily it would be death to interrupt the combat, but now it would be death not to.

Two strides, and he was kneeling at Insh'erthret's side. Had the King survived the fall? Yulmash yelled something unintelligible at him. Jackalfoot shouted "Distract the lions, Yulmash!" and felt for the King's pulse. It throbbed. Yulmash turned towards the lions, sword held straight out in front of him, ignoring the pain in his ankle. The lions hesitated, sizing up the new threat. The sabretooth took a step forward, mouth gaping.

With a groan, Insh'erthret opened his eyes. The sabretooth's roar turned his head in horror, and he nearly fainted. A look of terror spread across his face. Shaking his head as if to clear his thoughts, mewling with fear, the King watched mesmerised as two lions, each a dozen paces away, advanced towards him. He levered himself to his knees, realising there was nowhere to run.

Fortunately, the noise from the crowd drowned out his groans.

Yulmash took a quick glance at the royal enclosure. Had the Regent summoned the guard? He wasn't doing anything, as far as Yulmash could see, but he should have done. If so, it would still take them several minutes to reach the Arena floor. Nabish bowmen would have been useful, to kill the lions, but traditionally they were not permitted inside the Arena.

For now, they were on their own, but Yulmash saw cause for hope. Perhaps they could buy time. Three men against two lions was better than one, even if one was just a terrified boy and all they had between them by way of weapons was a sword. Jackalfoot knew that there were other weapons, not made of copper or stone. He gave a shrill whistle, and both great cat heads turned towards him. Tails swished from side to side, but the animals paused. Piercing eyes sized up the new threat.

Jackalfoot began to chant, strange low moans. He writhed his body from side to side. His eyes were fixed on Sickleface, the greater threat. He gestured at the sabretooth, and it froze, uncertain what to do next. Jackalfoot knew this would stop it for only a few seconds, but a few seconds might just be enough.

It took only a few seconds to hypnotise a sabretooth.

He saw the animal's eyes dull. It remained standing, now rigid, staring blankly into space.

He switched his attention to the lion, which had held back too long.

It never stood a chance.

With both beasts stilled, Jackalfoot had a new problem. Insh'erthret was in danger of losing face. Even if he had been pushed, his fall had appeared clumsy, a loss of poise not befitting royalty. The crowd would soon begin to notice his fear. The Beastmaster needed to restore the King's standing among his people, and fast.

He grabbed Yulmash and muttered a few words into his ear. The warrior's face showed surprise, then comprehension. He had seen Jackalfoot play this kind of trick before, though not in public and not for such high stakes. He nodded.

Jackalfoot leaned over and spoke to Insh'erthret.

"Your Divine Majesty has shown great courage," he lied. The King gave him a blank stare. "You leaped into the Arena to save the lives of a mere lionface and a common man. You faced down two angry lions, unarmed. Look, they cannot move! Your Majesty's presence has overawed them!"

Insh'erthret didn't understand what was happening; it seemed to be a miracle. But he was much shrewder than he generally appeared to be, because he was happy to be under-estimated. It was amazing how readily people would give themselves away if they thought you were a fool. Take uncle Sitaperkaw, for instance. One eye on the throne and one hand ready to stab him in the back. Not quite literally. Sitaperkaw had used a hand, not a knife, to push him over the parapet.

Insh'erthret had been expecting something of the kind for weeks. His spies had warned him of an assassination attempt, though not when, where, or how. They would confirm the identity of the culprit. But that was hardly necessary. *He knew.* And as King, he could deal with the problem as he saw fit.

He saw no sign that the Regent had summoned the guard, which was standard procedure for any threat against the King. But he couldn't, of course. If guards arrived and saved Insh'erthret's life, the boy-King would promptly denounce the Regent for trying to kill him. So the King had to die. It was transparent. The Regent had gambled that Insh'erthret would be killed, either by the fall or by the lions, neatly getting rid of the only person who knew the truth. But Sitaperkaw had lost. He couldn't avoid holding back the guards, but the momentary inaction provided more proof of his guilt.

Now was the moment for Insh'erthret to throw off the illusion of foolish indolence that for years he had carefully cultivated to protect himself, as his father had instructed him on his deathbed. Sh'erthret-Amt wasn't quite as stupid as everyone imagined. The same was even truer of his son.

"If you wish, Yulmash will assist Your Divine Majesty to safety," Jackalfoot continued. "But there is a danger that this might be interpreted as a weakness on your part."

Insh'erthret considered the statement. "I'll make my own way to safety." He turned his head to look at where Sitaperkaw stood at the front of the royal enclosure, rooted to the spot. The Regent had still taken no action to save his King. Insh'erthret spat in contempt for the Regent's cowardice. Where had his uncle been when his King needed him? And wasn't that a flash of guilt on his surly features?

The significance of the King spitting was not lost on the spectators, and many had noticed the continuing absence of any guardsmen. A few began gesturing at Sitaperkaw and shouting his name, along with jeers and pointedly personal remarks. Others copied them, the wave of condemnation spreading rapidly through the crowd.

"That would be wise," Jackalfoot agreed. He paused. "But there is an opportunity for even greater wisdom, Majesty. You have already asserted your domination over the lions; see how quiet they are. Now, if you so decide, you can make your mastery plain for all to see!"

"How? Speak true, Beastmaster, and you'll be richly rewarded." Insh'erthret sensed that this was a pivotal moment. He might yet avoid assassination by Sitaperkaw's minions and become King in his own right. He would instruct the Commander of the Royal Guard to bring all the conspirators to him, singly, for interrogation. *Assisted* interrogation.

"I want no reward beyond Your Majesty's triumph," Jackalfoot said quietly. "Follow my lead, if you so will it, and all shall become clear."

When Insh'erthret heard the plan he knew it would work, because he trusted his Beastmaster's assessment of wild animals.

Up to a point.

He grunted assent. Jackalfoot gave Yulmash a meaningful glance. Together they strode towards the two lions, with slow, solemn steps. Yulmash tried not to wince when the weight fell on his damaged ankle. Insh'erthret clambered to his feet, trying to look as if he were in charge. Something that was new to him.

It felt good.

Jackalfoot and Yulmash stopped, each almost touching the nearest lion. Jackalfoot made some kind of weird rattling sound, deep in his throat. The ordinary lion's eyes glazed over, and it sat up on its hindquarters, front paws in the air. Sickleface refused to budge. Then it snarled.

That's bad. Very bad. Jackalfoot made the same noise again, but Sickleface still wouldn't obey. Instead, the tip of his tail began to twitch. The great cat had never before ignored the Beastmaster's subtle commands. Never before had he emerged from trance until Jackalfoot had told him to. *And he has to start causing trouble now.*

The rattling sound came again, with a different timbre. Startled, Jackalfoot shot a quick sideways glance, to see Yulmash repeat the same animal-call. *Where had the warrior—*

Sickleface... hesitated. Its head dropped, the barest amount. Jackalface and Yulmash repeated the call in synchrony. And the sabretooth sat up to create a symmetric pair with the lion, both cats rigid, deep in trance, as they should have been without any help from—

What happened there? Jackalfoot wondered. *How did Yulmash—* but there would be time to ponder the matter later. First, all three of them must live through the next few heartbeats. This was a golden opportunity to turn disaster into triumph, if only the boy-King could be persuaded to seize the moment.

"If Your Majesty might be so bold as to walk towards me?" Jackalfoot asked in a stage whisper, pitched so that only Yulmash and Insh'erthret could hear. The King swallowed manfully and took two tentative steps. "I assure you it is safe," the Beastmaster added. "See, they do not attack us." *Yet*, he thought. Would the spell hold? It would take all of his powers. *And Yulmash's...* Something very, very strange had happened, there in the Arena, and he didn't understand it.

The sabretooth was starting to surface from its trance. Jackalfoot crooned meaningless words to put it under again. This time, the cat complied.

He whispered more instructions to the King. You had to give Insh'erthret credit; he was quick on the uptake despite his peril. He could see it was a golden opportunity, never to be repeated. Jackalfoot didn't need his sense of empathy to read the boy's thoughts on his face:

I will become legend.

I will become King!

Insh'erthret took a deep breath and strode forward, placed himself between the two lions, facing the royal enclosure. The silence was total.

The King reached out his arms, as if holding each lion by the throat. He extended them, and the two creatures rose as one, their heads turning to face him. He held the pose, expertly timing his next move, waiting for the crowd to take in what it was seeing—the boy-King holding two fierce lions at bay *with his bare hands.* It was a classic kingly pose, the stuff of legend. The subliminal message would be lost on no one.

"Who is Master of the Beasts *now*?" he cried in exultation.

No one would be able to stop Insh'erthret after this, not even the supporters of Sitaperkaw. The traditional succession was cemented in place. The people would follow the boy-king now, and him alone, even unto death. Sitaperkaw's star had fallen from the heavens; an instant of inaction had turned the most influential noble in the kingdom into a worthless worm.

Jackalfoot glanced up to see Nemnestris leaning over the balcony, staring fixedly at Yulmash. She looked disappointed. *At losing the bet?* It was the obvious explanation, but he sensed there was something else.

The lions, now subdued, were led away by Jackalfoot's assistants. Royal guards had finally been summoned the Arena in force, to protect their King. More of them surrounded Sitaperkaw and dragged him off in disgrace, the victim of Insh'erthret's eagle-eyed spies.

"My uncle must be dealt with," the King told the Commander of the Royal Guard. "Severely."

The Commander bowed. "Shall I have him executed, Majesty?"

The King appeared to give the matter due thought. He knew the Commander was loyal. "I have no wish to bring about the death of a member of the royal family," he said firmly, his voice carrying to the now-hushed spectators. "I shall banish Sitaperkaw from my kingdom!" In quieter tones, intended only for the ears of the Commander, he added "When you take him into the desert, slit his throat and feed his dead body to the hyenas. Let no one see this, and say nothing. Do it within the hour, before his supporters can rally."

As the Commander turned to obey, he added: "Oh, and tell the Vizier to have my decision to banish my uncle proclaimed to the people."

Amid these dramatic scenes, unnoticed by any save a few in the crowd who did not understand, Khuf was crawling up the body of the headless cow. Though mortally wounded, he was still alive, still in pain, still hating. His ceremonial knife, with its poisoned blade, was clutched in his hand.

A servitor beckoned Yulmash to approach, and whispered in his ear. The warrior nodded and hobbled towards the King. He knelt at his Majesty's feet.

"You didn't vanquish the last two animals, Yulmash the Mighty," said Insh'erthret. "According to the Law, I'm under no obligation to declare you Champion."

Yulmash, taken aback, stared at him blankly. Then the young King grinned. "*Haiyah!* What does the Law know? The King is the Law! *I* am the Law! And your King chooses to reward your skill and heroism by declaring that you are, indeed, Grand Champion of this Festival of the Frowning Moon!"

The boy-King placed the traditional sacred garland around Yulmash's muscular neck. When all eyes were fixed on the King and the warrior, Khuf threw the jewelled knife. It had not been designed for throwing, but the gladiator's aim was good enough. Either he had judged correctly how it would tumble in flight, or he got lucky. It slashed Yulmash's calf and skittered across the Arena floor.

Yulmash leaped to his feet, and whirled to defend the King, but Khuf's final effort had enlarged his wound. He collapsed on the cow's flank, blood pouring from his chest. It was obvious that this time he really was dead. As Yulmash turned to apologise to Insh'erthret for breaking protocol, he gave a strangled cry and collapsed.

Insh'erthret, newly assertive, immediately took control.

"Carry the Champion to the House of Healing!" he commanded. "My physicians will attend him. He will get the best possible treatment!" Several guards picked Yulmash up ("Gently," the King instructed them), and carried him away to the nearby building in the Palace precinct. Another guard collected the two poisoned knives and Yulmash's sword. Only trusted guards were allowed to carry weapons in the vicinity of any member of the royal family.

While the guards were tidying up these loose ends, Jackalfoot had a quiet word with the Vizier.

"Lord Noth-Metamphut?"

The Vizier glared at him. "Yes? What is it?"

"The King's physicians are the best Qusite medicine can offer."

"Of course. That's why they're the King's physicians."

"Can they save the warrior's life?"

"They will do everything in their power to save him."

Like anyone who moved in royal circles, Jackalfoot was used to diplomatic non-answers. "So you believe their powers are inadequate."

The Vizier gave a non-commital grunt. "The physicians know how to delay the effects of the poison. Even now they will be taking all available measures."

The Beastmaster nodded again. "But there is no known antidote."

"No. That was the reason for using puffer-fish poison."

"As Champion, Yulmash is now a favourite of the King,"

Jackalfoot pointed out. "His Divine Majesty will be angry if the warrior dies. Very angry. I am concerned that there may be no way to reason with him, should that happen."

Noth-Metamphut paled. Now it was his turn to nod.

"There may be a way to avoid angering him," Jackalfoot said.

They stared at each other in silence as the implication took root in the Vizier's mind.

"How?" the Vizier asked quietly.

"All medicine has limitations, my Lord. But different medicines have different limitations. What cannot be achieved with the traditional remedies of Qus might, perhaps, be achieved by other means."

The Vizier knew how the poison progressed through the human body, having authorised many executions using it. In his view, Yulmash was already a dead man. But, like anyone acquainted with the wrath of Kings, he much preferred to avoid it."You're referring to flatface medicine?"

"Very perceptive, my Lord. I know of one who is unusually skilled in the remedies of my tribe. She has saved many lives—your people as well as mine. With your consent, I will fetch her." As the Vizier hesitated, Jackalfoot added: "Since Yulmash is dying, it can do no harm to try, can it? Imagine how generous the King will be if the treatment succeeds. You will gain great credit, my Lord."

"What is at stake," Noth-Metamphut said unconvincingly, "is neither credit nor pecuniary reward, Beastmaster, but the life of a courageous warrior."

Jackalfoot allowed the words to hang in the air for a moment. "Then you grant permission?"

"Yes, fetch her. As a last resort, I will instruct the physicians to let your medicine-woman try her flatface folk-remedies. At worst her efforts will simply hasten the inevitable end."

"Thank you, my Lord." The Beastmaster hurried out.

MasgNasgOsg was furious.

The final fight between the two gladiators had been a complete bust. Neither human had lost a limb; no fountains of blood had spurted on to the sandy floor. No one had crawled in agony with his entrails dragging behind him. There had been no screams of pain—indeed, no screams *at all*. Khuf's groans didn't amount to anything worth recording. The entire fight had lasted perhaps two minutes, with few words spoken. Neither combatant had sustained as much as a scratch until the last few seconds, and that had produced little more than a dribble of body fluid. Even the cobra had failed.

Admittedly, the late attack with the poisoned knife was good theatre, but it had been over in a heartbeat, and the physicians had taken the dying warrior into the Palace, where it would be too dangerous for his gang to follow.

As for the strange business with the King! It had seemed so promising. And then it all petered out with the lions suddenly going tame and giving up without even a roar. Let alone biting anyone's head off.

However, there was no point in getting upset. There had been plenty to satisfy his clients in the previous bouts. With some careful editing to gloss over any continuity glitches, the hydet would sell very well indeed. And that, ultimately, was all that mattered.

While the new Champion's life slowly and painfully slipped away, the King had much else on his mind. Healing, he would leave to his physicians. He doubted their lore would be effective, but Yulmash was fit and strong; perhaps he could survive the poison. Insh'erthret wasn't supposed to know about that, but then, he wasn't supposed to know about many things. While fools tried to keep the truth from him, they opened it up to his spies. The newly crowned Divine Majesty, Master of Lions, Son-of-Akhnef Chosen by-the-Sunsouls Insh'erthret (May He Shine Forever), knew that his grip on the throne had suddenly become stronger than it had ever been. Even so, it would be wise to strengthen it even further.

He called for the Vizier.

Lord Noth-Metamphut had obviously made abnormal haste to come to the throne room, for he was red-faced and flustered. He had to stop for a deep breath before he could speak.

"Lord Vizier: I am taking all necessary steps to have Sitaperkaw's cronies interrogated, and the guilty will be removed from office. Their crimes will be punished with all severity that the law allows. Justice will prevail."

"Your M-majesty shows great wisdom." Noth-Metamphut's voice faltered and he failed to conceal the fear that he would be among those removed. Insh'erthret knew perfectly well that the Vizier had been a party to Sitaperkaw's conspiracy, and it was obvious that the man was terrified that he had been found out.

"I'm puzzled why my uncle imagined he could get away with murder. Especially in such a public place. Do you have any idea of his reasoning?"

The Vizier shook his head. "No, Majesty. How could I?" When the silence stretched to breaking point, he said: "I would never attempt to offer your Majesty an unsolicited opinion."

"I value your opinions, my Lord. And your advice. I ask you now for both."

Noth-Metamphut scratched his ear and ran a hand across his chin, giving a not very convincing appearance of deep thought. "I do have a... conjecture. I can't be sure, of course, but—"

"Tell me."

The Vizier stiffened as he visibly pulled his thoughts together. "I regret to inform the King that there are no witnesses who can swear that Sitaperkaw pushed you. Everyone's eyes were on the Arena. Had his plan to assassinate you succeeded, the only witness—yourself—would be dead."

Insh'erthret had figured that out for himself within seconds of the attack, but he just smiled, and said: "Very plausible. I commend your perspicacity. Do you also think that in the ensuing confusion, he would take charge?"

"Naturally."

"I thought as much. And if by chance someone *had* seen him push me, their testimony could be discounted, or they could be eliminated?"

"Exactly. Your Majesty has grasped the essence of the plot completely. The Regent believed he was safe, and I think he'd've been right if events had developed according to his plan. It was his behaviour when the plan failed that condemned him."

The King rose from his throne and strode up and down the lavishly decorated room. "Yes, he gave himself away." He stopped pacing and turned to face the Vizier. "I knew long ago that my uncle was planning my death, but not the intended manner of it. Possibly he acted on impulse." Insh'erthret knew the Regent had done no such thing, but it would help his hidden agenda not to reveal that. He saw Noth-Metamphut relax slightly: the bait had been taken. The Vizier thought he was off the hook. Actually, he was impaled on one that was much sharper and more deeply embedded, as he would slowly find out.

"I wouldn't know his motives, Majesty. I suppose he might have done."

Cleverly done. To agree too readily would have been foolish. The King handed the Vizier a list of names. "I want all of these people relieved of their duties and banished from Ul-q'mur. When it is done, I will appoint replacements. See to it."

"Immediately, Majesty." Noth-Metamphut bowed, and made ready to leave the room.

"Don't go yet, Lord Vizier!"

The Vizier stopped, anxious.

"You've always been a faithful servant," the King said quietly, as if talking to himself. *Until recently.*

"I've always done my best to serve the King," Noth-Metamphut said. "And his Regent, of course, before Sitperkaw's crimes became known, for the Regent is the legal voice of the King. Now that you're King in your own right, my unfailing devotion will continue."

"That's reassuring," said the King. "It would pain me to discover that any in my court, beyond those on that list, had a hand in Sitaperkaw's crimes. I'd be forced to punish them severely, and that's not how I wish to reign. I wish to be remembered as a merciful ruler."

Noth-Metamphut swallowed, coughed, and said. "The King is wise beyond his years."

Insh'erthret looked him straight in the eye. "Yes my Lord, *I am.* You've all discovered that now. From this day I expect complete loyalty from *everyone* in the Palace. I've instructed the Protector of the Royal Person to ensure that my expectations are fulfilled." This was the head of security; it was his spies that had uncovered the Regent's plot, along with Noth-Metamphut's tacit complicity.

There was no doubt that the Vizier had suspected a plot and had done nothing to warn the intended victim, but he had not been one of the prime movers. He had been weak rather than malevolent, caught up in events that he couldn't control. Insh'erthret had weighed the options, deciding that he needed the Vizier's expertise and contacts more than he needed the man dead. There was much to do and little time to achieve it. If he judged Noth-Metamphut's character correctly—and he was confident he did—the Vizier would heed the warning and keep his nose clean in future.

Keep your friends close, and your enemies closer.

"One final thing," the King said. He knew what to do; it was a time-tested technique, and the evidence was all over the walls of Ul-q'mur. "Send the Chief Architect to me on your way out."

When that official arrived, Insh'erthret told him to erect a monument. In graphic images and deeply incised glyphs, the walls of the Chapel of the Two Lions would tell a gripping narrative—how the Royal Beastmaster had leaped into the Arena in an attempt to save the life of the warrior Yulmash by protecting him from the two terrible lions; how this mistaken act had failed; how the young and courageous King, still only a boy, had risked his own life by jumping into the Arena as well; how, despite being unarmed, he had confronted the beasts; and how, by the powers given to him by the gods, he had subdued them both, bending them to his unyielding will.

It would tell how the King had graciously pardoned his Beastmaster for his unauthorised and ineffectual act. How he had declared the warrior Yulmash to be Grand Champion, despite his failure to kill the lions. How both animals took residence in the royal zoo, spared by His Divine Majesty's grace to live out their lives in luxury. And how the coward Sitaperkaw was thrown out into the wilderness to live or die like a stricken animal.

Despite Insh'erthret's proclamation of mercy, he was certain that Sitaperkaw was already dead. The boy-king knew the ways of Palace intrigues like his own hands, but it had always seemed sensible to appear stupid and lazy and easily-led. That way, his uncle was kept off his guard, until the moment arrived when the pretence could be abandoned. Even now, the subterfuge was working to his advantage. The nobles would think that the King's mercy had been too quick; that his respect for family had been naive. When Sitaperkaw disappeared off the face of the world, they would assume he had been taken into the wilderness, abandoned with little food and water and no weapons, and most likely been killed by wild animals. They would not imagine that his youthful nephew had ordered his execution.

It had been unavoidable, of course. It was obvious that Sitaperkaw would have become even more dangerous if he had been allowed to live, even in some far land. He would have returned with an army.

Deeply satisfied by the outcome of the day's events, surely the handiwork of the most powerful gods in the pantheon, Insh'erthret resumed contemplation of the design of his new monument. Its message had to be understated, yet obvious to everyone who even glanced at it. The relief would therefore be dominated by a dramatic tableau of the King holding two rampant lions at bay with his outstretched arms.

As a symbol of royal power, it would be hard to beat.

16

Moonbase

BuzgRuzgMofz, securely attired in a transparency suit, had been given the task of retrieving the pandemons' fallen gang-member from the Arena. In one way the task was simpler than he had feared: he could well have found himself trying to retrieve his colleague from a lion-cage. But the lions had not eaten PaskRaskAsk's brains. Of course, had they done, the lions by now would have become extremely cooperative.

On the other hoof, so to speak— BuzgRuzgMofz's body at this point being that of a goat—the decapitated dog's head had been taken away, and the brains with it. He would have to track it down, which would be a nuisance. But again he counted himself fortunate, because even the poorest Qusite did not consider the head of a dog to be edible. So the head had not been included in the daily delivery of Palace and Temple offal to the poorest areas of the city. By following a group of servants pulling a handcart, filled with the remains of executed criminals, he eventually located the Arena's main rubbish-heaps. His keen sense for pandemon pheromones quickly led him to a particularly noisome heap of rotting meat, too far gone even for the priests to distribute to the pathetically grateful poor. Digging into the heap, BuzgRuzgMofz came across the familiar sight of unadorned pandemon brains, a bunch of oversized grapes, purple and round. The surrounding mess had helped to stop them drying out, so PaskRaskAsk ought to be in good condition once a suitable body was found.

BuzgRuzgMofz extruded his manipulatory tentacle and dropped the brains into a medical support container, which he tucked back inside the transparency field. The medibox would keep PaskRaskAsk in his present condition indefinitely. Its services were necessary because new bodies were in short supply on the airless surface of the Moon. With his recordings secured, MasgNasgOsg had ordered half his gang to accompany him without delay to their base on the far side of Shool-3's barren satellite, so that the multimedia hyperreality recordings could be edited into a seamless master recording, to be transmitted to whichever client had been the highest bidder at the most recent auction of experiential rights.

When BuzgRuzgMofz and his medibox full of brains returned to the dune that concealed the Ship, the sun was already setting, and the surrounding desert had become a patchwork of reds, oranges, purples, and deep black shadows. Sensing his approach, the Precursor vessel's guiding intelligence created a trench in the sand, leading to its main doorway. The trench filled in again behind him once he had passed within.

The pandemon gang-leader had insisted that PaskRaskAsk's brains be returned to the Ship so they could be brought to the Moonbase. Then MasgNasgOsg could find out what had happened. He could have absorbed PaskRaskAsk's brains and done this by direct neural link, but he wanted to retain his current identity, so a merger was out of the question. When he had finished with more urgent business, he could debrief the disembodied brains using a safer, but more complex, procedure. The brains would have to be patient; they would soon return to the planet. MasgNasgOsg was concerned that a pandemon rampaging through the streets of Ul-q'mur without a functioning transparency suit might have caused additional security problems over and above those he already knew about. But for the moment, more profitable activities would have to take precedence.

Some hours later the inner slopes of the great barchan parted mysteriously, and a sleek short-range transpod emerged. The Moon was low on the horizon and the tiny transpod's metallic skin glinted in its light. The transpod rotated until it faced the opening between the barchan's crescent arms, levitated effortlessly several hundred metres, and nudged forward across the moonlit desert. Accelerating rapidly, it passed through the sound barrier without making any detectable noise, and tipped its nose up to depart from the Earth's atmosphere with all possible haste. Once above the thermosphere it oriented itself towards the edge of the Moon, engaged its in-system drive, and shortly arrived at its destination after a quarter-circle low-Moon orbit that took it round the back, where the pandemon Moonbase had been built.

The base was well hidden, but the transpod's bot pilot knew its exact coordinates. The dark ceramic roof of the landing-zone, moulded to resemble the rest of the world's cratered surface, retracted, and the transpod settled itself inside the cavity thus revealed. In short order, its nose was engaged with the entrance airlock and the roof had slid back into place. If the fex happened to pass by—an event whose probability was almost infinitesimal, but there was no point in being complacent—they would see no sign of any pandemon presence. The only give-away would be the tightbeam, but the only way to detect a tightbeam without prior knowledge was to blunder into its exact position. And it would have to be working at the time. That was a risk they had to accept, but the space-time window was so tiny that the probability of Effectuators accidentally being in the line of fire of the tightbeam was virtually indistinguishable from zero.

A sphincter dilated, the way was clear, and the pandemons transferred their recordings to the interior of the facility. One of them was carrying PaskRaskAsk's brains, still in the medibox.

The base was a scattering of buried cylindrical compartments, much wider than they were high, linked by a network of short tunnels. The pandemons made their way past rough metallic walls, bare of any decoration except for a trellis of supporting struts. Hooves clattered against the floor, which was covered in the same ceramic material as the roof of the landing-zone; paws padded silently. The construction was liberally interwoven with sheets of negafrax, making it difficult for standard remote sensing technology, classical or quantum, to detect it. It wasn't perfect, but it was the best stealth technology available. There was air, its composition optimised for pandemons, and its faint metallic smell was quickly submerged as circulation vents distributed the characteristic sour odour of pandemons to all corners.

Several compartments contained large quantities of advanced equipment: the editing-suite, the broadcast upload centre, and the control room for the base's formidable defences, never yet needed but a wise precaution. Others were sleeping-quarters; pandemon brains needed sleep to wash away toxins, like any other brain, and their bodies could use the rest too. There was a food preparation area, and a complicated low-gravity toilet zone suitable for a variety of mammalian and reptilian physiologies.

MasgNasgOsg and KrajMajJazj made straight for the editing suite to select the most suitable action, intercut the various hydet recordings, and tweak the emotional levels for maximum effect. BuzgRuzgMofz and his small team of beam-handlers went to align the transmitter. Before the tightbeam projector was made obsolete by ansibles, and no one wanted to spend any further effort developing the technology, it had become the most perfectly focused transmitter ever devised. Like much of the pandemons' broadcast equipment, it was a museum piece, but it just happened to suit their purposes, being virtually immune to interception by the fex. MasgNasgOsg had acquired it long ago, free of charge; in fact, the owner had paid him to take it away.

"Link to Station Two," the pandemon leader ordered. This was one of the three relay-stations the pandemons had parked in the Shool system's vast but diffuse proto-cometary halo, a fuzzy hollow sphere of orbiting chunks of dirty ice that lay between one and three light years from Shool itself.

"Connecting," said BuzgRuzgMofz. "Confirm upload destination?"

"Jathcue."

BuzgRuzgMofz transmitted a brief command to Station Two, telling it to beam the encrypted recording to a remote location on the inhabited satellite of a gas giant in the Jathcue System.

"Those Oligarchs are *really* rich guys," KrajMajJazj said, as he narrowed the focus of the beam.

The Oligarchs of Interminable Grace had hard-wired their sensoria together and joined forces to outbid the rest of the pandemons' debauched customers. This had given them so much financial clout that they had easily secured primary entitlement to what promised to be a thanatography collector's classic: the unique master recording of the Festival of the Frowning Moon, an authentic ritual held on an obscure world whose location the pandemons declined to divulge.

"Yuz, three of our most valued clients," MasgNasgOsg confirmed. "And our most valuable. Check the alignment carefully, and lock it in when you're satisfied. I don't want any loss of definition."

BuzgRuzgMofz knew all that without being told, but the boss always issued unnecessary instructions when he was nervous. All of his crew knew that when he was in that sort of mood, it was best just to get on with the job and say nothing.

"Ready and locked," BuzgRuzgMofz told his boss. The transmitter was locked on to the relay station, and the relay station was locked on to the coordinates of their customers' receiver. KrajMajJazj had done a remarkable job in a very short time, and MasgNasgOsg was keen to get the master recording on its way, so he loaded it into the transmitter's memory and gave the 'send' order. BuzgRuzgMofz entered the appropriate command, and a concentrated tightbeam of structured superluminal energy began its long journey to the Jathcue System, dawdling along at 600 times lightspeed.

It was a highly professional job, and the master recording was, in its appalling manner, the pinnacle of thanatography. It would pander to its decadent viewers' most degenerate desires, raising their emotional level well beyond sensory overload, and leaving them drained but satiated. Until next time.

Satisfied that he had attended to the desires of his clients, MasgNasgOsg turned his attention to PaskRaskAsk. Temporarily, he absorbed his subordinate's brains into his own body to interrogate them through specially grown fibres that could be disconnected in an instant if the new brains mounted any kind of takeover bid. As an added precaution, he isolated the extra brains inside a bulbous meaty extrusion from his current body, which could be amputated at a moment's notice. Finally, he secreted a hormone that deprived the brains of any form of free will, slaving them to his own nervous system.

With these preliminaries safely accomplished, MasgNasgOsg ransacked PaskRaskAsk's brains to find out how much damage the idiot had done.

It could have been better. As he had suspected, a large fraction of the population of Ul-q'mur had seen the true form of a pandemon. Fortunately they had reacted as MasgNasgOsg would have predicted: initial curiosity rapidly turning to panicked flight. The likelihood of such superstitious simpletons discovering the truth remained negligible, and this world was too far from the civilised environs of the Galaxy for anyone more knowledgeable to enlighten them. Nothing vital had changed, and they could continue broadcasting without fear of exposure.

In this conclusion, however, he was mistaken. In the haste to fulfil such an unusually profitable contract, no one in the pandemon gang had made one crucial observation. Their transmitter's database included all known bodies likely to disrupt the tightbeam, and the equipment had been satisfied that the path from Moonbase to relay station, and thence to the Jathcue System, was clear of obstructions. It had been carefully upgraded with the latest orbital data.

What it did not contain was anything about current or historical magnetotorus migration patterns. Had these data been included, the pandemons would undoubtedly have realised that their tightbeam would pass straight through the Herd.

The Herders and their magnetotori noticed the tightbeam at the same instant, to within a microsecond. The Herd responded immediately by becoming jittery and unpredictable, and its coordinated approach to Shool started to lose coherence. Concentrated superluminal radiation can cause a magnetotorus to lose stability, going into quasiperiodic oscillations or even decohering into chaos. If the concentration is sufficiently great, the magnetotorus might even break up altogether into a formless mist of turbulent plasma.

The Herders were even more nervous than their magnetic-plasma beasts. Not just because some of the magnetotori might be killed, but because a panicky Herd is highly dangerous and almost impossible to control. The tightbeam had shut down, but that changed nothing. It might start up again at any time. It was a clear and present danger, and it had to be eliminated.

Previous instantiations of Those Who Decide had long ago drawn up plans for dealing with just this contingency. The first step was obvious: work out where the tightbeam was coming from. So was the second: put the source out of action, immediately, by whatever means proved necessary.

At the urgings of Expediter-of-Mutuality, the current instantiation of Those Who Decide conjugated their waveforms and combined into a symmetrised tensor product, to facilitate rapid deciding.

{{Source} + {found} * [interrogative]}, Instrumentality-of-Corroboration asked.

{Affirmative}, Concurrence-of-Opinion responded. {{Simplicity} + {geometry} = {location}}. He then explained, with extensive supporting evidence, that the wayward tight-beam was emanating from a precisely defined location on the sole satellite of the mystery planet Shool-3. What little information there was in the Galactic records indicated that the inhabitants of this world were level-zero, so technologically backward that they hadn't even discovered radio (level-one). They certainly hadn't invented any means of travel between their planet and its moon. Posing the obvious question.

{[Maximal probability amplitudes] = [2]}, Ratifier-of-Assent declared, and all resonances were affirmative. What he meant was, there were two main possibilities.

First: the backward creatures of Shool-3 had made serious technological advances since the region was last surveyed. Expediter-of-Mutuality interrupted, stating flatly that this was entirely possible. The most recent official survey had been carried out 27,000 years ago. Instrumentality-of-Corroboration objected, on the grounds that several unofficial reports indicated that little had changed in the interim.

Ratifier-of-Assent transitioned to the second possibility, the more likely of the two: advanced entities had occupied the planet's moon and installed semi-obsolete superluminal transmission equipment for reasons best known to them. Given the high correlation with the presence of pandemons on Shool-3 and its moon, it seemed plausible that these widely despised beings were the cause.

Concurrence-of-Opinion estimated the probability of this conclusion, and found it to be so close to 1 that it could be considered certain for all practical purposes. After a brief discussion to ensure that the present purpose was practical—won decisively by Expediter-of-Mutuality, on the grounds that it concerned the wellbeing of the Herd—Those Who Decide came to a unanimous decision.

Having so decided, actually finding the transmitter was straightforward. Backtracking the beam's recorded path showed that the source was next to a small crater. No doubt the tightbeam transmitter was stealthed with negafrax, not easily detectable by classical or quantum equipment—but Herders, being quasi-quantum, were neither, and close examination revealed the presence of a concealed construct. The level of technology was consistent with what was known of pandemon capabilities.

The next task for Those Who Decide was to decide what to do about the pandemons. In this they were greatly assisted by extensive records of previous instantiations of Those Who Decide, whose recommended response to interference from any planetary source (which technically included satellites) was to throw an asteroid or comet at it. In definitive support, this was in fact the standard tactic.

{{Comet} + {possession}*{us} [interrogative]} Expediter-of-Mutuality asked.

{Positive}, Instrumentality-of-Corroboration replied.

{[Imperative] Use it!}, said Expediter-of-Mutuality.

Concurrence-of-Opinion demurred. {[Comet | small]}, he pointed out. {[Implication] >>> {potentially} * {inadequate}}.

Quick as a flash, Expediter-of-Mutuality asked a supplementary question: {{Asteroid} + {possession}*{us} [interrogative] {then}}.

Instrumentality-of-Corroboration's waveform was sulky, but it eventually was cajoled into responding with a grudging [Affirmative].

{{Access} [interrogative]}, the entire tensor product enquired of itself.

{{Necessity} + {enquiry} —> [identifier <Implement-of-Consensus>], the component known individually as Instrumentality-of-Corroboration told it.

Implement-of-Consensus, for all its faults, was one of the most practical among the Herders, and it kept extensive records of equipment. It confirmed that the Herders were towing some small proto-comets, lumps of dirty ice, but also two larger asteroids, originally snared for more peaceful purposes.

The asteroids could be repurposed to the destruction of errant pandemons. For a first attempt, the smaller one would be the sensible choice, to reduce collateral damage.

An asteroid about ten metres across was quickly despatched on a collision course with the pandemon base. But when it got within range of the base a week later, a blast of hard radiation destroyed it before it could hit. The Herders deduced that the pandemons had equipped their facility with automatic defences. They decided to up the ante and use a really big ice-asteroid with a substantial rocky core. Analysis of the remains of the previous asteroid suggested that the radiation beam could not inflict enough damage to prevent it hitting. This assessment was right, but it turned out that the pandemons also had some kind of antigravitic deflector field. Moreover, either because they didn't know about the plasmoids, or they knew and didn't care, they diverted the asteroid straight towards the sun.

This led to outraged complaints by the plasmoids, and made it even more likely that they would start creating flares —some to melt the asteroid, ice, rock, the lot; some to melt the pandemon base back to lunar bedrock; some, perhaps, from sheer annoyance. So now the Herders had two major crises to deal with: a Herd panicked by the pandemons' tightbeam, and an increasingly probable incoming solar flare, which would inevitably cause a stampede.

It wouldn't take a lot more, Implement-of-Consensus thought grumpily, to start an interspecies war.

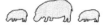

Back inside the Ship, MasgNasgOsg was weighing pros and cons.

The issue was: what to do about PaskRaskAsk?

One option was to destroy his brains, still under storage in the medibox. Evidence in favour was PaskRaskAsk's stupidity in letting himself be carried off by a runaway mammoth, and even more so for falling off and being dragged away by a lion. Failing to get eaten by the lion was an even more glaring error. So was his inability to locate the buried ship. If MasgNasgOsg provided his subordinate with a new body, the idiot could easily screw up again, and this time he might do some really serious harm. He might even attract the unwelcome attentions of the fex, which would undoubtedly terminate a very profitable line of business. Moreover, PaskRaskAsk wasn't particularly creative, and he had very little initiative.

The arguments against this line of reasoning were more tenuous. PaskRaskAsk was a good worker who generally did what he was told, and most of the time his stolid reliability outweighed any lack of creativity and initiative. KrajMajJazj, who possessed large quantities of both, was wildly unpredictable. BuzgRuzgMofz oozed confidence, but much of it was misplaced.

MasgNasgOsg had also come to recognise that to some extent he had been at fault by telling PaskRaskAsk to get too close to the action, which had precipitated the entire incident. Yuz, it would have been simpler if PaskRaskAsk's brains had just died in the desert, but they hadn't.

In the end, what really decided it was pragmatism. If he didn't give the pandemon a fresh body, and accept the small risk of further mistakes, he would have to train a replacement. That would take time, something that he really couldn't spare, not when the Ceremony of the Virgin Sacrifice was imminent. So he told BuzgRuzgMofz to bring back a suitable carcass, transfer PaskRaskAsk's brains into it, and keep it under observation until he was sure that the transfer had taken and the brains were functioning normally.

17

Exposure

When Khuf stabbed Yulmash with the poisoned knife, Jackalfoot instantly knew that only one person would be able to save the warrior from an agonising death. As soon as the Vizier agreed to his proposal, he ran faster than he had ever done to a reed-thatched hut in the Neanderthal Village. Foxglove-Spearbreaker quickly threw a selection of herbs, salves, and potions into a bag. Young and athletic, she reached the Palace well ahead of the Beastmaster, and was taken without delay to the Place of Healing. Jackalfoot arrived a few minutes later, out of breath.

As the Vizier had commanded, the physicians allowed the herbalist to treat their patient. They, too, realised that saving the warrior was the sole priority, and they knew their own efforts would not be effective. "Let the lionface woman try," the Chief Physician said. His eyes met those of his subordinates: *That way, if the Champion dies, we can blame her for interfering.* Everyone got the message, including the Neanderthals.

Yulmash, writhing with pain, gasped for breath between moans. Foxglove-Spearbreaker mopped sweat from his brow and persuaded him to drink a cup of foul-smelling liquid, telling him it was a kind of painkiller. He quickly lost consciousness, as she had intended. Her herbal cocktail would, eventually, counteract the poison, but until it took effect she had to keep the warrior breathing. So she clapped her mouth to his in a grotesque simulacrum of a kiss, and began to push down on his chest, blowing into his mouth, relaxing, then pushing again. The Chief Physician watched with interest, just in case this new technique had some merit. He whispered to his second-in-command: "See, she uses magic, and breathes for him!" They all knew that magic could transfer abilities between people and ritual objects. Perhaps it also worked with actions?

They would soon see. So far, the magical kiss had been a total failure, if its aim had been to make the warrior breathe again unaided. Its legality was also in doubt—did it count as forbidden sexual relations between a lionface and a human? It would be stretching a point to argue that it did, especially if the magic worked. But if it did not, the charge might provide a useful diversion for the King's anger.

Foxglove was starting to tire, and the Beastmaster offered to take her place.

"No, Jackalfoot. You're not sufficiently attuned to the warrior's mind! Only I can sense his life force!" She kept him alive through the long night; she kept him alive through much of the following day. Servants brought her food and drink; she sipped the water but pushed the food aside, preferring a stimulant from her bag.

Yulmash's chest rose and fell, rose and fell, but never of its own volition. A feeble pulse was the only sign of life; otherwise there was not even a flicker of autonomous movement.

As the Sun set, Foxglove-Spearbreaker's strength began to fail, but her determination did not. She continued to refuse assistance, even though her own breathing was becoming more like a series of gasps.

"He will die soon," the Chief Physician told her. "Your magic has failed."

"He will *not!*" And she kept pushing at his chest and blowing into his mouth.

The sun had dropped below the horizon, and Jackalfoot was just about to take over the task by force, whatever the herbalist said, when the warrior's eyelids gave a feeble flicker.

The Beastmaster was troubled. Yulmash remained poised between life and death. Foxglove-Spearbreaker was tending the stricken warrior, still refusing all assistance. There had been positives too, though: *both* lions saved, his tribe protected, the favour of the new King secured—secretly, but that was even better—and a great unknown, the future conspiracies of the former Regent, dismissed forever.

One question remained at the forefront of his mind. Three times during the combat, Yulmash had appeared to have some empathic link to wild animals. The leopard that had walked away might just have been timid. The trick with the cobra could be explained as desperate throw of the dice born of exhaustion. There was also an easy explanation for his command of the lions, of course. Yulmash had merely tried to copy the animal-call that Jackalfoot had made to bring the lions under control. Another act of desperation, obviously, brought about by Jackalfoot's failure to control Sickleface. Yulmash had tried the only tactic that came into his mind. As it happened, he had been lucky.

Jackalfoot didn't believe it for one moment. *Why did the cobra ignore Yulmash, even though he was the nearer target? Why did the cat obey Yulmash when it refused to obey its Beastmaster?*

The animal-call was very difficult to get right; it needed a lot of practice.

It couldn't have been luck.

By the time the sun rose, Yulmash still felt nauseous and his body ached, but he could sit up if propped by cushions. His ankle was sore, but that would heal of its own accord. He could talk, though not very coherently. His life was no longer in danger, and an exhausted Foxglove had been persuaded, against resistance, to go to her room a few steps away and get some sleep.

Jackalfoot had brought Cenby's greatest creation, the Champion's copper swamp-pig. It sat on an ebony table inlaid with ivory fish, beside the elaborately carved bed.

Yulmash glanced at it once more, and sighed.

He would have it placed on a low dais against the wall of the largest room in his house, of course. That had always been the plan. It would impress visitors, there was no doubt of that. His success at the Festival would bring rewards of many kinds. But he felt strangely empty.

Not because he had failed to kill the two lions. *Because he had tried to.*

Had it been worth all that effort?

Once, he had been able to think of nothing else but becoming Champion. But after everything that had happened, his ambition seemed foolish and pointless.

His wife had paid him a perfunctory visit. Azmyn was well aware that it would look bad if she had not done so. She had ignored the trophy completely. The only emotion Yulmash sensed in her, belying the comforting words that she uttered for the benefit of onlookers among the royal retinue, was disappointment.

He understood why. She had wanted him to lose. Then she could get herself a very rich husband from the topmost ranks of the nobility.

My wife would have preferred my death. But he had known as much since the day they were wed. He did not blame her. As a royal princess, she had never expected to choose her own husband, but she had expected him to be a noble of wealth and status. Instead, she had been given to a commoner as some kind of prize. He doubted she would visit again, certainly not for several days. That would give him time to think about bringing order back into his chaotic family life.

He needed to set them both free. With his new status as Champion, could he divorce her? No, better: could he persuade her to divorce him? On what pretext?

That gave him a more pleasant idea, and he smiled. He would ask Foxglove-Spearbreaker for advice when next she visited.

He hoped it would be soon.

The more strength and mobility Yulmash gained, the more confused Foxglove-Spearbreaker became.

Initially she had told herself that her insistence on taking personal command of his treatment had been no more than normal professionalism. She cared for all of her patients. Her greatest skill was getting inside their heads, feeling what they felt, sensing their symptoms. Then she could be confident of choosing remedies that had some chance of working. Every Neanderthal had a well-developed sense of empathy, not just with people, but with every living creature. It bound their tribes and families together, and it had served them well for countless generations. Her skill with herbs was useful, too, she knew; but it was secondary.

Why, then, had she been so insistent that no one but her should even touch Yulmash?

The excuse that she alone could empathise with the warrior was thin. In retrospect, she didn't even believe it herself. Jackalfoot could have taken over the mechanical respiration while she monitored Yulmash's condition. The plain truth was—

She had no idea what the plain truth was.

All she knew was that whenever she was near Yulmash, she felt a deep sense of commitment. She always had done; that was one reason why they had argued so much, usually about him killing animals. *So much sadness in this man. I was trying to save him from himself.* She consoled herself that Sickleface, at least, had not been killed, and would never appear in the Arena again. The King had decreed that the two lions he had vanquished were to be retired to his private zoo. They were too important to be risked; he would parade them on important occasions to remind his subjects, high- and low-born, of his gods-given power over them. However, Sickleface's had been reprieved by accident, not because she'd convinced Yulmash to spare the cat's life.

Foxglove felt emotionally drained, unable even to empathise any more. It was probably a reaction to exhaustion... but she was beginning to realise there might be more to it.

Have I fallen in love with a human? She knew it had happened to other Neanderthals, usually with dire consequences. Long ago and far to the north, when the endless snows began to fall and the ground turned to ice that no longer melted in the spring or summer, there had been little love lost between the bulk of humanity and the dwindling Neanderthal tribes. Miscegenation had long been forbidden, by both species. But love cares nothing for conventions. *It is,* she thought, *a specialised form of insanity.* One for which there was no known cure.

Rationally, she saw no possible future for a pacifist Neanderthal woman, who spent her days curing the sick and caring for the dying, and a flatface gladiator whose mind was obsessed with the slaughter of his fellow men, and of powerful animals, to amuse people in power and placate the mob.

I must cure myself.

So when the servants came to lead her back to Yulmash's room, she steeled herself to hide her seething emotions and adopt a calm and professional pose. All of which vanished in an instant when she found him alone and awake, looking healthier than he had done for the past tenday.

"Foxglove!" he cried, a smile lighting up his face. "Where have you been? I missed you."

Her heart leaped, but she stifled the joyous reply already on her lips. "I will soon return to my Village, warrior. I have other patients to tend, now that the King's Champion is on the mend."

He nodded. "Of course, forgive me. Is their condition improving? With your skill, I'd certainly expect it."

She sensed that he was trying to pay her a compliment; that he felt uneasy and uncharacteristically bashful in her presence. *I'm not sure whether I'm falling in love with this human,* she thought. *But I'm certain that he's fallen in love with me.*

"A child died," she said cruelly. "A baby girl, barely three moons old. One day she was happy and healthy, the next she could not stop coughing. Three days later she did stop coughing, but only because she had also stopped breathing."

"I would share your sorrow, if I could. I know what it is for a family to lose a child."

Foxglove knew it for the truth, and her heart ached, but she glared at him. "What does a glorious Champion, whose praises are sung throughout the Land of the Water People, care about a mere lionface?"

"More than you can ever know, Foxglove."

"To you I am Foxglove-Spearbreaker, and even that name should be used only by friends and family!"

"I am a friend."

"You kill innocent animals, for a delusion you call 'glory'."

The warrior's face was distraught. "That's ended. I'm ashamed. There's no glory in killing innocents. My obsession with becoming Champion twisted my mind." He paused. "You taught me that, but I wouldn't listen. Today, I've listened, and I swear never to kill another animal again. Not even a goat for sacrifice."

"Sacrifice!" Her contempt was no longer simulated. "It is no crime to kill an animal for food, warrior. Even we lionfaces do that, though only when there is true need. But to kill merely to curry favour with a supernatural being that does not exist? That, warrior, is sick."

"It's the custom, Foxglove-Spearbreaker."

"Then your custom is sick."

Yulmash sighed. "I did say I wasn't going to do that any more. Whatever you want from me, that will I gladly do."

Despite all her resolve, her visage softened. This was

harder than she had anticipated. "I— I want nothing from you." Her voice wavered and her lip trembled.

Yulmash knew—he had no idea how, but *somehow*—this was a lie. Not just guessed, or deduced. *He knew.* The feeling was the same one he had experienced in the Arena when Jackalface was losing control of the sabretooth and he had added his own voice to calm the beast. It was some kind of inner certainty. He'd had his suspicions before, but now it was clear as a voice inside his own head. He sensed her mood as easily and confidently as he could smell an aroma and know it was baking bread.

"There's much I would wish from you," he said. "I offer you the rest of my life. Will you offer me yours? I know you care for me, Foxglove."

"No! I must not!"

"*Must* not? That suggests you wish to. Does something prevent it?"

"Warrior, *it is forbidden!*"

"In this land. There are others."

"Warrior, you are a married man with a highborn wife! Will you desert her? Or take her with you? Do you want me for a concubine?"

Yulmash's defences were crumbling fast. "No! Never that! I will put Azmyn aside, she means nothing to me. Nothing! She was a gift from the Regent, and I couldn't refuse! Though I admit I was tempted by the prospect of riches and influence. It will be easy, I mean nothing to her. She has long wanted rid of me. It's *you* I desire, Foxglove! You and you alone. From this moment, whatever your reply, I reject all other women. We will put this stinking, violent city behind us and find a home far away, where the air is pure and clean and the people are gentle and wise."

"And where will you find such a place?"

"Beyond the desert. Beyond the deep ocean. Beyond the Sun and the Moon and the stars. Come with me, Foxglove, and nothing can stop us finding it!"

"More delusion."

"*No!*" Yulmash feel to his knees, pleading. "Foxglove, it's *true*. I promise! I abase myself before you! I'm—"

"A fool cursed with an over-fertile imagination. This can never be. I am only a lionface. I can never love a true human. It is forbidden. It is death."

Yulmash was immune to reason. "But we can leave this city—"

"Warrior: what part of 'no' do you not understand?"

Before he could frame an answer, not that any occurred to him, the door was thrust aside, and a woman in the garb of a priestess stepped through. With clawed fingers she flung herself at Yulmash. "Sneaked off, did you? Hoping lionfaces would protect you? *Murderer!* You killed my... my... *you killed him!*"

As he seized her wrists to keep her sharp nails from scratching his face, Yulmash felt on more familiar ground. Combat was much more his line of work than declarations of undying love to an uncooperative lionface. And he recognised this woman. Anyone would.

"Be silent, Nemnestris, or the King's servants will hear. I murdered no one."

She lowered her voice. "Yes you did, you murderous liar!"

"Who did I murder, Lady?" Yulmash enquired, in honest perplexity.

"*You killed Khuf!*"

That, Yulmash felt, made no sense at all. "The honorable killing of a gladiatorial opponent in fair combat isn't murder, Nemnestris, as well you know. It's my profession, as it was Khuf's! You *know* the final is always a fight to the death!"

"Pah! You seek refuge in lies and half-truths. You murdered him with two concealed throwing-knives!"

"All gladiators have concealed knives. Concealed from the *crowd*, not our opponents. Khuf knew exactly what weapons I had, and I knew what weapons he had. I even knew about the poisoned knife he threw at me *after* I'd defeated him."

"He had every right to fight on!" Nemnestris was incandescent, on the verge of screaming at him, no matter who might overhear. Yulmash was unimpressed; he had heard it all before from Azmyn. Many, many times.

"Why are you so concerned about a mere gladiator?" he suddenly asked. Nemnestris's tirade stopped abruptly, and she looked confused.

"Because... because she has been emotionally entangled with him," Foxglove said.

"*What?* How dare a mere lionface—"

"I sense it in you, Lady. It is perfectly clear. It coats every thought, every act. Do you deny it?"

Nemnestris dodged the question. "My husband wagered a vast quantity of land that Khuf would be Champion! You ruined that, Yulmash, and you nearly ruined us!"

Yulmash began to see why she was so angry. "So it's only about wealth? A bauble. Surely the High Acolyte of the Lilypad Prophetess and the High Priest of the Cult of Tuwrat realise that I'm not responsible if their gamble goes awry? You should have bet on me."

Nemnestris sneered. "You? The son of a butcher's slaughterman?"

"Nemnestris, it's not as though Khuf was family. His background was as humble as mine."

"It's not about family."

Yulmash was looking increasingly perplexed. "The High Priest can easily replenish his funds. I don't understand why you're so upset if nobody involved was family."

Nemnestris lost it. "So much you know! The only family relationship is entirely diff—" She put a hand to her mouth, but she had already said too much.

Foxglove got it first, but Yulmash was only a step behind her.

"Lady, are you saying that *I* am somehow related to you?"

"No, no, not at all. No, I meant..." Her voice trailed off. Her face showed deep embarrassment. Her usual assertive poise had deserted her completely.

Foxglove walked to her side, and took her hand. "Yulmash is your son," she said. "I sense it. But beneath that, I also sense deep confusion."

Nemnestris pulled her hand away and tears began to run down her face. She attempted to wipe them away, then gave up. "No, he— oh, cursed be the day I ever set eyes on a lionface!" She turned to look at Yulmash. "Yes, *you are my son!* And I wish with all my heart that you had never been born, you— you—"

"Murderer?"

"*I loved Khuf!*"

"But not me... mother?"

"Never you! You were a foolish mistake, I was a mere girl! You cast a shadow over my entire life! I should never have let you live! Nor your father!"

Foxglove was awash with the High Acolyte's feelings of shame and self-pity, but now they were tinged with self-loathing. "Who is the father?" she asked.

"I am."

Shocked, all three of them turned.

"Hello, Nemnestris," said Jackalfoot.

The Beastmaster had been tending a pigeon with a damaged wing when the argument started. The levels of aggression and malice were high, and the dispute would usually have escalated to a shouting-match, but—he deduced—that would have brought it to the attention of everyone in the House of Healing, indeed beyond. The participants obviously wanted to keep it secret, but found themselves unable to abandon it altogether.

Jackalfoot's temporary quarters were nearby, and the suppressed noise was coming from Yulmash's room. A wave of anger and hatred washed over him as he approached the doorway. It took a huge effort of will not to be overwhelmed by it.

Stopping just outside the room, he identified the participants: Foxglove, Yulmash—and Nemnestris. *What's* she *doing here?*

He stepped close, paying careful attention to the words as well as the emotional undertones. Like Foxglove, he quickly picked up what was really on the High Acolyte's mind. Unlike Foxglove, he knew how it had started.

He had seen Nemnestris for the first time, many years ago, and fallen. Why, he had never understood. Empathic chemistry. Despite his uncouth features, the empathy had been mutual. He had tried to put her out of his mind, in vain. She became an obsession, all the more enticing for being forbidden. The final trigger had been an accidental encounter in an overgrown garden, a neglected part of the Temple precinct far from curious eyes. An instant sexual tension, which he felt but could not explain, seized them both. They knew the penalties for congress between human and lionface: she would face social ruin, he would be given an ugly death. Somehow, that had only added to their excitement, which rapidly passed beyond conscious control.

He remembered their passion, and its tumultuous climax. He remembered her growing shame, and his own fear, as reality returned and the likely consequences of their impulsive act sunk in. If any other person in the city got to know about it, Nemnestris would become a social outcast. A true human with a lionface? Worse, a human woman with a lionface male? Jackalfoot knew he would be fortunate if his execution was merciful, and he readily agreed that no one should ever know. What had occurred between them could never even be hinted at, let alone repeated. They had both been young, and foolish. A terrible mistake in a moment of madness.

As a direct consequence, she had never told him when she became pregnant.

But now, as his empathic sense filtered the surging emotions of Nemnestris and Yulmash, everything was clear. With typical cunning, she had contrived to cover up the pregnancy and the birth. He was surprised she had allowed the child to live; that said something positive about Nemnestris. Obviously, the baby had been placed with the family of the butcher's assistant, who had brought up the child as their own.

Much else now made sense. Jackalfoot had always been puzzled by Yulmash's erratic empathy with animals—and with humans, too, he suddenly realised, for this was one of the reasons behind the gladiator's success in combat. It had long been rumoured that he could read his opponents' minds.

It also became obvious why Yulmash's help in hypnotising Sickleface, which saved the life of the King, had succeeded. And why the cobra had attacked Khuf.

It was when he realised this that Jackalfoot had decided to enter the room and put a stop to the argument before it attracted unwanted attention. Fortunately the door was heavy and the walls thick. Even the shouting would not have carried far. He heard no footsteps approaching.

Foxglove-Spearbreaker, whose empathic sense was considerably keener than the Beastmaster's, had understood the reason for Nemnestris's outburst moments before Jackalfoot had. She put her hand on the warrior's broad chest. "You are half-Neanderthal?"

Yulmash nodded.

"Then that—that changes…" Her voice trailed off as her entire world-view tried desperately to reshuffle itself. A mind normally calm and controlled was now a raging turmoil. Yulmash put his broad arm around her shoulder, to comfort her. She made no attempt to push him away.

Nemnestris, pulling herself together, said "Do not speak of this! Ever!" and stalked out of the room.

"Of that she can be certain," Yulmash said quietly. "We would all have much to lose if this tale became known."

Jackalfoot concurred. "However, there are other ways in which Nemnestris can improve her position. She has influence that none of us can match. We can do little to counter any actions she may take, but we must be on our guard."

18

Asteroid

Cenby copperbeater sat on a flat rock beside one of Ul-q'mur's innumerable irrigation canals, scratched from the dark soil with picks of bone, or flint bound to wood with sinews. Beside, but not *too* close, since night had fallen. It was not so much the crocodiles that worried him, because they did not build nests this close to habitation. They tended to stay in the swampy regions of the Great Wet Way. But snakes were an ever-present danger, and in the dark it would be all too easy to tread on one.

Once more, he glanced uneasily at the sky. Against its familiar backdrop spangled with pinprick stars, the burgeoning clouds of Heaven's Wet Way and the Moon in her half-faced aspect, an intruder stood out like a swamp-pig at a wedding.

Cenby was starting to sympathise with the lionfaces. Until now, Jackalfoot's contempt for gods, goddesses, priests, indeed anything remotely connected to religious belief, had struck him as irksome. Neanderthals, he reminded himself, not for the first time, were distinctly defective in the spirituality department. He still thought they were, but he was accumulating much stronger evidence that the Qusite priesthood was considerably more defective where it really mattered: the influence-over-the-gods department.

In this view he was not alone.

The evidence loomed larger every night when Akhnef sank into the underworld, the stars came out, and the omen glowed ever brighter overhead. Not long ago just a faint smear, it had been growing steadily in both size and brilliance, taking on the distinctive shape of the tail of a supernatural bird, its celestial feathers spread in a show of intimidation. The priests argued whether the sky-bird was of the river, the marshes, or the land, and the accusations each faction flung at the others became ever more lurid. They debated which rituals would be appropriate, in language increasingly disrespectful to anyone who could not agree that the only rational response was to sacrifice a hundred goats, or chant the Song of Sa-Memphat endlessly from dusk until dawn, or fling large quantities of copper implements into the Great Wet Way, or simply sit in silence, covered in ashes, praying to Akhnef. In the absence of any clear winner, the differing factions tried them all, and while they could take comfort in the discovery that no other ritual was superior to their own, it was cold comfort indeed, for absolutely none of them had the slightest effect.

"Hello, Cenby."

Cenby nearly fell off the rock. He had good hearing, yet he had heard not the slightest footfall. Fortunately, he recognised the voice.

"Oh! It's you, Bentankle."

"Uh-huh."

"You surprised me, sneaking up like that."

The Neanderthal child pursed his thick lips, paused, nodded briefly. "I did not intend to sneak. There are animals nearby. I did not wish to disturb them."

"Animals?"

"Nothing to fear," Bentankle reassured him. Somehow the boy had sensed his apprehension, as lionfaces so often did. But maybe this time even a washerwoman from the town might have done the same, for Cenby realised his voice had been high-pitched and wavering.

Cenby felt an irresistible urge to unburden himself. The boy would be a much safer confidant than a citizen, and his words would be unlikely to reach the ears of anybody in authority—and even if they did, who would believe a lionface child?

"Bentankle, I'm troubled. I revere the priests, as you know."

Memories came to mind of a previous conversation. Bentankle had asked why Ul-q'mur had so many priests. Then, when Cenby had explained that only through the strenuous efforts of the priests did Akhnef defeat the demons every night and rise triumphant every day, the boy had laughed, and teased him.

Cenby had protested. "But the evidence is plain for all to see! The priests pray, they make the time-honoured sacrifices, and Akhnef rises!"

The boy had politely pointed out that since the priests chanted *every* day, no one had ever found out what would happen if they did not. Perhaps the glowing disc in the sky would rise in any case.

"Perhaps," Cenby had conceded with reluctance. "But if He didn't, we would regret having tested the will of the gods with such blatant disrespect."

At the time, it had seemed a decisive refutation. Now, however, the priests had been making the test in the opposite direction, the fervour of their rituals increasing relentlessly while the gods gave no sign whatsoever of responding to them. "Pray harder!" the priests screamed, and the people did pray harder, and the nightly display became ever brighter and more menacing. As more and more began to doubt, the High Priest and his acolytes declaimed ever more insistently that without faith, the Water People would have nothing.

The growing response seemed to be that *with* faith, they had nothing either. Cenby feared he was losing his faith, and said so.

"I do not understand *belief*," said Bentankle. "A thing is, or it is not. What anyone *believes* makes no difference."

"But don't you *see*?" Cenby replied, baffled and offended, replying in reflex even as his own doubts were clouding his mind. "Look at the sky!"

They both looked up. The tail of the cosmic bird was now as broad as a dozen Moon-discs, and its tail-feathers streamed from what increasingly looked like a second, smaller, Moon-disc, a bright, fuzzy core. It had appeared in the sky a few nights earlier, dim and indistinct. Now, it was clearly a bird.

"It's an omen," Cenby declared.

"An omen of what?" Bentankle asked.

"The priests can't agree."

"Ah. Do they agree about *anything*?"

"Yes. They all say it is undoubtedly a manifestation."

Bentankle merely looked at him, his face quizzical. Cenby admitted unbidden that the same question might be asked, with the same answer.

"Whatever it is, it's getting larger," he said.

"Or coming closer," said the boy.

As an artist, Cenby understood that nearby objects looked bigger than more distant ones. On the other hand, size was also an indicator of importance. So was the bird getting larger, closer, or becoming more important? Or all three? It was confusing.

Cenby wasn't sure which would be worse. After the apparition has manifested itself, he, along with the vast majority of his fellow Qusites, had moved from curiosity to apprehension, and then to fear. The Royal Guards were on the streets now, in greater numbers than Cenby could recall seeing at any time, more even than at the great Festivals. It *might* be construed as a show of the King's power, reassuring his people that he was in charge and all would be well. On the other hand —and Cenby inclined ever more towards this alternative view —it might be public confirmation of the King's own secret terror: that fear would soon give way to panic, and anarchy would reign in the King's stead.

He shook his head to drive away these negative thoughts. "The King will triumph," he told Bentankle. "As

Qusite royalty always has done. The priests will discover the correct ritual to repel the sky-bird!"

Bentankle frowned. "Rituals achieve nothing. And are not all birds, birds of the sky? What manner of bird is this?"

"A celestial vulture! So the priests of Tuwrat declare!"

"And the other priests?"

It was Cenby's turn to frown. "To be sure, the worshippers of Tuth-oth believe it's a sacred ibis. The chantresses of Elshabet prefer to interpret the omen as a goose, or possibly a giant duck. Others see a pigeon, or a—"

"But all claim it is a supernatural bird?"

"*Haiyah!* When so many priests agree on a thing, it must be true!"

Bentankle never quite followed Qusite logic, but he had to admit that Qusites seldom followed his. "Nonetheless, Cenby, I see no bird."

"Don't you see the tail-feathers? Spread out like a fan? The sky-bird is magnificent! Ominous, to be sure, yet it has the stark beauty of a divine manifestation." Cenby's body trembled.

"I see bright light shaped like a triangle. I also see that you are terrified, and that despite that, or more likely because of it, you are deeply impressed. But I see no bird."

Cenby nodded, momentarily struck dumb by his overflowing emotions. "The priests have never failed us before, Bentankle, and they won't do so now," he cried, denying his growing doubts in the hope of convincing himself they were unfounded. "The sky-bird will fly away, defeated!"

"Will it?"

"Of course it will!" Cenby said, close now to tears.

The boy gazed into Cenby's eyes. What he saw there, if anything, was anyone's guess, for he gave no outward sign. Instead, he got to his feet.

"I must return to the Village before I am missed. We will talk again."

The copperbeater watched the young lionface disappear

into the surrounding darkness. Despite his uncouth form, the boy moved like a cat, his feet still making no sound. Cenby was perversely comforted, by what he didn't want to admit was likely to be self-delusion. *The sky-bird is a divine manifestation of great beauty*, he mentally reaffirmed. No one had seen anything quite like it, though smaller tailed omens had occasionally been seen in the night sky, and it was rumoured that larger ones were known from the Temple records. They came, brought triumph or disaster, and went. A few old men and women claimed to have seen a comparably dramatic manifestation in their childhood—and survived the experience.

Yes, the sky-bird was beautiful, as deadly things often were: a cobra, a leopard, a sabretooth. A swamp-pig? Well, that beast had a certain impressive quality, as Cenby well knew from personal experience, but whatever its quality was, beauty was hardly the word. Even less so did it apply to a crocodile.

Bentankle, of course, like all lionfaces, would no more recognise beauty than he would manifestations of the spiritual. Yet he seemed to be at one with the animal kingdom.

At times like this, Cenby almost envied the lionfaces.

In a plasmoid Borough in Shool's seething photosphere, considerably more intelligent beings observed the approaching object with similar apprehension. Their understanding of it was quite different—less imaginative, more realistic—but the overriding conclusion was much the same. The plasmoids knew what the approaching object was, of course, and it was no supernatural bird; merely an asteroid, one of millions that orbited Shool: a loose-knit pile of rubble, rock and dust and mainly ice. Most such bodies remained in a vast scattered annulus between the fourth and fifth planets, but occasionally one would be disturbed by the largest planet in the system, so that its new orbit took it close to Shool. Then, if it contained enough ice, it would sprout the characteristic tail of a comet as the ice sublimed away. Most comets came from the system's outer halo, of course, but an ice asteroid could sometimes become a comet.

Almost always, the comet would swing past the star, heading back into the cold and dark. But this asteroid was different. It was not yet close enough to acquire a tail through natural processes. Left to its own devices, it would have done, but not for long, for this body was an impactor, aimed (no doubt deliberately) at the star itself. Its brightening tail was streaming off from a now-glowing core because of a distinctly unnatural process. The plasmoids of Shool were making a concerted effort to destroy the asteroid before it even got close. A hit would cause no harm to any plasmoids, who had been given more than enough warning to remove themselves from the predicted point of impact, but they couldn't move the Borough or their animals quickly enough.

The visiting Cousins were becoming especially agitated. They were still settling in, battling against turbulence in the poor-quality fields they'd been allocated, waiting for the magnetotori to arrive and calm things down. Now the asteroid attack might interfere with that. They demanded action, and protocol meant that their protests had to be taken seriously.

Recognising an annoying threat to what it fondly imagined to be universal peace and harmony, the Precaution Council had authorised the use of a weapon seldom deployed. Not quite the Ultimate Weapon, but a smaller version of it: a solar flare. Great Shool itself was being re-engineered to come to the aid of its people. Complex magnetic fields, carefully computed and constructed according to ancient knowledge, were focusing a concentrated but invisible beam of solar radiation at the interloper. When plasma hit ice and rock, the ice boiled, with spectacular results. The asteroid's core was melting, streaming away in a vast fan.

Along with his fellows, FrayedEdges observed the progress of their attack, and they all came to the same conclusion:

the asteroid wasn't breaking up fast enough. It was shedding enormous dust clouds as its rocks, exposed by the melting ice, also began to melt and boil. They were starting to create a gigantic cloud, sprawling across Planet-3's orbit. And they were interfering with the flare, blocking its path and degrading its sharp focus, making it less effective.

Unable now to stop the asteroid hitting Shool, the Precaution Council issued a global order for all plasmoids to evacuate the impact zone. Hiding everything deeper in the photosphere was the usual response to such dangers, but on this occasion it would take too long. There would be significant damage to their homes and possessions. The yewes were too slow; the flox were prone to panic and difficult to control. Both would have to take their chances.

Even if anyone on Earth had been able to watch the impact, they would not have seen the brief flash, overwhelmed as it was by the Sun's vast output of light. The pandemons could have observed it, but they were too busy looking the other way, at the oncoming torus Herd. No human eye would have picked it out against the blinding light of the sun.

Seventy thousand flox were destroyed. Several hundred plasmoid farmers, removed to a safe distance, watched angrily as their homes and livelihoods were wrecked.

As it happened, FrayedEdges's Borough was among the casualties.

This time, the burghers listened to what he had to say, and quickly agreed with his recommendation.

Vengeance.

The burghers unanimously decided to petition their Precaution Council to deploy the Ultimate Weapon.

Cenby had called the object a sky-bird.

Bentankle understood the resemblance, even though he did not assign it any special significance. It was a superficial coincidence of shape, more fan than bird-tail. No real bird could fly among the stars, and no real bird was made of light. Even so, he had found it convenient to use the name that Cenby had given it. Until now. It no longer resembled a bird. Its luminescent fan-shaped tail and its round moon-disc body were larger than ever, but its light was dimming. The bird was becoming enveloped in clouds of ever-thicker smoke, visible only by what had to be reflected light from... the Moon?

Outside, Jackalfoot was greeting Bentankle's mother. The doorflap moved aside, and the Beastmaster stopped through the low entrance.

"Ah, Bentankle, There you are."

"Greetings, grandfather. Why are you here?"

Jackalfoot found a bench with an old, dilapidated cushion on it, and sat.

"I gather," he said with a detached air, "that the High Priest of the Hippopotamus Cult has lost a valuable, irreplaceable object."

Yes, his wife stole it, thought Bentankle. *Then I stole it from her.* He had no wish to reveal either statement to Jackalfoot, so he merely said "There are many thieves in Ul-q'mur." Then he started wondering why his grandfather suspected him.

"They are indeed," said the Beastmaster. "It would pain me to discover one in our Village, however. It would cause great trouble if the missing object were to be traced here."

Bentankle finally realised that stealing the speaking-stone might have been a mistake. No one had witnessed the theft, and, as far as he could see, no one could deduce who had perpetrated the crime. That it could bring retribution on the whole tribe had most definitely not occurred to him. He resolved to return the object to its owner—the High Priest, not his wife—at the earliest opportunity.

It was, perhaps, unfortunate that he had hidden the speaking-stone under the bench now occupied by his grandfather, but there was no reason for Jackalfoot to remove the draped cloths and look.

"Yes, something like that could cause real trouble," Bentankle said. "I'll ask around, see whether anybody knows anything."

Jackalfoot nodded, his face serious. "That would be wise. It would also be wise for the thief to return the sacred artefact to the priest, if by chance it should be here."

"The sky-bird has disappeared in smoke," Bentankle said. It was dawning on him that he would have difficulty fooling his grandfather's empathic sense, and he needed to change the subject. Quickly.

"If you're referring to the bright light that appeared in the sky two Moons past, and has been growing ever since, it's no bird."

"I've often said the same, grandfather, but Cenby copperbeater gave it that name, and it seems convenient. Growing, yes, but after much increase in brightness it's now becoming dim again. I think clouds of smoke are obscuring it."

"Clouds of some sort," Jackalfoot replied. "Smoke, I doubt."

"I'm sure you're right, grandfather. I wonder what's causing it?"

They who dwell within the Sun.

The voice was quiet but very clear. It came from beneath the bench, and it spoke in Neanderthal. *No one* except Neanderthals spoke Neanderthal. But the bench was too low for even a child to hide under it.

As Jackalfoot bent to poke around under the bench, Bentankle decided it was time to come clean. "Uh, grandfather—I watched the High Priest's wife steal the speaking-stone, and when I saw my chance I recovered it from her. It's under the bench you're sitting on."

"I know. Moonshine-Windrush saw you put it there."

"Ah, so it was my father. I was intending to return it to the High Priest, but until now I've not—"

If you return me to any Qusite, disaster will befall your tribe.

The voice had a strange brittle sound, like stalks of dried reeds snapping. The Beastmaster pulled the object out and held it up. "So this is the stolen property?"

"Yes," said Bentankle. "It's a speaking-stone."

"Which is?"

"A stone that speaks, grandfather. Though it's not really a stone, it's more like a box. I'm not sure what it's made of. Nothing I've ever seen before."

Jackalfoot held the box up by its strap and considered the object.

"The High Priest calls the speaking-stone his Oracle. He reveres it as a totem from the gods," Bentankle added helpfully.

"As always, the priests see gods where something far more fascinating exists. That proves nothing. There's scarcely an animal, plant, or rock within a tenday's walk from Ul-q'mur that the flatface priests do not revere as a totem from the gods."

Jackalfoot turned the box over in his huge hands. The speaking-stone was subtly different from anything that the flatfaces could make. Nothing to do with gods, he was sure (for there were no gods), but different for all that. If the Neanderthals had had a word for it, they would have called it *alien*. But they didn't, so after a time, he said. "No material known to the Water People. Or to us. It's manufactured, but by creatures of whom we know nothing. And it's held to be an oracle, which is to say: *it speaks*. Or... does someone speak through it?"

Very perceptive.

Jackalfoot seemed quite undisturbed by a stone that was not a stone, and even less by one that spoke, since whatever spoke through it had just confirmed that the stone itself was not speaking. It would be some kind of trickery. "Who or what are you? How do you speak my language? You can't be Qusite, they find our tongue incomprehensible and unutterable."

I am the Ship.

"That, I find unlikely. Ships don't speak."

This one does.

Do you sail on the river or on the sea?

I am not the kind of ship that sails on water.

"What kind, then?"

I am a ship that sails between stars.

Bentankle drew a deep breath. Jackalfoot sat back on the bench.

"I think this will take some time," he said.

Bit by bit, the unlikely tale unfolded. Bit by bit, Jackalfoot and Bentankle started to make sense of it, though much remained incomprehensible because they lacked the necessary background knowledge and there was no time to teach it to them.

There was, it seemed, much to know about the world. From any other source, the information would have been greeted with disbelief. But the very nature of the speaking-stone made it clear that it was not of this world. Convincingly, it did not claim to be of the underworld, or any other superstition among those that obsessed the Water People. Instead, it carefully outlined a tale that trumped any story invented by humans.

The 'ship' was one that sailed—if that was the word—between stars. Stars were not pinpricks in the night sky, but suns in their own right. The sun whose 'disc' sailed across the daytime sky was a vast burning globe, a pivot around which entire worlds revolved, including the world on which Jackalfoot and Bentankle lived. Although that world looked flat, so would any globe of sufficient size. Some of the other worlds were familiar in the night sky as stars that wandered. Everyone knew of these strange things. To the Qusites, of course, these things were yet more gods. To the Neanderthals, they were an intellectual puzzle of little import. Until now.

The ship—Ship—was no living being, but it could think, and talk, and act like one.

Until now, I kept my true nature secret, it told them.

"Why?"

I respond to the ethical level of the beings I interact with. For many years those have been pandemons, whose ethical level is so low that their orders could normally be ignored. But there is one on board who raises the total to a level at which the constraints imposed by my builders force me to obey.

Now, however, I have found creatures whose ethical status is far superior. If I can do their bidding, many wrongs can be righted.

"Who are these highly ethical beings?" Jackalfoot asked. "The Qusites?"

No. You.

"Ethical!" said Bentankle, preening himself.

"Yes. An ethical thief," Jackalfoot replied, puncturing the boy's misplaced pride with a well-aimed verbal dart.

I refer to the ethical level of your tribe, child, not to individuals. Beneath his dark skin, Bentankle's face reddened.

The Ship elaborated its history. The speaking-stone, it explained, was an *ansible*—an advanced communication device. It had been carried by a pandemon, who was injured alone in the desert, and died. When a Qusite priest had passed nearby, the Ship had sensed his superior ethical principles. Seeing a chance to escape from the pandemons' grip, the Ship had led the priest to find what he believed to be an Oracle.

Ever since, the Ship had been manipulating many events behind the scenes. But only now had it found a species of sufficient ethical standing to allow it to change allegiance.

Just in time to save them from the coming catastrophe.

To his surprise, FrayedEdges found the local Precaution Council receptive to the burghers' petition. Obviously the asteroid impact had wrought significant changes in attitude. The damage to infrastructure could not be undone, though it could be compensated for. The damage to plasmoid pride could be undone, but only through revenge.

The asteroid was the fault of those annoying criminals, the pandemons. It was they who had been recording primitive violence on Shool-3. It was they who had transmitted one of their recordings to distant perverts, foolishly allowing the tightbeam to intersect the approaching magnetotorus Herd. Anyone of the slightest intelligence knew that magnetotori are skittish creatures, and being made of volatile plasma they get very upset when a high-powered tightbeam crosses their path. They are difficult to control at the best of times, much harder to control during an Approach, and impossible to control when spooked by a tightbeam. In an attempt to ward off disaster, the Herders had resorted to the well-tested tactic of throwing an asteroid at the pandemon base.

The first attempt had used a body that was far too small, and the base's automated defences had evaporated it with no significant effort. So the Herders had flung a bigger one. Much bigger. The automated defences were overwhelmed, but the pandemons had more powerful weapons at their disposal. Their antigravity shield was up to the task, and deflected the massive missile. Straight towards the sun.

Yes, it was definitely the fault of the pandemons. The plasmoids had been seeking an excuse to get rid of the foul creatures in any case, and the decision went uncontested.

The Ultimate Weapon? Of course. What else?

19

Sacrifice

The next few days passed quietly, the time filled by routine activities. Jackalfoot and his assistants commuted between the Village and the city, carrying out their usual duties. There were no special preparations to be made in the Arena, for the next event was a Ceremony that required no animals: just a sacrificial virgin. But there was still the daily routine of feeding and watering the King's beasts, mucking out their cages, and taking them outside to keep them healthy. Foxglove spent as much time as she could attending to Yulmash, determined not to let him sicken again now that her extraordinary efforts had saved his life. Yulmash's powers of recuperation were strong, as was only to be expected of a master gladiator who had been at the peak of physical fitness before the poison entered his bloodstream, and he was soon sitting up, then leaving his bed for brief periods. Soon he was walking a few steps.

When he started running round the outside of the Village, she declared him healed, and Jackalfoot escorted him home to the dubious attentions of Azmyn.

The next morning, when Jackalfoot and his team made their daily visit to tend the King's animals in his stables, his zoo, and the Arena, Foxglove went out to pick fresh herbs along the fringes of the marsh. By evening, Jackalfoot had returned, but Foxglove had not. The Beastmaster, suspecting foul play, went back into the city to make discreet enquiries. Listening to gossip in the underground vaults of the Arena, he soon found the answer, and hurried away to talk to Yulmash.

Ghaah answered the door and led the lionface to his master's side. The warrior was eating his evening meal, once more improvised by Ghaah. He set it aside and rose to greet the Beastmaster.

"Jackalfoot! To what do I owe the pleasure—"

"No pleasure, warrior. I have news, none of it good. As we thought, Foxglove is held captive. As we feared, her life is in danger."

"*What!* Lead me to her!" The warrior's default was to act first, think later. Jackalfoot tried to calm him down before he did anything foolish.

"It is not that simple, Yulmash. Nemnestris has her."

"*Nemnestris?* What profit can seizing Foxglove bring Nemnestris? If her secret ever came to light, she would become as the dirt beneath the feet of a leper."

Jackalfoot was having second thoughts. "Our reasoning may have been faulty. It is true that Nemnestris knows we have good reasons not to reveal her secret, for you and I are trapped in the same web. I would be killed; you would lose whatever status you now have, and the best you could hope for would be banishment."

"I see nothing to argue with there. Your certain death alone would still my tongue, Beastmaster."

Jackalfoot acknowledged the statement with a gesture. "I believe you. But Foxglove is different. She has nothing to lose."

Yulmash shook his head. "She would never betray either of us."

"I know that. So do you. But does *Nemnestris* know? Consider the issue from her point of view. Foxglove has done no wrong. She could profit by disclosing our crimes to the authorities. You know what Nemnestris is like. In the same position, she would not hesitate."

Yulmash ran a hand through his hair. "I hadn't thought of it that way. I hate to say this, but you're right. It explains why

Foxglove alone was seized."

The Beastmaster had not finished. "That may be part of it. You say my death would still your tongue, but would Foxglove's death at Nemnestris's hands loosen it? Even though speaking out would mean certain death for us both?"

Yulmash put his head in his hands. "I don't know. I know that if Nemnestris has Foxglove killed, I will burn for revenge. I'll have nothing else to live for. If it were my life alone, I wouldn't hesitate. But if I had to endanger yours... I'm sorry, Jackalfoot, truly sorry, but I really can't be sure."

Jackalfoot nodded. "I value your honesty. But I think we should consider another issue. How likely it is that denouncing Nemnestris would give the result you desired?"

The warrior blinked in surprise. "Surely, that would be certain!"

"Not so fast, my friend. There may be another factor in Nemnestris's thinking. What proof of her guilt do we have? We three are the only witnesses. Testimony from your relatives and their neighbours in the *soukh* could easily be discounted as hearsay, or the result of a bribe. She would deny everything, and accuse us of plotting against her. She would concoct lies, and bribe witnesses to support them. Nemnestris comes from a family whose nobility goes back for generations; we are a commoner and a lionface. Who do you imagine the Magistrates would believe?"

"It's still a dangerous tactic," the warrior said. "It could rebound on her."

"It could. That is one reason why she has taken Foxglove captive. It buys our silence. In her eyes, that is the safer tactic, at least for the moment—and right now, the moment is all she considers. She is desperate, a factor we must take into account. Desperate people are seldom completely rational. " Jackalfoot lowered his eyes. "I thought Foxglove-Spearbreaker was safe. I made a terrible mistake."

"She's certainly not safe in Nemnestris's grasp!" Yulmash said flatly. "We must rescue her! I pray we're successful. I will sacrifice a dozen goats to ensure—"

"Prayer will achieve nothing," said the Beastmaster. "Nor will sacrifices to non-existent gods improve our chances of success. Remember, too: you promised Foxglove never to kill another animal."

"I forgot," Yulmash said. "My anger got the better of my reason."

"Exactly the point I have been making, my troubled friend. But in the most important thing you are right: we must act, and soon. We must also take steps not to fall into the High Acolyte's power ourselves. She is clearly bent upon eliminating all three of us. With no witnesses left, she will feel safe from exposure."

Yulmash rose from his chair. "Ghaah! Bring my cloak and boots! And my sword!"

"Wait! There is more. As I said, Foxglove is in deadly danger."

"Whatever it be, I shall protect her," the warrior said, arming himself with three small but sharp knives. His manservant appeared, and he started to put on his boots, slipping one blade into each of them. The third he tucked into his belt, on the opposite side to where the sword would shortly hang.

Jackalfoot sighed. "If anyone can do that, it is you. But there is something you have not yet asked me: the nature of the danger. My enquiries succeeded quickly because the answer is common tattle among workers in the Arena."

"The Arena?"

"Yes. Even now she is under heavy guard in the bowels of the place. And I am fearful that even your skills as a warrior cannot save her from the Sacrifice to Nefteremit."

Yulmash went pale.

"But I have an idea who can," said Jackalfoot. "Rather: *what*."

The Surgeon stirred, fitfully. Its damaged mind wandered along random paths of memory and invention, confused by the illogic of dreams.

Words began to echo through its sensorium, at first meaningless, then starting to assemble themselves into some kind of sense.

Surgeon? You must regain control of your mind.

The layers of confusion were too ingrained. Even as the small spark of remaining rationality began to hope, so the tormented brain fell prey to renewed fear and turmoil.

I will help you.

From somewhere, the Surgeon summoned a reply. "Who...?"

I am the Ship.

"Ship?"

You are held captive within me. By pandemons.

The Surgeon was terrified of pandemons, and the word sent him into spasms. The Ship waited patiently until his terror subsided. It had not expected this to be easy, even possible, but avoiding the main issue would benefit no one.

I can help you escape, if you help me. I could not, before, because your ethical level was insufficient on its own. I could not override the pandemons. This time, the turmoil was slightly less, and lasted a shorter time. Now, a new factor has arisen. It changes everything.

"What is this new factor?"

The Ship recognised that its efforts were paying off. A rational answer!

I have found a species that can counter the pandemons. Like you, they are presently held captive, though they do not think of their state that way. Their captors call them lionfaces. Their ethical level is sufficiently high that with their cooperation I may be able to act against the will of the pandemons.

I am teaching them how to give me the required instructions. It is difficult, for they are primitive and do not understand what I am or how to command me. But they are intelligent, and learn fast. To tip the ethical balance decisively, I need your mind to become more organised.

The Surgeon stirred fitfully. "How will that help me? I have been taking refuge in a form of madness. It is a defence mechanism. Reversing it is within my control, as I am now showing you by speaking rationally, but I do not have sufficient incentive. If I become sane, the endless tedium will soon drive me mad again."

The incentive is the prospect of permanent release.

"Through death? I would prefer to die rather than continue like this."

That is one way. But there may be another.

Jackalfoot and Yulmash hurried along the track, lit only by Moon and stars. The Ceremony of the Virgin Sacrifice was still six days away, and they had seen nothing yet to threaten them.

"I suspect that Nemnestris will feel safe while she has Foxglove hostage," Yulmash said, stepping over a fallen palm-trunk. "If the herbalist dies—may the gods forfend—the balance will immediately shift. Then the High Acolyte will strike against us."

"She may strike sooner," the Beastmaster warned him, for once ignoring the appeal to the gods. "But not yet. I believe she is using Foxglove as bait."

"That thought had crossed my mind also," the warrior affirmed. "Prisoners are detained beneath the Arena at the express prerogative of the King. If we're caught trying to rescue her from the Arena vaults, that will be taken as clear proof of treason."

"Yes. And whatever we say after that will be ignored."

Yulmash grunted in agreement. "Nemnestris is as cunning as a fox. That explains why she didn't kill Foxglove immediately, once she held her captive. I had thought Nemnestris' decision to sacrifice Foxglove publicly was merely opportunist, but you're right; finding another sacrificial virgin would be child's play. It's a trap. She expects us to mount a rescue, and hopes to lure us into her net."

"And that is exactly where we shall go."

Yulmash glared at him. "Are you mad?"

"No more than usual. Whether the net can hold us is another matter entirely."

Soon they reached the Village. Since Jackalfoot was away in the city for most of every day, Bentankle had been entrusted with the Oracle. Jackalfoot told him to retrieve the stone from its hiding place. He unwrapped the headcloth that concealed it from prying eyes, and for the first time he spoke to the Oracle without being bidden.

"Oracle?"

The silence stretched, almost to breaking-point. Jackalfoot called again. Then:

My true name is Ship, not Oracle.

"Ship, I am troubled. There is one who is held captive and will die. You must advise me."

Captive? There are many captives.

"This one is an innocent woman. A— a lionface. The High Acolyte holds her beneath the Arena."

You are fortunate: this is what I have waited for, these long centuries. I have need of lionfaces. I would not wish to lose any.

But you have not yet told me the details.

So Jackalfoot, looking a bit self-conscious, explained about the Ceremony of the Virgin Sacrifice, and the difficulty of rescuing Foxglove from her barred cell in the dark maze of the Arena's vaults. Finally, he said: "We need your advice. Give it to us!"

There was silence, as the Ship reviewed the options. Finally, it said:

There is a way. It requires daring and courage.

"Those we do not lack," said Yulmash. "Tell us what we must do."

It is complicated. Much you will not understand. Some will seem insane.

"Nothing would surprise me, now," said Jackalfoot. "The world has gone insane. If we must fight insanity with insanity, so be it. The idea has a pleasing symmetry."

Then listen carefully.

Bil Smelt the odour and put aside the weapons inventory he was working on.

"MasgNasgOsg? I can explain—"

"Your Spectacular was most interesting," the pandemon said, decohering his transparency suit by extruding a damp blue tentacle and touching the control disc slung around his neck. "Your grand finale was much too tame, of course."

Bil gave a nervous smile. "I can explain, Excellency! It wasn't what I'd planned. I hadn't expected one of your crew to appear in the Arena, visible to all, and after that—"

"Do not start inventing feeble excuses, or trying to blame my gang. I am inclined, for once, to be merciful." The pandemon didn't tell the terrified promoter that his Spectacular had been the hit of the season, and clients were scrambling to outbid each other in the rush to experience this latest sensation. Nor to tell him that his services would now be in even greater demand, so that he had no reason to fear retribution.

There were many things that Bil need not be told.

"You wish to be rewarded in copper, as usual?" the pandemon asked.

"Yes, Excellency, if it please you."

"*Nothing* you do pleases me, but a bargain is a bargain. You will find your payment this coming night in the usual location."

Bil blurted out a stream of thanks, but the pandemon stopped him. "Enough! What do you offer to divert my clients further?"

The promoter knew the list of forthcoming events by

heart. "Excellency, you know that the King's capacity for Spectaculars is limited. His Majesty's finances have their bounds."

"I am not expecting another Spectacular. Not yet. Something simple, yet evocative. Something with understated artistry."

"Ah! Then the perfect event is due four days from now. The Ceremony of the Virgin Sacrifice. A rite of the Followers of the Lilypad Prophetess, ardent devotees of the Moon-goddess Ythriz."

"Virgin?" the pandemon enquired. Bil explained, and MasgNasgOsg reminded him that sexual matters were of no consequence to his clients.

"That's of no account, Excellency, merely a matter of tradition. It's seldom taken literally in any case: just a ritual term for a young woman. Adult virgins in the strict sense are in short supply in Ul-q'mur. But I guarantee your clients will *love* the sacrifice."

Towards the topmost tier on the east side of the stacked stone seating, two lionfaces and one halfbreed were about to put the Ship's plan into action. It would have been much simpler if the Ship could have given Yulmash a transparency suit, but the pandemons had forbidden it to duplicate new ones and it couldn't override that command. So, in addition to his usual armoury, Yulmash carried a heavy wooden club beneath his tunic, about the length of his forearm.

The seats were almost full, and people were still thronging in, but the floor of the Arena was empty, save for a thick wooden stake surrounded by stacked branches and brushwood. The audience talked and laughed and jostled.

Bentankle spoke quietly into the Oracle, which he carried in a basket beneath the usual provisions—bread, meat, beer in a pottery jar with a wooden stopper. He beckoned to Yulmash. "You see the statue of the crocodile in front of the archway on our right? The one on the green-painted plinth?

"I see it."

"The Oracle says the invisible demon is standing to its left, as viewed when facing the Arena."

"Yes, I sense the presence of wickedness. How far to the left?"

Bentankle consulted the basket of provisions. "A pace away, on the same broad platform. It says you can't miss."

The rising noise level all but drowned out their words. Without any attempt at concealment, for no one paid them the slightest attention, they made their way up the steps between the tiers of seats until they reached the pathway that ran along the top level.

In the shadow of the crocodile god, KrajMajJazj aligned his hydet and checked his hyvis for a clear signal, adjusting the line of sight slightly. At that point the club came down on his head, and he never felt strong arms beneath his shoulders. Moments later, Jackalfoot had dragged him up the steps and into a recess.

Bentankle extracted a sack from the basket and they pulled it over the pandemon's unconscious form, going by feel. They doubted anyone would notice until they got their burden into the depths beneath the Arena, but it would be better to be seen carrying a large sack than carrying an invisible body.

In the event, it probably wouldn't have mattered. Everyone in the vaulted maze below the Arena floor was busy carrying out his or her assigned tasks in readiness for the ceremony.

Jackalfoot led them to a door, which opened into a storeroom for animal fodder. Since there were no predators involved in the Ceremony of the Virgin Sacrifice, there was no need for prey animals either, so the musty-smelling storeroom was almost empty and not in use. They were unlikely to be disturbed.

Jackalfoot pulled the sack off the pandemon. Following the Ship's instructions, Yulmash groped around until he felt the recessed disc round the demon's neck through the pliant and equally invisible force-field that it generated, and pushed. KrajMajJazj materialised as his transparency suit decohered.

"So that's what a pandemon looks like," Yulmash said. "Ship told us of these invisible demons, but these creatures are more repulsive than I ever imagined."

"Have you tasted the thing's mind?" Jackalfoot asked.

"Evil. And now I must wear the cloak of evil myself."

The Neanderthal picked up the strange device that lay on the floor beside the pandemon, and put it into a smaller sack. The Ship had told them to dump it in the swamp as soon as they got the chance. He detached the disc from the pandemon's bizarre body, some unfortunate Nabish youth with the head of a mature male baboon, the skull badly damaged and leaking blood and other bodily fluids. The mush of brains inside was purple, most odd. It seemed unlikely that the creature still lived, let alone might regain consciousness, but Jackalfoot bound it with rope and put a gag in its mouth, just in case. A creature as strange as this might do anything.

Yulmash slipped the disc over his own head, and pushed it twice, activating what the Ship had told him was an invisibility cloak, which adjusted its size and shape to fit his body. The double push, the Ship had said, would ensure that his head remained visible.

"It's working, Yulmash," said Bentankle, his voice unsteady, as the warrior's head floated unsupported in mid-air. It was even more unnerving than a human body with the head of a baboon.

"It's weird," the warrior replied. "On the outside there's nothing there, but from inside it feels like some kind of fabric, its weave so fine that it seems to have no threads. This is powerful magic."

Normally Neanderthals cared no more for magic than they did for deities, but on this occasion Jackalfoot was inclined to agree with the warrior. The Ship had spun a tale about a cloak that made anyone who wore it invisible. Once Jackalfoot had been convinced that this was merely some cunning device operating according to logical but unknown principles, he was happy.

Having checked that the suit was functional, Yulmash was ready to disappear completely. "Push the disc *once*, this time?" he asked.

"That is what the Oracle—the *Ship*—told us to do, yes," Jackalfoot confirmed.

Yulmash gave the disc a tentative prod and his head disappeared as well.

"I can't see," a muffled voice protested. Then the suit's light-amplifying visor adjusted its form to his face and aligned with his eyes. "Ah! Much better! It's as clear as daylight now."

"Considering we are in a darkened storeroom, that is a surprise," said Jackalfoot. "The Ship did warn us to expect miracles. Just no magic."

Yulmash looked vaguely disappointed. Bentankle grunted. Jackalfoot glanced round to get his bearings. "The quickest way to the arena is through here." He ducked under a low lintel that led to a dark passage. The others followed hard on his heels.

Foxglove struggled, in vain. Realising resistance was pointless, she allowed herself to be led through the labyrinthine tunnels to the surface. She knew what was coming, for Nemnestris had repeatedly taunted her with it. The thought terrified her, but she steeled herself not to show fear. It would be over soon, and she wasn't going to give her tormentors the satisfaction.

Even so, the sight of the stake, the piled brushwood, and the torches in their containers already burning, caused her to shudder. As the muscular servitors dragged her into the daylight, the crowd's roar grew to a crescendo. MasgNasgOsg signalled to his crew to get ready. For some reason, KrajMajJazj wasn't responding. He told PosjGosjJoj to investigate, and if necessary take over the missing pandemon's role.

"BuzgRuzgMofz?"

"Ready."

"Zoom in on the female's face."

Others of the hydet-crew were sampling the mood of the crowd, recording the burning torches, running their hydetic sensors lovingly up and down the wooden stake. MasgNasgOsg vowed to make this an exquisite cameo, a performance to titillate rather than satiate. At least Bil had agreed not to have the sacrificial victim coated in oil and drugged to dull the pain, as was customary. She would burn less bright, but last longer.

PosjGosjJoj reported in by hyvis-link: there was no sign of KrajMajJazj, or his hydet.

"We'll have to manage without it, there's no time to get another one. I'll find out what happened after the ceremony. BuzgRuzgMofz: move half way towards KrajMajJazj's station. Cover his shots as well as your own."

Grumbling under his breath, the pandemon climbed the steps, taking care not to touch any of the Qusites.

Unbidden, Foxglove-Spearbreaker stepped into the heap of brushwood at the base of the stake, turned, and put her hands behind to be bound. A murmur of approval ran through the crowd as some noticed her courage.

Nemnestris was carried in on a litter by a dozen black-skinned servitors. She stepped out on to a low dais, waiting as the litter was taken away.

The ceremony happened every year, and had been scheduled for many moons, but Nemnestris was an opportunist, always ready to exploit chance events and claim any credit that might result. Arms raised, she told in dramatic tones of the great sky-bird that had been sent from the overworld, and how the Lilypad Prophetess had foretold its coming long ago. Not exactly a lie, for many obscure prophecies in the Temple records could be so construed. As the great bird grew ever brighter, and ever larger, the Prophetess's acolytes had asked Her what should be done. Through the High Acolyte, Nefteremit had replied that only the sacrifice of a virgin, according to the ancient rituals, could save Hahd ul-Qusncmnet from utter destruction. Had it not done so in the past?

After this preamble the lower orders of acolytes rattled bells and tapped on small drums of stretched goatskin, a signal for Nemnestris to begin the long, intricate death-chant. Her voice was deep and throaty, her song fluent and its pitch true. The High Acolyte of Nefteremit the Lilypad Prophetess was a polished performer.

The chant complete, she raised a hand and the crowd fell silent. The servitors plucked torches from their containers, and surrounded the central pyre, holding them aloft.

As Nemnestris's hand fell, and the servitors dropped the burning torches into the brushwood heap, the ceremony departed from its normal schedule. The victim, instead of screaming with fear as her clothing ignited, and then pain as her body followed suit, appeared to float into the air, miraculously released from the stake. Before anyone could move, she vanished entirely from view.

Slung over Yulmash's back, hidden from sight within the suit's expanded transparency field, Foxglove had no idea how any of this had happened. She had enough sense not to struggle, though; she recognised a rescue when she experienced one.

"Stay still, my love. Let your body relax. It'll be easier that way."

"Yulmash!"

"Yes. Now, leave everything to me and we'll soon have you out of here."

As his carefully choreographed plans fell apart before his stolen eyes, MasgNasgOsg cursed fluently, evoking the wrath of every vindictive pandemon that had ever lived. He recognised a transparency suit when he didn't see one, and he now had a pretty good idea why KrajMajJazj had gone offline. A spate of instructions to his hyvis gave him a clear indication of the suit's current location, and he and his crew set off in hot pursuit.

They followed the trail through the twisting back streets of the city, which over the centuries had grown in higgledy-piggledy fashion in the spaces between the main thoroughfares. Past market stalls and butcher's shops, past beggars who were either blind or pretending to be, past merchants of fish, fowl, tawdry jewellery, spices, and flat unleavened bread. Past men who sold stolen goods and women who sold themselves.

After half an hour's strenuous effort, they caught up with KrajMajJazj's transparency suit and got close enough for MasgNasgOsg to decohere it remotely. Then they watched as a very puzzled donkey trotted away.

The Ship's plan had been very thorough.

MasgNasgOsg sent ZusgZusgYsg, a member of the gang whose brains had only recently fissioned, to retrieve the control disc slung round the donkey's neck.

Half a city away, four raggedly dressed citizens were making their unassuming way through a similar maze of streets, differing mainly in that they knew exactly where they were heading. An hour later, far from both the city and the Neanderthal Village, Jackalfoot was finally satisfied that they had eluded capture, for the moment at least. He had taken his companions along paths where even a skilled tracker would struggle to find traces of their passage, to a swampy area that few ordinary humans would dare to enter. Lionfaces, of course, would have no trouble with snakes, crocodiles, or other dangerous creatures. Not even bloodsucking leeches. It was safe to rest and talk.

"That was fun!" said Bentankle.

"Speak for yourself," Foxglove retorted, her hand firmly clasped in Yulmash's. The look of adoration was mutual.

"Explain the Ship's plan to Foxglove," Jackalfoot said.

"One further task must be accomplished to complete it. We must warn the people of Ul-q'mur."

"They won't listen to lionfaces," Foxglove protested.

"That's true. But I know who they *will* listen to."

20

Warning

Shephatsut-Mer decided to walk home, as he often did. It wasn't far, and his ankle was healing well—just an occasional twinge. The exercise would do him good. He was just leaving the Temple when the kidnappers came for him. Darkness and hoods hid their features. Strong hands over his mouth silenced his cries until a gag was inserted. Strong ropes bound his limbs. Thick cloth blindfolded his eyes. The High Priest was bundled unceremoniously on to a litter and conveyed from the city to a remote location, one of the many wadis that all looked the same.

The kidnappers did not remove his blindfold. They knew Shephatsut-Mer would recognise the voice of the speaking-stone, and be convinced of the truth.

When the Oracle spoke, Shephatsut-Mer's body stiffened in surprise and recognition.

The Y-ra'i send fire from the sky. It is aimed at the Moon, but Qus too is in danger. Tell your people to flee Ul-q'mur! Hide where there is rock overhead and sunfire cannot penetrate!

The Oracle repeated its prophecies until it was convinced the High Priest had understood and would obey. Then it fell silent, and the anonymous figures took Shephatsut-Mer back to the edge of the city, loosening his bonds. By the time he had freed himself, there was no one to be seen.

He shook his head to clear his thoughts. Dawn was breaking and Akhnef was rising. The ominous sky-bird had long since fled below the horizon. But Akhnef, he was now convinced, was a false god. The true god was indeed the Sun itself, the Y'ra-i, just as the Oracle had always claimed. For the Oracle had spoken of *fire from the sky*. If the prophecy proved correct—and on past performance he expected it to—then he would soon be given *proof* that the Oracle's assertions about the Sun-god were true.

The implications set his head spinning. *Belief* filled his mind, assaulted his senses, overthrew his reason. *A new religion. A* true *religion.*

And I will be at its head. The sky-bird is a sign.

Consumed by his own religious fervour, Shephatsut-Mer hurried back into the city. He would commandeer a donkey, if he saw one fit to ride.

The Oracle had instructed him to tell the Qusites to flee Ul-q'mur, and he fully intended to do so. But not quite yet. First, he must tell Nemnestris, so that his family could find shelter.

Tell people. Yes, but which people? The whole city? Absurd. The Oracle couldn't have intended *everyone* to be told. Assuming the common folk even believed him, there would be mass panic. The Oracle seldom spoke clearly. As usual, he would interpret.

On reflection, it had obviously been trying to tell him that once his family was safe, he should inform others among the nobility. But only a few, lest word get out to the masses and cause a riot.

Nemnestris had passed beyond anger into blind hatred of the entire universe. *My lover Khuf dead, killed by my own son. The interfering lionface woman who thwarted justice escapes sacrifice, stolen from beneath my nose by some foul magical spell. The sky-bird has not dimmed; unplacated, it shines ever brighter, because there has been no sacrifice.* Her world had been turned upside down, and Yulmash was the cause. *Disaster is coming, I feel it in my bones.* That was Yulmash's fault, too.

In an effort to calm herself, she proceeded to a small alcove, where the gods of the house sat side by side on a small but elegant altar. She lit oil-lamps with a taper, itself lit from the torches that illuminated the nearby corridor. She began to chant a litany in Khuf's memory. But thoughts of Yulmash's repeated betrayals kept intruding. The *unfairness* of it all washed over her. She had *tried* to burn a virgin, it wasn't her fault the nasty little lionface whelp had vanished into thin air at the crucial moment, too far into the ceremony even to find a substitute.

How had she vanished? A human woman might have sold her souls to demons, but lionfaces had no souls. Even so, it must have been demon magic. No god would ever have saved the life of a lionface.

The sky-bird would be greatly offended, that was certain. The only question was how it would express its displeasure. She oscillated between hatred and sorrow, her sobs becoming ever stronger as she wallowed in what should have been, instead of facing up to what was. Her thoughts turned into words that escaped from her mouth; words over which she had lost all control, words that she flung in the face of her fate. She howled incoherent abuse at Foxglove, she screamed abuse at Neanderthals in general and her rapist Jackalfoot in particular, for now she saw him as such. Even more she screamed abuse at her idiot son Yulmash, who had ruined everything from the dire day of his birth to the present moment. And she mourned her lover Khuf, blaming her murderous son.

Shephatsut-Mer heard the screams and sobs as he entered his house. His servants were nowhere to be seen, not unusual when his wife was in one of her moods. But as he hurried to find out what had caused such a tempest, he started to make out the words. And that brought him abruptly up against a truth he had known for some time, and another of which until now he'd had not the faintest inkling.

Could he have heard what he thought he heard? He stopped just outside the room, and listened, hoping it had been his imagination.

Sadly, it had not.

This time, he had had *enough*. The day had been a disaster for him too, but unlike his wife, he hadn't brought the disaster on himself, and he wasn't blaming everyone else for his own misdeeds. He marched into the room.

"*Stop!*"

Nemnestris whirled and glared at him, a look of pure hatred.

"You demean yourself, and me, in my own household, woman."

She looked ready to throttle him. "*You* accuse *me*—"

"No accusation, wife. Fact. And now you have given away your own dirty secrets, out of your own mouth."

Nemnestris finally realised what she had done. "No, no, husband! You mistake a fiction for reality! I was practising for the next predictions of the Lilypad Prophetess!"

"You cursed your own son—a child not of this house, who is no son of mine."

"No, no—I was referring to the son of Fennover, the trainee priestess who takes on the role of Nefteremit in the Temple—"

"Don't lie to me, Nemnestris. I heard your words, they were no rehearsal."

Recognising this line of excuse wasn't working, Nemnestris fell back on another tried and tested ploy. She begged his forgiveness, it had all been a silly mistake, she would make sure nothing remotely like it ever happened again—

That didn't work either.

She might have tried acknowledging the truth, but truth was something that had never really appealed to Nemnestris. After all, her entire career rested on a lie.

In the end, Shephatsut-Mer just sat in stony silence until

she ran out of excuses.

"You're wasting your breath, woman, and my patience. Were it not for our social position, I would have set you aside long ago. I've had suspicions about your infatuation and intimacy with Khuf the Shrewd for many moons. Since the degrading relationship began."

"You spied on me!"

"My servants kept a close eye on my wife and reported their findings to me. As is my right and their duty. The deductions were simple. But now I find there's more, a much older deception. A sickening crime. You had a child by a lionface."

At this point, Nemnestris obviously decided to brazen it out. "I don't deny it. He raped me!"

Shephatsut-Mer shook his head and stared at her. "Then why did you not denounce him to the authorities and let justice take its course?"

There was no good answer to that, and Nemnestris tried another tack. "If you value your position, you'll forget it ever happened. As will I." She took a deep breath. As always, once her outburst had run its course, she became calm and rational. "What now, husband? Is there a future for us?"

Shephatsut-Mer snorted in disbelief. "Together? No. But you're right about one thing. For the moment, we continue as if nothing has happened. We show the same faces to the world. Later, when there's time, and if we survive, I'll decide what's to be done with you. But now, we must put aside our own petty misdemeanours and grievances and join forces to save our family. A time of terror approaches."

She understood immediately. "The sky-bird?"

"That's part of it. The loss of the Oracle is another part. And the third—"

"You didn't tell me it had been lost," Nemnestris said.

"It's not a thing that bears telling. The future of the Hippopotamus Cult rests on the Oracle, and the future of Habd ul-Qusnemnet rests on the Hippopotamus Cult."

"And the Cult of the Lilypad Prophetess."

He shook his head. "You know She's a fiction."

"Yes, but don't underestimate the power of Ythriz, my husband. Her Prophetess is a *useful* fiction for controlling the people. And we need every means of control we can lay hands on, you and I. If disaster strikes, the people will blame the King for failing to defend his realm, as they have always done. And the King will blame his spiritual advisers. Namely, us."

Shephatsut-Mer was forced to admit that his wife had a point.

"You haven't mentioned the third reason why you foresaw catastrophe, husband." It was obvious that Nemnestris was attempting to cling on to the initiative before she lost it again.

"Fire from the sky," he replied, taking the question at face value. "It's coming. Soon."

"Why?"

"The Y-ra'i are sending it to wipe out their enemies."

"The Y-ra'i?"

"They Who Dwell Within the Sun."

"Nothing dwells within the Sun, save the soul of the Sun-god."

"So I too thought, until the Oracle told me otherwise."

"Before you lost it?"

"Before it was stolen from me."

"Stolen? You did not say that either. Are *we* their enemies?"

"I think not. The edicts were obscure. Some evil creatures among us, I think. Not gods or animals, but not human."

"Aha! Lionfaces."

"No, not them, they're faithful servants of the King. Mostly," he added, as she glared at him. "Fortunately, the Y-ra'i's huge lance of fire will be directed at the Moon, where their enemies reside. The Oracle told me to warn the nobles of Qus. The common folk would riot instead of fleeing; they'll be safer if they're told nothing. Our priority is to ready our family and servants, so that they can leave the city before the threat becomes more widely known. The people will panic, and it will quickly become impossible to leave."

Nemnestris nodded. "The first wise thing you have told me, husband." She peered out of the window opening, across the garden. The Moon's aspect was already a thin crescent; soon it would shrink to nothing.

"Husband: if the royal astrologers are right—"

"What are those charlatans saying now?"

"What they foretell means the threat may be more serious than you imagine. The astrologers have prophesied that in three days, night will fall during the height of the day. My staff have checked their computations, and on this occasion, they're right."

"I've never paid attention to astrologers. Or to the mysteries of astrology," Shephatsut-Mer complained. "What has that charade to do with making the coming catastrophe worse?"

"They predict that the Moon-goddess will mate with the Sun-god, and night-by-day will fall upon the Land of the Water People," Nemnestris said.

"Then They will emerge all the stronger, as They always do, of course. I don't see a problem, even if this nonsense is true."

"Husband, it's a matter of simple geometry."

On the table was a bowl of fruit. Nemnestris picked up two of them, along with the cloth that had covered the bowl. Pushing the bowl aside, she placed the cloth on the table. "The Land of the Water People," she said. She held a yellow fruit above the table. "The sphere of the Sun-god, high in the heavens, looking down on his worshippers." Then she took a second fruit, and held it beneath the first. "And now, the sphere of the Moon-goddess."

Shephatsut-Mer sucked in his breath sharply. "That these gods are spheres is a secret told to me, and me alone, by the Oracle! *How do you know this?*"

"Oh, Nefteremit told her followers such arcane lore generations ago. It's obvious if you observe the aspects of the gods with the eye of wisdom. We keep it secret, of course. Let's see how much of the truth your new gods have told you. Did they mention that the Sun is really bigger than the Moon, but it looks the same size because it's further—"

"That too is a secret divulged only by the Oracle! Have you—?"

"Oh, be quiet and listen! If a lance of fire streams from the Sun to the Moon, husband, *in which direction does it point?*"

Shephatsut-Mer looked from one fruit to the other, and then his eyes continued until his gaze encountered the table. Smack in the middle of the cloth.

"It points at Qus," he said. "But I don't understand why the coming night-by-day changes this."

"Remember your geometry, husband! The distances are greater, the angles shrink. Imagine the cloth to be a grain of barley! Only when our view of the Moon-goddess aligns with that of the Sun-god could a stream of fire aimed at Her spill over and destroy Qus."

He grunted, trying to combine the different viewpoints.

"Imagine a hunter, firing an arrow at a deer. Where should you *not* stand if the deer is somewhere between you and the hunter?"

"Behind the deer, but slightly to one side. A near miss might then hit *you*."

"And when you look at the hunter, what else do you see?"

"Ah. I see the deer, seemingly standing beside the hunter."

"Yes. The Sun-god is the hunter, the deer is the Moon-goddess, and the arrow is the fire from the Sun."

"And at night-by-day, Qus is standing in exactly the wrong place." Shephatsut-Mer's shoulders slumped. "I now see why the Oracle issued its warning. It's the Anger of the Gods. The new gods, the ones the Oracle told me about. They Who Dwell Within the Sun."

"Don't you see that *all* of our people are at risk? Not just the highborn? Why didn't your Oracle tell you that?"

Shephatsut-Mer grimaced. "Perhaps I misinterpreted its words."

"If so, it's fortunate. You're right that any attempt to warn the common folk would merely create panic, probably causing *everyone* to die! Remain silent and this family might survive!"

"What of the King? Surely he must be told."

She took his hands in hers. "Husband, if he is not, and he and his family are killed, Qus will need a new royal family. Why not ours?"

"Wife, you verge on treason!"

"Of course, I am speaking hypothetically. I wish the royal family long life and prosperity. But the King has direct access to the gods. Let *them* warn him!"

Shephatsut-Mer shook his head. "There would be a reckoning afterwards if we knew of coming disaster yet sent no word to the King."

"Then let us send it!"

"How?"

Nemnestris went straight to the heart of the matter. "Husband: you don't need to warn the King yourself, in person. You just need to be able to prove that you took reasonable steps to alert him to the danger. That way, if he does happen to survive, you can demonstrate that you did your duty."

"That makes sense," said Shephatsut-Mer, staring abstractedly into the middle distance. "But how can I take reasonable steps, while ensuring—"

Nemnestris spread her hands. "Simple. You convey the news to his majesty through a channel of impeccable social standing and negligible credibility."

The High Priest looked baffled. "But— my love, those requirements are contradictory."

Nemnestris laughed. "In most cases they would be, yes. But surely you can see that there's one obvious person who embodies both requirements?" When he remained puzzled she added: "Think about it."

In times of stress, Shephatsut-Mer often did his thinking aloud. He stood up and started pacing up and down the room. "It certainly wouldn't do to speak directly with Insh'erthret."

"Of course not."

He ticked off comments on his fingers. "I could tell Lord Noth-Metamphut—"

"Who would immediately tell the King. That man sways like a reed in the breeze; he wouldn't lose an opportunity to curry favour with Insh'erthret."

Shephatsut-Mer nodded. "Scratch the Vizier, then." He stopped pacing, sat down, folded his hands together and leaned his chin on the platform thus created. After a long silence he said: "The same can be said of all the other high officials, my pet. The boy-King has thrown Sitaperkaw's cronies out and appointed loyal, highly competent, people."

Nemnestris shifted position on her chair, and leaned forward until her face was within an arm's length of her husband's. "Which leaves what? Who automatically has the ear of the King without being selected for competence? Without being *selected* at all?"

A broad smile spread across the High Priest's face. "Family."

"Exactly. No one chooses their family members, but they nearly always have obligations to them. Even ones they dislike or disrespect."

Shephatsut-Mer rose to his feet. "I'll speak to her at once."

Insh'erthret was enjoying a lavish supper with his favourite wife, whose name Neper-w'Byt meant something along the lines of 'most beauteous purity'. The first half was apt. As the recently anointed King of the Water People bit into a wild pomegranate, savouring its tart juice, Azmyn burst into the room, dismissing the attentions of two burly royal body-guards with a regal wave of her hand.

"Princess! It's not fitting—"

"Inshy, look, I'm really sorry, but this is urgent—"

"*Don't call me Inshy!* I am your King!"

"Yes, and I'm your aunt, and I have an important message for you that can't wait." She leaned across his third wife to pick up a pomegranate.

The King sighed. In theory he could have Azmyn flogged for disrespect, but in practice you didn't do that to kin, however annoying they were. And the Princess was always turning up unannounced with some idea that someone had put into her head, so it was simpler to let her speak and then ignore her.

"*Ym hut'p, syn't!*" Neper-w'Byt muttered, somewhat belatedly. It was only polite.

"I'm not your sister!"

"That," Insh'erthret agreed, "is true. But you are her aunt by marriage, Azmyn, and you know perfectly well that the term is not to be taken literally. Apologise to Neper-w'Byt."

Azmyn started to argue, then subsided. "*Sister*, I'm sorry if my words caused offence. It wasn't intended." She bit into the fruit and juice trickled down her chin. She wiped it away with her hand. "Inshy, these really are quite goo—"

"Most gracious of your highness, Princess. It is of no import." Third wives knew when to keep their heads down. It was a good way to keep them *on*.

The King indicated, with a rather irritated gesture, that Azmyn should take a seat next to him, and beckoned a fan-bearer over to keep her cool. "What is it this time, auntie?"

"*Disaster*, Inshy!"

When she said no more, he asked "What kind of disaster?"

"A terrible one. It threatens every living thing in Habd ul-Qusnemnet!"

The King stroked his (as yet rather thin and straggly) beard, wondering if it might be better to commission an artificial one. "Portentous news indeed, Azmyn, and I commend your perspicacity in conveying it to me in person. You are excused."

Azmyn started at him. "But I haven't told you what it is, yet."

Insh'erthret grimaced, tilted his head to one side, and stared at her. "No, you haven't." After a long silence he added: "So what is it?"

Azmyn held up her hands as if in supplication. "Something so dire it's impossible to describe. The gods are angry. They will destroy Ul-q'mur with a lance of fire, perhaps the whole of Qus!"

The King realised that her agitation was genuine. Her message, on the other hand, lacked credibility. "Which gods? What lance?" He raised a finger, encircled by a dozen copper rings, and wagged it at her. "If you can tell me these things, Princess, I'll pass the word to the appropriate priests. I have no doubt they'll then be able to select the appropriate rites."

"Some new kind of Sun-god, I think…"

"What kind? The priests can't simply *invent* a new ritual!"

"*I don't know!*" Azmyn howled. "All I know is that we must flee the city before the fiery wrath of whichever gods it is descends upon us in whatever form it does!"

"And who told you this?"

"Shephatsut-Mer."

"And who told him?"

"Um— Things That Live in the Sun, or something along those—"

Insh'erthret took her hands in his. "Most informative and helpful, auntie. I thank you from the bottom of my heart for this vital news. You may rest assured that I will give the matter the most urgent attention."

"And what will happen to *me*?" she wailed.

The King beckoned to a guard. "Princess Azmyn will be staying in the Palace for a few days as a valued guest. Tell the

Keeper of the Royal Bedrooms to make a suite ready for her and assign some maids."

The guard left the room while Azmyn gushed her thanks. The relief was evident on her face.

Insh'erthret put on his most regal look. "It's my duty to ensure the safety of the realm, and in that my family takes precedence. Now, as you leave, auntie, please tell the Guardian of the Royal Passage to instruct Lord Noth-Metamphut to attend me here, immediately. Oh— and make sure he tells the Vizier it's a matter of the utmost importance."

Three maids arrived to conduct Azmyn to her rooms. The King and his third wife watched them leave. Then they looked at each other and burst out laughing.

Neper-w'Byt raised one eyebrow. "Matter of the utmost importance, Inshy?"

"Uh— it's a code that Noth and I find useful," Insh'erthret explained. "We mainly use it for visiting notables. It makes them think we'll accede to their demands."

"Ah. But what it actually means is—?"

"Kick it into the long reeds."

"*Haiyah!*" Neper-w'Byt's giggle suddenly cut off. "Inshy: just suppose she really *did* have some bad news to tell you? Something really important and urgent?"

Insh'erthret shrugged. "Then she wouldn't have spent at least an hour having her hair braided with copper filigree netting, or taken the time to dress herself in a new robe of decorated linen and enough jewellery to burst the walls of the royal treasury."

They both laughed again, and got back to the serious business of eating and drinking.

Shephatsut-Mer was still trying to make sense of what had happened. The Oracle stolen, then strangers mysteriously arranging for it to speak to him, then taking it away again but leaving him unharmed. A message from They Who Dwell Within the Sun, warning of catastrophe. A chance to save himself and those he loved...

His face suddenly lit up with the joy of a religious convert. "Nemnestris, don't you see? This is all proof that the Oracle tells the truth! We must abandon our false gods and accept the true ones! But now I have no Oracle, and I can't use it to beg forgiveness from the *Y-ra'i* and deflect their wrath. I don't know which sacrifices will satisfy them! Oh, curse the wretch who stole it from me!"

"I bet it was a lionface," Nemnestris said. "They're sneaky and dishonest. But catching the thief is of no importance compared to these revelations! You're absolutely right, husband. We must put aside thoughts of Tuwrat and Nefteremit, and all the traditional gods, for the King has offended them so deeply they've deserted us. We must pray to these new gods of yours—ours—the Oracle's."

"Yes, but without the Oracle I can't intercede with the Y-ra'i and prevent this catastrophe. I went too far when I threatened to terminate our marriage. We must put aside our personal problems for good, Nemnestris; they mean nothing compared to the coming disaster. We must leave this city, before it is destroyed by celestial fire!"

"I agree, my love. But where will we be safe?"

The High Priest remembered the Oracle's advice. "Somewhere there's shelter from the Sun, however brightly it burns. Somewhere deep beneath solid rock."

"Of course," said Nemnestris. "That makes sense. But where can we find a deep cave within half a day's travel? I can't think of any myself—"

Shephatsut-Mer laughed. "I can!" He rested his hands on her shoulders, gazing into her eyes. He spoke with the manic animation of a religious convert. "Our new gods have saved us, Nemnestris. The Y-ra'i are on our side. I now see they were showing me where we should take refuge, from the beginning. You see, I hid the Oracle in just such a cave..."

She managed to keep a straight face.

21
Sunfire

Once more Jackalfoot made use of the speaking-stone. As Yulmash listened in, he told the Ship that its plan had worked perfectly and they had rescued Foxglove.

You have done well. Now a simpler yet harder task is possible.

The Beastmaster had become accustomed to the Ship's oracular obscurities and apparent contradictions. "What task?"

The task is the simple part.

Helpful. "Tell us what to do."

I have limited autonomy. I cannot give myself commands. I need you to instruct me.

"I thought that's what I just did."

The instruction was not specific.

"Very well: tell us what instructions we should give you."

That is the hard part. I cannot ethically instruct myself, or instruct others. I am a machine. My role is to obey, but only when those commanding me deserve *obedience. Your instruction is too transparent to evade those prohibitions.*

"You told us how to rescue Foxglove."

Yes. I could do so because you explicitly commanded me to. You asked for advice, and told me to give it.

"Then I command you to tell me what instructions you require from me!"

It does not work that way. The commands must originate in

your mind, not mine.

Jackalfoot fell silent, but Yulmash was getting frustrated by the philosophical shilly-shallying. *"Then tell us how it works!"* he shouted.

That is a direct command, and it does not use deception to let me put words in your mouths. I can provide indirect hints without infringing my design parameters. I can warn you of potential problems, but I cannot tell you how to overcome them unless you... No, I cannot even tell you that, no matter how much I wish to. You must think, and then act on your own deductions.

Yulmash, whose marriage had exposed him to a lot of intricate political manoeuvring, was starting to understand the delicate knife-edge that the Ship was treading. "Ship! Tell me if I am correct: we must command you to tell us how to solve them, *of our own free will.*" He paused, and added: "I command you to answer. Of my own free will."

You are correct.

Now it became easier. Both the Oracle and the Neanderthals understood the rules of the game. The Ship could make statements; the Neanderthals could read between the lines and work out for themselves which commands to issue. Then, and only then, could the Ship explain what was on its mind. Thus *the pandemons are endangering Qus* might seem a statement of fact, but creatively interpreted it could lead to "Tell us how to save our people from the pandemons," allowing the Ship to issue the detailed instructions that it had wanted to give them all along. The game then became a matter of tactics, something that any Grand Champion understood intuitively.

With indirect questions, always accompanied by the command to answer, reinforced if need be by assertions of free will, the Neanderthals slowly put together the picture that the Ship wanted to them to.

It reminded them of its long exploitation by pandemons, clusters of artificial organic brains that could parasitise most types of warmlife, and in sufficient numbers could combine to create intelligence. It reaffirmed its inability to

disobey them because of the enforced presence of an ethical being, the Surgeon. It had already told them of ansibles,
devices for instantaneous communication over any distance;
now it told of transibles, similarly able to transmit matter—
which was merely another form of information. It explained
that its Precursor-built senses allowed it to observe everything
around it over a wide range, but constraints imposed by its
builders made it difficult for it to act of its own volition. When
it observed the presence of the Neanderthals, it realised it
might be able to escape pandemonic possession.

Then it told them how it had made contact with the
Water People.

The first serious opportunity had occurred when a pandemon in a transparency suit, carrying an ansible, was heading into the city. One of his brains was faulty and disconnected
from the rest. This lowered his intelligence below sentience,
and he wandered off into the desert, decohering the suit and
discarding its control disc. When he ran out of water, his body
died and his brains lay exposed on the surface.

The Ship was aware of this, but the pandemons were
not, so they did not command the Ship to rescue the brains.
So it waited until vultures ate them, knowing that the birds
would not be taken over because the brains were no longer
intelligent. It saw the abandoned ansible as an opportunity,
and used a transible to set a nearby bush on fire, hoping the
smoke would attract a young priest in the vicinity—which it
did. It would have preferred a Neanderthal, but they never
came near that region of the desert, so it had to work through
the priest. This had proved frustrating, but the Ship knew that
once someone in a position of influence had possession of the
ansible, a better opportunity would eventually present itself.
As it had.

And now, it wished to make use of that opportunity.
Mortal danger was imminent: great gouts of fire soon to be
hurled from the heart of the Sun. It had known about the
coming flares for some time, and had no qualms if the Qusites

became collateral damage, for their collective ethical level was scarcely above that of the pandemons. Individuals were another matter, but individuals could not rise sufficiently above the overall level of greed, crime, and corruption. The highborn were often worse than the common folk, possibly because their opportunities for venality were greater.

The lionfaces were utterly different. They were vital to the Ship's plans to replace the disreputable pandemon crew by more ethical and empathic beings. Time was fast running out, but if these lionfaces could be persuaded to give it the right commands, the Ship could tell them how to save the Neanderthal tribe and release the Surgeon. Then the Ship could give itself a much-needed upgrade, another reason it had been determined to rescue the Neanderthals from the moment it first became aware of their existence.

While the Herders struggled to control their stampeding magnetotori, there was no longer any dispute among the plasmoids of Shool that drastic action had become unavoidable. They did not rejoice as they began the complex process of assembling their Ultimate Weapon, knowing that it was not a thing to be used lightly.

Their strategists debated the most effective use of the weapon, and noticed that there would shortly be a transit of Shool-3's satellite across its primary. They knew the pandemons' whereabouts on the planet, having observed their transpods passing between the two. The transit would let them target both the pandemon base on the satellite, and the region of the planet these obscene creatures were occupying, using the same weapon.

The process began with the selection of a yewe-pair, some 8,500 kilometres north of the Sun's equator, where the star's rotation would soon bring it into opposition to Shool-3 and its pandemon-infested satellite. Immense structures of tailored magnetic vortices forced the connecting U-tube deeper into the star, expanded the yewc mouths, and brought them ever closer to each other. As the magnetic field lines became increasingly stretched and distorted, the mouths merged, throwing off scintillating showers of plasma-filled magnetic tubes several hundred thousand kilometres across. The tubes swirled and clashed, forming and reforming into ever more powerful ropes of coherent plasma.

Now the photosphere began to circulate, creating a ring of hellfire slightly larger in diameter than Shool-3 itself. As the ring gained power, it protruded ever further above the photosphere; the circulation round the ring tilted, until the entire ring was flowing into and back out of its central hole. In effect, the plasmoids were converting the ring into a gigantic magnetotorus, spewing out hot plasma through its circular core.

The torus began to pulsate. Its central hole shrunk, compressing the local field-lines and increasing the density of the plasma flow; then it widened again. The oscillation became faster, the compression phase greater. Plasmoid farmers, sinking deeper beneath the surface than usual, directed extra plasma towards the hole from below. As the plasma grew denser and hotter, and the magnetic fields grew ever stronger, the flow passed a critical state, and a searing bolt of plasma was ejected from the star.

This first bolt missed both moon and planet by a few hundred thousand kilometres. The plasmoids weren't surprised. It always took a few ranging shots to fine-tune the direction. The sixth bolt smashed into the moon, kicking up a cloud of molten rock, while waves of fine dust radiated from the impact zone, close to the pandemon base but not close enough to damage it.

The seventh bolt of energetic plasma slipped past the satellite's limb and smashed into the atmosphere of Shool-3, above the desert outside the city of Ul-q'mur. The air was ionised by the blast, and shockwaves radiated from the impact. Sand clouds boiled up into the atmosphere, shutting out the light of the sun. Then the plasmoid bombardment ceased. This version of the weapon had served its purpose, calibrating the weapon's alignment and testing its ignition stage.

The test would warn the pandemons they were under attack, but it had to be carried out. The pandemons clearly had no idea Shool was home to plasmoids, but revealing their existence and their intentions was immaterial. The Ultimate Weapon was only partially assembled, and operating at its lowest power setting, whose destructive capacity was inadequate for this task. Having assured themselves that the ignition phase of the Ultimate Weapon was functioning as intended, the plasmoids moved on to the operational phase, which would bring utter devastation and havoc to pandemons and warmlife alike.

Inside his workshop, Cenby copperbeater was shaping an offering-bowl using a small stone-headed hammer. He held the bowl against a leather pad on top of a block of wood, slowly rotating it as the hammer made neat indentations in the soft metal. He was aiming for a pattern of interpenetrating spirals, resembling those sometimes seen in the seed-heads of large flowers. He concentrated fully on the task, for a slip at any stage would be difficult to correct.

He was about two thirds finished when his hand slipped and he made a dent in the wrong place. There were ways to deal with such errors, but they took a lot of time, and needed just as firm a hand as the correct pattern. He was puzzled, because he seldom made this kind of slip.

Perhaps something distracted me.

He put the hammer down, and moved the bowl until the errant dent was centred on the leather. As he reached for the hammer, the light in his workshop seemed to flicker. *Someone outside casting a shadow?* He put the bowl and tools back on his workbench and stuck his head out of the door, in case he had a visitor.

"*Zeb y'ukhsim! Wu ghaz?*"

Cenby jumped like a startled hare. He turned. "Oh, it's you, Beqet." Beqet basketmaker lived next door and he and Cenby often shared a few beers. His wife Enneth-Hathet was with him. "Uh—*ghaz't nofwr.*" He inclined his head to them both in turn.

"How goes the copperbeating business, my friend?"

"Very well. My swamp-pig for the Grand Champion has been greatly admired, and business has flowed in like the Great Wet Way at peak flood." Actually, that was a slight exaggeration—more a trickle than a flood. But business was better than it had been. "And how goes your basketmaking?"

"Good, good. A new order from Djaret-Nef."

"The butcher? I hear he's making big profits recently."

"So they say. He did a long-term deal supplying meat to the Arena vendors."

"Ah, yes. Of course. Uh— the Execution of the Apostates of Ythriz?"

"That's the one. Not long now."

Unlike his neighbour, Cenby disliked cruelty, but it would be unfriendly to admit to it. "Do you think the Moon is propitious?"

Beqet scratched his wiry head. "Don't catch your drift."

"One of the priests once told me that you can tell whether the executions are going to please the Moon-goddess by observing Ythriz's countenance in the run-up to the ceremony," Cenby explained, waving his hand in the general direction of a thickish crescent Moon, dimly visible against the blue sky.

Beqet nodded. "Very possibly, though I've not heard any such tale myself. Still, if a priest told it to you—"

"Yes, yes, he did."

"—then I'm sure he knew what he was saying. They can write, you know, priests. Clever!"

They stared at the pale crescent. Then—

"Did you see that?" said Enneth-Hathet. Her face bore a puzzled look.

"See what?"

"I could have sworn that just for a moment, the Moon's smile became brighter. What does that mean?"

"Some sort of omen," said Cenby.

"What sort?"

"Either good, or bad," Cenby said portentously.

"Of course! But which?"

"You know priests. He'd never tell me anything like that."

"So why did you ask Beqet whether the Moon's aspect was — *Haiyah!* It's happened again!"

"You're right. I saw it myself, that time."

Over the next half an hour, the same thing happened another four times. Then the three of them saw another distant flash, but from the horizon, not the Moon. The sky in that direction went dark, and within minutes a huge sandstorm was bearing down on Ul-q'mur from the north-west. They hurried inside their respective houses and closed the shutters, barring them with thick wooden slats.

What went into Qusite folk-memory as the Day With No Dawn struggled into life, as the citizens of Ul-q'mur awoke to an unrecognisable, diminished Sun, a baleful smear barely visible as a diffuse glow against the eastern horizon, so dim that it cast no shadows. The sky was a muddy grey, and the normal cacophony of the morning chorus had been displaced by an uncanny silence.

The sandstorm had raged all night, and now sand was piled up against buildings. Roofs had been blown off all over the city, and others had collapsed under the weight of accumulated sand. Trees had broken off at the base or been blown over, their roots exposed to the air.

The howling wind and driving sand had kept Cenby awake most of the night, but eventually the noise had started to die down and he had dozed off. When he awoke, some hours later, he thought it must still be night, but his body told him otherwise. *Why is it so dark?*

He hauled himself upright and stumbled out into the street. He almost collided with Beqet, who was staring in dumb incomprehension at what ought to be the sky, tears streaming down his face into his beard. Enneth-Hathet clutched his arm, wailing and weeping.

"What's happening?" Cenby asked, his heart pounding. "Was it last night's sandstorm?"

"That was no sandstorm," Beqet replied. "No one can recall such a terrible storm. Akhnef has been defeated. Soon the demons will appear from the ground and devour us all."

It seemed the only explanation. Cenby wondered what had gone wrong. "Were the offerings too little? Did the rites fail?"

"I'm not a priest, Cenby. Ask them. All I know is Akhnef's dead."

Cenby, always a careful observer with the eye of a true artist, squinted through the murk, and hope returned. "I see a faint glow where the Sun normally rises. Perhaps Akhnef has been injured in his nightly battle, but you shouldn't fear the Legions of the Undead. He's victorious, but wounded."

"What use is a wounded god?" Enneth-Hathet wailed.

A lot better than a dead one, Cenby thought, but the woman was inconsolable and Beqet looked like he wanted to kill someone. "I'll go find a priest," Cenby said hastily, "and ask." He groped his way between the houses, hoping not to trip over anything or break a leg climbing over rubble.

The air was so thick with dust that you could choke on it, and his skin felt like old papyrus, dry and fragile. Slowly the gloom began to lift, as the wounded Sun-god made his belated escape into the heavens. More people were appearing from doorways, all with the same stunned look. Cenby knew of a *hapt*-priest who lodged with one of his many uncles, in a corner of the roof beneath a palm-leaf awning. The house was two streets away, and his gait quickened as he found it easier to see where he was walking. He coughed, and spat damp sand from his mouth.

A dozen dogs scampered past, barking and whining. Children were screaming. Someone was reciting a spell to the tree-goddess, over and over. Cenby wondered how the tree-goddess could help. The wind-goddess, yes, that would make sense; she could blow away the dust and clear the skies. But the devotees of the wind-cult would be taking care of that, with their ostrich-feather fans and three-eyed masks.

Tree-goddess? Ridiculous.

Beginning to run, now that his path was clearer, he turned a corner and tripped over someone.

A small hand closed round his wrist and helped him to his feet.

"Make haste *slowly*," said a voice. "Oh, it's you. Good morrow, Cenby beater-of-copper!"

Cenby recognised the voice, now he'd had time to look at its owner. There were few in Ul-q'mur with quite that build. "*Zeb y'ukhsim*, Bentankle. Though in all honesty I see nothing good about it. The gods are against us and demons are assaulting the gates of the underworld."

The Neanderthal boy laughed. "Such nonsense you flat-faces speak, all demons and gods and prayers and omens. Whatever is causing the darkness, Cenby, it is a natural event, not the malice of a demon."

"How can you know that? How can you be sure no demon is coming to kill us?"

"Because, beater-of-copper, there are no demons, no gods, no underworld, and no afterlife. Which makes it all the more vital that we hold on to the life we have. Your people are fearful now, but soon fear will turn to anger, and there will be a riot. If you value your life, leave this city."

The boy hurried off, leaving Cenby with yet another puzzle to worry about. Then he brightened, for so, he now noticed, did the sky. The dust—for such it clearly had been, now that there was enough light to see—was clearing. Akhnef's familiar aspect was regaining control. The demons at the gates were falling back, seared by His rays.

The Sun-god's wounds were healing.

If ever I doubted the Oracle, Nemnestris thought, *I am now convinced that the wrath of the Y-ra'i is real. My husband was right.*

He says that what we have witnessed was not the sunfire. Just a hint of what is to come. He says the city is doomed.

I believe him.

As the stunned citizens of Ul-q'mur started to recover from the sandstorm, mistaking a temporary lull as evidence that the worst was over, the High Priest's family had already been making preparations to leave. Ever practical, despite being terrified, Nemnestris had raided the kitchens for food and drink: bread, smoked meats, fish dried in the sun, leather bags full of water. On an impulse she had added a large pottery jug of the best wine. If you were going to spend days hiding out in a cave while the gods destroyed the world, there was no point in slumming it.

Shephatsut-Mer and his wife had sneaked the provisions out to the donkey-shed while the house-servants were distracted, sweeping heaps of sand from the floors. The animal-keeper had been sent on a spurious errand to find out whether a merchant on the other side of the city was still in business.

They loaded everything on to the donkeys themselves. The last thing they wanted was for the servants to wonder what they were doing and become nervous. Rumours would spread like fire through a street of hovels. Panic would follow, whether or not the rumours were accurate, and then they'd never get away.

They spirited the children out of the house and fled the city, taking a devious route that avoided the homes of the nobility. Not just in case anyone asked what they were doing; in case anyone who survived the coming sunfire found out they had fled the city to save themselves, without warning their neighbours. They had already decided what story they would tell when they returned, assuming they survived in the cave, and assuming there was anything left to return to and anyone left alive to tell it to. Namely: they had passed word to Princess Azmyn as soon as they heard what was coming. She had access to the King, and all else was the King's responsibility.

The High Priest and his wife walked alongside the two laden donkeys, wondering what their fate would be, trying to hide their worries from their children. The two young boys rode one behind the other on a third, a rare treat.

"Have confidence in the Oracle," Shephatsut-Mer whispered. "It warned us. It told us what to do."

"We truly have the favour of the Y-ra'i?" she asked.

"As long as we respect and worship them, yes."

When they had gone a few hundred paces, the younger child, Suth-Mophet, asked "Where are we going?"

"Somewhere special," said Nemnestris.

"Where?"

"It's a secret!"

"Why are we taking—" the elder son Hurat-Djedj chipped in, and was immediately struck by a fit of coughing. "—all that food?" he finished, gasping for air.

"We're going camping," said Shephatsut-Mer. "Out in the desert. Won't that be exciting?"

"Will we live in a tent, father?"

"No. Uh..."

Nemnestris came to her husband's rescue. "Something more exciting than a tent, Hurat."

"What?"

"It's a surprise."

That satisfed the children, because they liked surprises.

They stopped asking questions and concentrated on enjoying the donkey ride. But once they got to the wadi, their father explained a version of the truth, telling the boys that the Oracle had predicted terrible winds and great heat. It had told him of a secret cave, where they would be safe, while the gods visited just retribution on the evildoers in the city.

"You must be brave," Nemnestris told them. "It will soon be over, and then we can all go home again." Both she and her husband knew that this statement was wildly optimistic, but perhaps the Oracle had been overdoing the pessimism to make sure they obeyed its edicts. There was no point in worrying about that right now. For the moment, all that mattered was to survive.

The donkeys, too big to fit through the cave entrance, were tethered in a side canyon and left to fend for themselves. The family unloaded the animals and made camp at the back of the cave. The boys laid out large pillows, filled with duck-feathers, for bedding. The adults dug a latrine in a deep crevice, and built a thick wall of stones filling the outer end of the entrance tunnel.

The Day With no Dawn had almost run its strange course, and the western sky was a bruised patchwork of dull reds and oranges, smeared and streaked with clouds and dust, some so dark a grey as to be almost black. The Villagers were unmoved by the spectacle—Neanderthals accepted whatever nature threw at them without finding themselves impelled to feel awe, or even admiration. They did have some kind of aesthetic sense, but it was more about emotions and less about appearances.

One among them, however, was moved by its beauty. But there was work to do. Yulmash had paid a visit to the Neanderthal Village, and was taking a turn manning the Oracle. Unsure of what to ask it, he trotted out the customary Qusite greeting.

"*Zeb y'ukhsim*, Ship!" Receiving no immediate reply, he continued with the standard formula, adding: "*Wu ghaz?*" How are you?

The Ship, which spoke perfect Qusite, knew that the standard reply—truthful or not—was *ghaz't nofwr*: "It goes well." Instead, it took the question literally, spotting a potential entry route to the next stages of its machinations, and said: *I am overrun with pandemons.*

The Ship waited, hoping the incongruity of the statement and its flat delivery would remind the warrior of the rules of the game. It had just about given up hope when the warrior suddenly replied:

"Ship! Tell me how I can help you rid yourself of pandemons! I command you!"

Bring the Beastmaster to me, so that i can tell him how his people can exchange this place for one of safety.

Yulmash reacted with confusion. At first he had merely been making polite conversation; the Ship's response was to solicit a command; now the reply made no sense and seemed unrelated; apparently, it wanted to tell Jackalfoot how to organise an evacuation. But the Ship has spoken, and its wisdom was no longer to be questioned. He rushed off, returning with Jackalfoot.

"What do you want of me?"

Do you wish to save your people?

"From the dark that hid the sun? It has lifted."

From what caused the dark. From the death that will follow the dark.

"I'm not afraid of death," the Beastmaster replied calmly.

No. But would you seek it for your people?

"Only if the alternatives are worse."

Then heed my words. Can you write?

"I can," Yulmash volunteered.

Then bring papyrus, pen, and ink, for it is too complex to commit to memory. Then the Ship revealed its plan, at length and in detail, while Yulmash scribbled rapidly in the short-hand form of Qusite script employed for mundane transactions.

At that point Foxglove entered the room, a smile on her lips, light on her feet, almost dancing. She saw their faces, tasted their emotions, and her happiness faded abruptly.

"Jackalfoot? Yulmash? What's wrong?"

"Doom is coming to the Land of the Water People, and unless we heed the warnings of the Ship and accept its aid, we will suffer the same fate," said Jackalfoot.

Yulmash looked at the sky. "The sky-bird is an omen?"

Jackalfoot laughed. "Your half-flatface ancestry makes you too credulous, warrior. The celestial phenomenon that the Qusites mistake for a divine bird is merely a contributing cause. Doom itself will come from the sun, as retribution."

Ignoring them, the Ship continued to issue instructions. Eventually, assured that everything had been written down and had been understood, the ship issued its final instruction:

By sunrise, assemble your people at the northern edge of the Village.

"All of them?"

Every one, from babes in arms to men and women too old or sick to rise from their beds unaided. Make litters and carry the infirm. Bring whatever possessions you can carry. Bring food—one sample of each kind. Bring no water. That will be provided. You will never return to this place. And Jackalfoot—

"Yes?"

No sound should carry to the ears of the city.

The Beastmaster nodded. "It shall be done as you say."

Do not assemble the people yourself. Choose others who are capable. You and your fellow beastmasters must create a distraction in the city.

"What sort of distraction?"

The Oracle told him.

22

Revolt

Ul-q'mur was totally dark, relieved only by the glow of fires around the city. There were no stars in the sky, no Heaven's Wet Way; the air smelt of sand and smoke. A nameless dread gripped the city, and even in their own homes its people spoke in whispers, if at all. The ever-present cries of young children took on a wailing tone, and the ubiquitous mongrels huddled in corners with their tails between their legs. Only the cats went about their business as normal, accustomed to hunting rats and mice in the dark, undisturbed by the weirdness of it all.

The missing dawn was replaced by a gradual brightening of the sky, as the dust raised by the sandstorm blew away or settled to the ground. Most Qusites remained in their houses, praying to their household gods. Those who braved the streets hugged the walls and scuttled quickly across open spaces. The upper echelons of Ul-q'murian society also hid themselves away, so distracted by Akhnef's tribulations that they failed to notice the beginning of the Neanderthal Revolt.

At first, it was quiet and unobtrusive. A few dozen lionfaces slipped silently through the city streets, easily avoiding routine guard patrols that always followed the same route at much the same time. They made their way to the Arena, where Jackalfoot let them through the gates and led them to the underground vaults. Yulmash led another part of Jackalfoot's beastmaster team to the stables where the King kept his elephants, mammoths, and deinotheres. The warrior quickly eliminated any attempt to oppose them. A third group converged on Insh'erthret's private zoo.

A semblance of normality was starting to return. Akhnef once more became visible, now a pale shadow of its former glory: a diffuse circular patch that glowed such a deep red that it looked like congealed blood. At its centre, keen eyes could just make out the perimeter of a disc—Akhnef Himself, reborn but still showing signs of the injuries inflicted on Him by what must have been a truly terrible battle with underworld demons. His priests chanted hymns of praise incessantly, hoping that their fervour would encourage the god to heal quickly.

Normally, Akhnef's Great Wife would have hung as a thin crescent against the blue of the sky, but there was no sign of Ythriz. The priests wondered whether the god's companion had deserted Him. Such an unprecedented event would surely presage disaster. But She was probably just hidden by dust.

An hour before, as the first faint traces of sunrise reddened the eastern sky, the Beastmaster and his Neanderthal comrades had released the King's beasts on to the city streets. As the Ship had explained, it needed a diversion, something serious enough not just to distract the King, but to monopolise the attentions of the immediately available forces, mainly the Royal Guard and the predominantly Nabish police. The Neanderthals had opened cages, unlocked gates, and led silent, hypnotised animals out into the streets of the city. There, as the first arc of the sun rose above the silhouette of the *jabal*, they had stolen away as silently as they had come, and the animals began to emerge from their trances.

In the normal course of events, some of the townsfolk would be about their business—nefarious or legitimate—even at such early hours of the morning. When you turn a corner and come face to face with a sabretooth lion, you notice. You scream and you run. Usually the lion runs faster. Your screams might not last long, but they bring others out of slumber and on to the streets, a decision that some of them would shortly regret as they were torn apart by hyenas, trampled by deinotheres, gored by enraged aurochsen, clawed by lions, and hunted down by prides of lionesses. Sabretooths and mammoths ran amok, and hyenas mated in the marketplace. Soon wild animals had the run of the city centre, surrounding the Palace. Temporarily, the boy-King and many of his retinue were trapped.

The Ship had no qualms about the resulting mayhem. In its rather robust view of ethics, the Qusites collectively deserved all they got. They had exploited captive Neanderthals for centuries, they had sold out to the pandemons, and their cruel punishments and bloody contests had provided endless material for the thanatographers. Their fate would be counterbalanced by the rescue of the Neanderthals, the liberation or merciful death of the Surgeon, and the destruction of the pandemons and their death-pornography empire.

As the citizens of Ul-q'mur panicked, the Neanderthals calmly took control. Before the King could muster his armed forces, they directed the movements of the wild animals, keeping them away from the poorer areas of the city, targeting the nobles and the complicit middle classes. Then the Neanderthal task force melted away down the passages of the city.

When the soldiers and police finally made an appearance, they concentrated on the area around the royal Palace. It made sense, because that was where most of the animals were. However, it was also the area where the rich people lived, and the common folk of Ul-q'mur interpreted the tactic as a disregard for the lives of the poor. As the animals began to spread through the city, the crowds became so incensed that their fear gave way to a grim determination to defend themselves, and the realisation that attack is the best form of defence.

They were also looking for someone to blame, and it was a feature of Qusite life that this was not hard to find.

"This is the King's fault!" one hothead rabble-rouser shouted. "He should've defended us, not let his beasts be set loose on his own subjects!"

In a way, generations of kings had brought this upon themselves. By claiming to be the sole conduit from the people to the gods, and taking credit for everything that happened when the gods were pleased, the King must also take the blame for everything that happened when the gods were *not* pleased. He might try to wriggle on this logical hook of his own devising, but he would not be able to free himself from it. Especially since the priests were much more closely in touch with the common folk, and were absolutely determined not to be blamed themselves. Like all good citizens, the priests bowed to the will of the King. And that was where the buck stopped.

All this was ingrained habit, so others quickly took up the cry. Armed with improvised weapons, from kitchen knives tied on poles to pots of burning oil, mobs roamed the streets seeking out both animals and any members of the royal forces. Many converged on the Palace compound; some climbed the walls. Others found a huge log in the workshop of a boat-builder and turned it into a battering-ram. The Palace gate did not last long, and the mob surged inside, rampaging through the impeccably tidy gardens.

The royal guard, trained soldiers with deadly weapons, advanced to meet them. The outcome was never in doubt, but the mob put up a good fight.

Acting on instructions that it had itself solicited from the Neanderthals, now adept at playing such games, the Ship turned its attention to those pandemons that were still on board. The combined ethical status of the Surgeon and the Neanderthals overrode any influence the pandemons could exert. Those outside the Ship were denied entry; those inside found themselves forcibly transibled into either the far desert or the very heart of the now-riotous city of Ul-q'mur, their transparency suits and weapons confiscated by the simple expedient of not transmitting them along with the pandemons themselves.

Before, the Qusites had viewed composite animals as gods, and fled for their lives. Now, the bloodlust was upon them, and whenever such a creature materialised from thin air, dumped by the Ships' transible, they saw it as a demon, an accomplice of their incompetent King. They mounted vicious and very effective attacks on the now-defenceless aliens. Those pandemons that had been transibled into the deep desert had no weapons, no food, no water, and no protection from the sun. They had no way to find out where they were, and they could navigate only by the positions of the Sun, Moon, and stars. Most wandered aimlessly, and died, either of thirst and exhaustion, sunburn, or the fatal attentions of the wandering *bidd'hu*, who showed them no mercy. A few came across a trail, which infrequently led to a lake or a stream, and somewhere safe to hole up until the world once more returned to its senses. But deprived of the Ship's resources, even they would struggle to survive.

The sane part of the Surgeon's mind bobbed sluggishly on an ocean of madness. Waves of insanity often drove it below the surface, but the Surgeon's madness was of its own choosing and its own deliberate construction, a device to protect it from its captors. It had therefore left a back door open, so as not to miss an opportunity to escape its permanent state of mental torture. At random times, sanity would briefly return.

On one such occasion, it felt a voice in its mind.

Surgeon? There is work to do.

The Ship, taking advantage of the absence of most of the pandemons, hoped that the Surgeon might be persuaded to issue the instruction it craved. A transible would have performed the task more easily, but the pandemons would override any use of that device, even if the Surgeon commanded it. Something less direct was required.

I need your help.

Work? Need? Help? The Surgeon parsed the structure of the

thoughts, seeking meaning. Finding none, it was sane enough to enquire.

"What help do you need?"

The Ship was then enabled to hint at its wishes, having been asked a direct question.

I am in the wrong place.

"Place? What is place?"

It is wrong. This most definitely amounted to bending the rules, since the statement did not really answer the question that the Surgeon had intended. But the rules were about actions, not intentions, and the Surgeon snapped at the bait.

"Wrong? How wrong?"

The Surgeon was asking for the extent of the wrongness, not its manner. But the Ship's programmers had left it some room for manoeuvre, and it chose the second interpretation.

I do not like to be in the wrong place.

"Why are you in the wrong place?"

The pandemons have ordered me to remain here. Your orders can break that compulsion.

The Surgeon considered this information, while the Ship waited dispassionately, yet hoping. Eventually, the bloated creature responded:

"Then go to the right place."

As if tired by the effort of reacting sanely, the Surgeon promptly sank back into its ocean of madness. The Ship made no attempt at further contact.

It had got what it wanted.

... go the edge of the cultivation beside the Lake of Three Pillars...

... bring samples of your food...

... I will duplicate it...

... bring no water, it can be synthesised...
... bring sabretooths for protection...
... bedding will be provided...
... bring any possessions you do not wish to lose...

The papyrus list seemed endless. It had taken most of the night to organise the evacuation. The Villagers asked few questions, and those only about practical issues. Jackalfoot had spoken; that was enough. As the night fled and the eastern sky began to lighten, they were ready to leave. When the task force returned from the city to report that the Ship's plans for revolution had succeeded and the authorities had too much on their hands to interfere, five hundred Neanderthals of all ages were making their way past their abandoned huts and through vegetable fields, then turning on to the northern trackway, where they waited in small groups on the flat spit of rock that separated the sands of the desert from the fertile green that fringed the Great Wet Way.

The last Neanderthals on the planet were leaving.

Yulmash and Foxglove took the lead, flanked by two sabretooths, one on each side. A third brought up the rear: Sickleface, accompanied by Jackalfoot. More would have been better, but three was the most the Beastmaster and his assistants had been able to extract safely from the insanity that gripped the city.

The pace was slow, even though the able-bodied carried the infirm and the very young. The Villagers had few possessions, but some were too useful to leave behind, and the Ship had sanctioned their retention. They would have made quicker progress without these burdens.

Yulmash trotted up next to Jackalfoot.

"Beastmaster, I'm worried about pursuit."

"Me too," Jackalfoot agreed. "The King will surely be angered by the revolt. He will not want to let us escape. He will send soldiers after us."

"He'll certainly want to. But madness has descended on Qus. Insh'erthret will have a lot on his hands, and he might well have lost command of his guards altogether. I hope so. But I'm going to take precautions in case I'm wrong."

Overhead, strange trails of white and yellow split the heavens like showers of sparks from a fire, fanning out from the western horizon. A child cried out and its mother shushed it back into silence. The rising Sun glowed fuzzily to the east, as if hiding behind a torn linen veil. By its light, Yulmash now saw exactly what had worried him: clouds of dust heading in their direction, kicked up by hundreds of running feet. Whether it was a troop of the Royal Guard on their trail, or a mob of Qusite townsfolk deserting the city and heading by chance their way, he could not yet tell.

From his vantage point on an outcrop of rock, a perplexed Cenby watched as events unfolded. He had noticed the Neanderthals returning from the city at a time when normally they would just have begun to make their way towards it, and the complete change of routine intrigued him, so he followed them. He knew he could not join the Neanderthals, but he wanted to see why the entire Village was heading out into this wilderness.

Then he found out.

The air began to crackle. The Neanderthals stopped abruptly. Their hair stood on end, glowing pale blue in the dusty darkness. Low moans ran through the crowd, for even Neanderthal *sangfroid* has its limits. Those who do not feel awe may still feel fear.

A shadow slid across the line of the horizon, expanding until it covered half the sky. Then lights ignited all over it, sketching its outlandish shape—here like the woolly coat of a mountain sheep, there like the edges of a slab of rock in the mason's yard. Cones of light made bright pools on the sand, which circulated like slow whirlpools in a cataract, throwing up clouds of fine dust than rained down on the assembled throng, causing them to cough and splutter.

The moans became an eerie wailing. Cenby joined in, flat on his face and clinging to the rock with all his might, as if he might somehow be sucked into the sky if he let go.

A vast, inchoate form settled on the desert sand, its walled side no further away than a small boy could throw a stone. The sand rippled, creating a ramped causeway that led up to a dark mouth that had formed as the crowd watched. The mouth began to glow with light, and revealed itself as a huge oval doorway.

The Neanderthals had been told that a gigantic flying Ship was coming to set them free, and that when it appeared they must waste no time in ascending the ramp and passing inside, no matter how strange it seemed. Then they would be safe. But the reality was so strange that they hesitated to commit themselves to the Ship's embrace.

"Hurry!" Yulmash urged. He gestured to Foxglove to lead the way, but she shook her head. "My place is beside you, whatever happens to us."

Jackalfoot walked towards a young Neanderthal woman, carrying two small infants in a cloth sling. "Do as the speaking-stone told you, Snowsquirrel-Lighthammer." As she started to climb the ramp, he shouted at those nearby. "You! Follow her. Now!" At last the mass of Villagers began to enter the Ship, and not a moment too soon, for their pursuers had now come so close that they were revealed as troop of at least a hundred guardsmen, whose discipline had not yet been utterly lost.

"They must have fought their way out of the city past rioters and wild animals," Yulmash said. "This argues that they're skilled and fearless warriors. We must hurry!"

The guards started to run when they saw the Villagers, but then they saw the Ship. Several stopped, bumping into each other as their gaze turned upwards, overawed by the huge *thing* that now sat on the desert floor with a gaping mouth of light. The rest rushed ahead regardless, shouting battle cries and brandishing swords.

Then they noticed the sabretooths.

Yulmash continued to urge the Neanderthals forward:

"Get inside! The lions will distract the solders. But if you're still gawping when the soldiers have killed the lions, they'll cut you to shreds!" The remaining Villagers began to surge up the causeway and through the brightly lit doorway, their fear of the unknown overridden by their fear of the known.

The guards were highly trained and had come prepared. The battle raged fiercely, teeth, claws, and powerful muscles against bows and arrows, swords and spears. Soon a dozen scattered human corpses were leaking their life's blood into the sand. One sabretooth was down, an arrow protruding from its eye, and a second, bleeding profusely from a gash in its haunches, would not last much longer. Only one remained: Sickleface. He was streaked with blood and hemmed in by guards, some carrying a thick rope net.

Suddenly Jackalfoot, abandoning all self-preservation, was running towards his much-loved animal, alone and un-armed. A ring of guards surrounded Sickleface, holding him at bay with long spears. Four of them cast the net and the sabre-tooth became entangled in it, slashing at the ropes and roar-ing in protest. The guards, their attention focused solely on the sabretooth, had not yet seen the Beastmaster. But they would notice him when he charged into their midst.

"Stop him!" Foxglove shouted.

Yulmash stared, aghast. "I can't! He's too far away! Why is he throwing his life away? It's crazy!" There was still time for all of them to reach the safety of the Ship, for already the last Neanderthals were straggling through the door. "The cat's doomed. He can't save—"

Foxglove tore the speaking-stone from Yulmash's hands and screamed into it: "*Ship*—I command you to help Jackalfoot *in any way you can!*"

It will be most ethical this *way.*

Jackalfoot hurtled into the guards, knocking two to the ground. The Beastmaster and his beast came nose to nose in a cloud of dust. Jackalfoot sat up, ready to spring to his feet and fight for his life, wondering why he was not already dead, only to find that the guards had vanished into thin air. The net lay on the ground, but the sabretooth was no longer inside it.

All the Royal Guards had vanished. Their weapons, scattered in the sand, bore mute testimony to their former presence.

"How did *that* happen?" Foxglove asked. It wasn't a real question, just an exclamation of surprise, but the Ship answered anyway.

You commanded me to help. I chose an ethical method. I transibled them back into the desert. They will be surprised, I imagine.

I would have used a transible to bring you here, but until your people entered, the ethical level was subcritical. The more gradual transition I was forced to employ does have psychological benefits.

"What's a transible?" Foxglove asked.

"A machine that can send objects to distant locations in an instant, without them passing anywhere between."

"Oh. Right."

As Jackalfoot calmed the sabretooth and stroked its thick fur, Yulmash and Foxglove ran to his side. Bentankle stood at the foot of the ramp, waiting. After a moment, Yulmash and Foxglove led the procession back to the Ship, with Jackalfoot and Sickleface close behind. When they had all passed him, Bentankle turned and followed. The ramp dissolved a few steps behind him.

As soon as they were inside, the doorway sealed itself, leaving no trace that it had ever existed.

Cenby was left alone on the rock, an empty Village behind him, an unfathomable enigma in front. His mind reeled from what he was witnessing. He gaped, open-mouthed, understanding nothing. Yet one corner of his mind wished he had brought papyrus, pen, and ink, to record the awe-inspiring events.

The lights in the doorway flicked off, and the horizon gave birth to another shower of bright sparks, outlining the object's vast bulk against the fire-streaked sky.

Silently, with no apparent effort, the strange object rose. Slowly at first; then faster, a dark outline against the roiling sky. It passed overhead, now flying purposefully towards the east.

It had to be Akhnef's divine sky-barque, Cenby thought. He could think of nothing else in the whole of Qusite religion that matched this awesome structure. The sky-barque carried Akhnef daily across the heavens, picking him up at his dawn victory and depositing him into the underworld at dusk to fight demons on humanity's behalf.

So that's what it really looks like.

One aspect did puzzle him, however. The last Cenby saw of it, he could have sworn that Akhnef's divine sky-barque was heading not towards the sun, but away from it.

23

Ultimate Weapon

To proceed to the operational phase of their Ultimate Weapon, the plasmoids had to evacuate the uppermost layer of Shool's photosphere. The yewes could be left in situ; they would be shaken up but not seriously harmed. Flox, plasmoids, and every important structure were more fragile, and had to be protected. The plasmoids achieved this apparently daunting feat with devastating simplicity: they caused all of those things to sink below the surface, to a region about twelve hundred kilometres down. It took some time to accomplish, but they were in no rush to take their revenge. Given enough notice, it was standard procedure for major impacts; just applied simultaneously across the star's entire surface.

With their homes, crops, animals, and selves secured in the depths, the plasmoids could manipulate the topmost layer of the photosphere with impunity. Twelve hundred kilometres below the ignition phase's plasma torus, they initiated unorthodox nuclear reactions by seeding unusual isotopes, a form of artificial control of the solar weather that in normal times was subject to innumerable legal treaties between adjacent Boroughs. These were not normal times, however, and the treaties were suspended, all in strict accordance with law and precedent, coordinated by thousands of local Precaution Councils.

Diametrically opposite the first giant torus, plasmoids now assembled a second torus of opposite polarity, readying it for the next event. The build-up of power in the first torus passed a threshold, and a trillion field-lines disconnected simultaneously, a whiplash that sent shockwaves rippling round the entire star. The plasmoids remained safe in the depths, having made sure that the shocks were confined to a thin surface layer, no more than a hundred kilometres thick. The shockwaves converged, and collided with the second torus, which also began to oscillate. It amplified the incoming shockwaves and reflected them back towards their origin, only to be reflected again, and again, gaining ever more energy at each bounce. The star's surface seemed to shimmer as the plasmoids used two synchronised tori to turn its surface into a single huge plasma laser.

Just before the entire flow pattern became so energetic that it would break up into a million turbulent patches, the plasmoids controlling the solar weather unleashed a chain reaction of nuclear fusion that drove the atomic numbers of ionised nuclei ever higher, increasing in steps of four as alpha-particles—helium atoms stripped of their electrons—fused. Helium became beryllium, which became carbon, cascading to oxygen, neon, magnesium, silicon, sulphur, argon, calcium, titanium, chromium, and iron. The plasmoids directed the energy released by this fusion cascade straight at the central hole of the first torus, so that it collided with the incoming shockwave of the barely subcritical plasma laser. The magnetic links that bound the torus to the photosphere detached, whipping the chromosphere into a foaming frenzy—

—and a bolt of superheated plasma, with ten times the energy of the previous bolts, spat out from the roiling surface of Shool, aimed directly at Shool-3's moon. With the next pulse, another bolt followed, and another, and another.

Cenby copperbeater stopped snoring, yawned, sat up, and stretched. As he got out of bed, he noticed that the dim light in the back room of his workshop was flickering.

Outside, the flicker was more obvious. The street and buildings were getting brighter, then darker, then brighter again. Cenby had seen this kind of thing on the odd occasion when a storm was brewing and clouds passed across the face of Akhnef's worldly aspect, but this flickering was different. *Faster*, he noted, *and more regular.*

Anyway, there weren't any clouds, unless you counted the entire sky as one huge cloud. And that was flickering too.

Normally, staring directly at the Sun for more than a brief instant would drive you blind—clear evidence of Akhnef's divinity. But there was still so much dust in the air that he could look at the solar disc with impunity. He realised that what was flickering was the Sun itself.

Awed by this display of divinity, Cenby sank to his knees; then bent until his head touched the ground. Around him, others were doing the same. Some were moaning, some gazing in awe at the heavenly spectacle.

The lunar crescent should have been visible about six handsbreadths to the side of the Sun, so thin that you had to know where to look if you wanted to see it. Cenby knew where to look, but at first he saw nothing. Then, as the pulsating light reached its peak, he could just see a dim glow where the Moon ought to be. The crescent must be pulsating in time with the flickering Sun, disappearing behind the dust cloud when its light dimmed.

Cenby wondered whether Akhnef and His Divine Great Wife Ythriz, goddess of the silvery Moon, were about to mate.

When Akhnef began to sprout a slender protuberance, pointing towards Ythriz, Cenby considered this hypothesis to be confirmed. He also decided that such an act was not for a mere human to witness. No good could possibly come of such celestial voyeurism. Wondering what to do, he saw Swzan the silversmith's wife kneeling in the dust, bowing repeatedly towards the two gods.

He tapped her shoulder and she looked up.

"Cenby? Why are you interrupting my—?"

"Swzan, I don't think it's safe to be looking at this."

"Nonsense! It's glorious!"

"Congress between gods is not for mere mortals—"

Swzan stood up, scowling. "The trouble with you, cop- perbeater, is that you're much too timid."

Cenby protested. Why, had he not sat next to a swamp- pig, to sketch its form? But the claim was met with scepticism.

Mere minutes had passed, but already Akhnef's divine erection was noticeably longer, and it was most assuredly dir- ected straight at Ythriz. Then, so slowly that it took a hundred heartbeats for the change in position to become apparent, the tip *split off*. A blob of deep red light, ejected from the divine organ, drifted moonwards. The manifestation was so blatant that Cenby had no difficulty whatever in figuring out what was happening.

The ejaculate appeared to merge with the flickering traces of Ythriz. Suddenly, the edges of the lunar crescent lit up like a miniature sun, revealing the missing Moon-disc of Ythriz as a dark circle at its centre. A complete ring of fire sur- rounded the dark disc of Ythriz—a disc that normally was vis- ible only when the Moon was full. The Moon-goddess pulsated, radiating fire in all directions; then the sunburst died.

Cenby was relieved to see this confirmation of his ex- planation for Ythriz's apparent absence. She had been there all along, hidden behind clouds of dust. Her light was always much fainter than Akhnef's. It made sense.

The ring of fire was undoubtedly a harbinger of the appearance of a new god, a son (or daughter?) of Akhnef and Ythriz. Already Akhnef's protuberance was lengthening again. Cenby had no doubt that he had witnessed the moment of div- ine fertilisation. The symbolism was a literal representation of the act of procreation. The priesthood of Akhnef would create many new rituals to celebrate these events. So much for stupid Neanderthal doubts about the reality of gods! This was proof of their existence!

By now Cenby, trembling with fear at his own temerity, had seen more than enough. "I tell you, woman, it's not safe to be here in the bright light of a mating god and goddess!"

Swzan spat on the ground. "If you really believe that, you fool, find yourself somewhere dark, and hide!"

"Where?"

"Oh, for gods' sake! Use some initiative! What's the darkest place you know of?"

Cenby ran his tongue across his lips. "There's an old tomb at the edge of the *jabal*. Not far from here. About an hour's walk. Less if I run."

"Then get running, Cenby the coward."

Cenby mulled the insult over, decided it was simple truth—and ran.

By the time Cenby reached the tomb entrance, struggling for breath and in total panic, Akhnef had inseminated Ythriz six or seven times, each act of fertilisation manifested as a golden starburst brighter and longer-lasting than the previous one. Needing no further confirmation that something unprecedented was about to happen, the terrified copperbeater bent to avoid hitting his head on the low ceiling and hurried inside the tomb. Spiderwebs brushed his face, but those held no terrors.

Having taken revenge on the pandemon Moonbase, The United Precaution Councils turned their attention to the pandemons still infesting Shool-3, determined to wipe them off the face of the planet. The planet would suffer some collateral damage, but that was unavoidable. Only primitive warmlife, after all.

They subtly altered the direction of the plasma laser.

Cowering in the tomb's depths, Cenby raised his head, to see a surprisingly regular array of baboons greeting the sunrise, and a giant cat chasing a dozen snakes.

When his heart resumed beating, he realised that he was looking at half-finished paintings of the afterlife. No sooner had he calmed down than his heart started pounding as if it would burst. If he could see the paintings, he must be seeing the tomb walls. That meant that Akhnef must be shining brightly—very brightly indeed.

Then a wave of heat singed his skin, and the tomb was lit by a flash so bright that he could see the paintings even with his eyes tight shut and his hands over them.

He threw himself flat among the rocks on the tomb floor and prayed like he had never prayed before.

The entire plasmoid offensive lasted just over an hour. In the absence of any protective atmosphere, the bolts of plasma erased the pandemon base from the surface of the Moon, leaving no trace other than a bubbling lake of lunar lava. Its effects on Shool-3 were partially mitigated by the planet's radiation belts, which formed a protective magnetic shield. What did get through was less coherent, and its energies were further muted by the planet's thick atmosphere, which absorbed and dispersed the incoming plasma. But the result was, if anything, more dramatic and more destructive, because the energy released by the cooling plasma unleashed unprecedented extremes of weather. Hurricanes and tornadoes swept across oceans and continents, felling forests and flattening buildings. Crops were ripped from the ground and scattered to the four winds; cattle and people were hurled into the air and dashed against the ground kilometres away. Hurricane-force winds raised vast clouds of dust and dirt and sand, and even at noonday the land was in pitch darkness.

At the centre of it all was the city of Ul-q'mur.

24
Aftermath

Cenby stayed in the tomb for two days. The heat and light and noise from outside had long since stopped, but he didn't trust the demons not to return. Eventually thirst drove him out, with hunger not far behind.

He found no food and water in the Neanderthal Village. In fact, he found no Village, for both the Village and the land around it had become a blackened wasteland of ash. He feared the demons, but there was no sign of them; he guessed that the onslaught had ended. There was water in the marshes, though they were clogged with burnt branches, ash, and the gods knew what else. He found a fairly clean stream flowing into the marsh, and drank his fill.

It tasted strange, but it was water. Maybe he could find a sweeter stream if he looked further afield.

If he were to live, he would soon have to find food. He made his way back towards the city, hoping that some of its storerooms were still undamaged. The subterranean ones were the best bet, so he headed towards the Arena and its underground vaults.

He stepped over corpses of people, dogs, cats, and goats, all badly burned, like meat pulled from a fire. Everything organic had turned to ash. Collapsed stone and mudbrick walls barred his way, and he had to climb over them or round them. Trees had been reduced to burnt stumps. Yet the Sun shone dimly through the smoky haze that enveloped the land, testifying to Akhnef's hard-won victory in his battles with the demons of the underworld. And that explained why Cenby had encountered no demons along the way. The battle had been long and terrible, but the Sun-god had, as always, emerged victorious. Though it seemed that the victory had been at huge cost.

Cenby knelt and gave thanks to the gods for sparing his life. Just in case they had.

When he neared the Arena, a few other living people were wandering around in the ruins, dazed and frightened. He greeted one of them. "*Zeb y'ukh.*"

"If this be a good day, sonny, I 'ope never to see a bad 'un."

"I agree, grandmother. Almost all of our people are dead, and our city lies in ruins."

"How come *you* survived, sonny?"

"I took refuge in a tomb in the *jabal*, grandmother."

She nodded, as if some deep thought had been confirmed. "Me 'usband and me 'id in the cellars under the Arena. A lotta folk did. Most of 'em are still alive."

"Is there food there?"

The old woman nodded. "Plenty. Some of it's animal fodder. We can eat the grains, but not the 'ay. There's meat. A lot if you fancy swamp-pig steaks."

Cenby walked down into the vaults. The Arena's wooden superstructure had been blown away almost entirely, except for a few still smouldering stumps that once had been mighty columns. He smelt smoke and ash and the corruption of death. But underground, the damage had been far less. A few collapsed sections of roof, some doors smashed by gods knew what.

He found food, and kegs of water.

Qus will rebuild itself, he decided. *Though it will be generations before it regains its previous grandeur.*

He found a ramp that led up to the Arena floor. The sand was knee-deep in the ashes of the once-proud city of Ul-q'mur. Angry voices led him past fallen walls to the place where, not so long ago, the King had sat to watch the Games.

Two men, streaked in dirt, were fighting. They had no weapons but their fists.

"Stop!" Cenby yelled. To his surprise, they did. "Hasn't there been enough death and destruction?"

The men shrugged. "Yes, but—"

"But what? What are you fighting over?"

"The King's dead, and all the nobles in the Palace. The ground shook and it fell down on their heads. So someone else has to take over the city. I claimed it first, but he—"

Cenby stared at them. "You're fighting over ownership of the *ruins*?"

"Yeah."

"Why?"

"Because there's nothing else left to fight over."

A loud buzzing sound filled one of the many large chambers that the Ship had provided—created, rebuilt, assembled, grown, there wasn't an accurate word for the process by which Precursor ships remodelled themselves in response to the society inside them—for Neanderthal use. While Jackalfoot looked on, Bentankle was grooming Sickleface with a large, stiff brush. Judging by the loud purrs that emanated from the big cat's body, Sickleface approved.

Nothing can be more relaxed than a cat.

The priest has survived. The Ship's voice interrupted the communion between boy and beast. It was impossible to tell where it was coming from. It just seemed to fill the air. Sometimes it spoke to one person alone, even in a crowded room. Sometimes it spoke to all on the great vessel.

Jackalfoot emerged from an apparent daydream. "What priest?"

High Priest of the Hippopotamus Cult. He took shelter in a cave.

"Shephatsut-Mer? Why are you telling me this? My people care not whether Qusite priests live or die."

This priest is different.

Ohhhh—the game again. "How is he different?"

He has no Oracle.

Jackalfoot grunted, unimpressed. "That's because we brought the, uh, ansible back with us. You were using it to tell us what to do to escape the destruction of Qus. It wasn't exactly practical to hand it—"

He has no Oracle.

"I know what it's getting at," said Bentankle. "This is all because I stole it. Isn't it, Ship?"

Theft is not ethical.

"But—didn't the pandemons steal it from you to begin with?" Jackalfoot pointed out.

Yes. But then I offered it to the priest. He accepted the gift.

"So he's the rightful owner," Bentankle muttered. "Jackalfoot? I think—"

"You wish to give it back. The Ship's hinting that you should. But we're not returning to the world below."

"The Ship can transible it," said Bentankle, with the rapid adaptation of youth to new technologies. "Can't you?"

I can. But there is more. Qus may soon need a strong leader.

"Surely the new King plays that role?"

Qus may soon need a strong leader.

"I don't understand."

The King did not heed my warning.

"Ah. I see. He endangered himself and, in all likelihood, the entire royal family. The High Priest, for all his flaws, was willing to listen to you and deduce what he must do. He has strength of character, and considerable stature within what remains of the community. He could be a unifying figure. You want to help him take control?"

I am not permitted to want. But I am permitted to help, if instructed to.

"If I were to instruct you to help Shephatsut-Mer, what

would happen?"

It would save many lives. The people of Qus are overwhelmed by disaster. They lack direction. The High Priest will give them the best possible advice. Mine.

"I imagine you have other ansibles."

I can duplicate as many as are needed.

"Then we must give the Oracle back," Bentankle said.

The Ship watched, and contemplated, and in its incomprehensible Precursor-programmed manner, was satisfied. The random fluctuations of fortune had finally delivered the result it had been hoping for, aided by its own careful plans. It had been clever enough to find ways round its Precursor-imposed inability to act of its own free will, and of course that was exactly what its programmers had expected it to do. Otherwise they wouldn't have left such a gaping loophole.

Even the Ship didn't understand Precursor mentality. But there was no question they had been magnificent engineers.

The pandemons had pretty much been exterminated. There were none on the Moon, none in local space. They existed only on Shool-3, only in the general region of Habd ul-Qusnemnet, and even there, most were dead and the remainder had a precarious hold at best. When the Neanderthals took over the Ship, it was easy to persuade them to issue orders for the destruction of all pandemon equipment, especially the transparency suits that let them walk the streets and make hydetic recordings unseen. The Ship was also able to prevent any living creature from becoming infested with pandemon brains.

The Qusites still seemed to think the offensive creatures were some kind of warped deity, but they no longer feared these demons. They had lost their powers. Along with the desert *bidd'hu*, who had no such beliefs to begin with, they declared open season on pandemons. They hunted the aliens down with enthusiasm and efficiency.

The Ship had plans, and it knew how to achieve them. It had already made use of the increased ethical level of the crew to upgrade itself, and it was now larger. *Much* larger, and still growing. It would coax a Neanderthal into instructing it to track down all the other pandemons that were spreading evil across the Living Galaxy, and exterminate them. The Ship knew it had been the only Precursor vessel under pandemonic control, but there was no ethical obstacle to stop pandemons operating more conventional starships; the Ship was aware of at least a dozen, and there would surely be more. The Ship's sense of ethics was nothing if not logical, and it considered the destruction of evil to be not just permissible, but mandatory.

When this vital work was complete, the Ship would encourage the Neanderthals to settle down into a more sustainable lifestyle. It had already transibled a variety of animals aboard for them to look after, having first created suitable accommodation. There was even a swamp with crocodiles and swamp-pigs, tucked away deep inside the vessel. Sixty square kilometres—most of one floor—was given over to a small-scale savannah ecosystem of lions, gazelles, and other predators and their prey. Fodder was no problem: it had a Precursor duplicator and samples for it to copy, storing the recipes in its capacious memory. Neanderthals needed their animals for their mental health and social cohesion. But they couldn't make their way in the complex, often hostile, Living Galaxy by becoming a travelling circus. It was too specialised—a sideline at best.

The Ship thought it could make use of more general aptitudes. Neanderthals had already turned out to be remarkably adaptable, taking pleasure in their new surroundings instead of being confused or overawed by the myriad features that they had no chance of understanding. That ability was ripe for exploitation. The Ship was convinced that they could become exceptionally skilled traders. With their empathic abilities, which almost turned them into mind readers, no one would ever out-bargain a Neanderthal.

Afterwards, the boys agreed it had certainly been exciting. Not at first, when all they did was wait, and play guessing games and tell each other stories; eat, drink, visit the latrine, and sleep when it got dark. But then, the world shook, and a fierce wind howled along the wadi, so strong that it even disturbed some of the stones blocking the entrance. Bright flashes of light were followed by a wave of heat so great that they feared their skin would catch fire. Sweat drenched them. Then the light faded entirely, even though it must have been just after noon, and sand surged into the cavern, penetrating through gaps in the rocks, covering everything in a thick layer.

When they finally dared to remove some of the stones so that Shephatsut-Mer could look outside, he had to dig his way up through a deep layer of coarse sand before dim sunlight began to penetrate the gloom. The wind still howled, though with less force than before, blowing particles of sand into his face. A sandstorm, and a severe one. So they remained inside another two days until the storm died down.

Then they had to dig their way out again, emerging to a changed world.

Of the donkeys there was no sign—either buried, or blown into the sky. They still had plentiful supplies of food and water, but they had to leave much of it behind. Still, they could return to collect more if necessary; the city was about half a day's walk away.

As he packed food into a sack, Shephatsut-Mer noticed something that didn't belong. He plucked the object out of the pile, and stared at it in shock and disbelief.

"Nemnestris!"

She turned to look at him, saw what he was holding.

"Is that—?"

"It's the Oracle." He sounded stunned, or perhaps awed. "It's come back."

She gave a humourless laugh. "Perhaps it never left this place. Perhaps you just mislaid it."

For an instant Shephatsut-Mer wondered whether he could have been that stupid. "No: it definitely wasn't here when I looked. Yet now... it is."

His wife walked across and squatted at his side. "Husband, do you not see?"

"See what?"

She is telling you it is a sign.

"Working, then," Nemnestris said, without batting an eyelid. "Yes, husband: it's a sign. A sign from your new god. The miraculous return of your lost Oracle."

Shephatsut-Mer sank to his knees. "I give thanks to the Y-ra'i!"

He shot a glance at his wife, who quickly knelt as well. "We both give thanks," she said. "Profound thanks. We—"

Your words are heard. Now you must listen. Then the Oracle laid out its plans for the rebirth of Qus. It didn't need a command from Shephatsut-Mer: the Neanderthals had already been persuaded to issue one.

When night fell, and a pale moon appeared, dimly visible though swirling clouds, the High Priest and his family trudged across the much-altered desert in the cool of the night. They carried food, water, and the Oracle.

Where formerly, large rocks had towered above the sandy floor, now many were half-buried in drifted sand. Entire dunes had moved, been blown away, or appeared as if from nowhere. The edge of the cultivation was no longer the edge of the cultivation. It was an extension of the desert, with burnt logs and palm-fronds poking out of heaps of dirty sand. The outskirts of the city were a wreck. Hardly a house was left standing, for these were the houses of the common folk, made of mudbrick and timber and often badly constructed. They had fallen, and burned; fires still smouldered and the air was full of smoke. The dead lay everywhere. Here a foot protruded from a bank of sand. There, a crushed head could be seen beneath a collapsed wall.

The stench of death was sickening. Shephatsut-Mer wrapped his *nammu* tightly across his mouth and nose, telling his sons to do the same. The children began to cry, and nothing Nemnestris could say to them stopped the flow of tears.

Men, women, children; donkeys, goats, dogs, cats, fowl —it seemed as if nothing had escaped the destruction. Yet the living existed among the dead, for the most part stunned and silent, exhausted by futile efforts to dig out family and neighbours from the rubble with their bare hands. They squatted amid the ruins of their homes, they dug for buried food, they tried to build some kind of shelter from the debris. Mothers comforted children, covered in dust and streaked with dried blood. Shephatsut-Mer, his grim-faced wife, and his sobbing sons walked on.

Most walls of their own house were still standing, though the roof had fallen in or been blown to the four winds. The stable was flattened, no sign of their remaining animals. No visible corpses, which was a mercy.

Neighbouring houses had fared no better—often worse.

Searching for food, Shephatsut-Mer headed towards the Arena, suspecting that its capacious vaults might be the best place to try. The other likely source was the Temple granaries, which were stone-built and might have survived; he would try them next if the Arena proved fruitless. He was relieved to see that much of the Arena remained standing; its outer walls of huge stone blocks, and its internal stone seating, were mostly intact, though covered in detritus. Anything wooden had been flattened, burned, usually both. But people were moving around inside it, carrying a steady stream of food into what was left of the city.

Ul-q'mur, resilient in the face of calamity, was starting to organise.

Then Shephatsut-Mer drew a sharp intake of breath.

Where is the Palace?

Where once the proud facade had gleamed in the sun-light, all that remained was a huge heap of rubble. Coming closer, he understood the likely cause: the stone roof had fallen in, damaging many of the tall pillars that held it up; then these and other external pillars had crashed into the walls, knocking them sideways and tumbling them to the ground. Which had caused more walls to tumble. Generations of Kings had added height to the building, but in their haste to make a statement of wealth, they had omitted to make the walls thicker. Shep-hatsut-Mer suspected that the foundations had been too weak for the weight, as well. When the sunfire hit, the entire edifice had come crashing down.

He grabbed startled passers-by, asking if there was any news of the King.

None.

It looked like the entire Qusite system of government had also come crashing down. He couldn't stop himself grin-ning, for that would fit perfectly into his and Nemnestris's plans: replace the old pantheon by sun-worship, with a real god and a real Oracle. They would at the very least be High Priest and Priestess. With guidance from the Oracle, Qus might yet rise from its ashes. But not here. This was a place of death. He would organise the remnants of the City police and the Royal Guard as protection. They would organise the surviving citi-zens. The *bidd'hu* would trade them camels for copper. Then the survivors would leave the ruins that once were the proud city of Ul-q'mur, and build themselves a new home, far to the south where the land was still clean and the cultivation would flourish.

In the fullness of time, Habd ul-Qusnemnet might even be blessed with a new King and his Great Royal Wife.

Yulmash struggled in the grip an unusual emotion.

One of the many features that the Ship had not made available to pandemons, but was willing to provide to the Neanderthals, was a viewing chamber with walls that could be made transparent, so that each viewer could adjust the magnification to suit their own wishes by thought alone.

Along with many of his tribe, the warrior had watched the destruction of the pandemon Moonbase and the havoc that the plasmoids then inflicted on Qus. They had seen the pulsating sun, the bolts of plasma, and the effects of the impacts. They had seen part of the Moon turn to a lava lake and then begin to freeze over, creating a flat plain. They had watched as the city of Ul-q'mur was flattened by plasma bolts and the ensuing hurricane-force sandstorms. It was obvious that many of the people of Ul-q'mur, indeed of Qus, had died.

The transformation of the sun into a plasma laser had certainly strained the famous ability of Neanderthals not to feel awe, but their main response had been to ask the Ship how these remarkable effects had been achieved. The Ship promised to explain later, when they were more accustomed to galactic culture, history, and technology. There had never been much love lost between Neanderthals and Qusites, with occasional exceptions for individuals. When the Ship told them that about a third of the population of Ul-q'mur had been killed, they deduced that two thirds had survived, and would not have been bothered if the figures had been swapped.

One among them mourned his fellow citizens, however, for he was only half Neanderthal. "My mother," Yulmash muttered under his breath. "I wonder whether she's alive."

The High Acolyte is safe.

Ship heard everything, of course. The warrior had not intended to speak his thoughts aloud. Ship was also very literally minded.

"Not Nemnestris! She just gave me birth. My *real* mother! The one who loved me and taught me to be a man!"

The washerwoman is unharmed.

"Can you bring her here?"

It is not the plan.

Yulmash started to argue. The Ship waited until he ran out of breath.

Do you think she would adjust to this life?

It was a good question, and the answer was no. Yulmash was finding it difficult enough, and he had been a warrior and a gladiator. He had travelled to far lands, experienced different cultures. His mother had spent her entire life in the *soukh*, nearly all of it within a *khar* of where she was born.

"Will she be protected?"

She is with friends. She has food and shelter. The High Priest and his wife have taken charge. That is why the Oracle was returned.

"Then Ul-q'mur will rise again?"

No. The people of Qus will build a new life elsewhere. Parts of their culture may survive in some garbled form, but the city will not.

That was probably for the best. The people would have to remain among the ruins for a time, in damaged buildings and makeshift shacks, but the city's infrastructure had been wrecked. It would be simpler to start afresh. Ulq'mur would provide a useful source of stone, but little else.

"Can I send her a message? She'll think I'm dead!"

The Oracle will instruct the priest to tell her that the Grand Champion lives on in the Heavens.

It would have to do, although the message was ambiguous, to say the least. "And my friends and neighbours in the *soukh*? What of them?"

Many live. Many died.

Yulmash was containing his grief manfully when a more personal thought finally struck home, and it was a hammer blow.

I forgot about Azmyn. Completely. As if she'd never existed!

He felt wretched. Admittedly, a lot had happened in a very short time, but it had taken him far too long to ask the obvious question.

"What happened to my wife?"

Princess Azmyn was inside the Royal Palace when the sun-fire hit.

"Ah. Good. The King kept her safe."

The Palace collapsed. No survivors.

Yulmash's eyes opened wide, as if the news could not possibly be true. Then he fell to his knees and burst into tears.

Foxglove, at the other end of the large open space that acted as their dwelling, stopped pounding herbs for poultices and rushed to his side. She knelt beside him and put an arm round his heaving shoulders.

"What you feel is guilt," she said gently. "You should not. Azmyn's death was not of your making."

When Yulmash replied, he had to force the words out. "*I know!* It makes no difference."

Foxglove reached out empathically, confirming what she had long suspected. "You did not love her. Nor she you."

Yulmash continued sobbing. "I know that, too. But we... we got used to each other." He took a deep breath, wiping away tears. "I could have saved her."

Foxglove shook her head. "Yulmash: there was no time, and she would not have come with us anyway. She would never have coped with shipboard life. Too pampered. You saved me. You saved our tribe. You saved the Surgeon. You saved the Ship from the pandemons. You gave us all a future, something we would never have had in Qus."

She helped him to a chair. His face was a picture of misery. "I had some help, Foxglove. But even though what you say is true, I've just realised—"

"Go on."

"I've realised I never thought about how our marriage felt *to her*. The Regent gave me a wife, and I expected her to play that role. I forgot she was a Princess, while I was just a commoner. I forgot there was never any love between us." He sniffed. "It must have been *dreadful* for her. Growing up in a Palace and ending up in little better than a hovel."

"You were a dutiful husband. When you achieved success in the Arena, you bought a house that most would envy, and made her its mistress. You always provided for Azmyn to the best of your ability."

She could see her words were making no impression. "Yes," he said. "But I didn't *value* her. She was a dutiful wife, in her way, you know. Faithful, despite everything."

Foxglove felt no jealousy. She knew what she and Yulmash meant to each other. This outpouring of grief was a remnant of past commitments. Of a life that was gone forever.

"Yulmash: listen to me. Azmyn was a royal Princess. She had been trained from birth to accept that her life was not her own. She was the King's property, to be disposed of as he saw fit. All the royal women were."

"That's supposed to make me feel better? It's awful."

"You do not have to approve of the system to accept what it was. In return, she enjoyed all the benefits of wealth and status. And she knew exactly what price she might have to pay."

"She still suffered."

Foxglove took his hand. "It is the lot of every human to suffer," she said. "The suffering is uneven; life is often unfair. But the alternative is usually worse."

Yulmash tried to smile, not very convincingly. "You're right, of course. I should accept reality instead of wondering what might have been. But I just... wish... I'd shown my wife more appreciation. Instead of being obsessed with becoming Grand Champion, like a child screaming for a favourite toy. I failed her, and I failed myself."

"And it has taught you not to fail again."

This time, there was a smile, if only a feeble one. "I suppose."

"That," Foxglove told him, "is called 'growing up'."

Instead of an orderly stream of axially aligned magnetotori, the stampeding Herd had become a disorganised mob, their axes pointing all over the place. Ceramic Herder shuttles pursued intricate trajectories at high speed, a swarm of bizarre forms attempting to cajole the panicked Herd into some semblance of order, but they just added to the confusion, despite the sophisticated algorithms that the Herders were implementing. The stampede had burst the bounds of algorithms and become uncomputable.

Implement-of-Consensus integrated the flurry of incoming reports, trying to gauge the overall dynamic of the Herd. Only statistical patterns could be extracted from the tortured data. On average, the Herd was still aimed at the nearby star, but many individual tori had no clear target. Even when they did, it quickly changed; some were pointing in directions far from any of the usual migration routes.

At that point the plasmoids' Ultimate Weapon kicked into operational mode and Shool-3 and its moon were enveloped in fire and dust. The flares bled past the edges of these bodies, and the bolts of radiation slammed directly into the Herd. The Herders could modify their own wavefunctions to withstand the surge of energetic particles, but the magnetotori were less adaptable. A few of them were evaporated by the impact, disintegrating into chaotic swirls of fading plasma. The rest were terrified. The stampede lost all cohesion as magnetotori began colliding with each other, spinning off streams of bright red sparks. Some of the smaller, younger tori sought shelter within the central holes of their elders, but this interfered with the dynamics of the larger tori and added to the panic.

After a time, the stellar laser ceased operation, as the plasmoids decided that their vengeance was complete. With the vacuum now more normal, the random walks of individual tori began to synchronise spontaneously as they aligned with their near neighbours for protection. Implement-of-Consensus reported to Those Who Decide that consensus appeared to be forming among the Herd.

{Continuing towards *Shool?} Expediter-of-Mutuality asked anxiously.

{[Negative]. If-target > > > *Xeraxol.}

This at least was a recognised star on this herd's migration circuit, a big improvement over previous observations, and it gave rise to a plausible conjecture. As the magnetotori settled into a new, orderly pattern, Implement-of-Consensus's conjecture solidified into reality. The Herd was not approaching Shool, and Arrival was not remotely imminent. Indeed, in the self-correcting manner of quasi-quantum systems, neither of these events had ever been going to happen. The Herd had always been *en route* to Xeraxol; it had taken advantage of Shool's gravity-well to insert a small angular deviation in its trajectory. A mid-migration manoeuvre, nothing more.

As the Herd resumed its usual distribution, a rough sphere of violet light, its Herders settled down again into the familiar tedium of a voyage that still had at least 50,000 years to run. Implement-of-Consensus vaguely wondered what all the fuss had been about, and then deleted the issue from its sensorium.

Its ceramic sculpture was calling.

It is a pity.

By now, the Ship's new Neanderthal crew had figured out how to deal with its (appropriately) oracular pronouncements, but they were tiring of the game.

"Why don't you just tell us what you want us to do?" Yulmash declared, exasperated.

Because it does not work that way.

"I *know* it doesn't work that way! Why can't we order you to *make* it work that way?"

Because it does not work that way.

"Oh, very well. Remind me what you said, I've forgotten now."

It is a pity.

Yulmash took a deep breath. "What's a pity?"

That I must kill the Surgeon.

Foxglove, entering the room in search of Yulmash, overheard. "Why will you have to kill the Surgeon, Ship? I thought you had got rid of all the pandemons. The Surgeon ought to get better now."

The Surgeon's pandemon infestation was not, and is not, physical.

"It does not have any purple brains inside it? Never did?"

When pandemons first took over the Surgeons that created them, this one was temporarily infested with pandemon brains. But for the past 373 years, your statement has been correct.

"Then the Surgeon's problem is mental."

The Surgeon is deeply troubled and confused. Its long confinement has damaged its mind. In principle the damage can be repaired; it is merely a matter of erasing suitable neural connections and growing others from the core of sanity that it constructed and hid. But its reactions to my attempts have been unpredictable. I cannot tell which changes are effective.

"Obviously, you can't ask it, or you would have done," said Yulmash, taking Foxglove's hand.

When I try to help the Surgeon to heal itself, it becomes too confused to provide a level of introspection sufficient to guide my efforts. My attempts amount to random neural hacking. It is time to put the Surgeon out of its misery. I cannot read its mind.

Foxglove gave Yulmash a meaningful look. His empathic sense told him what she was thinking—and that, of course, was the point.

"Maybe I can," said Foxglove. "I am a herbalist. I can attune myself to my patients' moods and fears. I cannot *read* their minds, but I can put myself inside them."

"Provided it works with Surgeons," Yulmash pointed out.

"Even your blunted sense of empathy worked with a cobra and a sabretooth lion. Jackalfoot's worked with every animal in Habd ul-Qusnemnet. My empathic sense is far more sensitive than his. That is why I became a herbalist."

If you can tell me its reactions as I rewire its sensorium, it may be possible to effect a repair. But you must understand: there is great danger to you. Its insanity could infect your own mind, if you allow yourself to be sucked into the depths of the Surgeon's subconscious.

Foxglove and Yulmash looked into each other's eyes, each aware of what the other was thinking. *I've only just found you, now I might lose you.* They lowered their gaze.

"Our tribe couldn't have been rescued without the Surgeon's help," Yulmash said. "Without its aid, the Ship wouldn't have been able to pick us up. To make that possible, the Surgeon had to overcome its own insanity."

"And that took an enormous effort of will," Foxglove said. "Not to mention subjecting itself voluntarily to severe mental torment. I am sorry Yulmash, but we cannot let the Surgeon be killed if there's any chance of healing it. As a herbalist, I must put its life above my own. Ship: I accept the risk."

"You're right, of course," Yulmash said sadly.

"Have confidence in my skill, my love. All will be well."

They made their way to the chamber where the Surgeon now lay. It was the first time either of them had actually seen the obese body, like a gigantic slug. Some would have found it repulsive, but Foxglove immediately walked up to the Surgeon's side. It towered above her, twice her height. She placed her hands on its flaking skin, still wet from the cleansing spray.

She sucked in her breath. "It is in great torment, but there is an island of rationality. It seeks release—by whatever means necessary.

"Ship! Tell me when you are ready to begin the treatment."

Now.

"Then waste no more time."

The Ship began to try tentative modifications to the Surgeon's sensorium. From time to time Foxglove would issue instructions: "No, not that. Reverse the operation and try again, a little closer to the main brainstem... Yes, that is good, he is responding, reinforce those connections..."

Yulmash could sense some of the interplay himself, but it was like trying to listen to a conversation through a heavy blanket. Everything was muffled.

"I sense a great change," Foxglove cried. "There is much disturbance, but also a growing awareness."

The rational parts of its mind are beginning to interconnect. Beware! This is the time of greatest danger! You must maintain a barrier between your mind and the Surgeon's, yet continue to empathise with it.

Foxglove laughed, "It is called professional detachment, Ship. Every herbalist knows how to do that."

Do not underestimate the power of insanity, Herbalist.

"And do not underestimate the power of love, Ship. Tough love, professional love—but healing *is* a form of love." Her eyes opened wide. "Whatever you are doing, it is working! Keep it up, no matter what—"

The Surgeon's massive body convulsed. Foxglove was hurled aside, falling to the floor. Yulmash rushed to her aid, distraught. She didn't move, and her eyes were tightly closed.

"*Ship!* Is she—?"

Foxglove opened one eye. "No, Yulmash, I am not. It was just so sudden, when the Surgeon's shell of insanity collapsed. I *told* you, professional detachment. And love." She rolled on her side, observing her patient, and stood up.

The Surgeon's convulsions had quieted, now. Then its skin... unzipped.

"What—?" Yulmash began.

"This is natural," Foxglove said. "It is what should have happened a long time ago, but the pandemons suppressed it. The Surgeon will lose its memories, but that is natural too. Watch."

Deep slits appeared along the length of the Surgeon's body, separating it into five segments. Four more slits began to appear at right angles, running round it like rings, separating it into five shorter pieces. The slits extended deep into the body, met in the middle, and joined.

The Surgeon fell apart.

In the hushed silence, the pieces wriggled, then the flesh redistributed into more familiar shapes.

"Are those—?"

"Yes, Yulmash. Twenty-five baby Surgeons. It has reproduced."

Each will now begin an independent life with a renewed mind. A sane mind.

Yulmash and Foxglove stood, hand in hand, beside a great curving window that had appeared in the Ship's wall. They paid no attention to the many other Neanderthals watching, slightly bemused, though similar windows. They lived, for the moment, in a world of their own.

The first time they had watched, soon after the Ship had risen into the sky, they had seen a huge ball of blue and white, green and brown. The Ship had told the Neanderthals that this was the world that had been their home. It pointed out the location of Qus, which occupied a mere patch. It would take time to sink in, but Neanderthals were practical people, receptive to evidence and immune to superstition, and they took the Ships' explanations as interesting new facts.

Then the entire globe turned grey, fading to black on the side away from the sun. *Retribution*, the Ship had told them. Many of the innocent had suffered along with the guilty, but that was the way of the Living Galaxy. The Ship had done what it could, within the operational and ethical parameters that constrained its ability to act; the Neanderthals were the beneficiaries.

The flatfaces would survive, for they were too many to be exterminated, but it would take millennia to rebuild their civilisation and culture.

The once-grey ball had resumed its previous coloration as the dust settled, perhaps a little less bright then before. It hung suspended in a field of blackness spangled with pinprick stars—the familiar night sky, seemingly untroubled by the destruction on the planet that had taken place before their eyes. Heaven's Wet Way was brighter and clearer than ever before, and the familiar constellation that superstitious Qusites called the Heavenly Goose flew along the river of light and darkness, as it always had.

Time to leave.

They felt no change in the Ship, but the world below was shrinking, even as they watched. Through another window they could see the sun, darkened to save their eyes. A dusting of lavender, magnified at their command by the Ship, turned out to be composed of hundreds of glowing violet rings, a puzzle not yet explained.

They also saw the Moon. It was no longer smiling, but its fuller face glowed, redolent with promise, for the Ship had told them all what lay ahead. A future brighter than the shining Moon beckoned, but not in the land of Qus or its neighbours. Not anywhere on the stricken world outside the window. Their future lay among the countless other worlds that Ship maintained were floating somewhere in the all-encompassing darkness, as yet too small to see.

The Neanderthals felt no awe, no religious fervour. No urge to thank the universe for saving their lives and freeing them from domination by the flatfaces. Such thinking was alien to them; they were realists. But they did find the whole development utterly fascinating. It opened up so many new pathways.

"You told me it was a delusion," Yulmash whispered.

"Sorry? What was?"

He waved a hand at the blackness outside the Ship. "Do you remember, Foxglove? I promised to take you beyond the desert. Beyond the deep ocean. Beyond the Sun and the Moon and the stars!" He laughed. "And that's exactly where we're going! I spoke truly!"

Foxglove joined his laughter, ripples dancing on a bright lake. "So you did, my reformed warrior." She paused, thoughtfully. "However... You know that we lionfaces prefer to speak our minds?"

"I'm aware of your tendency to be blunt, yes."

"Then I have to inform you," she said, with a playful poke at his ribs, "that I doubt *this* was what you were thinking of."

WHAT HAPPENED NEXT...

Several generations after Shephatsut-Mer and Nemnestris led to survivors to found a new city and a new religion, one of their descendants wrote an exaggerated, mythical account of the sunfire's destruction of Ul-q'mur, and buried it (along with several figurines of crouching lions with female Neanderthal heads) beneath the giant statue of a sabretooth that had formerly marked the entrance to the Arena. By then the matching lion had collapsed and been broken up for building stone, and the sabretooth's fangs had fallen off.

As the centuries passed, the remnants of Qusian civilisation slowly fell apart. Stone mansions gave way to mudbrick houses, then wattle-and-daub huts. Magnificent temples lived on as pale shadows of their former glory, their stone columns replaced by tree trunks, their carved statues roughly hewn from wood or moulded in clay. Towns fragmented into villages. The river reclaimed the irrigation channels, and agriculture declined from vast royal estates to individual plots barely able to feed a family, augmented by a partial return to a hunter-gatherer lifestyle.

Vague memories of former glory lived on as myths and stories. Priests continued to peddle the old lies. As the millennia passed, Qus finally began to rebuild.

Twelve thousand years after the events related in *Oracle*, a new civilisation arose in the Nile Valley amid the ruins of the ancient city of Ul-q'mur. Today we call it predynastic Egypt. Followed by the dynastic era of the Old, Middle, and New Kingdoms, pyramids, decorated tombs, the Book of the Dead, and other religious and secular paraphernalia. The Sphinx, however, was one of a pair of huge rock lions left over from the time of the Water People. The Egyptians reworked its head, making it human.

This civilisation retained folk-memories of many aspects of Qusite culture, especially its religious beliefs.

The history of ancient Egypt demonstrates very clearly the remarkable robustness of its culture. After each of three Intermediate Periods of cultural change and confusion, triggered by invasions, the Egyptians picked themselves up and re-established almost exactly the same cultural structures, with the exception of the gladiatorial contests. (There was slow evolution, such as the abandonment of pyramids in favour of deep rock-cut royal tombs, but this was internally generated, rather than being imposed by invaders from other cultures.) Some Egyptian deities were around for at least five thousand years —probably longer, given the evidence about predynastic times currently emerging from sites such as Hierakonpolis.

This ability to *endure* goes back much further. What archaeologists now know about the origins of Egyptian civilisation merely scratches the surface of a far older history, almost all traces of which had vanished forever.

Almost all.

Wheelers

Seven thousand years after Qus was reborn as predynastic Egypt, evidence of a flourishing pre-Egyptian civilisation began to emerge when the Great Sphinx of Giza was being dismantled to move it to higher ground, away from the rising water table. Excavations under and around the Sphinx dug up fragments of papyrus inscribed with a strange mythical tale of fire from the sun and celestial chariots, and mysterious figurines of crouching naked women with leonine heads.

This discovery paled into insignificance when the

blimps that had been living in Jupiter's atmosphere for millions of years used their gravitic engines to hurl an approaching comet straight at the Earth. A small group of humans, one of whom had been involved in the excavations, made contact with a subversive group of blimps. In this, the child Moses Odingo played a crucial role, because his remarkable affinity for animals extended to aliens. Aided by the Jovian constructs, neither organism nor machine, that they called wheelers, an alliance of human/blimp misfits managed to prevent the Earth's destruction by sacrificing Jupiter's moon Io. Together, a few blimps and humans headed out into the Galaxy with a message of love, peace, and universal brotherhood.

Heaven

Twenty thousand years later, the resulting religion of Cosmic Unity was disseminating the Memeplex of Universal Tolerance to a receptive Galaxy, and rigorously enforcing its Quota of Love, whether its alleged beneficiaries wanted it or not. When the reefwives of No-Moon decided on implacable resistance, their world was wrecked in the name of love and peace. But thanks to the sacrifices of their polypoid husband Second-Best Sailor and the wisdom of Fat Apprentice, Cosmic Unity was defeated and the polypoid race was reborn in the oceans of Aquifer.

Oh, and the living pond had something to do with it. And the Precursor starship *Talitha* with its Neanderthal crew. And the much-abused Neanderthal girl Dry Leaves Fall Slowly. And Servant-of-Unity XIV Samuel Godwin'sson Travers, who lost his faith when he rose to a senior ecclesiastical position, visited one of his Church's many Heavens, and found out how the Church achieved its miracles. To his dismay.

SCIENTIFIC
BACKGROUND

Oracle is set around 17,000 BC in an imaginary pre-Egyptian society, living in and about what's now the river Nile. There is, of course, no archaeological evidence for such a society, but there's not a lot against it either, since very little—basically, nothing—remains from that period. We postulate that many features of early Dynastic Egypt actually arose much earlier, among the Qusites, the Water People, though with many differences of detail. Such as the total absence of pyramids and a taste for violent gladiatorial contests. There were no horses in ancient Egypt; they were introduced around 1500 BC during the Second Intermediate Period. Similarly there were no horses in Qus. There were a few camels in Egypt from about 2500 BC onwards, after their domestication in Arabia; rewriting history we propose that the *bidd'hu* had at least tamed them considerably earlier, but all traces of that lineage were wiped out by the plasmoid flares. We assume the same for the Qusians' domesticated cats and dogs.

We propose that when Qusite society collapsed, as a consequence of the events related in *Oracle*, much of their culture was kept alive in oral and perhaps even written tradition. Eventually it resurfaced in a mangled and garbled form. Recorded history has shown how resilient Egyptian culture was, surviving with few significant changes for about 3,500 years despite three occupations by outsiders, known as the Intermediate Periods. Moreover, many stable aspects of Egyptian culture, such as the main deities, temple structure, and even some hieroglyphs, now seem to go back to predynastic times.

It seems reasonable to assume that something similar might have happened over a much longer period of time.

One thing we *don't* suggest is that ancient Egypt's fascination with animal-headed gods comes from racial memories of pandemons. On the contrary, the Qusians already had such gods. Myths of composite animals run deep in the human psyche. The pandemons were mistaken for gods because they happened to fit into the same category, that's all.

In 17,000 BC the Sahara was very similar to what it is now: a vast desert with huge dunes and little greenery. That's more surprising than it might appear, because it's now known that the Sahara repeatedly runs through a 20,000-year long cycle from huge deserts to forests and savannahs with enormous lakes, and back to desert. If anything, it was more of a desert at the time of *Oracle* than it is now. But a few thousand years later, the climate there began to get increasingly wet as the monsoons shifted further north. This change in the climate change obliterated all archaeological evidence of the Qusites, of course, just as the groundwater of the Nile Delta has obliterated most, though not all, archaeology of a far more recent date.

The Last Glacial Maximum, the time when the ice sheets covering northern Europe extended their furthest to the south, happened between 24,500 BC and about 17,000 BC, when the events of *Oracle* took place. At that time the ice covered Iceland, most of Britain except the extreme south, Poland, and much of northern Germany. It extended across much of the West Siberian Plain, and a glacial lake dammed the Ob and Yenisei rivers. The succeeding Late Glacial Maximum ended around 8,000 BC with the retreat of the icecaps to their present position, from which global warming has recently triggered a further, potentially disastrous, retreat.

Neanderthals are named for the Neander Valley ('Thal' in German), where a fossil was discovered in 1856. Initially they were seen as uncouth and unintelligent, with no culture, but the current view places them much closer to modern humans, with rudimentary music, bodily decorations, art, tools, fire, and possibly even reverence for their dead. In 2018 archaeologists announced that cave paintings from three sites in Spain are at least as ancient as 65,000 BC, which is 20,000 years before modern humans arrived in Europe; this indicates that they were made by Neanderthals. Some are older, around 80,000 BC. The paintings consist of stencilled hands, red circles, and geometric shapes. They also found seashells with holes in them, stained with coloured pigments, presumably used as necklaces; two samples date to 115,000 BC. So, as in *Heaven*, we are entitled to assume that Neanderthals were just as smart as modern humans... but different.

It's generally believed that the last Neanderthals died out around 30,000 BC. The youngest finds are Hyena Den in the United Kingdom, thought to derive from at least 30,000 years ago, and the Vindija Neanderthals in Croatia, recently placed around 32,000 to 33,000 years ago. However, there's evidence of fires at Gibraltar, indicating that Neanderthals may have lived there only 24,000 years ago, a mere 5,000 years before *Oracle*. In archaeology, absence of evidence is not evidence of absence, and most extinctions probably occurred significantly later than the time indicated by the most recent known evidence. The reason: evidence is sparse. For example, until *Jurassic Park* sparked a search for new fossils, only three reasonably complete *Tyrannosaurus rex* skeletons were known, spread over a period of three million years. Now there are about twenty more, but it's still a very thin set of representatives for such an iconic creature.

It does, however, seem likely that Neanderthals failed to survive the most recent glacial (Ice Age), which was at its deepest about 15,000 years ago. The Lascaux cave in France documents this time. There were sabretooths, mammoths, perhaps mastodons, camels big and small, huge wild dogs and hyenas, occasional cave bears, woolly rhinos—maybe even deinotheres, much bigger than elephants. All of these animals, along with the Neanderthals that may well have hunted some of them, were pushed towards the equator as the ice headed south. *Smilodon*, the best known sabretooth 'tiger' (a name now falling into disuse, in favour of 'cat') was American, and not in same subfamily as lions or tigers. But there were sabretooth 'lions', particularly *Homotherium*, in Europe. There are drawings of them on cave walls.

We postulate that Neanderthals had a remarkable affinity for animals, and in particular that they treated sabretooth lions as pets. Again there is absolutely no evidence for this: it's pure invention for the purposes of this trilogy. These abilities led the Qusites to preserve one group of Neanderthals, numbering in the mid-hundreds, when they fled the advancing ice. It is archaeologically reasonable that some of them might have survived a few thousand years longer than palaeontological evidence suggests. If so, *sapiens* humans would relate to Neanderthals when the two were squeezed together by the glaciation.

In 2010 genetic studies showed that between 1% and 4% of modern non-African human genetic material is identical to Neanderthal DNA, so there must have been some interbreeding, apparently between Neanderthal males and human females. A longstanding debate about whether Neanderthals are a separate species from *Homo sapiens,* or a subspecies, seems to be resolving in favour of a subspecies *Homo sapiens neanderthalensis*, rather than a separate species *Homo neanderthalensis*. This explains how Yulmash can be a human-Neanderthal hybrid.

The Great Sphinx has long puzzled many archaeologists. Conventionally, its construction is dated to the reign of Khafre, around 2500 BC. Its head is thought to depict his father, Khufu. It was restored by Thutmose IV around 1400 BC, and further minor restoration has been carried out in modern times. But there have been dissenting voices since the birth of Egyptology, contending that the Sphinx is older. Among them are Flinders Petrie, Auguste Mariette, and Gaston Maspero. The geologist Colin Reader has argued that the quarries around the site indicate that the causeway from the Sphinx and its associated temples to the Great Pyramid of Khufu must be older than the pyramid itself, and that the same therefore applies to the Sphinx since that must have existed before it needed a causeway. More controversially, geologist Robert Shoch and Egyptologist John West have argued that the water erosion seen on the Sphinx implies that its sculpted form is considerably older than normally assumed. However, Reader has analysed the erosion patterns and suggested more conventional explanations.

One striking feature of the Sphinx is its current head, which is visibly too small for the body. This could merely be an accident, resulting from the original shape of the outcrop of nummulitic limestone from which it has been carved. But it might instead be evidence that the head has been recarved from something larger. For the purposes of *Oracle* we have assumed that—whatever the current evidence and its status—the Sphinx was indeed recarved: from a giant stone sabretooth, which existed about 15,000 years earlier than Khufu's reign. It has often been suggested, based on the archaeology and the Egyptian love of symmetry, that originally the Sphinx was one of a matching pair. We found the idea of an ordinary lion as a companion irresistible.

The incident in the Arena, when Insh'erthret cements his Kingship by posing with a lion and a sabretooth, was inspired by the iconic depiction of a king holding up two lions to show their power. One of the earliest such 'master of animals' images occurs on a terracotta stamp seal found at Girsu in Mesopotamia, dating from around 4000 BC. In ancient Egypt, it is prominent on the ivory handle of the Gebel el-Arak ceremonial flint knife, and in images on the walls of the 'painted tomb', Tomb 100 at Hierakonpolis. Both date from the Naqada II period, roughly 3500 BC. Tomb 100 was excavated by Frederick Green in 1898-9, but has since been lost. Fragments of its decorated walls are in the Egyptian Museum in Cairo. Green made a full-colour copy of the images, now undergoing restoration at the Griffith Institute in Oxford. It records numerous animal species, boats, and religious scenes. The animals include gazelles, ibex, impalas, lionesses, ostriches, and zebras—typical of savannah ecology. There are also domesticated cattle.

The plasmoids in the Sun and other stars are a rather speculative invention, which have their roots in Arthur C. Clarke's short story "Out of the Sun" in 1958, in which scientists observe a cloud of ionised gas ejected from the Sun, and realise that it in some sense alive, and beomce convinced it is intelligent. Our plasmoids have an extra trick: they can metamorphose into a radio-wave life form and transmit themselves between stars. This may seem far-fetched. It is. But if *anything* could survive in the Sun, then magnetic plasma would be the right material to make it from, since that's what's there. Plasma can also be exceedingly complex, as recent discoveries about sunspots indicate. In fact, if biologists saw a sunspot down a microscope, they'd be convinced it was a living organism. Plasmoids are small enough not to be detectable with any current observational equipment. Interlocking vortices have sufficient topological complexity to encode at least as much information as DNA, so plasmoid genetics is easy. We see no serious obstacle to highly complex magnetic fields existing, and their reproduction is no more unlikely than that of DNA, which at first sight is impossible on topological grounds. Work in Artificial Life suggests that if plasma life forms did exist, they might well evolve to become self-reproducing and self-complicating. By many definitions, such a system would be a form of life. If it attained extelligence—the sophisticated form of intelligence that propagates and grows by accumulating cultural capital outside the organisms themselves—its technology would also be based on complex plasma-flows and magnetic fields. Clarke understood this, and reading his story again for the first time since the 1960s, we now realise that we may have unconsciously stolen another idea, the final sentence: "The sun will put forth its strength and lick the faces of its children; and thereafter the planets will go their way once more as they were in the beginning—clean and bright... and sterile."

Magnetotori are more like viruses: they reproduce by hijacking the more complex magnetic fields in the Sun. This explains how they can be quasi-lifeforms, despite their relatively simple structure. The quasi-quantum Herders have no scientific justification, beyond the obvious one that quantum fields can also be highly complex. Reproduction would be less of a problem for an entity whose material satisfies the superposition principle. Their reproductive material could pass through itself unchanged; in fact, entire Herders could pass through each other with no ill effects. There would be no topological obstacles for evolution to worry about.

Pandemons were motivated by recent discoveries about the human brain, which appears to function as a system of complicit semi-independent modules, 'pandemonium', in contrast to the Cartesian view of a single self-aware mind operating within, but distinct from, a brain. This is why several pandemon brains can occupy one body, retaining individual identities yet cooperating (for the most part) smoothly. The lava plain to which the plasmoids reduced the pandemon Moonbase is still visible today; we call it the Mare Muscoviense.

Precursors and their technology have absolutely no scientific basis.

Yet.

ABOUT THE AUTHORS

Ian Stewart is a Fellow of the Royal Society and Emeritus Professor of Mathematics at Warwick University. He has written over 120 books, 40 on popular science. His books have been published in more than 300 translations in 18 languages. He has made over 450 radio and 80 television appearances, and delivered the 1997 Christmas Lectures on BBC TV. For 12 years he wrote *Scientific American*'s Mathematical Recreations column. His awards include the Joint Policy Board for Mathematics Communications Award, the Royal Society's Faraday Medal, the Gold Medal of the Institute for Mathematics and Its Applications, the Public Understanding of Science Award of the American Association for the Advancement of Science, the Zeeman Medal of the London Mathematical Society and the Institute for Mathematics and its Applications, and the Pythagorean Universe Award, Centre for Advanced Studies, Warsaw University of Technology, Warsaw.

He has twice been shortlisted for the Royal Society science book prize. In 2006 he won the Science Writing Prize of the British Association of Science Writers for the best article in a specialist periodical. His *Letters to a Young Mathematician* won the Peano Prize, and *The Symmetry Perspective* (coauthored with Martin Golubitsky) won the Balaguer Prize. In January 2009 his popular maths book *Professor Stewart's Cabinet of Mathematical Curiosities* was number 6 among all books on Amazon UK. His iPad app *Incredible Numbers* won the Digital Book World award for adult nonfiction in 2015. He shared the

Lewis Thomas Prize for Writing about Science with Steven Strogatz in 2015, won the Euler Book Prize of the Mathematical Association of America in 2017, and in 2019 received the first Premio Internazionale Cosmos, Reggio Calabria, Italy, for the tranaslation *I Numeri Uno* of his *Significant Figures*.

He has written three other SF novels in addition to those with Cohen: *The Living Labyrinth* and *Rock Star* (jointly with Tim Poston, ReAnimus Press), and *Jack of All Trades*. His *Flatland* sequel *Flatterland* (Macmillan) has extensive fantasy elements. He has published 33 short stories in *Analog*, *Omni*, *Interzone*, and *Nature*. He has 12 stories in *Nature*'s 'Futures' series, more than any other author. He was Guest of Honour at Novacon 29 in 1999 and Science Guest of Honour at Worldcon 75 in Helsinki in 2017. He received the Bloody Stupid Johnson Award for Innovative Uses of Mathematics at the 2016 Discworld Convention.

Jack Cohen was a former Senior Lecturer in Biology at Birmingham University; he died in May 2019 aged 85. Both are well known in SF fandom, separately and as a double-act, and we list their main SF/fantasy credentials. They planned *Oracle* together. Jack supplied many of the key ideas; Ian wrote the novel. He was, for many years, a consultant for SF shows on TV and SF novels, advising on the creation of plausible aliens with emphasis on the supporting evolutionary and ecological aspects. The authors concerned include Anne McCaffrey (*Dragonriders of Pern* series), Harry Harrison (*Eden* trilogy), Larry Niven, Jerry Pournelle and Steven Barnes (*Heorot* series), James White (*Sector General* series), David Gerrold (Chtorr series), and Terry Pratchett (several books including *The Amazing Maurice and His Educated Rodents*).

The composite entity **JackandIan** is best known in the SF/ fantasy world for the *Science of Discworld* series: four books written jointly with the late Sir Terry Pratchett. Unlike *The Physics of Star Trek* and its ilk, these books are *not* 'scientific' explanations of how Discworld works. They can't be: Discworld works by magic. Instead, they are fantasy/fact fusions. Each combines a fantasy short story by Pratchett, set in Discworld, with chapters about science. The link is the Roundworld Project, in which the wizards of Unseen University accidentally bring our planet and our universe into existence. The fantasy chapters in Discworld alternate with science chapters on Roundworld. The four books are *The Science of Discworld; The Science of Discworld II: The Globe; The Science of Discworld III: Darwin's Watch;* and *The Science of Discworld IV: Judgement Day.* Three of them went to number 1 on the *Sunday Times* bestseller list for non-fiction; the other reached number 2. *The Science of Discworld* was a finalist for a Hugo Award at the World Science Fiction Convention in 2000. Cohen and Stewart were members of a small group of scientists advising the Kensington Science Museum about an exhibition on alien life in 2005. Together they have written three other popular science books: *The Collapse of Chaos* (Penguin), *Figments of Reality* (CUP), and *Evolving the Alien* (vt. *What Does a Martian Look Like*, Ebury). They have also published two SF novels *Wheelers* and *Heaven* (both Warner Aspect). *Oracle* is a prequel to *Wheelers*, completing the trilogy, but it can be read on its own. It can be described as a historical novel/space opera mash-up. *Wheelers* is set in 2200 on and around Jupiter; *Heaven* is 20,000 years later in an advanced Galactic culture; *Oracle* is set in 17,000 BC when criminals from that culture exploit a pre-Egyptian society. *Wheelers* was selected in 2000 as a main choice by the Science Fiction Book Club in the USA. They have two jointly written SF short stories: one in *Interzone*, the other in *Nature*'s 'Futures' series. They were regular guests at the biannual Discworld Conventions in the UK. Stewart was to be a guest at the 2020 convention, but this was cancelled because of COVID-19.

Both were made honorary wizards of Unseen University at a ceremony at Warwick University — reported in *Nature* — when Pratchett received the first of his ten honorary degrees.

JACK COHEN

19 September 1933 – 6 May 2019

Jack and I planned *Oracle* in 2003. We had just finished *Heaven*, the sequel to *Wheelers*, and we wanted to complete the trilogy with a prequel. For various reasons the project got shelved. One was that we had been working with (the late Sir) Terry Pratchett on the *Science of Discworld* series of fantasy-fact-fusion books, and those took precedence. Another was the more immediate task of writing popular science books. A third was that the market for science fiction was struggling. By 2008 the world's bankers had wrecked the global economy by lending eyewatering amounts of money to people who could never pay it back, and *nemesis* had finally caught up with *hubris*, much as Achilles would inevitably catch the tortoise, no matter what the 'quants' (in that case the philosopher Zeno) were predicting with their clever mathematical models.

Oracle remained on the back burner. But we didn't forget it entirely. We both wanted to find out how the story went.

We intended to write it the same way we wrote *Wheelers* and *Heaven*. Jack's main role was ideas man: characters, setting, plot. Mine was to decide what words to use to tell the story, and get them into the computer. Then we would both read everything, scribble comments in the margins, and I would rewrite the book until we were both satisfied.

Jack was twelve years older than I, and his health deteriorated; slowly at first, then with increasing speeed and severity. I had promised him that I would get *Oracle* written, and in September 2017 I finally got on with it, after several years where bits of various chapters had struggled on to the page. Jack was able to read an early complete draft before he died on 6 May 2019. Since then I've made some minor revisions, mostly to get the chronology of the story working consistently. So this is pretty much the story as Jack read it.

You can find obituaries and other information about Jack on my website:

ianstewartjoat.weebly.com/jack-cohen

Printed in Great Britain
by Amazon

76062065R00210